Johnnie Spot Perfect
& The Twelve Tribes of Jesus

Book Two: Thy Kingdom Come

BRIAN SMITH

1st Edition

This is a work of fiction. Names, characters, places and incidents are either the product of the author's imagination or are used fictionally. Any resemblance to actual persons or organizations, living or dead, is entirely coincidental.

Printed and bound in the USA.

ISBN: 978-0-9991641-2-9

Jesus said this:

"Be perfect, therefore, just as your Heavenly Father is perfect."

***

"Enter through the narrow gate…
For wide is the gate and broad is the road that leads to destruction, and many enter through it…
But small is the gate and narrow is the road that leads to life… and only a few find it."

***

"If you want to be perfect, go, sell your possessions and give to the poor, and you will have treasure in heaven. Then come, follow me."

As testified by Matthew,
Your Brother in Christ
Chapter 5:48
Chapter 7:13-14
Chapter 19:21

Preface

There are many mysteries which are shielded and hidden within the historical confines of the Holy Bible by the Holy Spirit. These mysteries are not inherent, nor are they meant to be fully understood or known until the Lord God of the Most-High, Himself, makes them known and directs His revelation of all things known, at His perfect moment of pre-determined time, pre-set and pre-ordained by Him, in the future. I, the author, believe that these mysteries are not meant to be fully understood by this generation, nor by the next generation, nor by any generation to come, unless Christ comes first to give His divine enlightenment to those who have sought Him out and prayed in earnest for His Kingdom to return and bless followers of "The Way" for being patient… past, present, and future. This book is a heartfelt representation of the many struggles which we have all been dealt and seen played out in our lives—packaged into many forms—as the Holy Spirit deems appropriate.

The half-fictional journey which I take you on in *Book 2: Thy Kingdom Come* is a representational history lesson through a time and space where history is part fiction (of this world) and part divine truth (of the creational three unified worlds ruled by the Triune Deity: our Father-God in Heaven, His Son Jesus Christ who is Lord and Savior to the world, and the Holy Spirit). The part of mankind and His creation which is the Holy Truth of nations, known as our salvation, is often overshadowed for convenience's sake, lost in conjunction with our spiritual growth, or avoided for sin's sake.

Neither is good as a stand-alone entity for our human spiritual existence, for both are an integral part of our recipe for gaining insight into the reason why God made us, which is the sole reason we are here: to reciprocate the love He gives to us back to Him, each of us asking nothing in return, but gaining everything back, through the holy blessing of living a fruitful eternal life, existing in Heaven with Him in us, as His children.

In Book One, three great and powerful, evolving, and formidable world cultures collide—specifically the Greek, Hebrew, and Latin—some two millennia ago. A Jewish zealot, Saul (who later became known as Paul the Apostle), was the man God chose to be His ambassador to show His will to the lost and dying multi-religious and multi-racial world in a specific pre-ordained and post-prophesied war-torn time. Before Saul (reborn as Paul), it was Abraham (formerly known as Abram) who was the appointed proxy of God's voice and will for an era of time spanning five millennia. Between Abraham's visit by God on the mountain and Saul's visit by Jesus on a horse, it was Moses who was given God's voice with full authority to perform miracles and lead His chosen people, the Hebrews, into a new land, carrying the message of His covenants—those of obedience, faith, and loyalty—to be established as earthly pillars of law, order, and justice, known as the Mosaic Law.

At the time of Jesus' earthly life, at least one-third of our world (earth) was in some form of war and/or battle for lands and people to submit to control by surrounding countries, which still defined the rule of expanding worldly occupations, both then and now. Mankind still lives in the world of materialism and not in the world of divine truth, thus not much has changed by seeking God's will and oversight, with the same worldly death and chaos by the angels' count that plagues the earth in any single epoch in time. This is the nature and design of earth until Christ comes again to rule with peace, differentiating the two worlds of Heaven and Earth. This is also the one understanding which can remove and wash away the stains of enmity which lurk in the hearts of all men who call themselves globalized, civilized, and evolved. The angels know the faults of man and will testify for and over him—both good and bad in the end—for men believe themselves supreme as they walk this earth.

Around the Year of our Lord 200 (Anno Domini), God gave His full voice to another remarkable but unknown man, Tertullian, a Berber whose voice has fallen silent through the years. He, with the help of the Holy Spirit, called for and designed a lasting dialog to develop Christian beliefs as a Triune Order of Three Spiritual Heads, or Triad—Father, Son, and Holy Spirit—who are one and the same, separable but also inseparable. In so doing, he keep the Trinity message exact, not falling back into the single Jehovah belief in the aftermath of the birth and fulfillment of the prophecies of Christ's coming. Tertullian wrote down and petitioned the Holy Spirit's Truths for the acceptance of the Triune Trinity God-Head, as separated into three entities which could exist in three phases (or more) at once. Tertullian's words and vehement messages arguing for a Triune God led the doctrinal leaders of the day to understand and then unify their beliefs during their ecumenical councils in early Christian development days, which became the solidification period of the Roman Catholic Church. (The word "catholic" today means "unified.")

The Roman Catholic Church has stood unwavering now in its unified message for all mankind since the physical walking of Jesus Christ on earth. It has been tested on a daily basis for its stance and promotion of its unified doctrines concerning inalienable human rights, including—but not limited to—the appeasement from dictatorial suffering and freedom from political persecution. As a separate non-secular and powerful union of faithful believers, its armies, past leaders, and top-down structure of self-government have unified into a Triune spiritually based religion which believes that a worldwide reformation is needed to free humanity of its suffering, just has Moses freed the slaves from Egypt under the Pharaoh some 2500 solar revolutions (years) ago.

Then in the year 1483 Anno Domini, God sent forth a new protestor's voice—that of Martin Luther—to take the message of salvation and Good News, i.e. the "Unified Word." as written and transcribed mainly in Latin and translated it into German, which could unlock the power of a new formed church movement. His followers were free to study the Word themselves, unbridled and without the oversight of organized religion, and to remain unified apart from the Mother church. Thus, they could now educate others without having to go through the process of being indebted to a binding papal government that began charging money for salvation, which can be seen today in an education system of secular colleges and universities in a similar, insidious, and destructive pattern. Note that the Holy Roman Catholic Church and almost all of its socially imperfect problems have been addressed and altered, but all in accordance with God's will and God's timing, for all events are laid down and carried out in this age because God controls everything and everyone, while man never controls anything but his own destiny, though many may disagree with this.

When Martin Luther became the new voice of the Reformation movement which began after 1517 Anno Domini, the Protestants (i.e. protestors), as they were called, split into many different groups and factions, each adopting some, but not all, of his numerous writings by their own interpretations of God's divine will for mankind. And through time, there has been much written by theologians concerning these differences on what has come to be known as the "Five Solae." And with more time, and more demands by the Holy Spirit to spread the gospel to all corners of the earth, many different varieties of churches have sprung up from many different hearts of Christ's missionaries, all being believers in the "good of Christianity with the common root of Christ's heart," and all being "fishers of men," though fishing in different pools, lakes, and oceans for the diversity of the fish God created. This has often led to a theological question: why isn't the one and only unified universal church, the Roman Catholic Church, sufficient for all? The Holy Spirit's way to reach out and touch the diversity created in mankind dates back to the original division and conflict between Paul and Barnabas going their separate ways when the they split to be fishers of men in different areas, and they both were successful as God ruled their lives and led them to prosper, each yielding the fruit of the Holy Spirit among their own followers in their sermons, missions, beliefs, and writings.

This diversity of "fishing for men" through the ages has grown so that we, the body, have divisions in the Holy tree of life we call Jesus Christ. We share His common root, but we exist as separate churches, growing with many individual trunks waiting to be big enough to unite and bond to form one common trunk. It is my belief that the church of God's children must continue to grow and grow until it can unite into a large common trunk, finally unifying into a common root, which then becomes the servant people God created, lacking nothing as a single unified church all united in one love, one cause, and one purpose, without division or disharmony. But the ultimate question is: how will this happen, and when?

We know only for certain Jesus' lasting words of encouragement, instruction, guidance, direction, and fulfillment while He was here during his mortal life, as they were written down to last for all time, along with forfeiture of His life, living as he lived, doing as He did, and praying as He prayed, for all God created, and the world which exists, and all that is in it, for the Great Plan which is lived out in the people who call Him Lord. This is all we know; all else is speculation. All else is just scenes and props upon a stage, where the main story of beauty, blessing, and personal salvation takes place surrounded by the tenets of grace, submission, and mercy, finally reaching an eternal life, which is a relationship based on love, not hate.

As the author of this series of writings entitled "Thy Kingdom Come," I am often taken aback by the lack of the interest in the life-quest for one's own personal salvation. It should be, I believe, the zenith of all conversation by all people, everywhere at all times. It should be more than any one thing a person or group can discuss or pursue at any one moment in time, yet the topic is met mostly with lethargy in the westernized circles of life, with almost no exposure or education spent on its merits other than one hour per week. The masses of mankind have always loved to hide in the Passé Fair of the status quo in which they are led to believe they are released and obviated from any personal engagement in the discussion or involvement in the proper stewardship of bearing any banner (or cross) of Christ's love and blood He shed for them. But this is wrong. All must get engaged in the conversation… or fall to the trappings of false prophets and heinous crimes against humanity for which there is no forgiveness for naivety. Christ's thirty-three-year existence on earth was not some small, isolated event in the course of time, as often projected. It was prophesied and fulfilled by numerous historical events and evidence, yet people scoff at the events which created the world in which they live. The gift of Salvation, along with the message that God forgives, must be discussed and remembered each day as the one thing which makes the world and everything in it exist, for evolution is just a myth created by short-sighted fools with no Godly wisdom. Creation is an undeniable fact, and those who deny it exists need go no further than the mirror, where they would deny that they themselves exist, deny that their very own blood, sinew, and chromosomes exist, thereby sealing their fate along with the angels who denied God in the beginning of time.

To understand the inside-out and upside-down paradoxical message of love itself, one must first understand the Trinity's foundational message of giving first and receiving last via delayed gratification. Selfishness is banished, and the "whole self" is destroyed to reach perfection in the calling of service to others. So the question: How could Deity—who could do all things and be all things—give that all up to be whipped, spit on, nailed to a tree, and voluntarily suffer so terribly for us, for humanity? It is a simple but incredible story, with hundreds of eyewitnesses willing to die to retell it, with more evidence and fulfilled prophecy than any other story or theory ever presented in the courts of man's mind, heart, and soul. It is a story passed forth with passion and conviction to the depths of man's pandering soul, to gain knowledge of the grand design and be at one with the Creator, Himself. It is a story of pure love, untainted by self-interest.

Please, readers… do not make the biggest mistake of your eternal-lives, for the Lord's Kingdom *will* come, as He declares in

His prayer and praise to His father in Heaven[161], and when it does there will be only two groups: sheep and goats[162], those who will have been stewards of the blessings they have received and who have served with their loyal obedience, and those who will have frittered away their chance to multiply their blessings, just as in the parable of the investment of talents.[163]

I urge to now and each day to pray and brand these words on your heart which Christ said to his followers as you read through this book, for not every situation of daily Christian life is met with mercy in the next life, just for being good, as many are misled to believe:

---

[161] Matthew 6:10

[162] Matthew 25:31-46

[163] Matthew 25:14-30

Jesus said:

"Do not suppose that I have come to bring peace to the earth. I did not come to bring peace, but a sword. For I have come to turn a man against his father, a daughter against her mother, and a daughter-in-law against her mother-in-law—a man's enemies will be the members of his own household. Anyone who loves their father or mother more than me is not worthy of me; anyone who loves their son or daughter more than me is not worthy of me. Whoever does not take up their cross and follow me is not worthy of me. Whoever finds their life will lose it, and whoever loses their life for my sake will find it."

As testified by Matthew,
Your brother in Christ,
Chapter 10:35-39

James, a servant of God and of the Lord Jesus Christ…
to the Twelve Tribes ("Believers of Christ")
scattered among the nations:

Greetings! Consider it pure joy, my brothers and sisters, whenever you face trials of many kinds, because you know that the testing of your faith produces perseverance. Let perseverance finish its work so that you may be mature and complete, not lacking anything.

Attested and witnessed by James,
Your Brother in Christ
(Oldest brother of Jesus)
Chapter 1:1-4

Book II Contents

Chapter 1

Remembering a Tough Childhood in South Central Los Angeles in 2006

With Gangbangers as Parents

I am 37 now, but as I travel back in my mind to that place where I was raised, I can still see the scene of my momma's house where the two of us lived together alone in Watts. It was not a place of peace and harmony, but it was all I knew and all I ever cared about. My grandmother, Mamaw, used to tell me: *Ignorance is bliss*. Now that I am older, I have actually come to embrace this philosophy. Our little one-room efficiency apartment was really micro-sized, about 450 square feet total and quite cramped for the two of us. Since then I have seen closets larger than what Momma and I had to live in. I am half-black and half-white. My momma was a drug user, my father was her drug dealer, and I was Momma's only reason for living as long as she did. When crack killed her, I was sent to live with my grandmother in Texas. As a child I knew only the warmth of my mother's arms. We merely existed in our tiny apartment together. I slept on the couch when I had to and my mother on her twin-size bed that she had managed to wrangle into the back of our '74 Honda Accord hatchback and drag home, tied down with some clothesline from our backyard, and the two of us had set up together. I only had one set of shoes at the time, which had many holes in them, and did not know that most everyone in America did not live this way.

Momma told me that she had met my daddy in Texas at the "game of the century" in 1968, which was between the University of Houston and UCLA basketball teams. My daddy had driven for two days straight from Los Angeles to Houston to see "The Tower of Power" play the game, which was extremely hyped up by sports commentator Howard Cosell, who had thus far mainly announced football and boxing matches. This basketball game was being played in the huge air-conditioned indoor arena called the Astrodome in Houston, and it was known as the "8th Wonder of the world" because of its massive size. It held over 50,000 people and had a full-size roof and air conditioning, at a time in America when half the homes were still without centralized air. Momma said that Daddy's car had air conditioning, and it was a good thing, too, because it was a long trip back to California after UCLA lost 71-69. But one small thing made the trip home different than the trip there: Daddy had met Momma, a young girl, a fresh runaway from home, run fresh that very night, and she wanted to go home with him. It didn't matter to her where to—anywhere, as long as she could just get away from her mother. So, that fateful night in 1968, she got into the car with a man she hardly knew and headed for California, the land of palm trees and Hollywood. It turned out to be a huge mistake for her, but not a mistake for God. "Take me away from here; I don't care where... just drive!" she told him. The following year Marcus Johnson—that was my daddy's name—received a draft notice to show up for a physical and then training for the war in Vietnam. He was #38 in the queue to enter. But he was "in love" with new his new runaway wife. Or in any case, that's how my momma tells it. I think he was just in love with her body and the pleasures it afforded him, plus he was lazy to boot, so he just decided not to bother to show up for that physical. So there he was—all of a sudden a draft dodger, no longer able to hold a job where anyone could identify him through taxes or social security, so he turned to the streets and sold drugs when he could. He claimed it was love that kept him home, but it was really only the love of himself that he meant in his heart.

Momma always kept a box under her bed with pictures of herself when she was a little girl. It was her memory box, her "happy box," she called it. I never had a happy box, but I wanted one like she had. I remember only pain in that small place which to me was more a prison than a home. Even prison, where I spent a weekend later in life, was clean and the food was edible. I had less stress at California Juvenile State Corrections (CJSC) than living with Momma. I never blamed her for my life; I just knew I was different, and that the world was different for me than what I saw on television.

In the 'hood, my daddy's street name was "John," and some people even called him "Fluky John." He didn't like the name Marcus because that was the name on his police record, the name etched on his cell door when he'd done two years' time for dealing crack cocaine.

When I was six, Momma would take me to the park to play with Jamie, the son of another single mom. I was Johnnie Jr. (J.J.), and Jamie was my half-brother, but I didn't know that at the time. I just remember our moms pushing us on the swings, and we would go higher and higher into the sky forever as they talked about our dad,

John. It was all a blur to me, but I loved going high. It was a sensation I never forgot, and when I was older, playing basketball reminded me of flying like that as a child, being pushed by my mother in that swing. A few times I flew out of the swing and landed face-first in the gravel, and Momma would pick me up and dust me off, but I never cried. I'm not sure why, but the pain of hitting the ground seemed to be just something that was meant to be, so I always got up and climbed back into the swing because being high in the air was something that gave me joy, drowning out whatever pain or worries were plaguing me.

Jamie's mom had dark hair and dark skin, and my mom had blonde hair like me. My dad was very dark and he did not come home much except to bring a few groceries like boxes of macaroni and cheese or ramen noodles twice a month. Later I found out he would get food stamps for us from the government and then spend the money on whiskey. He made most of his money by arranging for my mom and Jamie's mom to go on dates other men to get money to pay our rent and buy drugs to sell on the street. Mom would say, "I should have never listened to that man because he created hell for me here on earth. You are my very best angel, Johnnie, and my only hope of happiness while I still breathe." She always seemed sad, and when we were a little older, I would try to push her in the swing when she sat and talked with Jamie's mother, but my little feet never could get her high enough to get her into the air so she could feel God's wind on her face, like she did for me.

"Johnnie," she once told me, "you will have a better life one day than me… I promise you! I am going to get you out of here someday and we are going to have a big house on a hill. We will be able to see the ocean from your window, and smell the wind as it comes off the sand dunes, and see the morning sun as it comes up over the ocean with boats and clouds on the horizon." It was her dream to move back to Houston and be close to Galveston beaches, before she went to Cal Berkeley to study political science with the dream to become a US Supreme Court Justice. There was no justice for her in college, though. She flunked out of school after meeting some weird liberal friends her first year of college who got her thinking about strange things, like social injustice and how inherently corrupt the world was, and how it supposedly all really worked. Supposedly it was all some sort of ploy against them, and they were all victims of racial injustice because of some uncontrollable "past events." They started smoking weed—or "pot," as they called it—and their relaxation time they called "pot parties." This is where she met my daddy, and this is where we begin the story of my life, the story of Johnnie Spot Perfect, the man they still talk about today in the NBA as the one who was determined to "never give up… or die trying."

Historically the 1960s through the 1980s in America was a time of quiet domestic and social change both internally and politically by the Holy Spirit, who controlled and orchestrated the vast happenings on earth. Much of what was going on was because not enough missionaries were being sent out to spread the gospel, and abortion, a repugnant insult to the miracle of creation itself, was a common practice across all races. There were no clean hands in the laundry room of life. Family standards were being broken up across the board with a barrage of no-fault divorce practices and false narratives crusaded by ideological members of the US Supreme Court, Hollywood producers, university professors, ill-willed attorneys, self-serving politicians, technology innovations, and poisoning of the food supply. Suicide rates were on the rise from the indifference and distraction of social messaging going on in the media rooms. On the surface, there was historical change with confusion happening everywhere. But in the mind, spirit, and soul, it was silent and deadly for the new generation, where victimization was put on television to make money for the corporate offices, while making surrogates and addicts of all peoples on many imperfect things that made others wealthier. God had made all things perfect, while man put his hands to making all things more imperfect in God's eyes, while justifying lies regarding everything to make an 'honest dollar' was aired in many forms of social easing, but the real victims were the good and loyal citizens and their families who had to put up with the world of globalizing media giants, who were nothing more than journalistic prostitutes selling their evil promotional wares. The digital revolution of stealing personal liberties via soft-selling social injustice had begun, and the victims were many on both sides, with no God in the middle to claim victory. The proud heroes of World War II were now dying at an unprecedented pace. They had fought for something they believed in—liberty and freedom—and now the world had forgotten what war really looked like. Along with them faded their hard-fought family values. Parents claimed that young males were too harsh and that they never hugged their children, so now children were being brought up to be friends with their parents, and "being good" was valued over being strong or right. Families were ruled now by family democratic voting, with wives and children outvoting their fathers in a form of emasculation that lowered generational male testosterone.

-- Remembering a Tough Childhood in South Central Los Angeles in 2006 --

The Holy Spirit watched in horror. The 1960s had welcomed in the age of free sex with easy access to "the pill," women's rights in the workplace, rock 'n' roll, and the digital age of cell phones and computers. Abortions were becoming as common as takeout food. A new voice was taking hold, cries of: "I want it now," "Someone else is responsible," "Just put it on credit," "Bill my insurance, please," "I need a new car and a bigger house," and "Who cares? We are all in this together!" The real problem was that the generation of the old guard which had lived by high standards of individual responsibility and saving money for a rainy day had given way to "Intellectualism," where a liberal arts degree meant more than common sense, and where football games on television had distracted men from taking their families to church on Sundays. The world was so busy being reborn into new liberal values that were based on character assassination and dodging with spinning questions to "show how smart a liar you can be" and working to get ahead, that no one really worried about day-to-day consequences. But over the long haul, an attitude of invincibility was setting in. The Cuban Missile Crisis had ended without a shot, so America ruled by virtue of its political will, and the War in Vietnam substantially hurt the political machines of both parties, but pulling out in retreat was not a sign of defeat. The aftermath question of the war was: who was to blame for the decay in the big cities? White Flight was common in the major suburbs, for they could no longer stomach the low standards forced onto them by the public school systems. The 55,000 young men who died in Vietnam, in an effort to root out evil in that part of the world, were merely a distraction from the civil disobedience happening on the home front, the women's liberation movement outwardly emasculating white men, the college street demonstrations, and the burnings of the American flag. There seemed to be no end to the young generation looking for answers and relief from the pain of not being able to live up to the standards the previous generation had set. The same had happened with the fall of the Roman Empire, the British Empire, the Spanish Empire, and all the others… great and noble conquerors who ruled for a long period of time, all supposedly invincible, but eventually all fell from their full power, might, and glory due to internal decay at home.

Once after driving home from seeing the old apartment where Momma and I had lived like sardines in an old tin can, I remember vividly a conversation I'd had with my dad on a Sunday afternoon while we were sitting on the couch together watching the six-o-clock news.

"What are you watching on TV, Dad?" I asked my daddy one day while he was sitting on the family's green couch that smelled like either a dead animal or rotten food lived inside of it.

"J.J., some white po-po man is beating a black n----r brother up on the ground next to his car!" he said. "Reminds me of when I was a teen in Watts—there was no justice by the po-po then!—so I bet there's gonna be a big fire burning tonight somewhere in a shop in south central LA, and I'm gonna be there helping!"

-- Remembering a Tough Childhood in South Central Los Angeles in 2006 --

"What about Momma?" I asked. "You know she's sick again. Aren't you going to help me take care of her tonight?"

"Your momma needs to take care of herself. I ain't helping her!" he said. "Nope, no way, never! She's so messed up now... she is just costing me more money than I got's... she's white, and her daddy has lots of money. He can come get her any time and take her back to his big castle in Texas. Me, I'm gonna get me some new shoes tonight from a broken store front!"

That was the second-to-last time I ever saw my daddy, and I don't remember much from the other handful of times I even met him. Momma said they used to love to go to the park together just south of the college where she went to school. They would laugh and poke fun at the outside world that was ignorant of the way things really worked... the world of the smart people who had all the answers, and who had their own television shows, and who were getting paid for doing things people used to frown at, like being in that new magazine called *Playboy*. Everyone wanted to be like Hugh, the immortal bachelor who had it all: the perfect life of good food, good clothes, and good sex.

These distant memories from my childhood are all hard for me to go back and face. Since my wife left me, all the money I made from my hard work in the NBA is now going to my foundation to help the poor, to those who grew up just like me… without a real home or real family. I love to go to orphanages now and watch the kids laugh and play. It always seems about the age of fourteen that the real world sets in, and the young kids can no longer laugh unless they have someone to laugh with… because there is nothing to live for if they have no family or home. But I was lucky enough to be adopted, and later on I laughed a lot.

It was just a normal day in Paradise for this generation, as the angels sang their praises and carried on with the duties of caring for each other. Selfishness and the desire to put one's self first did not exist in Heaven—it never had and never could exist there. Selfishness only exists on earth, which was designed, brought forth, and born in the Garden of Eden after the fall from grace. God was patiently waiting in the Center Garden of Heaven for this current age of non-enlightenment to be done… and for 'His Kingdom Come' period to begin. He had been watching over His twelve tribes of Israel[164] (Israel whom He had once called Jacob, whose father had been born Isaac, and whom God favored over Ishmael, and whose grandfather was Abraham, the father of God's eternal plan for His earthly creation). The Lord's angels carried out His divine volition. They were His numbered and ordered minions whose primary task was to keep the world in order and hold His plan together as it unfolded. His masterful plan had taken seven millennia to unfold since His last epoch, for the human genome of Christ's blood had to wind its way carefully and intricately through time to prepare the

[164] Deuteronomy 33: 6-25, Judges 5: 14-18

world. Christ's blood had to be spilled more than ten billion times before God could call his ten billion home. At that time He would then repopulate the world through His own Son, Jesus, who would rule again as in the days of old.

The Holy Spirit, who lived with His ten billion souls the Trinity created for themselves—for He was alive in each of them, and also alive in Paradise as He commuted amongst the Believers—now called for the accounting of the Twelve Tribes of Jacob, whom God had renamed Israel.

"COME FORTH! ALL YE TWELVE SONS OF JACOB WHO SET MY PLANS INTO MOTION," the Holy Spirit roared like a lion from his den. "REUBEN, SIMEON, LEVI, JUDAH, ISSACHAR, and ZEBULUN: stand next to your mother, Leah! GAD and ASHER, stand next to your mother, Zilpah! DAN and NAPHTALI, come stand next to your mother, Bilhah! And JOSEPH and BENJAMIN, stand next to your mother, Rachel! You were blessed by your father Jacob,[165] as I blessed him through Isaac, son of Abraham[166]. BUT BE SILENT AND SHAKE! I shall not speak to you this day, but only to your mothers, who have been called here to answer."

Then the Holy Spirit set them apart and lined them up, putting the twelve sons of Jacob on His right side and the four wives of Jacob on His left. "DO NOT SPEAK, ANY OF YOU!" He commanded. Then He called for His cherubim to attend the meeting, as well as the archangels: Gabriel, Michael, Phylamonas, and Verostices. "BRING ME the sons of Joseph, whose names are EPHRAIM and MANASSEH, and place them before me so that I

[165] Genesis 49
[166] Genesis 27

might look upon then, but do not bring ASENATH, their mother. And prepare REBEKAH, wife of ISAAC, from her separate place, so she knows that I call her, too."

The center of Paradise was not in harmony with the angels, or to the extremes of the farthest reaches of Heaven, for the unrest was being felt across all the dimensions of all three domains: Heaven, Hell, and Paradise (which also included earth on the lower chamber).

Upon Israel's deathbed, he had summoned his two sons, Jacob and Esau, ready to bless his older son, Esau; but Rebekah, with enmity in her heart—for Esau had married women of the Hittites, the unclean—had set out on an unrighteousness mission to undermine and deceive her husband, Israel, and make him give to Jacob, the younger brother, the total blessing. No longer did the birthright and blessing of being the firstborn in holy lineage,[167] as ordered by God, go to the oldest son, chosen by God himself. This was foreseen by Christ himself to be answered when he came to rectify the wrongs done by this deed, so that he might prevail as the firstborn and only born to the Father himself in the world, so that no prideful human genome dynasty could be established.

"Bring me EPHRAIM and MANASSEH!" the Holy Spirit ordered the cherubim. And so they were brought in to the trial of REBEKAH. "Tell me again who your mother was!" the Holy Spirit commanded them.

"Asenath, daughter of Potiphar," they replied simultaneously.

"And which of you received your father's blessing with his right hand?" the Holy Spirit inquired of the two.

"I did," answered Ephraim, who was younger than Manasseh.

---

[167] Genesis 27:37

"Do you know why?" the Holy Spirit asked, moving around them in a full circle as He inspected their glowing bodies of sainthood for their deeds.[168] They stood silent, for they knew who would answer for them.

Joseph, their father, also blessed by his father Israel, stepped forward to answer, but before he spoke, he asked to be represented by Verostices, who had been there in the original days, so that his words would not falter in the wake of the Holy Spirit's anger. Then Verostices stepped between Joseph, son of Isaac, and the Holy Spirit, to plead the younger brother's case.

"Oh, Holy One, You and You alone know the heart of Joseph when he was a slave," Verostices breathed, "for it was he who stayed pure and he who ran from the house of Potiphar and his wife when she tried to seduce and discredit him, so that he ended up in prison, a servant of the king there. There You gave him sight in the darkness, to see what no other could see.[169] Even the Pharaoh had no eyes for the future, but Your servant Joseph did, and You blessed him with many wonders of leadership and counsel, and you gave to him the daughter of Potiphar, so he could have two sons by that tribe. And of these sons, he placed the younger over the older so they could have their own community on the earth and be equal in the tribe of Joseph, and they produced many more tribes upon tribes, though they were—from the beginning—of the disloyal house and the pompous breed."

"Yes, Verostices, you are correct," the Holy Spirit responded, "for you are my witness to these things that did occur, and you held the hand of the one who would bring forth a ruler to the earth. And

[168] Genesis 48:15-17
[169] Genesis 39

which son of Israel did I then choose to be the human gene carrier of my Lord through the years right up to Mary, the Virgin, who would then set right the sins of Rebekah, to bear a firstborn without a mortal husband, to the second honorable Joseph, who would be the stepfather to My own divine and blessed Son above all, Jesus Christ, of Bethlehem?"

"It was Judah, from Leah, first wife of Israel, oh Most Holy One," Verostices replied. "For You declared, 'He is the one who will be praised by all his brothers because he keeps his hand on the neck of Your enemies; and he is like the lion, whom all dare not rouse; and he guards Your scepter, which will never deteriorate. Judah is the bloodline to the second Adam, the only man without sin."

"Yes, you are correct again, Verostices. Now bring me Rebekah!" The Holy Spirit declared. "I wish to ask her one question, and one question only…"

So they brought Rebekah, the one chosen to be the wife of Isaac, father of all good nations, and son of Sarah, unknown to Hagar.

The Holy Spirit rose up to the Heavens and then fell back down to Hades. He twisted and turned in agony, for Rebekah had not sought counsel with Him before unseating Esau from his position to receive the first-born blessing. Her pride had caused Esau, her beloved son and the good and faithful servant of Isaac, to lose his blessing.

"Rebekah," the Holy Spirit rumbled, low and sternly, "I ask you once and but once: Do you repent of your prideful deed whereby you neglected to seek counsel with me before you acted? For you are blessed highly here in Heaven and the Lord God has bestowed on you much responsibility, yet like Eve, you fell prey to Satan and cast your will above God's will!"

"You know my heart, Lord! I repent every day, and yet you ask me every day," she wailed, now on her knees. "Must my life run like a saga before my eyes that I must watch over and over again for eternity?"

"Yes, you must!" the Holy Spirit answered. "And even though you and the rest are forgiven and your sins are no more, the course of many has been altered by your actions, and to them you must make account. They will look to you for guidance, for you led them astray, and so the sin nature of the Twelve Tribes goes on. Oh, when will they turn to Mary, mother of Jesus, and repent as you do, so they can follow the woman who was faithful to God and not man?"

Verostices answered for Rebekah now.

"Oh, Holy One, You sent the twelve disciples of Christ out into the world to claim back the loyalty of the Twelve Tribes of Jacob, their father, whom You renamed Israel, but they have refused and are a stubborn lot. Then you sent St. Paulus out unto the Gentiles, for their own hearts are open to you because they were chosen last, like the second sons of Ephraim and Manasseh by many different women, but then you said to James, born the second son of Mary, brother to Jesus, with the same blood as Mary, his mother, that he would know who the Twelve Tribes of Mary's sons shall be in the new age of Jesus, Son above Mary, and Redeemer of Your new holy order, ruling even now over above Rebekah in the Heavens and on earth, challenging Judah for his might and wanting to fill in over her husband Jacob. This will not happen!"

"You are again correct, Verostices, angel of the day and protector of the night. Take Gabriel, Phylamonas, and Chalymina with you and check on my next mortal messenger, Johnnie Spot; then report back to me if he is yet ready for his great blessing!" The

Holy Spirit then dismissed those attending the trial of Rebekah and moved on to praise the Father in Heaven, and the Son Jesus, who both retained their place above Him in Paradise, for the great plan was being revealed once more….

The US-Vietnam Conflict

"Mayday! Mayday! Bird down… bird down! This is Sonny… Hercules, can you read me? Sonny, the Bird Man! Can you read me? Can you read me? Coordinates: Alpha-six-niner-two… alpha-six-niner-two … Mayday, mayday! Bird down! Need help! Can you read me?" Sonny repeated this message three times before he had to abandon his chopper and get out of there. It would be a terrible fall, and he knew there was not much time before the Viet Cong would be coming for him… a few minutes, maybe, at most. He scrambled to free himself from his harness. Just twenty minutes earlier he had been laughing and joking with his copilot, Bobby McIntyre, about how they would all be home for Christmas this year, riding sleighs in the badlands of North Dakota under an Aurora Borealis that didn't exist there, though that hadn't stopped them from talking as if it did. In his mind, Sonny could still see Bobby sitting across from him, in that white chopper helmet with the words "BOBBY" in big bold letters across the forehead. He looked over now and saw Bobby's helmet had blood all over it. Bobby had taken a 50-caliber bullet in the neck, which was gone now except for a small chord that was still attached to his head, which rested on his left shoulder, eyes still open, body hanging upside down. It was a shocking sight to Sonny that he would never forget. The war in Vietnam was at its height and the corpses were lining the tarmac every day to be taken home to loved ones. Their rescue chopper had been doing just that. Sonny and Bobby had been sent out to pick up a stranded patrol who was taking heavy fire when their back rotor was hit after liftoff, about thirty feet in the air, and the chopper began to spin uncontrollably. The windshield was blown out on the way down when Bobby was hit. Sonny knew it would be a hard landing.

The year was 1966. Rock-n-roll music of the Beatles had invaded the homes of America while the military of America had invaded the homes of southeast Asia. The world was changing quickly, while most global, social, and economic boundaries were being broken down. Once again, none of it was good for mankind, for man was chasing his dreams to make the world a more perfect place, while actually accomplishing the opposite. Both Bobby and Sonny had been part of the military draft. Sonny had grown up in south Texas, in Hidalgo County. His father had owned a crop duster company, which was where he had learned to fly, while the other boys were all out on the football field trying to win the girls' affections. Bobby was from Butte, Montana, and had spent most of his life herding cattle from the backside of a horse. But Bobby's time on earth was over now, and more than likely his family would not get to see him home. Sonny reached over and grabbed Bobby's dog tags as he jumped from the plane, yelling, "Follow me, boys," to the four crewmen and two wounded soldiers in the back. But there was no answer. When he put his foot on the ground, he could tell he had been hit too. His left lung felt like it was full of water, but Sonny knew it had to be blood from the fall. In survival training he had been told to run into the thickest brush he could find, because if he ran down a path, most likely he would meet the Charlies coming at him, which would be the end of him. So instead he ran right into the thorns and jungle brush, making several circles to stay close to the chopper, because it was his only way out. He could hear them coming. The rest of the patrol were now firing and using the downed chopper for protection. They were going to stick together, as they had been instructed, but Sonny knew from the air surveillance they did not have a chance. There were more than three thousand Charlies on the border of Cambodia not a few miles from where they had gone down. They could either fight to the bitter end, or end up in a POW situation that would certainly be worse than death itself. Sonny had an issued survival kit that was good for about six hours. One food bar, a pistol, a flare gun, and an injectable cartridge of cyanide in he wished to use it over being caught.

"My God," Sonny thought to himself, "this is not the way it is supposed to be. It should be someone else, not me. This is not my time to die… It is not my time!"

What good is it, my brothers and sisters, if someone claims to have faith but has no deeds? Can such faith save them? Suppose a brother or a sister is without clothes and daily food. If one of you says to them, "Go in peace; keep warm and well fed," but does nothing about their physical needs, what good is it? In the same way, faith by itself, if it is not accompanied by action, is dead.

Attested and witnessed by James,
Your Brother in Christ
(oldest brother of Jesus)
Chapter 2:14-17

Chapter 2

Forced to Texas and a New Beginning

1975

Young Johnnie was lost now more than ever… severely lost. He had nothing! Not even a real identity. He was stepping into a world of strangers where everything was new and foreign, almost as if he were in a new country with a new language. His mother had died of an overdose (drugs mixed with too much alcohol). His father, he had not seen in several years… not since he had walked out of his life on an early Saturday morning. And Jamie's mother, his momma's closest friend, was the only person he knew at all in the world, and she would not—could not—take him in nor care for him. She had so many problems of her own, and another mouth to feed was just not possible for her. It seemed Johnnie just couldn't catch a break in his young life.

The day he landed at California's Center for Foster and Adoption, Johnnie was mad at the world. More than that, he was bitter: his life's grapes had soured before they could become wine, and he wondered what he had done to deserve such agony, such abandonment. No one loved him and no one cared. He was alone, with nowhere to turn. So he had no choice but to get mean and tough quick… just to survive his meager, pathetic life.

He went through the usual questioning by adults. He was only nine years old, and he should have been in school, in the fourth grade, but that was not his reality. He was behind in his education compared to his peers and that would be a major hindrance in getting him blended into a normal family somewhere. While sitting in the main office, he heard one of the directors talking on the phone to a lady that she referred to has Johnnie's grandmother. She lived in Houston, but where that was, Johnnie had not the faintest idea. In fact, he did not even know where he was now… just a strange place where he was asked to wear strange clothes and flip-flops. It was sort of like the Juvenile Home where he had been before, when Childhood Protective Services had taken him, but a little different. At least people cared for him here and he got to eat with other kids, with parents sometimes sitting at the tables with them. He was told that these parents were looking to adopt children to be their own, but Johnnie wanted nothing to do with that business. He just wanted to get out and take his chances on the street, which he knew might be a big mistake, but he did not care. He felt confident he could take whatever punches came his way.

"Mrs. Gleason," Johnnie heard the administration lady say into the phone, "the state will pay for the transportation of both you and Johnnie if you will just come get him. That would be easiest for everyone…" Then they talked for a little longer, but the whole conversation made Johnnie feel uneasy.

Finally the lady hung up the phone. She got up from her chair and came to sit down beside him on the bench against the white wall.

"Johnnie, you are going to stay with you grandmother in Houston, Texas. Her name is Mrs. Gleason; she is your mommy's mother."

"I don't care!" Johnnie screamed. "I hate her!"

"How can you hate someone you have never met?" the counselor asked.

"Doesn't make any difference. I will run away when I can," he said.

"She sounds like a good person," she replied. "She says she looks forward to seeing you and wonders if you look like her late husband, Charles."

"Big deal! I don't want to go," he retorted.

"You have to go, Johnnie. There is no one here who can take care of you, and we don't have enough space as it is. Tomorrow you are flying to Houston. She will meet you at the airport tomorrow night. We will give you new clothes for your journey, and you will be in your new bed by tomorrow night."

"And what about… what about my mother?" he asked feebly, tears welling up in his eyes. "I want to see her again. I don't wants to leave her."

"Johnnie, your mother is in Heaven now," she said gently. "That just can't happen. You need to begin to look forward, not backward."

"But I want to be with her! She's the only person who ever loved me! I want her back! I need her now!" Johnnie screamed, swinging at the woman who was trying to console him. Two security guards rushed into the room, one man and one woman, and pulled little Johnnie off of the woman.

She stood up and spoke pointedly. "Johnnie, don't let hate rule your life, or you will die alone, with no one around to even show up at your funeral. Please forgive your mother. She didn't want to die. It just happened. She loved you, I know, and I hope your grandmother can help you get over this pain you carry." The two security guards pulled him out of the counselor's room and into the arms of a third security officer, who must have weighed three hundred pounds or more. Johnnie, who weighed no more than sixty-five pounds, was nevertheless fighting and struggling, yelling, "You can't make me go! I don't want to go!! You can't make me!!" Finally—desperate, exhausted, and feeling utterly alone—Johnnie slumped into a deep sleep.

When Johnnie was taken to the Los Angeles airport to fly to Texas, he had a big yellow tag on him that said, "Gleason." The stewardess seated him in the front row of the airplane, but Johnnie uttered not a word the whole trip. When asked if he wanted water or juice, he just stared straight ahead, not even blinking. Sometimes he just played like he was sleeping so he could avoid interaction altogether.

When they landed in Houston, the stewardess walked him out to the receiving gate, where a large, gray-haired lady was standing with her cane. She wore a blue-and-white dress with some sort of flower pattern that made Johnnie squint to be able to focus on her. She had on stockings that were rolled up to below her knees and then just stopped, and she wore horn-rimmed glasses inlaid with rhinestones that made them sparkle in the sunlight. Her hair had clearly just been done at the beauty shop and sprayed stiff with hairspray so it did not move when she walked. It looked more like fishing net you could see through than human hair. But none of this made an impression on Johnnie… he knew she was just another enemy who would let him down in his time of need. She also wore a yellow lanyard that said "Gleason" on it, and the stewardess seemed relieved to see her, but also felt a little sorry for her, because she knew the old lady was in for holy hell when she got this little S.O.B. home.

"Look, Johnnie, there's your new grandma," the stewardess said to him. She had to push him from behind to get him to step forward, but he looked away, as if repelled by the sight of his new grandmother.

"Well, hello there, grandson! I am so happy to see you! So, you do look like my Charlie. You have his eyes! And you know, he was one smart man. He was probably a genius in his own right. Everybody liked him, and I am sure everybody will like you too," she said to Johnnie, who was still trying to avoid any interaction with her at all costs.

"Johnnie," the stewardess said, "when you come back to California, I want you to tell me all about Texas. I hear they have longhorn cows there and oil wells where the stuff just shoots out of the ground by itself… and cowboys, too. Do you like cowboys?"

As Johnnie continued to stand there in silence, his grandmother realized that she had her work cut out for her, trying to find a warm heart in this seemingly cold shell of a little boy.

"Well, young man," she said, undeterred, "I have a room already for you. It has a window facing east, and when the moon is full, it will look like a big flashlight in the sky. I actually think we're gonna have one tonight, so let's go home and see if we can see what wonderful things God has hidden for us up in that sky of his." That was Mamaw's way of saying, "Young man, I really hope I can get through to you, because your life depends on it." She knew she had just a few years to set a good foundation for him at this tender age or he would be lost to the world, and maybe the underworld, if she could not break the cycle of violence in his life and give him something to believe in other than pain and despair. Satan would rule him then, and Mamaw was determined not to let that happen.

When they arrived at the house, Johnnie found it clean and neat... really overly clean and neat. A big yellow lab named Cojo rushed to the door to greet them as they entered. Cojo was not a very good guard dog unless no one was home, and then he became a nut-case barking machine. He had even attacked the mailman once, which was very atypical of him, but the mailman was new and had tried to open the door to put a package on the floor inside. Mamaw felt safe at night knowing her protector always slept by the front door.

"Do you want to see your new room?" she asked Johnnie.

Again, no answer.

"Cojo, go find your ball," Mamaw commanded the dog. Quickly, the dog ran up the stairs and returned with a tennis ball, setting it at Johnnie's feet. The dog then lay flat on all fours, stomach directly pressed against the carpet, and stared at the ball. Mamaw turned to Johnnie and said, "Why don't you try and take the ball from him?"

This was a challenge which Johnnie did not quite understand yet. He was still young, though he did understand greed and the word "mine."

"Johnnie, Cojo thinks the ball is his. He likes to play with people until they take the ball away and he thinks he won't get it back, and then he gets sort of angry. Why don't you just raise your hand like you are going to take his ball from him…" Mamaw said. This actually intrigued Johnnie enough that he raised his hand and slowly moved it toward the ball. He heard a low growl coming from the dog. When he put his hand back down, the growling stopped. He raised it again, and again Cojo began to growl. He moved it a little closer, and Cojo's tail began to thump the floor in a rhythmic fashion, while the growling grew more intense. As a small child, Johnnie had once been bitten in the park by a dog that was fighting with another dog… Johnnie had just been in the wrong place at the wrong time. These two dogs had gotten into a fierce fight over some scraps of fried chicken thrown into a garbage can on the side of the playground, and the fight had erupted when Johnnie's mother was throwing away a beer can. Johnnie had been too young to know what to do, and his mother had been too drunk to get him out of the way or protect him, so he had gotten bitten in the dog fight. And now he was living with a creature from canine hell, a fluffy psycho fur ball with a sad face that owned a ball that no one could take from him. Johnnie was suddenly fed up with this ridiculous situation and could not care less about the dog.

"Do you want to see your room?" Mamaw asked him again, but still no answer came. "Well, okay, so now you have met your new roommate…" she said. Then she turned to Cojo and said, "Cojo, go to your room!" The dog immediately grabbed his ball, made an about-face, and hopped up the stairs, taking a turn into the first room on the right.

Suddenly Johnnie spoke, for the first time since the tussle at Child Foster Services.

"I'm sleeping in the same room with that animal? I will sue you if that son of a bitch bites me!"

"Oh, my goodness, son, where did you learn such foul language? I used to wash your momma's mouth out with soap when she was your age and she talked like that. This isn't going to be any different for you, neither. I am not going to let you run away like she did and mess up my life twice, and you aren't going to run, either! So, boy, you had better get tough now or it is gonna be hell around here, and you have not seen hell until you are cold and hungry with no place to run to. Now follow me, and I do mean follow! Now march!"

Johnnie had never been given such bold instructions and was not sure what to make of the situation. All he had ever known was, '*Comme ci, comme ça*,' which had been his mother's fancy way of saying, 'Life always sucks, so whatever you want is fine.' Of course, being from southern California, the meaning got garbled somehow in its usage, and that attitude clearly was not going to fly in this Texas house. Jenny had been a daddy's girl, but Charlie and Jenny were both dead. Mamaw figured she had about ten years left before she would expire… a very short time to make amends for her daughter's mistakes. Jenny had just been a bad apple, she thought to herself. Nevertheless, she still felt remorse that she had not been able to prevent her from becoming a runaway child. Jenny's problems had seemed to start about age nine or ten, same as Johnnie was now.

Up the stairs they both went. When they turned right at the first door, they saw that Cojo was on the bed with his ball still in his mouth. It scared Johnnie, so Johnnie stopped at the door and would not step into the room. Mamaw told him to come over so she could show him something. She led him over to the big bay window that looked out over the street below.

"This was your momma's bedroom when she was your age. I finally got around to painting it and changing the curtains when I got the phone call that you were going to come here to stay with me."

"You mean, my momma really lived here? Right here?" he asked.

"Yes, sir, young man… right here! And this was her bed too," she replied. "I have taken all her things away and put them in storage, in the attic, to make room for you."

"They didn't tell me I was going to live where my momma had lived," he said.

"Okay, so now you know. Another thing you should know is your mommy climbed out of this window when she was sixteen and ran away. She never came back. I have screwed it shut so you can't climb out too. You are going to have to just suck it up and get along with Cojo or one of you is going to die, and I don't think it is going to be him!" Mamaw began to tease him, her way of saying, 'This is your home, like it or not, and you WILL LEARN TO GET ALONG.' Then she walked out and closed the door behind her. She wanted them to figure it out on their own. Johnnie would have to learn to negotiate, and better to do it with a dog than a person. He needed a new skill set, and she knew that meant getting him out of his comfort zone.

In the morning, Mamaw opened the door to see who had won the battle for the bed, and she found Cojo sleeping on it, with Johnnie on the floor, still in his clothes from the long trip. Cojo needed to go outside, so Mamaw took him to the back door and let him out to do his business.

That evening Mamaw sat Johnnie down on the couch. She wanted to talk to him about something.

It was toward the end of summer and Johnnie would need to be enrolled in the public school down the street, in fifth grade. There were forms that needed to be filled out, and immunization records to update, none of which were easy on Mamaw's social security and what little pension she had from Charles' forty years of service at the post office. But she was a trooper, a real sergeant at arms, and she would make sure everything got done quickly to get Johnnie into school.

The problem was, Johnnie had no original birth certificate, and Jenny never had told Mamaw what Johnnie's father's last name was, so she didn't know what name to put on all the school enrollment forms. But Mamaw had an idea: she thought this would be something that Johnnie might want to be involved with. He certainly had not taken a shine to his grandmother, and maybe it would help ease tensions between them if he could pick out an identity for himself. So she broached the topic with her grandson.

"Johnnie, young man, you are going to be going to school soon, and you need a last name for their records. So… well, I was wondering if you wanted me to use our last name, which is Gleason, as your last name," she asked carefully.

"No, I don't," he quickly replied. Mamaw always believed in honesty, so she said to him, "Well, we don't know your father's last name, so we have a little bit of a problem what to write down on your school applications."

Johnnie was quiet for a minute, mulling this new information over in his head. Finally he said, "I don't care. Just call me anything, or nothing... maybe nothing is a good last name. How about 'Johnnie Nothing'?"

"That is not a last name, Johnnie... that is a description. You cannot have a last name called 'Nothing'."

"What about 'Christ'?" he asked. "I hear you say that all day long! 'Oh my goodness, save me, my blessed Jesus Christ!' "

"Johnnie, you can't use that one either… that one is reserved and taken," Mamaw said resolutely.

"Is it a description?" he asked. Mamaw was becoming rather agitated. Her face was starting to redden, and she chided herself that she should have just used 'Gleason' and avoided this whole difficult conversation with this difficult child.

"Yes, well, the word Christian or the name Christ can be used as is a description or name, but it is certainly NOT your last name," she said a little more loudly than she had planned.

"I want a description…You always say 'Perfect Cojo this', and 'Cojo is perfect at that' and that he is the 'perfect' dog, and that 'dog' is 'God' spelled backwards. So I want my last name to be 'Perfect,' just like Cojo's last name. That way you will like me as much as you like Cojo when I am older," Johnnie said.

The boy's words and vulnerability and need for love and acceptance cut straight to the tender part of Mamaw's heart. Although she was at her wit's end trying to reason with the boy to pick out a normal last name, she couldn't look into his sweet little eyes and deny him this request. She took a big breath and exhaled a loud sigh.

"Okay. Well, young man, I think you will one day regret this choice, but I will see what I can do for you. Maybe this will make you happy…" she said to him, though she seriously doubted it.

For the next four mornings, when Mamaw went in to let Cojo out, she found Johnnie asleep on the floor. This told her he was non-confrontational, at least when it came to something bigger and better than himself, which was a good thing. She had been brought up in the east Texas Piney Woods, the Bible Belt, in the city of Tyler, to be exact, and she had gone to church as a young girl. She remembered two sermons in particular very clearly: 'Fear the Lord[1]' and 'Jonah could run but he could not hide[2].' Her father would say to her, "Babs, there are just two kinds of people on this earth: those who are servants of the King, and those who are enemies of the King, and I thank God each and every day that you and I both fear the Lord so we are on his good side. We should consider ourselves lucky to be considered his own children with eternal life… for he loves us just as I love you."

Each morning Johnnie would wake to the smell of bacon frying on the big turquois-blue gas stove. Turquois-blue stoves were all the rage in the sixties, and Mamaw had bought a blue enamel sink to go along with it. It had always made her very proud, when her Charlie had still been alive, to wake up each morning and cook him the same breakfast of oatmeal, eggs, and bacon before he headed off to work delivering mail. This morning when Johnnie came downstairs, Mamaw greeted him with the same question she always did: "How did you sleep last night, young servant of the King?"

Above the bed where Cojo slept was a piece of wood, an oval about 14 inches long and 8 inches high, which Mamaw had made at summer camp one year when she was just about Johnnie's age. They had done wood-burning projects that summer where the kids could make any design or creation they wanted, to give some outlet to their creative side, and Mamaw had chosen to make a big plaque that read

'Servant of the King, John 3:16.' She had varnished it with floor varnish, which she gotten from one of her father's garage shelves, to give it that shiny look and had hung it over her bed when she and Charlie first got married. And then when Jenny was old enough to read, Mamaw had moved it to over her bed, and there it has stayed since she had run away.

"Cojo won't get out of bed with his ball," Johnnie answered, while grabbing a chair at the breakfast table, tearing a piece of bacon with his teeth, and then proceeding to talk with his mouth full of food.

"Well maybe you just don't know how to talk to him," Mamaw replied.

"I tell him to leave and point my finger at him, and point to the door, but he only growls and then starts thumping his tail." Johnnie exclaimed. "I hate him! He's a beast."

"Oh, really? And how do you define a beast, young servant of the Lord?" she teased him.

"Why do you keep calling me that? My name is Johnnie Perfect!" he yelled at her in exasperation.

"Okay, Mr. Johnnie Perfect, now I have called you by your name, even though you have not earned it. Now answer me this: how do you define what a beast is?"

Johnnie mulled this over for a second, and then said, "Someone who is different than me."

"That is very interesting. So, Cojo is a beast, huh?" Mamaw giggled.

"What are you laughing at? Are you laughing at me?" Johnnie asked, enraged.

He jumped up from the table and pointed his fork in Mamaw's face. Without skipping a beat, Mamaw pushed the table back toward him, knocking him to the floor.

"Don't you even come at me like that again, young man," she said in a low and controlled voice, "or I will take you down and you won't get up!" Mamaw looked Johnnie right in the eyes, getting right up in his face, to let him know who was the boss, right then and there. It wasn't him, and that was something he would never forget for the rest of his life.

"Now tell me what you think of the plaque over your bed," she said coolly, changing the subject.

"I don't know," Johnnie replied, still somewhat shaken by Mamaw's show of authority.

"There is another rule in the house, and that is that 'I don't know' is not an acceptable answer," she told him. "What does it say?"

Johnnie sat down quietly but didn't answer.

"So, you can't read, neither!" Mamaw exclaimed. "Or can you? Here… what does it say on this?" she asked, handing him a round container of oatmeal. He just stared at it. "Lord have mercy, you are supposed to be going into the fifth grade and you can't even read. Your momma was just as stubborn as you. They don't give us a teaching manual at the hospital when we go home with our kids, but and I wish they did! I would have raised your momma differently so she would have amounted to something instead of just having her own pity party every day, wanting something in life for nothing."

"Don't you be talking bad about my momma!" Johnnie challenged her, but immediately backed down, remembering that Mamaw was boss.

"Honey child and dear servant of the King, she came out from between my two legs and I knew her better than you ever did! She was stubborn as the day is long. God still loves her, though, and she is saved. She accepted Christ at the age of twelve. I tried and tried to love her, but she never let me in… she let God in, but she never let anyone else into her cold heart, and look where she ended up. And you ain't going there, Johnnie, unless it's over my dead body! So, you had better shape up soon or a good ass-whooping is next in store for you, and I mean it!"

Johnnie knew she meant it, so he wasn't going to press his luck today. Tomorrow was the first day of fifth grade, so mostly he just sat around the house and watched Mamaw clean. She had given him only one towel and it was beginning to stink, so she showed him the washing machine and taught him how to turn it on. She gave him all day to wash his one towel, and when night time rolled around, he had still not washed it.

"It's time for bed, Johnnie. You didn't wash your towel today like I asked you very nicely to do," Mamaw said calmly, pointing him toward his room.

"Well I ain't doing it," he replied.

"Fine, no problem…" Mamaw said. "In the morning you will still have to take your shower as always, but you will have to drip-dry before your first day of school. I hope you make a good impression. If you are not showered and ready by 7:30 a.m. sharp, dressed and in the car, then I will come up there and give you a bath like you are still a baby. Do you understand me, young servant of the King?"

Johnnie let out a long, "Awwww…" and went up to bed. The corner was now his regular place to sleep, and his shoulders were starting to hurt from sleeping on the floor. He had stolen the pillow off of the bed when Cojo was not around, but Cojo was still king of the bed at night and king of the front door during the day. As Johnnie saw it, he, himself, was king of nothing, and a prisoner in a home where he had no say or opinion.

At 6:45 the next morning, Mamaw heard the shower running. Whether Johnnie was actually in it or not was a different story. At 7:30 Johnnie was in the car ready for school. His hair was wet, but he smelled bad.

"You didn't take a shower this morning like I asked very nicely to, did you, Johnnie?" Mamaw prodded.

"Yes, I did," he retorted.

" 'Thou shalt not lie' is one of God's Commandments, young servant of the King, so don't you start that with me. Better to learn now the fruits of you labor will be good or bad depending on the words you speak and how you say them, or you are going to have a tough life, my friend."

"I am not your friend," Johnnie snapped at her. "I am your hostage."

"Okie-dokie, young man. Today is going to be very interesting, I can already tell that," she muttered as she pulled out of the driveway and headed toward Michael Jordan Elementary School, three blocks away.

Mamaw was right. *Interesting* turned out to be a mild way of describing the day. *Catastrophic* was more accurate. By the second week of school, Johnnie was expelled for fighting. He was asked not to come back. This was something he could control when Mamaw was not around, and he liked fighting. He was getting bigger than the other kids in both height and muscles, and was at least six inches taller than the next biggest kid in the school.

Sonny Francis lived about a mile from Mamaw's house, and this night he had had a bad dream. He leapt out of bed in a cold sweat, hitting the floor feet-first with a painful thud against the oversized armoire he had bought at the flea market to hold his military memorabilia. He was having early morning flashbacks of the night his chopper had gone down five years before. Rosanne, his wife, had not slept much that night either. She had been listening to him snore and then stop breathing for at least a minute before starting up again. Just the day before they had been to the Veteran's Hospital in Houston where Sonny had been diagnosed with sleep apnea.

"What's wrong, honey?" his wife asked groggily.

"I had another terrible dream. I can't go back to bed." Sonny went in to the dining room and sat down at a table covered with about a dozen bottles of vodka and rum. It seemed drinking was the only thing that would help his pain. The more he drank, the more he was sedated, but the sedation was becoming a severe depression.

Sonny couldn't seem to get any internal relief from his past. It was the one thing in life he could not overcome.

"Vietnam is haunting me," he would say to himself. "Why can't God just take it from me? I am at peace with it, but I can't shake it… it travels with me in my subconscious like a weed in my field of clover."

On that fateful night in the jungle, Sonny had had to sleep with leaves piled on him so the communist forces could not find him, knowing that if they did find him, more than likely he would be forced to play Russian Roulette with a loaded revolver in his mouth until it finally went off, blowing the back of his head off in a form of sadistic mental suicide that the Viet Kong loved to force on their prisoners of war.

What Sonny—now back home in the States—did not realize was that the food here had become so commercialized that he was being poisoned as well as victimized to a state of chronic cellular suffocation. His blood oxygen was falling below normal levels and he was dying a full-body cellular death when he was supposed to be recharging while he slept. His body was not able to accommodate the massive amounts of preservatives put into commercial foods, so he would stop breathing at night, and then, when his brain became asphyxiated, his adrenaline response took over and he would jump out of bed in cold sweat, as if he were in a burning building with no place to go. It was a hormonal response phenomenon utilized by the body to stimulate it when all else failed. Savvy doctors called "fight or flight," but neither term seemed to be appropriate to him because it was happening in his sleep, and in his dreams. So Sonny's VA doctors classified him as another PTSD patient, an inefficient way to avoid long-term treatment to help him physically as well as mentally. A majority of doctors and scientists at the time had not put together the complete understanding of sleep apnea just yet; and yes, combat mental trauma was one of the most obvious factors in the fight or flight response, but the severe mental depression that went along with it caused by the acidic blood lower than a pH of 7.35 and corresponding low oxygen transport levels were, in the end, causing most of the onerous casualties of suicide from mental depression that a majority of post-war military families were extremely worried about.

The reality of going to war as a patriot and then coming back from war changed, but not accepted as a war hero, was a contributing factor to many of the GI woes, but not the only factor. Survivors were coming home to a world they did not know. After giving everything they had to a country to defend its liberties, they returned to a country now led by liberal media that were turning the world against them through propaganda, even worse than Joseph Goebbels had done to the Jews pre-World War II with Hitler and his Nazis. It was the ultimate form of character assassination and it had been working since the beginning of time, all the way back to the Salem Witch Trials, Mao Tse Tung in Laos, and even Jesus Christ himself, almost two thousand years before.

Five years had passed quickly for Johnnie living in Houston with Mamaw as his new life-coach, and now he was growing into a young man, with his body getting an adolescent dose of the hormones HGH and testosterone. Mamaw had enrolled him at St. Stephen's Catholic School for Boys, hoping and praying for the best. She had spent many a night on her knees, praying for Johnnie to find God somehow, somewhere, sometime… but she was losing hope. Johnnie seemed to always be hanging out with the wrong crowd. And he was getting so big now that she could no longer physically force him to do what she wanted him to do. She had resolved that she would probably point him toward the army recruiter's office once he hit the age of eighteen and let them handle him from there. But even getting him to volunteer would be a chore. She prayed for the military draft to come back like when she was a child (but without a World War of course) because she wished him no harm, but she was terrified he would end up on drugs like his mother if God did not intercede with a miracle.

One night she was praying in her bedroom, on her knees. She had just read Job, the oldest book of the Bible, written even before Genesis. In the book, God allowed Satan to do terrible things to Job in order to test Job's loyalty to Him. This was exactly how Mamaw felt now. Her daughter had been taken from her by drugs, her husband by cancer, and now her only grandson was acting belligerent in school and running with the wrong crowd. He would skip the school's required daily mass service and not turn in his homework assignments. She even took his bed out of his room as punishment, so now both he and Cojo slept on the floor, with one on one side of the room and one on the other. Things were turning out as she had predicted. His will was too strong, and now she was at her wit's end. The extra money she was spending to send him to a private school had drained her savings, and each year she had to beg for financial scholarships to keep him in.

But on this night, after reading Job and praying, a voice spoke to her heart. It was Shemenea, her personal guardian angel, who had been watching over her since she was a little girl and had been baptized in the Tyler Baptist Church when she was twelve and accepted Christ. The guardian angels were not allowed to intervene unless instructed by the Holy Spirit, and in Mamaw's case, the time had come to reward her for her faithfulness and devotion to her Lord, for being a servant with a good heart, and for putting others before herself.[170]

"The coach will call you, and you will let him take Johnnie," Shemenea whispered into her heart. Suddenly a great peace came over her, and she felt as if something good was going to happen, though she did not know what. She did not care anymore, because she knew everything was out of her hands now anyhow. She would be seventy on her next birthday. She had no family except those at the church who got together for game night every once in a while. Johnnie was beginning to leave the house when she would leave, so she had begun giving up her own freedom just to keep him home, but she could do it no longer. She needed God's help now, or both of their lives would be destroyed.

So on that night—right then and there—she decided to let him go, just as she had done with Jenny so many years ago. It was just as painful as back then, but this time was different… this time she was putting it in God's hands first. She could be an observer now, not an enforcer.

---

[170] Hebrews 6:10, Galatians 5:13, I Peter 4:10, I Samuel 12:24

At exactly 11:32 a.m. the next morning, the phone rang. Her favorite show, Oprah, had just started at 11:30 and she did not want to miss this one because it was on women getting older and living alone. But she remembered the voice from last night, so she jumped out of her La-Z-Boy recliner and went to the kitchen to answer the ringing phone.

"Hello, this is Babs," she said into the receiver.

Babs was short for Baby, which is what her father had called her, since she had been the youngest of three children, and born almost twenty years after her older brother and sister. They had basically raised her, the two of them, because their parents had both had to work to make enough money to pay the rent and food bills. They had all lived a hard life, but had all gone to church on Sundays, where her dad had always put one dollar in the church plate when it passed by him, even if they did not have enough money for Sunday dinner.

"Hello, Ms. Gleason, this is Coach Thornton, the basketball coach from the school, and I would like to talk to you a moment about Johnnie," the voice on the other end of the line said.

"I've been waiting for your call," she said. "What took you so long?"

"What do you mean?" Coach Thornton said.

"God told me you would be calling… and now you have done it. The answer is yes to whatever you're calling me about," she said to him.

"This is quite interesting, but, ma'am, the reason I am calling you is Johnnie has asked to join the basketball team, and I need your permission to let him play on the team. We will be traveling for away games, and I'm not sure what your schedule will be like when he gets back to the school, if anyone will be available to pick him up and take him home…"

This was not the phone call she had expected, and Johnnie did not deserve any perks for being a stubborn child, but she agreed anyway.

"The answer is again yes, but I must say one thing: he doesn't have a father figure in his life, so maybe you can be one to him. Now you enjoy your new role, because if you can't change him, then he won't change, and it will be a pity for us all." She hung up abruptly, and then melted into the kitchen chair, exasperated from the strain of dealing with this child. She had not even said *goodbye*, or *thank you for calling*, or *have a nice* day… she was just exhausted. It was in God's hands now and she had passed the torch to Coach Thornton. She was washing her hands of Johnnie, and all she could think was *good riddance*!

Three weeks had gone by and Johnnie asked her to watch him play. They had made him a 'forward,' whatever that meant. They were playing in the gym at 4 o'clock that afternoon, and out of curiosity, Mamaw went to see him play. He was a freshman on the team, and he couldn't dribble the ball or even keep up running as fast as the other boys, but he was tall! His height helped him, and the coach saw promise in him. He made two points that game, which was really an accident while he was fighting for the ball under the basket and it went in. At that moment he looked up into the stands and smiled at Mamaw. It was the first time—perhaps in his entire life—that he actually felt good about something he had done, even though it was only by chance, or perhaps divine intervention. But either way, this was suddenly—at this watershed moment—Johnnie's new ambition. Mamaw could see the spark in his eyes, in his spirit, and she knew he was actually working for something he wanted—for the first time in his life.

Needless to say, it was a rough year for Johnnie. His teammates had nicknamed him "Spot" because he was the only white guy on the team. Johnnie had light skin and the rest of the team had dark skin, a mixture of different cultures. The Catholic school had recruited mostly young black boys to play for the team, and several had problems with the law, which scared Mamaw to death. She figured Johnnie would soon fall into similar trouble and that would be the end of his new-found passion, the only thing keeping him afloat in life. But by some miracle, days turned into weeks turned into months, and it did not happen. Coach Thornton kept a tight grip on all his boys, and they seemed to respect him for his "make it or break it" attitude. They would be sitting on the bench if they even looked at him sideways or got out of line from the team spirit or philosophy.

Throughout Johnnie's freshman year he averaged about one point (which was really 1.3 usually on a free throw), one assist, and one rebound per game. Although this was far from what a stellar performance, Johnnie began to see value in hard work. He stayed at the gym more and went with the other guys after school to a court to keep honing his skills. All the attention he was giving to basketball did not help his grades much, but then he was never going to be an Einstein anyway. Johnnie was convinced this was would be his new career, his meaning in life. The problem was he was no good… at least not in his beginning.

One afternoon after school, Coach Thornton came by Mamaw's house with Johnnie. Johnnie had made it a practice of coming in the back door to avoid Cojo, but the coach insisted on entering by the front door. This time they both stood at the front door and rang the doorbell so Mamaw would come let them in. Sure enough, Cojo began his incessant barking when he heard the doorbell ring, and Mamaw opened the door to find them both standing there, staring back at her. Coach did not look happy.

"Well, come in," Mamaw said to them. "Is there something wrong at school?"

"Not really," Coach Thornton replied, "but we would like to visit with you just a moment if we could, please?"

Inside the house they went, past Cojo, to sit in the family room, which was really just a two-seated couch, a television, and a recliner on a multi-colored oval braided rug. Cojo came too, ball in mouth, and took his position beside the couch. As they sat down, Coach leaned over to get the ball from the dog, who immediately began to growl at him.

"See, Coach?" Johnnie said. "This is the dog from hell I was telling you about."

Unbeknownst to both Johnnie and Mamaw, the whole reason why Coach Thornton had come to the house was to have a teaching moment with Johnnie. For three years, all Johnnie had been able to talk about at school was the dog at his house that forever kept him in fear, and Coach wanted to find out if it was true. Coach had images of a German Sheppard, a Chow, a Cattle Dog, or a Rottweiler mix, but none of these was the case. Cojo was just a Labrador Retriever with a little poodle in him, but by no means a bad breed.

"What did you want to see me about, Coach?" Mamaw asked. "Would you like some ice tea or other beverage while you are here?"

"No, thank you, Ms. Gleason" the coach replied. "Johnnie is doing quite well at my practices, and I wanted to take him and a couple of the boys to watch the Hurricanes play next month. I was hoping that would be okay with you," he ventured.

Johnnie was taken aback because he had known nothing of this when the coach had asked to come to his house. He had assumed he was in trouble for making a ruckus in the showers the other day.

"We haven't enough in our budget for sporting activities," Mamaw replied, "so unless he gets himself a job and earns the money, I am afraid I can't help with that. Any extra money I got this year went to new tennis shoes and other things so he could be a part of the school."

The coach had one eye on Cojo and one eye on Mamaw as he spoke. He figured the big leather shoes he had on were no match for the dog's teeth, and if the dog did try to bite him, it would be a quick event with Mamaw sitting right there, so he slowly moved his foot toward Cojo's ball. The leery old dog growled as he intently watched the foot approach him. Johnnie—who saw what Coach was doing—watched in amazement and eager expectation as Mamaw continued to talk to them, unaware of the drama unfolding beneath her nose.

"Johnnie," Coach said calmly, "would you please go open the back door for me for just a second?"

Johnnie rose obediently. Then, just as he opened the door, Coach Thornton's foot snatched the ball from Cojo and he tossed it outside through the back door with one swift motion. Cojo leapt up and raced out the door to retrieve ball, and without hesitation,

Johnnie closed the door behind the dog as instinct, keeping Cojo outside for the moment.

"That's what we call a 'backdoor play' on our opponent in basketball, Ms. Gleason. And you, young man," Coach addressed Johnnie, "have just have had your first lesson in scoring on the court."

He winked at Johnnie, and they both laughed, but Mamaw missed the whole joke. She was still deeply mired in the thought of Johnnie needing to go somewhere that she could not afford to send him. Johnnie came back and gave the coach a high-five that confirmed they were a team playing together, and once again Mamaw missed the point.

"Well," she said to them, "the Bible says that if a man does not work, he should not eat.[171] Johnnie will be sixteen next month, and I was thinking it was about time for him to get a summer job so he would have money of his own to do some of these things he wants to do."

"Well, we actually have the job-part figured out for you, Ms. Gleason," Coach replied, winking at Johnnie.

"Mamaw!" Johnnie interjected breathlessly. "They're gonna pay me to run the scoreboard for the football games, and help keep score at the other sports event, like baseball and volleyball! Will you let me do it, please, Mamaw… please?" Johnnie begged, almost childlike.

This hit Mamaw square in the heart, almost like an actual fist. She knew this was an important breakthrough—the first time Johnnie had really asked for anything from her.

---

[171] II Thessalonians 3:10

"Well, Coach, it you think this is the right thing to do, and you drove all the way over here to ask, I think we have a deal, if you promise me he will stay out of trouble at these late-night events." Mamaw added, "And, Johnnie, are you going to keep up your end of the bargain?"

"Yes, ma'am!" Johnnie replied without hesitation.

"He most certainly will, or he will be off the team, I can promise you that," Coach Thornton replied.

"Ok, then…" Mamaw said, glancing warily from Johnnie to Coach, and then back to Johnnie.

Coach told Johnnie to let Cojo back in, because he was standing there at the door waiting patiently. Johnnie obeyed.

"Johnnie," Coach said, "did anyone ever share with you that 'dog' spelled backwards is 'God'?"

"No, sir, never heard it," Johnnie replied.

"Your Mamaw knows her Bible," Coach said. "She quoted Proverbs. She is a good woman, Johnnie. You are lucky to have her… she is teaching you well. And Cojo is not a bad dog… he only wants to play ball… sort of like you on the court yesterday. You just needed someone to throw it to you."

"Huh," Johnnie responded, mulling all this over.

"I know your Mamaw is a smart lady," Coach continued, "because she never told you that Cojo just wanted to play. She's waited this long to let you learn this for yourself. You and this dog are a lot alike! You both growl when someone wants to take the ball away from you, but all you really needed was someone to play with. Can you see the paradox in that?" Coach Thornton asked.

Johnnie was silent for a moment. Things were beginning to click into place in his brain. Mamaw smiled. This was exactly what she had been waiting for these past few years. She had been trying to get this message through to her grandson this whole time, but now that someone else was delivering the message, she looked smart instead of pushy. She finally had some backup, some fortification! It was a good day for God to weave his mastery into the tapestry of young Johnnie's new life. And this was where the fun began! Now it was just steps—one, two, three—for God to take over and mold Johnnie into what God wanted him to be all along: a servant of the King.

As Coach was leaving that day, he stood on the front doorsteps and he turned to Johnnie.

"When I asked you to let Cojo back into the house, did you know there's a Bible verse for that too?"

"No, Coach, I didn't," Johnnie said.

"Knock, and the door shall be opened to you; no one comes to the Father but by me." Coach Thornton turned and left, calling over his shoulder, "I'll see you at practice tomorrow Johnnie! We have a lot of work to do, so don't be late!"

Johnnie continued to grow and grow, and by his sophomore year, he was 6'4", 195 pounds, and a mere 15 years old. In the first four preliminary games that year, he averaged 12 points, 8 assists, and 15 rebounds per game—not bad for such a big boy! Mamaw began to come consistently watch him play and cheer him on. He was big enough that he learned to dunk the ball, and even had good coordination. He wore a size 18 shoe now, and Coach Thornton had to order special shoes just to keep him playing. The team was now a contender for state finals in the church league, to be played in Dallas that year.

By the end of the season he was averaging over 30 points a game and 18 rebounds. There were several really good players around the state, and even though Johnnie was just a sophomore, he made it into the top one hundred college prospects because of his size and talent. But also because Johnnie had a special skill that a lot of the other contenders lacked: an uncanny ability to make the longshot from past half-court. Several games ended with Johnnie—finding the ball in his hands and just a few seconds left on the clock—shooting and scoring from half-court! "Icing on the cake!" Mamaw called it.

Sometimes Johnnie would say to his opponent, "In your face!" as he blew by them to score. But Coach Thornton got after him for that and would bench him for five minutes when he was disrespectful to the other team. Coach Thornton was head of the local Chapter of the Knights of Columbus, and he knew what it took to be a Knight for the Lord. He had monthly meetings in his home and kept a Coat of Arms Insignia up in office so all the young men that addressed him knew there was an order they must abide by, and that their Coach was definitely not at the top, and that they certainly were not either. It helped everyone keep perspective when times got tough.

"Spot" was becoming the kind of player the scouts wanted to see play; and he was getting to be quite the 'big man' on the school campus. He loved all the attention he got for being a sports hero, but whenever he got a little too big-headed, Mamaw quickly put him in his place, sitting him down and lecturing him on the values of life.

One night, after she had gone to pick him up after a semifinals game against Bracken Christian School, she sat with him in the car at 2 o'clock in the morning in front of their house and would not let him go inside until he read her a page of the Bible.

"Go ahead and pick any page," she told him. "Just open it up and read it.... I don't care what. Pick from the front, the middle, or the back. God will lead you to the right page. There's something good for you to learn on each and every page. I'll hold the flashlight. Then we can go inside."

It was so late at night and Johnnie was almost unconscious from fatigue. He just wanted to go in and sleep, but Mamaw insisted. She always kept an old tattered Bible of Charlie's in the backseat, and now she reached back and grabbed it, laying it gently on Johnnie's lap. He looked at it a minute, thinking this was pretty stupid. He had just had his best game ever. He had scored 45 points, destroying the other team almost single-handily. Coach Thornton had called Mamaw from the Burger King on the way home, wanting to let her know Johnnie would probably be getting a college scholarship next year in his junior year, and could probably pick any college he wanted. Johnnie did not know this, however; he just loved the game and felt Mamaw was way out of bounds making him read the Bible at 2 a.m. in the car.

Nevertheless, Johnnie humored his grandmother. He felt a certain tenderness for her now. He was too big for her to hit with the belt like she had done once for leaving the door open and letting the air conditioning out. That made her checking account bounce a check, costing them $35 dollars they did not have, so they'd eaten peanut and jelly sandwiches for a week just to pay that bill. He opened the Bible to a random page.

"Johnnie," Mamaw said, "read it to me out loud, please. I want to hear what the angels are telling me at night, if it is true."

Johnnie thought Mamaw was a little batty, and at sixteen he was pretty sure he knew it all.

"Let's see," Johnnie said, cracking open the Bible. "It is the book of Matthew, Mamaw. It says Chapter Nine, and the story is called 'The workers are few'..." Johnnie swallowed hard and then began reading. " 'Then Jesus went through all the towns and villages, teaching in their synagogues, preaching the good news of the kingdom and healing every disease and sickness. When he saw the crowds, he had compassion on them, because they were harassed and helpless like sheep without a shepherd. Then he said to his disciples, "The harvest is plenty, but the workers are few. Ask the Lord of the harvest, therefore, to send out workers into his harvest field." '[172] Now we're on Chapter 10," Johnnie informed Mamaw, and then continued. " 'So he called his twelve disciples to him and gave them authority to drive out evil spirits and to heal every disease and sickness.' "[173]

"That is enough, Johnnie" Mamaw said. "I believe these words are confirming you are to be a servant of the King. You do not know it yet, but I do, and you have many years ahead of you which will make you wonder about the life God has given you and why it takes certain paths." She knew the meaning of what James (brother of Jesus) was saying when he began his greetings in the Bible

[172] Mathew 9: 35-38
[173] Mathew 10:1

referring to the twelve tribes, the same twelve which Jesus had referred to here.

"We are but links on a chain that goes on for thousands of years, and his chain in never broken," Mamaw said glowingly. "I think you are one of the strong links to hold the other weaker links together. I pray for you every night that you also will receive a guardian angel to lead you as mine has done. Without Christ in my heart and following him every day, I would have been forever lost and probably would have killed myself a long time ago, perhaps by some slow form of self-destruction, like your mother did. But this is not your course Johnnie. God has lifted you from out of the lion's mouth, and now you will rise to great heights. Just remember you can do nothing by yourself and all things come from the Lord.[174] Now it time for us to go inside and go to bed. We have the pleasure of one day living in grace and mercy as the Lord sees fit, so help us all, God!"

And with that, they both went inside and went to bed.

The following week Johnnie once again destroyed the opposing team, the Spartans, in the finals, performing like a champion. He scored a state record of 50 points in a final game, and got 22 rebounds. He hit twenty-six out of twenty-six free throws in a row. The other team tried constantly to foul him from the start of the game to slow the game and hopefully injure Johnnie, but this tactic just made him better and stronger. No player had ever made more than twenty free throws in a final game, hitting 100%, which made his performance even more unique than his last.

This time when he arrived back at the school on the bus at 2 a.m., the entire school of students, faculty, and coaches were there to

---

[174] Romans 11:36

greet him. The principal took him to the center of the football field and under the lights gave him a plaque, saying the world would come to know Johnnie as a great player and a great man, which he felt humbled to hear, but did not really believe in his heart. Even after all this, Johnnie still had too much baggage to get rid of. He was just playing for fun when he took to the basketball court. Where this all would lead, he did not know or care… he just loved to play.

Johnnie continued to grow and succeed in the game of basketball. By his junior year he was 6'5" and stunning the entire basketball world. His stats were better than the best that ever played basketball in high school. Some said it was because he had not seen any real competition yet, and some said it was all luck, but Mamaw said it was God, and that no one was going to stop him unless they killed him. "And that even that," Mamaw would say, "did nothing to stop Jesus' legacy, but only strengthened it!"

Halfway through his junior season, Johnnie was called into Coach Thornton's office after a good game. He was averaging 34.3 points per game that year so far, with nine assists and twelve boards. It seemed he was unstoppable, even from half-court. When he decided to shoot, it just went in.

"Have a seat, Johnnie," the coach said. "Congratulations. Do you know who St. Vincent was?"

"No, sir," Johnnie replied.

"Saint Vincent lived a long time ago in a place called Lisbon. He lived a great life that he believed in… and did you know that the word 'believe' comes from the two words 'by life'?"

"No, sir," Johnnie again replied.

"You see, Johnnie," Coach continued, "there are many different kinds of people out there, and the only way you know what they believe in is to watch and see how they live their lives. Many of them are hypocrites. They say one thing and do another, and that is why most people dislike politicians. St. Vincent knew world was filled with hypocrites, and he was led by the Lord to not let people see him do one thing and say something else. Unfortunately, the politicians did not like what he said, so he was brutally killed and his body was put into a sack and thrown into the sea. He was made a saint for upholding the truth of God and not letting pressure change his behavior. You, too, are going to come under a lot of pressure, Johnnie, because of your talent. And the hardest thing you will ever have to do is not change your behavior when the pressure comes. You must stay true to the One who created you, and you will be blessed by His protection. I want you to remember that as you grow old, Johnnie. You won't always have me at your side to coach you or Mamaw there to lead you, but you will have your Father in Heaven, and he will not walk out on you or turn His back on you, like your real father did."

Coach could see tears welling up in Johnnie's eyes. The truth hurt, and Johnnie had a lot of wounds that still needed to heal in his heart. At night sometimes, anger would overtake him and he would beat his pillow with his first as if he were hitting his father for leaving him, and then he would cry and scream out in pain at the loss of his mother, who had abandoned him at his early age, not by choice but by God's will. And this was perhaps Johnnie's biggest stumbling block in coming to Christ: knowing that God had taken his mother from him when he had needed her the most, making him an orphan without life to call his own. It just was not fair.

Coach could sense what he was thinking and said, "Johnnie, life is not fair, at least not in the ways most people measure it. Just think: you could have been born at another time, or place, or even to different parents, but that would change everything! Then you would not be *right here* with this chance *right now*! Not everyone is so blessed as you, Johnnie, and you can't let the past, or any hate that goes along with it, keep you from being everything that God wants you to be. He loves you and wants the best for you. Just please remember this as colleges all around the country start making their offers next week when the recruiting begins."

"Yes, sir," Johnnie whispered, wiping tears from his face with the back of his hand. "I won't forget." Then he rolled over on the bench where he was sitting and began to cry as Coach was walking out of the office.

"This is something you are going to have to face alone, Johnnie," Coach said gently. "I can't help you with what is going on inside if you… only with what is going on outside of you."

With that, he left the room, slipping a sealed envelope with the name "Spot" scrawled on it into Johnnie's sports bag. It was an invitation for the monthly baptism ceremony held in the main sanctuary at Coach's church on the fourth Sunday of each month. It was written on his Knights of Columbus stationery, and Coach had signed it, "Esto Dignus—Be Worthy."

In Paradise, the Holy Spirit called together his legions of angels and was lecturing them on how He hated lies (i.e. untruths). Yes, 'hate' was a strong word for the Holy Spirit and one He often avoided for the anger it could inflict, especially in those who knew better and were thus judged more harshly than the innocent who were just naïve.

"Just remember," the Holy Spirit said, "Our Lord Jesus volunteered to be sent to the lost world saying, 'I am the Way, the Truth, and the Life, and no one come to the Father but by me.' But the world did not listen."

This caused the Holy Spirit visible anger, and He continued, "For the souls of men who refuse to accept in their time of offering to choose selflessness over selfishness shall be called down. That is why there is no selfishness in Heaven, for if we let those in, it would be no different than the selfishness known on earth… utterly disgusting!"

"And also," the Holy Spirit continued, "the God Father came down and spoke to Moses on the mountain, where He gave him His Ten Commandments and carved them into stone tablets on the mountain, telling Moses that if He could carve them into the stone of a mountain without a hammer, then Moses should be able to carve them in to the stone-cold hearts of his followers; and that if people disobeyed, they would feel the wrath of the Holy Ghost upon their efforts, and enlightenment would be withheld until repentance had been cried out from their lips, so that their anguish could be felt for three generations, and the love of God would be needed to fix their brokenness, for nothing else could do that. For He commanded and still commands:

'I am the LORD your God, who brought you out of Egypt, out of the land of slavery.

You shall have no other gods before[a] me.

You shall not make for yourself an image in the form of anything in heaven above or on the earth beneath or in the waters below. You shall not bow down to them or worship them; for I, the LORD your God, am a jealous God, punishing the children for the sin of the parents to the third and fourth generation of those who hate me, but showing love to a thousand generations of those who love me and keep my commandments.

You shall not misuse the name of the LORD your God, for the LORD will not hold anyone guiltless who misuses his name.

Remember the Sabbath day by keeping it holy. Six days you shall labor and do all your work, but the seventh day is a Sabbath to the LORD your God. On it you shall not do any work, neither you, nor your son or daughter, nor your male or female servant, nor your animals, nor any foreigner residing in your towns. For in six days the LORD made the heavens and the earth, the sea, and all that is in them, but he rested on the seventh day. Therefore, the LORD blessed the Sabbath day and made it holy.

Honor your father and your mother, so that you may live long in the land the LORD your God is giving you.

You shall not murder.

You shall not commit adultery.

You shall not steal.

You shall not give false testimony against your neighbor.

You shall not covet your neighbor's house. You shall not covet your neighbor's wife, or his male or female servant, his ox or donkey, or anything that belongs to your neighbor.'[175]

"And when the people saw the thunder and lightning," the Holy Spirit continued lecturing His angels, "and heard the trumpet and saw the mountain in smoke, they trembled with fear. They stayed at a distance and said to Moses, 'Speak to us yourself and we will listen. But do not have God speak to us or we will die.' And Moses said to the people, 'Do not be afraid. God has come to test you, so that the fear of God will be with you to keep you from sinning.' "

[175] Exodus 20: 1-20

If any of you lacks wisdom, you should ask God, who gives generously to all without finding fault, and it will be given to you. But when you ask, you must believe and not doubt, because the one who doubts is like a wave of the sea, blown and tossed by the wind.

Attested and witnessed by James,
your Brother in Christ
(oldest brother of Jesus)
Chapter 1:5-6

Chapter 3

Mamaw's Influence and the Surprise Medical Report

That following year, as in every year, the NBA draft required a blood test of all those who put their names up for the draft. Johnnie put his up, before even thinking about the value of waiting and going to college. Mamaw thought Johnnie still had some maturing to do. Once it was in though, it was in. The owners of the pro-sports teams wanted to make sure the players they drafted were clean from addictive performance enhancers or mind-altering drugs. Each of the owner's franchise investments was way too valuable to skip this investigation, so Johnnie—along with all his teammates—agreed to the NBA blood tests. Johnnie had nothing to hide; he was clean. But many of the other draftees were trying to beat the system by asking friends to pee into their bottles for them or carry urine in from outside and use it in their medical testing tubes.

From Johnnie's very first day in Houston living with Mamaw, he could remember her saying to him, "Johnnie, what goes around, comes around, and God is watching you closer than Santa Claus, so you be a good boy, or you might just be surprised what will happen when you meet Him, because he won't be as nice as me!" From then on, Johnnie tried to live honestly, mainly out of fear… because Mamaw scared the cajoles out of poor Johnnie. Week after week she dragged him to Sunday services to listen to the sermons, but Johnnie never felt any conviction. He had a heart that had been hardened by ill-fate, and he truly did not want anything to do with God, whom he felt had abandoned him so early in his life.

But there was one secret Mamaw knew that Johnnie did not.

Before Charlie had died, he wanted to give a kidney to his twin brother, who had renal failure from long-term medication use for pain in his back. Charlie knew the risks of sacrificing a kidney at his age, but he did it anyway because he loved his brother like no other. Unfortunately, the surgery did not turn out well for either brother, and he paid the ultimate price with his life. Charlie passed away shortly thereafter from surgery complications, and his brother passed away from a blood clot that went to into his leg.

It was a horrible year for Mamaw. She barely made it through those hard times. She earnestly clung to her faith, which was the only thing that held her life together. It was later that same year, in October, that she heard about her daughter's death, and the new crisis of her only grandson, Johnnie, needing a home.

But before Charlie's surgery and tragic death, the surgeons at Methodist Hospital did a highly involved blood analysis, which involved a new DNA ancestry linkage test that was quite experimental. The attending lab physician came in and explained to Mamaw that they had discovered that both Charlie and his brother had a very rare gene on the X-chromosome called the 'James & Mary' gene.

This of course intrigued Mamaw. The doctor went on to explain it something like this: In 1972, a Franciscan monk, Bellarmino Bagatti, excavated a site in the Kidron Valley at the foot of Mount of Olives thought to be the Tomb of Mary the mother of Jesus. Then, when the James Ossuary was later discovered—thought to be originated from James, the brother of Jesus, because it came from the Talpiot Tomb—the two sets of bones were tested against each other using advanced DNA testing, and a match was found, which was dubbed the "James & Mary" gene. He explained that no one really knew for sure if these were the real family members of Jesus, but regardless, Charlie and his brother were carriers of that gene.

When Mamaw heard this, she exclaimed, "Holy Mother of God! Charlie could have had the same blood in his veins as Mary… and Jesus?! And just think how many more people out there might be actually in the family of Jesus, all related to the other brothers and one sister of Jesus, if they all had children. What a thought! If there were twelve grandchildren, could these be the lost tribes that James had referred to!"

Later that night in Charlie's hospital room, Mamaw looked down at Charlie in disbelief.

"Oh, my God," she whispered to him, "You really *are* a servant of the Lord, Charlie. I knew it the day I met you! You are related to Jesus, himself! Not in the really smart and miracle sort of way, but in the good old-fashioned, big-hearted, loyal sort of way," she joked lovingly with him.

Charlie, joking back, said, "Well, he and I both have something in common then: we both never thought much of jokes, did we?"

This made them both laugh. But it was true: Charlie did not laugh much because he was always too busy helping other people to stop for a moment, take a breath, and just relax or laugh. Charlie was one of those rare individuals who felt other people's pain by just looking at them. He could tell you immediately what their childhood wounds were before they had even spoken a word. Once he had seen a woman sitting on a park bench and he had turned to Mamaw and said, "You see that woman over there? She never had any children, and she comes here to cry sometimes when no one is watching. I can feel her pain, and I pray for her at night, and hope one day she realizes the Lord knows her heart and will make everything right in the next life." Mamaw never questioned him about his story. Somehow she just sensed that he was right.

But now there was the issue of monitoring Johnnie, this multi-racial boy, the sports phenom hellion born in south central L.A. (there, too, he had been a racial spot that stood out in the bad neighborhood). Mamaw did not want to drop the ball raising him, so often she found herself wondering: What would Mary do? How do you raise someone who is independent, won't take advice, and seems almost supernatural in the things he can do that others can't? Mamaw knew these mind-bending questions could only be resolved in prayer, so she would lie on the floor at the foot of her bed at night, after she'd locked the door, and pray, with tears in her eyes, that she not let God down this time, that she would raise this boy up as her adopted son without a worldly father. She needed a Heavenly Father for him, one that could take over once he was old enough to see the wisdom in good choices.

For now, it was all she could do to just try and lay a solid foundation on which God could build, and hope somehow a miracle would happen to lead this boy down the path to conviction. Heck, he could not even spell "God," his English was so bad! And in math, he tripped up at any sums higher than twenty, when he ran out of fingers and toes. No, Mamaw knew Johnnie was not the sharpest knife in the kitchen drawer, but he had common sense, something many of his peers lacked. And more importantly, he shared the same empathy for others that his grandfather Charlie had had, that an uncanny ability to feel others' pain, even to the point that it drowned out his own pain.

Before Mamaw could blink, Johnnie's senior year was over. He was a future NBA All-Star in the making, and everyone could see it. No matter where he was on the court, when he shot, it was almost a sure bucket. The Fab Four Colleges who always ended up in the

NCAA finals all wanted him. Nobody could defend his jump shot very well because he would always fall back from his shot, almost leaning backwards instead of forwards. Anyone who watched him play was amazed, because his technique was so different.

Johnnie could remember when his unique style had started churning in his brain. In 1988, when he had been only 8 years old, he was sitting and watching the NBA finals on television. The player to watch was #33, a center named Lew Alcindor. His favorite shot was the "unstoppable sky hook." After watching it over and over, Johnnie was amazed at the simplicity of the signature move: put your left shoulder on the other person's face and drop the ball from Heaven right into the bucket. Forget about charging up the middle to dunk it… this was much easier!

So now, Johnnie set up twelve personal spots on the court from which he was a deadly accurate shot. Therefore, Couch Thornton would often cut short his halftime speeches or the courtside huddles to let Johnnie take his shots from his favorite spots (usually at half-court). The team began to call him Johnnie "On the Spot" or just "Spot" because of the twelve spots from which he would shoot the ball perfectly. Johnnie never thought much about anything except the best way to put the basketball into the net. The fans did not know or care what his name was, but the media always had a field day focusing on the racial thing during his games, just as he had been judged in his earlier school years for being the best white-skinned kid playing in a predominantly black sport. His best friend Mack had even once told him in the ninth grade that he stood out like whipped cream on coffee, a remark that had never stopped echoing around Johnnie's head.

Early one Friday morning, Sonny got up and looked his wife Rosanne directly in both eyes. Then he spoke a solemn statement that had been brewing in his mind for several years but which he had finally found the courage to utter.

"Sugar, I have to do something different… something different in life. I don't know what, but I can't keep doing this. This job I have is killing me."

He had been flying helicopter air taxi for Methodist Hospital at the Medical Center for over a decade. His credentials as a helicopter pilot were spotless. Before that he had laid pipe up in North Dakota—where he had met Bobby, his copilot—for the oil companies to bring the petroleum-rich black gold down to the lower forty-eight states from Canada. Exxon had been a good employer, but when he came to Houston to work corporate, he didn't like it. Looking at a computer screen, telling people how to lay lines, and teaching classes was not his cup of tea. So he took a job flying air taxi for heart attack patients and other medical emergencies in and out of Methodist. The problem was he had to stay at the hospital a week at a time—one week on and one week off—and he missed his sweet Rosie too much when he was gone. He needed a change.

"God is going to figure it out for you," she told him, "so don't be in a hurry to take the chopper out again and again for a flight until you have a Godly flight plan, okay?"

"Sure enough, Baby," he replied, and then he headed off to Methodist for his one-week rotation. It was always hard on both of them, but Sonny had to fly; it was in his blood. Plus being in a chopper helped him cope with his memories of Bobby and the crash. Sometimes at night in the dark, he would tell his wife, "You know, Rosie, I think when I fly I am closest to God. I can look down on the people down there and think what it must feel like to be an angel."

Rosie would always respond, "Sonny, you are *my* angel, and don't you ever forget it!" Then she would kiss him on the cheek and hold him really close and tight, because touch was his love language, and without it he would probably take his own life, like so many of his Vietnam buddies had already done.

Today in Upper Paradise, the Holy Spirit called for Shemenea, waking her from her rest.

"Come forth and report!" He commanded.

Faster than lightning, Shemenea landed on the platform outside of upper Paradise and entered the gate through the angels' entrance. Mamaw's other guardian angel, Phylamonas, replaced her at Mamaw's side.

Shemenea had been one of the key organizers of The Way and had also been rounded up with her family to be present in one of the terrible holding prison death cells beneath the Coliseum the day Peter was crucified upside down and burned as a human torch. She had been marched out with one of the first groups to be martyred that day. Nero had brought in bears to do the deeds, and she had watched ever so intently as the bears approached all those helpless in the area that day. Never having seen a bear before and thus not knowing how gruesome her fate would be, she prayed to God, that Christ would receive her soul back as easily as He had given it. Then she had looked back toward Peter from the floor of the coliseum, staring for a second to see his response. Peter had put his hands together through the bars and held them above his head in a victory sign to give her strength in her final moments.

She had smiled, and then—without fear—rushed the three bears in front of her, while the other twenty or so prisoners ran backwards. The bears had seen the others scatter, but Shemenea charged and tackled one of the bears and then held on to it as if were her mortal enemy, wishing it were Nero himself. They had fought for a brief moment before she was ripped open by the mighty fore-claws of the bear in one mighty swoosh of death.

This single act of victory defiance over her captors had impressed the Holy Spirit so much that when she arrived in Paradise that day, she immediately became a warrior guardian angel to protect the ones He loved, especially those in the line of the Mary-James gene. Similarly, Stephen had been awarded for his martyrdom, and Phylamonas awarded defending his brother, Uriah the Hittite when he had pushed to the frontlines of the Battle of Kadesh with his brother Uriah against the Ammonites, in the sinful days of David for the lust of a single woman's touch.[176] So the three warrior angel souls made a good trio to guard Mamaw and Johnnie, ensuring that neither of them got off-track as they were prepared for the journey and mission before them.

Shemenea and the others came and went as the Holy Spirit dictated to them, to go and assist in Lower Paradise (and not for a

[176] 2 Samuel 10

single moment did Mamaw ever doubt that she was alone after Charlie had passed away). The guardian angels were not allowed to take care of their own mortal family lines, which was why Shemenea was assigned a guardianship in the Mary-James line, even though she stemmed from the Mary-Jude line herself. Her father was Jude, brother of Jesus, so she had been declared an enemy of the state and was martyred that day with the conviction by the Proconsul, at the instruction of Nero, for "peaceful demonstrations of terror" and for collaborating with "The Way, enemies of the State." Each of those in her group that day had been branded with a branding iron the day before with the Roman initials MPI, with meant *miserabilis probus infirmitas*, Latin for *the deplorables.* Their sentence, though, was one of mercy, and they were spared crucifixion, unlike other followers of The Way captured for carrying written messages to new churches in the Aegean Territories.

Today Johnnie had been called to join the NBA scouting finals in Pittsburg over the Fourth of July holiday. They were happening on July 5th and 6th. He would be gone from Mamaw for a whole week ("Thank You, Jesus!" he said to himself as he left Houston, ready to enjoy the solitude away from Cojo, the maniac dog).

Finally, he would be able to concentrate on the one thing he loved… basketball. It had become his only passion, his new God. On the night of July 4th, while other players were out seeing the sights and drinking beer under the fireworks, Johnnie was in the gym shooting and dunking basketballs till late. He shot over 1,000 balls that night and refused to leave until he hit ten half-court shots in a row.

All of the basic athletic skills of running, jumping, and endurance were measured there at the training camp in Pennsylvania, the state which boasted of Brotherly Love. There were the snake trials, where the players had to run around the cones on the court for agility, and the rim trials, where they were made to stand under the net and see how much of their arms they could get above the ten-foot rim from a standing jump. The horse trials—which Johnnie was already familiar with from his childhood—involved shooting twelve balls from twelve different spots on the court for thirty seconds each and seeing how many baskets could be made in six minutes. No player had ever made a perfect 144. One player many years ago, Wilt, had scored above 100, thus instituting the "100 Club," which only had eleven members over the years far since, with a high score of 118. But this summer Johnnie broke that record, shooting 122 of 144. It was his greatest day, and he knew it. He was soon to be offered big money to play for an NBA team, but he was sure Mamaw would have something to say about that!

The July 4th weekend over in Houston was always bad for Sonny because the hospital and urgent care emergency room visits always spiked, due to everything from fireworks injuries to car accidents. Sonny was no newbie to trauma, death, and injury, so after a hard week flying some additional hours as a new medevac for Methodist Hospital, Sonny took his usual break on his way home, stopping by American Legion Hall #472 in South Houston to decompress before going home to Rosanne. He had over twenty calls to make during the week. Many of the victims he rescued had survived, but the one that stuck with him most that week was a motorcyclist who had hit a guardrail in the rain and flipped his bike. He hadn't been wearing a helmet and was braindead when the chopper arrived. It was going to be up to his family to decide if he would live in a vegetative state for many years until he died or if they would choose to let him pass away after the doctors tried to bring him out of the coma at the hospital.

Sonny remembered his grandmother once advising him when he was 12 years old growing up in the crop fields of south Texas, "When you leave the house every day, you had better make sure you're saved going out that door, because you never know when it will be your time to be called home… don't wait until it's too late to repent!" Her words of warning rang in his ears every day since then. So Sonny repented every night before he went to sleep, just to make sure God knew his heart was one of reconciliation.

After each death that Sonny witnessed, he had to down a few drinks at the Legion Hall. He always thought it was funny that they called the U.S. Military place of solace, rest, and recruitment after the Roman Legions that once ruled the world by force and crucified Christ.

Little to his knowledge, this was going to be a special day for Sonny. The angel Verostices had made arrangements for the Baron of Corpus Christi (i.e. the Baron of 'the Body of Christ'), Texas, to be there. The Baron was not, of course, a real Baron—heck no, and far from it! That was just what his buddies called him because he looked like the Red Baron of Germany who had terrorized the skies in World War I, and he didn't fear anyone, even God himself (which was a mistake). The Baron's real name was Andy, and he had been a bombardier in both World War II and the Korean War.

Andy was sitting at the bar, drinking a cold brew of ginger ale when Sonny walked in. Something told Sonny to sit beside him, even though he usually headed to the pool table and played some Mickey Gilley or Merle Haggard on the juke box while he thought about his time in Vietnam.

"Hey there, old timer," Sonny jokingly said to Andy as he took a seat next to him at the bar. "I'm Sonny, the SOB who should be home with his sweet wife who's waiting there for him. But I just need a drink first. It's been one of those weeks, and I just can't go home until I have had some alcohol self-therapy. How about you?"

Andy cracked a smile and said, "Me too. I lost my best friend this week. He was my childhood buddy, Linney Donn. He and I flew together in Korea. He was the pilot, and I was in back, lining up the pay load to drop on the Commies for all the bad stuff they did around Seoul."

"Sorry to hear that," Sonny said. "My wingman buddy in 'Nam was Bobby, and I miss him every day, too. What kind of wings did he fly?"

"Anything with two wings," Andy said. "But God is telling me to go chopper now. I have a new company that is doing quite well, and I need to get around a little nimbler than just airport to airport, since I mainly just fly around Houston."

Sonny could not believe what he was hearing. His sweet Rosanne had been right!

"Well," Sonny began, "you're not gonna believe this, but…"

Within three weeks, Sonny was flying as Andy's personal pilot. His small business selling pipe to oil rigs had jumped the oil boom, and now they were drilling on the gulf coast shelf. West Texas crude oil had shot up from $24 dollars a barrel to over $55 a barrel, and now everybody and their mother wanted a piece of the action. It was now an official boom-or-bust feeding frenzy, almost like the Klondike Gold Rush.

Blessed is the man who perseveres under trial, because when he has stood the test, he will receive the crown of life that God has promised to those who love Him.

Attested and witnessed by James,
Your Brother in Christ
(Oldest brother of Jesus)
Chapter 1:12

Chapter 4

Johnnie's NBA Dream Comes True

On this day in Paradise, the Holy Spirit was busy, spending His time portioning out the exact amounts of each gift and talent that would be distributed to each follower of Jesus Christ who had not yet been born (i.e. reborn) and whom the Father God in Heaven had created with the Spirit (i.e. not evolved in the Spirit). The Holy Spirit was setting these gifts and talents apart for each and ahead as well, to as many as forty generations, so the links established would not be broken. The holy time of enlightenment and judgment for each soul was also being established and secured in each heart with a golden key. The Holy Spirit would be there in their hearts like a great and mighty bollard on a ship dock, available for the souls to anchor themselves to whenever they were surrounded by rough waters teeming with the evil of Satan and his angels of lies and destruction.

Then the Holy Spirit rested for a moment and called the sons of Asher to stand before Him. Asher was the eighth son of Jacob. He represented the Eighth Tribe of Israel several thousand years before Christ was to arrive. He was born the second son of Jacob's second wife, Zilpah, who was the servant of Jacob's first wife, Leah. Jacob blessed his son with these words: "Asher's food will be rich; he will provide delicacies fit for a king." And so, he did.[177]

And when it came time to assign talents to Johnnie Spot Perfect, the angel Chalymina stood before the Holy Spirit holding a scroll under his left wing and said, "Here, oh Holy One, are the instructions of the Father God in Heaven."

"Chalymina," the Holy Spirit said, "the scroll you carry is not silver, but gold, so this one must be another carrier of the seed of Mary, the mother of Jesus, is he not?"

"Yes, oh Holy One," Chalymina replied with great fervor and excitement.

"So this one, like the others, is also assigned a special service to provide to the Kingdom; he is another servant by the blood of his brother, Christ; and he also is to receive a special amount of blessing commensurate to his special amount of suffering?" the Holy Spirit asked, though he knew the answer to these questions already.

"It has been thus decreed as you describe it, Most High and Holy Counselor," Chalymina replied, again with fervor and excitement.

"Well then come," the Holy Spirit instructed, "be quick with this message as a beam of stardust on a fading shadow! Unroll this scroll and give it to me, that I might know the Father's holy words which I will use to bless this new soul as we, the Trinity, agree and wish him to be!"

Chalymina opened the scroll and laid it before the Holy Spirit, pausing for a brief moment, for he knew how all three—the Father in Heaven with Jesus Christ and the Holy Spirit at His side—would simultaneously understand the importance and depth of the

---

[177] Genesis 49:20

words that lay there before them on the scroll. This pause in Heaven would amount to five or ten thousand years of time on earth. Then the Holy Spirit shouted out the blessing as dictated by the Father in Heaven, so that all three worlds could hear:

"Unleash the power of the human Trebuchet, a favored weapon of war for siege against Satan and his angels!" For God used many tools of miracles to show His power to the masses, and this tool, the trebuchet, would be the tool which Johnnie would use to be remembered as one of God's people who had undoubtedly powers bestowed from God to conquer enemies and break down massive walls or barriers. But in Johnnie's case the barriers would be multi-racial, multi-religious, multi-cultural, multi-economic, and multi-generational. His powerful athletic trebuchet act on the basketball court for which God had uniquely crafted his body strength, skills, and determination would show to the world once again God's ability to still do miracles, just as Moses had done many miracles and opened the Dead Sea to let His people pass through the raging water to a new, unsure land of freedom, based on obedience and a constantly tested faith.

Even though it was Johnnie's intent to skip college altogether and go directly into the NBA, no one knew for sure his marketability status and if he really would be drafted early, due to his 'unique' personality. He was to many people who knew him a sort of lone-wolf. Mamaw saw both a certain intelligence and indomitable persistence—which both Charlie and Jenny had had—in her grandson, Johnnie, and her mailbox was getting so full of letters of college offers that the mailman was beginning to deliver them straight to the house. They would not fit in the box anymore! Mamaw was torn in what to do. She was annoyed by the amount of mail coming in, and some days she felt like moving just to get away from the inconvenience of Johnnie's new stardom. She kept wondering how God was going to use him, but she tried to be patient and just sit back and watch as the show unveiled itself.

One day, about a month later, there was a knock at the door, and the college recruiters began to file in and out, wanting to meet and talk with Johnnie. First it was the Iowa Jayhawks, the UCLA Bruins, then the Duke Blue Devils (although Mamaw would not let him play for any team called the Devils for sure; she preferred the Saints, but that was a football team), and on and on, like a revolving door. It got to be quite humorous… each of the recruiters knew each other by first and would talk to each other like family. Each recruiter (sometimes it was even the head coach!) was on a mission to have their school get the best players at the lowest cost, so they could pass the fees on to the students and pay the coaches more. To Mamaw, this was quite immoral and a real screw-job the schools were doing to the tuition-paying students, claiming that team sports and the entertainment they provided would give them a better education and better jobs, when really it was only self-serving for the regents, who lived in big houses and drove big cars, at the expense of the illusion of jobs available for higher education. Mamaw could see it, buy Johnnie could not. His hormones were raging, and all he could think of was which school had the best-looking cheerleaders, softest bed, easiest diploma, and best free food! What a roost! A true case of *Res Ipsa Loquitur*! The presentations were all the same: "Johnnie, if you come play for us, we will have the number-one team in the country. Everyone will pay to come see you play, and your name will be in the spotlight, and the world will know who Johnnie Spot Perfect is!" A Wolverine, or a Longhorn, or a Trojan… but Mamaw saw through all of it, and she laughed as she pushed each one out the door, being nice but firm, of course. Mamaw did not want Johnnie to be part of the college Ponzi scheme, where sports lured rich kids into financial ruin and poor kids into unmet reality expectations. She wanted him to just skirt the whole part of sin by misinformation and misrepresentation and go directly into the NBA, where money was paid to a person according to athletic skills without the lure of education based on need or having a politically correct mascot.

One night while Mamaw was praying, a voice came to her. It was Verostices. She could not see him, but she knew he was there. The voice was not in her head but in her heart. The Holy Spirit had woken her once again and put her at peace. Verostices' voice, under the direction of the Holy Spirit, told her that the city of Houston would remain Johnnie's home; just be patient, and everything would be all right. That was good enough for Mamaw, so she just patiently waited and told Johnnie he was to say "nothing to nobody" until he had heard from a Houston team. And then one day, about two weeks later, it happened!

A call came from Leroy McGinnis, the new player contact for the Houston Hurricanes. Unlike many of the colleges that wanted to see and speak with Johnnie, he asked if Johnnie could meet him at the Houston Arboretum and Nature Center on NW Loop 610. This was different. The Chicago Bulls and Detroit Pistons had already been by the house, Johnnie thought to himself, so why the Nature Center? Why not a fancy restaurant, or how about the Mercedes dealership so he could look at big fancy cars? Something to really impress and influence him!

Mamaw, who had a separate phone line in her bedroom, always listened in on the conversations. (Cell phones had not been invented yet, so one phone line had multiple phone jacks throughout a family house. Unfortunately, this has been lost as has most of the community family style of living where family members can protect their loved ones and separation is done early and children lose their childhoods all in the name of prosperity and technology. Something the Holy Spirit frowns upon as children are losing their identities and souls, becoming para-androids, and soon back to uneducated unskilled slaves and tyrannical slave masters and worlds of tyranny that Jesus came to abolish.

So one Sunday, after going to a Memorial Baptist Church service, Johnnie and Mamaw went to meet Mr. McGinnis at the Nature Center. Mamaw was wearing her finest church outfit, complete with pink horn-rimmed glasses and matching a pink handbag with purple, blue, and red rhinestones. She also wore her Sunday girdle that Charlie had loved so much because it helped accentuate her feminine figure so well, and he was proud that she could get it on even later in life, when time and gravity usually took their natural toll on women's youthful figures.

Mr. McGinnis drove up in a long, light blue Mercedes Coup that had only two seats and big tear-shaped tail lights. It just said '369' on its Texas license plate. Johnnie was very impressed! The light gray roof was rolled all the way down in the back (and it was electric and self-moving too!), and Mr. McGinnis wore oversized aviator sunglasses, with his hair shiny and slicked back with something maybe similar to Beryl-cream.

He jumped out of the car without even using the door (further impressing the young Johnnie! and greeted both of them in a loud and friendly voice.

"Howdy, ma'am, I am Leroy," he said in a long, southern Texas country drawl. Then he put out his hand to shake Johnnie's hand, saying, "Johnnie, young man, I am here to take you to God, make you prosperous, and show all the things that goes with it." He chuckled in a sort of funny way.

Mamaw winced slightly at his candor, but knew Johnnie would be accepting a position on a local team. She just did not know which. The University of Houston had already come knocking, but they were like the rest, just wanting to use Johnnie so they could build more buildings and part of the college sports Ponzi scheme. None of the colleges offered an educational degree in common sense, as far as Mamaw was concerned. They taught women how to think like men and play athletics like men, and they gave out liberal ideas like free birth control pills and condoms on campus just so they could keep them in school and make more money at the college footfall ticket gates. It was a form of insanity that Mamaw did not understand. The number of abortions in the country was now outnumbering births, so that the number of deaths at the hands of progress was only weighed by the scales of moral decay and depravity, like that which had the Holy Spirit to bring down the city of Sodom and Gomorrah many centuries before.

"How about a walk," Leroy said to them, pointing down the path at the end of the parking lot. "I like butterflies, and I would like to walk down to the pond area and see if they have any Swallowtails around." So the three of them walked together down to the pond, where they were greeted by an amazing cornucopia of beautiful butterflies.

"Coach Barricks likes to bring the team down here sometimes to get them grounded and back down to earth," Mr. McGinnis explained. "He thinks that sometimes all the limelight of living in front of television cameras all season puts debilitating weeds in the players brains so they can't think straight." They were all three silent for a moment.

"He brought me down here, too, when I was a young kid out of Tyler," Mr. McGinnis continued, "with no home to really call my own. He showed me the butterflies and then found a cocoon that had been laid on a milkweed. He proceeded to tell me how all of us find ourselves at some point or another in the weeds of life, and that's exactly when we have to be born again into something that is beautiful and can lift itself up off the ground from an ugly thing that can only crawl on its belly and eat what is in front of it, and be born again into something that gets to live off sweet nectar for its food and spend its life flying in the air from flower to flower, spreading life to each flower it touches growing in God's garden." Mr. McGinnis paused and looked over at Johnnie. He could see the boy listening and thinking as he stared at the flurry of butterfly activity before them.

"You see, Johnnie," Mr. McGinnis said gently, "we all have a purpose, and in the grand design of things, you have a purpose too. The team you chose to go with will either bring out your greater purpose, or it will cause that divine purpose to wither and die, like you yourself will one day. And then the purpose will have been given to you in vain. The Bible says, 'Of those to whom much is given, much is expected.[178] And, Johnnie, you have been given much."

---

[178] Luke 12:48

The boy continued mulling over the words he was hearing. *Much?* he thought to himself. Had he really been given much? All his life he had felt like he had been given nothing… or worse than nothing, even. But now, as he looked out at the butterflies, the words he was hearing landed on the finally fertile soil of his heart, and he believed them. He *believed* them! Yes… he—Johnnie—had been given *much*.

Mamaw, of course, was sold! It was the Hurricanes for Johnnie… the deal was done. Now she just had to convince him that would be his new home, with Coach Barricks. Little did she know that a miracle had just occurred in her grandson's heart, and that he would need no convincing from her; the Holy Spirit Himself had done all the convincing.

"So who will take care of Johnnie when I am not there?" Mamaw grilled Mr. McGinnis.

"I am sure Johnnie has a guardian angel, and if he doesn't, Coach Barricks will run him through hell until he asks for one," Mr. McGinnis replied.

Now all three of them were laughing together. Johnnie had always gone to church with Mamaw when he was younger—at first because she had given him no choice and later out of respect for what she believed—but he had never taken up the offer personally, either at her church or at Coach Thornton's—to be baptized and give up all his baggage and lead a new life walking in faith.

They continued around the short loop, and as they approached the parking lot, Mr. McGinnis said he wanted to show them one more thing. It was a very old crepe myrtle tree located at the northwest corner of the building, one of the largest trees reaching into the canopy.

Turning to them, he said, "My grandfather planted this tree for me when I was just a child before my father went off to the Korean War as a bombardier. He told me that all the trunks it had as individual shoots—there were twelve at the time—would one day grow and weave together into one great trunk. He told me this symbolized the Christian faith: one mighty trunk! I come here often to reflect on that. My father was later shot down over the jungles of North Korea, and the government said they never found his body. So this is my memorial, a living headstone for my father, representing the strife in my life."

Mr. McGinnis paused, looking at Johnnie and Mamaw, then continued.

"Over the years I have seen it do just what my father said it would do. The tree now has but one trunk, and it flowers for all the bees and butterflies when it is too hot for anything else to have nectar. My father was a wise man, Johnnie. He would have liked to see you play. You are twice as good as I could ever be, and three times as good as any player I have seen in the last twenty years since 'The Bird' came to town.

By this time both Johnnie and Mamaw were speechless.

As the three of them went back to the cars, Mr. McGinnis said to them as he jumped into his sports car to drive away, "Just remember one thing, Johnnie: time is fleeting, and you need to be preparing for an eternity with God, not a lifetime of friends, because those friends will not be around once you are placed in the grave, where all men live alone that are not saved."

"Yes, sir," Johnnie replied solemnly.

Then Mr. McGinnis said, "So, Johnnie, if our new owner and General Manager, Mr. Silverman, wants to choose you to play for us in the draft, what number jersey would you like to wear?"

"One... number One!" Johnnie quickly replied.

Faster than a chicken on a wandering June bug, Mamaw took her purse off her shoulder and gave it a mighty overhead swing, hitting Johnnie so hard on the back of his head he almost went to his knees from the jolt. It left quite an imprint of a flower on the back of his neck, and Johnnie quickly recanted.

"Four… I meant to say number Four! Number Four, please."

Mamaw quickly added, "Yes, Mr. McGinnis, please tell Mr. Silverman, Johnnie would be happy to play for his home town Hurricanes, and wear number Four. He knows that God is number One, and he ain't God, so let's not be getting all prideful and acting like Jesus almighty wanting to rule the world with the flick of your hand."

Mr. McGinnis looked at her with a hint of admiration in his eyes and said, "I like you, Mamaw. I will give Mr. Silverman the message. No one has worn number Four in Houston for a long time. I think we may have one in just the Spot's size."

Mr. McGinnis left and drove away, putting his hand up in the air and waving goodbye as he disappeared west into the sun. When he was out of sight, Johnnie exhaled a long, loud breath and kicked at the ground, considering all he had just heard.

Mamaw did not say anything all the way home, but let him think about everything, waiting for Johnnie to speak first. This was a decision Johnnie would have to make alone. When they arrived home, they entered in silence.

That night in her bedroom, Mamaw got on her knees and prayed to her Father in Heaven that Johnnie's life might be fulfilled in the way that the Holy Trinity desired. At that moment a sense of total peace came over her. It was like being dropped into a warm bath. She went limp and fell to the floor weeping in thankfulness.

She knew this was not her burden anymore; she had passed it along to the Holy Spirit and left it at the Cross of Jesus.

Sonny had hurried home to tell his wife about meeting Andy and the new job that he would be taking. He was talking so fast when he hit the door that Rosanne could hardly tell what he was saying. All she knew was that he was ecstatic and could hardly wait to pour them both a drink to celebrate the news.

"But… what's the news?" Roseanne asked. "What is going on?"

"Sugar, you're not gonna believe this, but I have been offered my dream job!" Sonny told her breathlessly. He started filling her in on all the details. It was the career he had been waiting for: no stress, no trauma, no more nightmares of seeing ghosts of dead people… just a normal job being a helicopter chauffer. It would be great!

"There's just one thing…" Sonny said, glancing warily at his wife. "I will be on call 24/7 for Andy, meaning I won't know my schedule. I may have to fly five days in a row, but then get five weeks off… or vice versa. Because even Andy doesn't know what his schedule will be."

When Rosanne heard this, her smile faded. What about summer vacations to the beach, or the annual family reunions in St. Louis? What about Thanksgiving, Christmas, and New Year's?

"Honey," she said, "did you accept the position?"

"Of course I did!" he practically yelled.

"What's the pay?" his practical-minded wife asked.

"Well... we didn't get that far." Sonny was starting to feel the heat of the moment, as the euphoria melted into anxiety. It was beginning to feel like an interrogation.

"Where does he work?" Rosanne prodded further. "Are you going to be flying out of the airport close to here?"

"Well, Sugar, it went something like this... he asked me if I wanted to work for him, I said yes, and that was that," Sonny joked. Only Roseanne was not laughing.

"Did you get his number? Or how about a business card? What is the name of his company?" she continued prodding.

"Andy just said to give Methodist my two-week notice and meet him back at the Legion Hall in two weeks to begin my new job. I said okay, and that's what I plan to do." Sonny glanced at Roseanne and continued, "...with your permission, of course, Sugar Bear... Honey Bun... my sweet, adorable Princess."

Rosanne shot Sonny a sideways glance out of the corner of her left eye. She had been down this road before. Sonny was not the most responsible person on the planet, but his heart was always in the right place.

"Now here's the sixty-million-dollar question, my handsome Prince Charming of South Texas, Flying King of the tomato fields, President of the Crop Dusters of America: Did you talk this over with God first before you gave your answer?"

Sonny smiled and said, "Yes, I did... that is a big 10-4, my precious wife!"

"Okay, then I will be your faithful helper on this journey," Rosanne said. "But if it turns out that you didn't talk to God first and this road you lead me down bears no fruit, then you'll see me packing my bags and heading home to my mother's house, where you can send me a support check on the first of each month."

They laughed out loud together, and Sonny picked her up and twirled her around the room a couple of times. Then they both fell on the couch in gleeful hysterics, a perfect picture of the love they had for each other. After cuddling for a few minutes in front of the television, they went to bed for the night. The next morning, Sonny would give his two-weeks' notice at work.

Now the end of the year was at hand and it was time for Johnnie's nineteenth birthday on Wednesday, December 28th. He was never fond of his birthday because he considered himself a "'tweener," one of those unfortunate kids whose birthday fell between Christmas and New Year. This meant he never got to receive two set of presents like all the other kids, who received Santa Clause gifts on Christmas and a separate gift for their birthdays.

"Why can't I have a birthday in the middle of the year, like everyone else?" Johnnie always complained to Mamaw every year at this time. He would only get one gift on his birthday and none on Christmas from Mamaw, who always explained to him that the gift of his salvation was the only present he deserved on Christmas Day, because Jesus was able to pay for it, and she was always broke.

This birthday was special because an amazing number of four-year free-ride scholarship offers were pouring in for the next college year of 1982, even though Johnnie had declared himself available for the NBA draft in the spring. Johnnie was not a great thinker or mathematician, so he knew college would be difficult. He was more interested in the money and having enough of it to fly back out to see Jenny's grave. He always wanted to take her flowers on Mother's Day, but had never had enough money from the small jobs he could get as a teenager around Houston, so he had decided no college for him. He was NBA-eligible, taking the job with Houston if he got it, and if he got injured playing in college or busted out in the NBA, at least he would have enough money to finally go see his Momma's resting place. Johnnie had spoken with several teams at length, but in reality now he was just waiting for the draft, and it was just a matter of who wanted him the most and was willing to trade up to get him if he went as high in the draft as he thought.

Mamaw had taken a few of her favorite items Charlie had left to her after he passed away to a pawn shop down on South Main Street to get enough money to take Johnnie to the tryouts in Pittsburgh ten months before. That was the best she could do. So as far as traveling again for the actual draft picks they would just have to watch on television from home and wait for a phone call.

And then that day of the draft finally arrived.

About 7:30 in the evening (Central Standard Time), Johnnie's guests started arriving at the house, each bearing some form of food to put out on the table for a potluck dinner. Coach Thornton and some kids from the high school team, along with their parents, had all been invited over for the event. Mamaw had invited a few of her friends too so they could pay Yahtzee in the backroom while everyone else sat around the television. The angel Verostices had already told her that Johnnie would be staying in Houston, so she was not nervous at all. The rest of the guests, however, were sweating bullets to see if he was going to make it in the draft at all.

Coach Buddy ('The Budster' as his friends fondly referred to him) Thornton was not nervous either, but he was a little tense. He had never coached a player like Johnnie and it would be his greatest accomplishment in life if he could see Johnnie propel to success. Coach Thornton was a widower, so he did not have anyone to share this event with. His wife had died of pancreatic cancer; even the specialists at MD Anderson Hospital had been unable to save her. She had died in the first round of chemotherapy, and 'The Budster' had never been the same person since. With her, a piece of himself had died, as well his fire for life. He had continued coaching, but he had lost his passion. He was truly broken inside.

But with Johnnie, he had regained some of that fire, but the wood in his heart was too wet to ignite fully. He still joked but never really smiled, and certainly never laughed until tears came out like he used too when his wife had been alive. Any show of enthusiasm was exactly that… a show. He did not understand how God could do this to him. He still had two eyes that could see but was blind. He eventually would see and understand God' perfect plan in this horrible pain, but the time had not yet come for God to reveal that to him. And now it was time for Johnnie's biggest day, and the hinge that Coach Thornton would hold onto for the rest of eternity.

This night would end up being a long night if Johnnie did not go in the draft early. A lot of it had to do with team dynamics and what the teams had left over in their budgets to spend on new recruits. Several of the leading NBA teams had already maxed out their budgets, and they knew that even if they landed someone like Johnnie, they might not be able to get him to sign a contract.

Mamaw had let each of the teams who courted Johnnie know that she would be the agent representing Johnnie and thus would be getting ten percent of whatever he was offered. She thought this was mighty fair for all the hell he had put her through and the sacrifices that she had made to get him to this point. She also wanted to get a bigger house for Cojo, who was tired of going through the back door where the screen had never been replaced.

Mamaw did not allow regular distilled liquor alcohol in the house, since she was a strict no-dancing no-partying practicing good old-fashioned Baptist from Tyler, Texas, so no one dared show up trying to sneak any booze in, or they would be given a big boot with a swift kick to the britches and then thrown out the door on their chin if she ever found out. Charlie was no longer around, but Mamaw claimed she kept Charlie's old army boots in the closet just in case she had to put one of them on and put a her toe to someone's rear end if she ever caught them disrespecting the Lord by becoming impure by drinking anything harder than wine, which Jesus himself drank on several occasions, and that made it all right with her. And that was the gospel truth according to Mamaw, and there was no arguing with her. And you had better not stay out past midnight, either, or you would find the front door locked, even if it was freezing outside. But Mamaw was known to take a bottle or two of Boone's Farm fine apple wine into her room in a brown paper bag at times when she felt lonely and close the door and then not come out until it was time to empty the trash. She was no saint either.

But tonight she was not having wine. This was serious business. Johnnie was going to become a man tonight; she could feel it in her bones. He was going to go out and live on his own and have his own money to spend (wisely, she hoped!).

Howard Cosell came on Channel 7 for the first thirty minutes that evening and discussed the main NBA prospects in this year's draft. They showed clips of Johnnie playing for his high school team, of the patented sky-hook shot he had developed. Howard did not say his full name, but referred to him as 'Hot Spot Perfect' (a name that would soon stick with him and his teammates in difficult times to come). Johnnie was also known for using his left hand to block his opponent's eyesight while executing his sky hook (the trebuchet move), which was really only annoying to the scouts and didn't do much to help his shooting percentages so far, and probably would not be tolerated in the pros. They also showed a clip where he made an around-the-back shot during a final game, and several clips of him taking 'granny shots' for free throws when his team was leading by 50 or more, just to annoy the other team. When a clip of Johnnie taking and making an around-the-back free-throw shot once (which Couch Thornton had chewed him out over and pulled him out of the game) came onscreen, everyone in the living room went wild with woops and cheers.

It was all quite entertaining as everyone sat around the television that night and watched how their friend taunted the other teams in the state and kept them off-balance with his trickster shots. He was a natural. But these shenanigans—although highly entertaining—could also be detrimental in the draft, indicating that maybe Johnnie was not a good team player, and would have to be let him go after a year. The idea was to give new players a one-year contract with an option to extend if they worked well with the team and made the goals set out in the written contract for points scored and defensive plays. There were verbal contracts also, but those were mainly between the players, sort of like warriors going into battle. Team leaders were easy to identify because they kept the team together at all costs. They knew the survival and win of the team depended on the solidarity and unconditional loyalty to the cause of the team, and playing together was the ultimate goal in every game.

The opposing team was always the enemy, no second chances and no excuses.

Finally it was time for the draft to begin. Johnnie had heard that Houston had wanted him, and that they were trying to make a deal with Chicago to let them have first pick, but at this point no one knew what had happened in the last ten minutes of negotiating before the cameras went live on the air. And then it was time for the first pick.

"...and the first pick," the announcer said, "goes to Houston!"

Mr. McGinnis walked out onto the stage beside the new owner and general manager, who had just bought the team during the off season. It was Andy, the Baron of Corpus Christi, who had recently struck it rich during the oil boom of the last decade along with a new valve patent to keep rigs from breaking a pipe under the water in the gulf exploration. He had leveraged his earning to purchase the team with one hundred million in collateralized debt to get the financing to do the deal. Andy was always known for his eccentric move-forward-and-never-go-backward ways, and he looked forward to this new challenge of making the team great or go bust trying. It would be the best fun he had had since being shot at in the war and going down in the jungle and having to be rescued by medevac choppers.

Mr. Silverman carried a jersey with him out to the podium, and the world waited with bated breath to see who the number-one pick this year would be. The Las Vegas odds makers did not have Johnnie going first because of his lone-wolf style of playing. He was young and had not been in the college ranks yet. He was untested. Plus, there were at least six players who would be NBA starters for years and had the experience. Regardless, Mr. Silverman knew how to make money, and marketing was one of his best skills. If he could get Johnnie to sign—and Mr. McGinnis thought he could with the backing of Mamaw—it would mean good ticket sales the first year, so Andy could retire at least twenty percent of his debt and amortize it over a longer-term note.

Then the moment came.

"So who will the 'Canes be selecting this year as their number-one pick for 1984?" the two asked each other.

Mr. Silverman quickly turned to the camera and unfurled the 'Canes jersey to reveal a big number four on the back and the name 'SPOT' above it.

The fans onscreen went crazy. They leapt to their feet and started cheering "Hot Spot, Hot Spot, Take that Shot!" over and over again.

And in Mamaw's house, Johnnie's friends began to cheer along with the television.

"Hot Spot, Hot Spot, Take that Shot!"

Johnnie, screaming with excitement, jumped up onto the couch and started dancing. Mamaw was standing right there, and it was first time she did absolutely nothing when he was out of control. He was now in God's hands. She gave him over to his guardian angels and said a prayer, thanking the Lord for getting him this far.

Now her life could go back to normal… or so she thought.

Sonny was watching the NBA draft from his house that night also. He was interested in who Houston was going to choose. He had gone to a couple of games but just about fell off his chair when he saw Andy walk out on the stage as the owner of the 'Canes!

"Rosie!" he screamed to his wife, who was in the back of the house doing laundry.

Certain that Sonny must have hurt himself and needed help or an ambulance, Roseanne ran stumbling into the TV room, an alarmed expression on her face. Rosanne had an incurable form of inherited macular degeneration called Stargardt's Disease. In early adulthood the retina just starts to peel away from the back of the eyes so that eventually everything is sketchy, like a puzzle with pieces missing in front of you. Roseanne could see enough to get around, but when startled like that she would fall over furniture and lampshades just trying to get through the house quickly, almost like trying to get around a dark house in the middle of the night, half asleep.

"Look who is on TV!" Sonny yelled as he pointed at the screen. "It's Andy! And he owns the Mighty Hurricanes! He is the owner and General Manager. Holy Moses, I have seen it all now! It's a frickin' miracle!"

"Sonny!" Rosie exclaimed, "Hold your tongue! No cussing or yelling! I just about killed myself getting in here to you!"

Then she grabbed his hands they began jumping and yelling on the couch like two kids.

Across town that very moment in his living room, Johnnie was doing a similar dance for joy. Everyone was yelling and jumping at once… except Mamaw of course, who was jumping and yelling on the inside.

Two weeks went by, and Sonny went back to the Legion Hall to meet Andy. It was going on 7 p.m. They had agreed to meet at 6:30, and Sonny was beginning to wonder if he had gotten the time wrong. Inside was no Andy.

Then all of a sudden, Sonny heard a strange noise outside, getting steadily louder. Racing over to the window, he was surprised to see a chopper hovering there. It was Andy! He was motioning for Sonny to come outside. Sonny ran outside, and Andy opened the side door and motioned him to climb aboard. Without having to be asked twice, Sonny jumped on in.

"How do you like my new princess?" Andy asked. "Just bought her! Want take a ride over the city?"

"Hell yeah! Let's go!" Sonny screamed. He was so happy to be flying again—and with someone who felt like a long-lost friend—that he almost wet his pants in hysterical laughter. It was like being a kid again. He was grinning from ear to ear.

"Just picked her up today," Andy yelled over the chopper noise, "and she is gonna be yours to take care of!"

"Oh my God," Sonny muttered to himself in disbelief. "My sweet Rosie was right—just have patience and keep the faith, and God works things all out for those who love him and keep his commandments."[179]

"Phil, from the airport, just brought 'er over for me to come pick you up," Andy explained. "We're heading back to the hanger, where she'll sleep for the night, and then I'll drive you back to get your car."

"This is so cool, Andy!" Sonny replied, "I mean, Mr. Silverman," he corrected himself.

"You'll be working for my company, Silverman Interests, Inc.," Andy replied. "In the morning I'm going to send Leroy McGinnis over to set you up with Betty, my secretary. She'll see that you get what you need."

"That all sounds great!" Sonny laughed. "I can't wait to tell my sweet wife about this when I get home!" he continued, still shouting over the roar of the chopper blades and rotor whirling around them.

"Great," Andy smiled. "Now, I just need to let you know that I have two rules, and as long as you don't break those two rules, you get to keep the job."

Okay, here we go, Sonny thought to himself. Here come the things I don't want to hear.

Andy lifted one finger in the air and said, "First, I require complete loyalty, like Jesus Christ has for his Father in Heaven. I am not God, of course, but sometimes I sure act like it, so no questions are asked when I ask you to do something."

I can do that, Sonny thought to himself, nodding.

---

[179] Romans 8

Then Andy raised his second finger and said, "And item number two…" Andy then smiles and says, "What you see, hear, and discuss with me and my staff goes nowhere. It is an absolute code of silence between you and me and the company." Andy looked pointedly over at Sonny, gauging his reaction, and then continued. "Now, you can tell you wife where you are going and when you will be back, and the nature of the task, but we will have no business leaks or company secretes divulged, or you will be looking for another job. Do you understand?"

"Totally, Andy… I mean, Mr. Silverman. It will be just like I am in the military again with you as my lead commander. I love it!"

"That is why I chose you, Sonny. I knew I could count on you. One of these days I will tell you about the dream I had the night before we first met. I knew you would walk through that door that day and be my right-hand man in the skies. God told me to go there and wait till you arrived. I had been there since 1 o'clock, and then you showed up! This is bigger than all of us, Sonny." Andy glanced over at Sonny again, pausing. "Just be patient, and you will understand later, my brother...."

My Son, do not forget my teaching,

But keep my commands in your heart,
For they will prolog your life many years…
And bring you prosperity.

Proverbs 3:1-2

Chapter 5

#1 NBA Player Enters the Real World

The Holy Spirit called up the soul of sleeping Barnabas, the one once called to validate Paul's testimony, and He spoke unto him.

"I have created many wonderful and poignant signs and miracles in the world for mankind to see and to praise only Me! And yet still many do not believe but adhere to Charles Darwin's false theories. I am a jealous God! Shame on them! From Job to Johnnie I have put wondrous things in the sky, in the oceans, and on the lands. I have put rich dirt under Man's feet to stand on, air to breath for oxygen, trees to recycle the air, water to drink, rain to replenish the lakes and rivers, polar ice caps to create the seasons and make the rain fall, and knowledge to take the things out of the ground—everything man needs to sustain himself and his family, and to grow in peace. And if these were not wondrous miracles enough, I raised my Son from the grave for man to see, showed him my power of resurrection over death, and yet many still do not believe. I cleanse their lands each day with my breath like angels sent to cleanse their bodies, I wash their beaches with my power to roll back and forth the oceans to and fro like Michael ordered to blow his mighty horn, and I grow their food with my sun's rays which they cannot see nor touch nor understand, its heat bringing forth life from nothingness. And then I make them lie down to be alone and rest their souls under the moon, my earthly clock, so they can recharge their earthly bodies made from the ground and have enough energy to last for the next day, yet still they are a stubborn and prideful lot and have no use for anything but their own selves. If I chose to eliminate the sun one day, they would all be dead within a mere seven minutes, just as I created the world in a mere seven days. Therefore, I tell you the truth, Barnabas: I will give them one more sign that they must obey… a symbol, a living tree that will show them how to grow and become one nation, just as you prayed over the eleven disciples to the Jews to be one tree made of many sprouts, and then I added Saul to them, my chosen one, to bind them together to make them one united trunk in the days after the resurrection. I shall call this new tree from which they will learn and whose branches will become one trunk the "B-a-r-n-a-b-a-s Tree" of the Loose Strife Family (common called the Crepe Myrtle)."

The Holy Spirit paused, looking at Barnabas, who listened patiently, head bowed. Then He continued:

"I shall plant the Barnabas Trees in a foreign land and then have it brought to my Christian nations to show them how they are to live as the Twelve Tribes of Christ and within one age, the 'Age of Non-Profits.' It will grow in all nations, more plentiful than the cedars of Lebanon; it will flower in the heat of the year, with leaves which will represent the holy union of man and woman in pairs only, and the sending out of its disciples in pairs as strength to spread the gospel. And when one shoot is taken off by either animal or Satan or man, it will grow back three time more to become a stronger trunk. The fusion of its trunk will not be denied! And the love of

Christianity—just like the trunk of the tree of Living Truth in my Son, which I have named for all Christ's loyal followers—will never fail either. For the trunk only gets bigger and stronger each time a branch is removed, until it becomes the mighty Tree of Life foreseen by John,[180] covering both sides of the river, where once two rivers stood with the Tree of Life in the middle in the Garden of Eden, now One mighty Tree made of ten billion souls are united into the Tree of Life, and the rivers below it I have merged into one. I have pushed their waters together and they have fed the Tree of Christians so that it will grow and they will feed My tree. This is the answer that so many have waited for: a sign that Christ died for them so they too shall be a sprout of the tree, that they may grow under my sunlight, and they, too, shall be united into one Tribe, with one trunk, and have leaves that are paired two at a time with Christ as one, and their flowers are of many colors, which are more than the seven races I created which will be seen to bloom in the heat. And the fruit of the tree will be the healing of nations prophesied by John during his revelation from God. And then My Son will come to reign on the throne again for which He was sent, and the love of the Father in Heaven, who sent his Son, will not have been in vain. The common symbolic crepe myrtle tree will also be given the family name Lystra, in honor of my favored son, Saul, who was stoned in the city of Lystra, and was left for dead, yet I resurrected him there, like my son Christ, and I put him back on his feet to go with you, Barnabas, into Derbe, that together you might persevere in the spreading of the Gospel, and that all would see and hear and be astonished by their words and their deeds, that all might come to the cross and find salvation through the acceptance of the blood that was shed for

[180] Revelation 22:2

them.[181] But still the people are stubborn fools, and they deserve nothing at all, except perhaps one more chance to accept the blood of Christ that was shed for them and to have relationship with Me for Eternity. Yes, I am giving them one more chance, for the sake of you, St. Barnabas, born as Joseph, and cousin of John Mark, leaders of my faithful request. Amen."

Johnnie was now officially an NBA player; not a starter, but nonetheless a player on the roster. He had to win that position like everyone else, and now it was time to practice under the guidelines of Coach Barricks. Everyone had settled into the program and had had a couple days of loosening up and when Coach rounded everyone up and had them sit on the floor facing the retired jerseys hanging on the south wall.

Then Coach started talking to his players in a point-blank manner.

"Just so everyone is clear here: I am the coach, and you are the players. You do what I say, and we'll all win and be friends."

There were a few giggles from the veteran players who had heard this speech before, but not Johnnie. He was taking this all very seriously.

"I am not your mama!" Coach continued. "I am not your friend! I may not like you and you may not like me, but here we are together because the owner and General Manager have faith in both

[181] Acts 14: 19-20

you and me, that we can win and bring some glory to this game and our city name. I have a job, and that is to win! You have a job, and it is to play. Even if your ass is on fire, you can't put it out until the game is over with a "W" for our side. Should you fail to win… well, then I fail as your coach, and I hate failing. And I don't fail! Should any of you have problems outside of the team, do not bring them here! We do not have time for your petty personal life nonsense. You are getting paid big bucks to win games, not sit around and cry because you made bad decisions outside of this place, so if you need to find God, then do it on your own time. If you need to go to the bathroom, then do it on your own time. And if you need to have a drug problem, then do it on your own time. And speaking of that, if anyone here is caught doing drugs of any kind, even eating too many candy bars for extra caffeine, I will personally escort them to the poor-house and see they get a lifetime supply of misery… crying that they once had a chance at the big leagues and blew it. Because there are no second chances on my team. You will either produce wins and play as a team, or call your mama and get yourself a bus ticket back to whatever God-forsaken hole you climbed out of before you came here. Now does everyone understand me? Am I making myself perfectly clear??"

"Yes, Coach!" the team all replied in unison.

"Does anyone have any questions?" Coach Barricks yelled out.

"No, Coach!" the team once again replied in unison.

"Then it is time for our team attitude-adjustment drill to kick off the first practice of the year," the coach replied.

This coach was different. He wanted the players to play as a team. Whoever was the first player picked in the draft—whether he was the first pick or the last of twenty-four picked in the first round—Coach always did the same thing. He made an example out of him to humble him around the other players. It was not an envious position to be in on Coach Barrick's team.

"Johnnie, please stand up," coach said sternly. You were chosen number one, so you get the first chance at this drill. "Do you know where you are standing, Mr. Johnnie Hot-Shot Take-that-Shot Perfect?"

"Yes, Coach, in Hurricane Stadium," Johnnie replied.

"Wrong, Johnnie, you are in the eye of the Hurricane. It is a raging around you and where you stand is calm. The game is for you to get outside of the eye of this Hurricane, but you won't be able to, because if you do, the team member who lets you out will then go into the eye and not be able to get himself out. It is a simple game. We do not play this one with a basketball. It is just you against the rest of the team. When I blow my whistle twice, the game starts or stops, and until then you must try to break out of the grip of the eye of the Hurricane. And now I want to wish you luck!"

No first-choice player had ever been able to do it, and Johnnie would not be able to either. The coach blew his whistle to begin the humbling exercise and the team players formed a three-deep ring around Johnnie that was an impenetrable barrier, a brick wall. He ran into the wall with all his strength, but the team held tight. It was exhausting for Johnnie, to say the least. He ran at the circle five or six times and was pushed back, and then he tried to fight through the circle by unclasping the hands of the unified team, and still he was thrown back. When he had little strength left, he got down on the floor and tried to crawl through the circle but he was jumped on by the rest of the players and now, he could barely move or breathe. The coach then blew his whistle, because he had made his point, but by this point Johnnie was a wreck of the person he had been before the practice started. He had no ego anymore, but he knew he had to earn the respect of the team or her would be just another bench warmer that saw season one come and go as a one season blow-away.

When Johnnie got back to the lockers and showers, someone (he thought maybe it was Antonio, but he had no proof) had put a poster inside of his locker of some terrible pictures which were supposed to frighten him, or at least help him deflate his ego. It essentially said that this was not tennis or golf where one person was the whole team; this was basketball, and everyone had to play as a unit or they would get picked apart like Texas road pizza by a flock of menacing turkey vultures.

Johnnie needed consoling after trying to free himself from the team-made hurricane, and it was Ben Tucker—who seemed to be the nicest guy on the team—who came up to him and started a conversation.

"It's a golden rule around here we never talk about what goes on inside the arena, especially the initiation drill, or Coach Barricks will have us out the door with our bags packed and gone overnight," Tucker told him. "I hope we didn't rough you up too bad."

"I'm fine," Johnnie said. He looked down the hall and saw some of the guys looking back at him to see if he had gotten the message that any playing to the crowd as 'Hot-Shot Johnnie' would not work in Houston; maybe in another town but not here. "I got the message."

"You know all these guys signed contracts to perform, and they need to make their production points to get their bonuses at the end of the year, so if you take all the shots, they might get pretty mad, even if you hit 100%," Tucker explained.

"But that's not fair to me..." Johnnie said. "If I can hit 100%, then we would certainly win."

"As long as you only think about yourself, Johnnie, then you'll go nowhere in life. That's the hard, bare-bones truth! Like it or not, we were put her on the earth to serve, and that does not mean serve ourselves."

"Ok, well… I guess we'll see then," Johnnie replied. He looked down the hall to see if he could catch a glimpse of Orlando, to see if he would look away, but he was nowhere in sight. Probably scared and hiding in the back next to the whirlpool where Johnnie had seen him before practice started. Johnnie had not bought into the 'servant' message yet. He was still waiting for his time to shine, and even get revenge if he had to; for no one was going to get away with bullying him into submission. It was in his genes, which he got from his dad's (the drug dealer) side, of course.

Tucker went straight home that night to share with his wife about the new kid-phenom whom they had gotten for the 'Canes, Johnnie Hot-Shot Perfect. Coach Barricks had shortened the practice that day into short five-minute drills, and Johnnie's performance was better than anyone he had ever seen play.

It was Tucker's fourth year out of Purdue, and he had failed to make his 250 offensive points required to keep his position on first team last year. As the Hurricanes number-one point guard, Tucker was a master dribbler with the ball, possessing complete control. He never missed a bounce or step. He could fake out or assist with a blind pass with the best of them, but he knew his position was up for grabs this year now that Johnnie had been drafted. Tucker was the leader of the team, even though he was not the oldest. He knew how to judge a person for their character and not their words. So far Johnnie had been pretty quiet and had been staying late after every practice to make sure he could try his hook shot from any spot on the court. He had seventeen special places he called his 'sweet seventeen' where he almost never missed, and his favorite was at half-court, the real show stopper he had become famous for at such a young age.

Tucker sat down to have dinner with his wife, Evie.

"Ben," she said, not taking her eyes off him while she spoke, "you have that worried look on you face again… the one you get every time something big is about to happen. What is it this time?"

Ben and Evie had met in college and had a sturdy marriage, unlike a lot of the players on the team, who could not be trusted to be faithful when they were on the road for out-of-town games.

"Johnnie is toooo good, Evie!" Tucker exclaimed. "I think I am going to ask for a trade. Denver is looking for someone like me. Their GM contacted me last week… I just didn't want to tell you until I was sure about The Spot's 'Hot Shot' abilities, and now I am a believer as well."

"But can he do it here in the Pros?" she asked. "You know, it's a whole new game here. And I hate the cold weather."

"I know, Baby," Tucker said. "I really can't figure out what to do. In a few weeks the regular season will be in full swing, so I guess we probably just need to wait and see how he does his rookie year. Hey!" Tucker said, grinning, "Maybe you should set him up with Melody! Then he'd totally lose focus on his game, and I might have a shot!"

"Well you said it now, you bozo," Evie teased him. "You want him in our family? My sister needs someone reliable, and not some rocket-jock-strap on an ego trip!"

They both laughed and finished their meal. Tucker felt much better after talking with Evie. She always put him at ease. Still, he couldn't help wondering if he was going to have a job next year or should start looking around now. The only other thing he could do was be a high school basketball coach, and the pay was like night and day. They still had two little kids to raise and put through braces and college, after all. He was starting to think maybe he should have finished that chemistry degree before going pro. But best to not look backwards nor worry,[182] he consoled himself. That wasn't Biblical.

It was 12:04 a.m. when Sonny and Rosanne were wakened by their phone ringing.

"Oh no, something bad must have just happened," Sonny mumbled, grabbing for the phone from a dead sleep.

"Sonny, wake up… this is Andy. I need to go fishing," the voice on the other end of the line said coolly.

"Andy? Er, Mr. Silverman, do you know what time it is? It's the middle of the night!" Sonny said directly into the phone.

---

[182] Matthew 6:25

"I know exactly what time it is. The fish are biting tonight. Meet me down at the hanger in fifteen minutes or turn in your resignation in the morning. This is important!" Then he hung up on Sonny.

"What was that all about?" Rosanne asked Sonny groggily.

"Don't really know… Mr. Silverman says he wants to go fishing." Sonny grumbled.

"But it's the middle of the night!" Roseanne said.

"That's what I said, but he says this is important, so I need to show up now for find another job."

Without another word, Sonny rose and slipped on his dirty clothes from the day before and began to head out the door.

"Aren't you even going to quickly change your socks and underwear? That's disgusting!" Rosanne exclaimed.

"I now have twelve minutes to get there and it is a fifteen-minute drive. After midnight I should be able to run a few lights and make it," he called over his shoulder after kissing her quickly. Then he trotted out the door.

Rosanne just sat there with a bewildered look on her face, unable to get back to sleep for at least another hour.

Andy was there at the hanger waiting for Sonny when he arrived.

"Let's fire up this helo-bird and head for the coast," he said.

"Don't we need a flight plan and fuel first?" Sonny asked.

"It's already been taken care of this afternoon. We are ready for take-off. Go due east. We are headed to my oil rig and platform twenty-five miles off the jetties at West Bay in Galveston."

Johnnie glanced at the fight plan and saw it was, indeed, good to go.

"Can we at least stop for coffee somewhere along the way? I think the Channel Bar and Grill stays open all night."

They both laughed and climbed into the chopper, buckling their harnesses for the hour-long flight.

When they were approaching the platform rig, Andy said, "The fish really are biting out here tonight."

"You have to be kidding me, Mr. Silverman," Sonny replied. He was thinking: 'Well, when a person is rich enough or just plain too smart, they must be a little cuckoo as well.' This seemed to hold true from Mozart to King George to the Hapsburgs.

"Put her down there next to my other bird I bought. We are meeting Coach Barricks and Mr. McGinnis here tonight," Andy said.

"Interesting," Sonny muttered, thinking to himself, '...a basketball meeting in the middle of the night in the middle of the ocean on an oil rig platform... how much more clandestine can you get!?'

Sonny landed and looked across the platform, where he saw both Coach Barricks and Leroy McGinnis smoking big cigars and holding fishing poles at the edge of the rig. It must have been a hundred feet down to the water, but the rig was lit up like a Christmas tree, so the waters below were filled with fish attracted to the lights overhead. There were all kinds of fish down there and all kinds of other activity as well, from sea turtles bobbing around for a while and then drifting off to sharks passing through and gorging themselves on the trout that seemed to be eating shrimp stirred up by the changing tides.

Andy climbed out of the chopper and instructed Sonny to wait there. "Catch a few winks of shut eye," Andy said, heading off to the other two men.

"Hello, Coach!" Andy called out to Barricks. Leroy was by his side. They were discussing the team and what the season was going to look like with the new #1 player selection.

"Hello, Mr. Silverman," Coach said.

"Did McGinnis tell you why I wanted to meet out here?" Andy asked.

"No, sir, he just said you wanted to have a private meeting and that the 'Canes arena was not the right place."

"Okay, then, I will tell you something straight up that you need to know: Johnnie's Mamaw called Leroy last week and told him that Johnnie is related to Jesus!"

"Ha! Now that is one I have never heard before!" Coach exclaimed. "So what's big deal, Andy?"

"Whether it is true or not, it will affect ticket sales, and we don't need any bad decisions to happen suddenly, so we need a plan. He is our #1 pick, so everyone will be following him as long as he is making points, and if they think he is related to God, all the better... maybe."

"So, why did his Mamaw call Leroy in the first place and say such a thing? I think she needs to get a new life," Coach replied.

"Funny," Andy said, "that's pretty much what she said about you. She said Johnnie told her about the initiation drill he went through. It didn't bother her, but she felt like maybe you were not saved. She said she wanted you to live for Eternity and not just for basketball."

"Okay, so let her get her own team and try to win a few titles then," Coach laughed.

"On a more serious note, Coach, she was referring to Johnnie's blood test he had to take to enter the NBA. Mamaw's doctors told her that her late husband was a carrier of the 'Mary-James gene,' which is the line of the family of Jesus, which means Johnnie is a carrier, McGinnis said. "And she claims Johnnie will be doing something for the whole world to see that will show Christ is still King of the world."

"I asked her what she meany, but she said she did not know exactly, just that the angels had told her it was going to happen," Leroy said.

"Now I know why you didn't want to have this meeting at the arena. If this got out, the media would have a field day and we would never recoup the momentum of the expectation, always looking for that each game," Coach said.

"So, what's the plan? McGinnis asked.

"We have to find him a girlfriend," Andy replied.

"What the ----!? Coach cried out. "That's all we need is another major media distraction and meltdown around here."

"No, I'm serious," Andy said. "He needs a good helper! There is no way on God's green earth this boy is going to be a stable useful person until he finds the right person to keep his head on straight. That means finding a soulmate... until then he is no good to us."

"Well let me know how it goes… this is not my department," Coach Barricks added.

"Leroy, please keep your baby-blue eyes peeled for a nice girl for him, okay? We don't want any ding-dong who will cost us the sixty million we bet on him and lose what we have invested so far in his future," Andy said, addressing the cause of financial success as well as Johnnie's success.

"Got it, Andy," he replied.

"Okay, the sun is coming up, and the fishing is over. Let's get back to work. We have a lot to do before the first practice game next week," Andy said, thereby calling the meeting to adjourn.

Then he turned and headed back to the chopper, climbing in and waking Sonny.

"Fire this bird up and try to outrun the sunup. I need to get some shut-eye when I get home before my 10 a.m. meeting at the Board of Directors."

"Gochta' covered," Sonny said, "and that's a big 10-4, Mr. Silverman… I will get you back to the hanger ASAP!"

Slightly after liftoff, Andy turned to Sonny and said, "Do you know any nice single girls we could maybe set up Johnnie Hot-Shot with?"

"I know of possibly two... they are both nurses at Methodist Hospital. Is that what you are looking for?" Sonny asked.

"Yes!" Andy replies, "Perfect! I have one of those, myself: my wife, Daisy. She is a great caretaker. Just what Johnnie needs! And we need someone who is not on some crusade from old childhood self-esteem wounds, or afraid of changing diapers and being a mother. Nurses always make better mothers and wives, you know, just ask around. And nurses are educated, too, with great work ethics and common sense, not like my niece, with a crazy political science degree, which means absolutely nothing to most people."

"I will call around and find out what they are doing these days. They might be engaged already, who know. So what do I tell each of them?" he asked.

"Ask them if they want to go for a helicopter ride next week and see the city at night with my wife, Daisy. See if one or both can meet at the hanger on Thursday at 5pm. I will take care of the rest." Andy had it all planned out. "Whichever one my wife likes best, we'll invite to his first game."

"Sure thing, Boss," Sonny answered with a vocalized grunt and a quick salute to his 'copter's helmet visor.

Then Andy said, "Do you know if any of them go to church?"

"One is Catholic, and the other is LDS Mormon," Sonny said with a smile.

"Not a problem, my good friend, as long as they both believe in a greater power and go to church once a week… that is fine. Daisy and I are Messianic Jews, but I think you know that already. And you're Presbyterian right? And Johnnie is Baptist. We Hurricanes are a motley lot, aren't we? That's what Leroy told me."

"Correct," Sonny said with a grin.

"Well, this will be a real hoot," Andy said. "All we need now is one liberal Methodist who likes fine wine to round out our group."

"Well… that would be my amazing, wonderful, talented and beautiful Methodist wife, Rosanne, you are now speaking of. Can she vote on Johnnie's new wife too?" Sonny eased in the big request.

Sonny then fell back in his big chopper seat laughing out loud and acting like he was had just been stabbed in the heart. They both smiled at each other and gave a thumbs-up together. It was a great time that night and the beginning of a great joint adventure.

About an hour later they landed, and Sonny headed back to his house to tell Rosanne all about what had happened (which was nothing, of course, according to Mr. Silverman). But at least she was going to meet Andy's wife soon and get a fun helicopter ride at the same time.

The Holy Spirit then called for the sleeping spirit of Tertullian to be wakened and brought forward.

"Quintus Septus Tertillianus, come forth!" the Holy Spirit demanded. "I created you the day of Jesus' Resurrection," He and She said together, having two heads at this time, not just one. The Holy Spirit was known to have many head-forms and many body-forms, and whatever form the He-and-She Godhead took at any given moment was an indication of how the Holy Spirit would rule over Lower Paradise at that moment.

"I remember now, oh Holy One," Tertullian replied.

"And do you remember why?" the Holy Spirit asked.

"To continue with the power of the holy pen, your instrument of the Gospel: the power of Words and of your Miracles," Tertullian replied.

"Correct. You were and remain my good and faithful servant in whom I am well pleased," He and She answered.

"Your will is my hands, my Creator," Tertullian replied.

"So, one hundred years after St. Paul and one hundred and fifty years after My Son Christ, you wrote for my treatise that might understand the truth of human pain, salvation, damnation, blessing, and diversification, did you not, oh master of the holy pen?" the Holy Spirit inquired.

"I did as you asked of me," Tertullian replied.

"So once again, explain… so that the Heavens might rejoice in your written answers," the Holy Spirit proclaimed.

"The Creator is a Trinity, a Triune God, not a sole being, for a sole being is too much like the sole being of man, that he might get mixed up and think of himself as God in total first, My Lord But man shall not have any gods before you," Tertullian said. "That you created him to bless himself if he lives according to Your will, and if not, he will damn himself, if he lives outside Your will. For it is not your design to damn him but to allow himself to destroy his own future by not repenting of his sinful, imperfect ways."

Tertullian paused, and then continued.

"That you gave to him the angels to help lead him if he will just rely on them for guidance through Your holy design and seek Your conscience of internal guidance placed by Your holy design, led by the Father in Heaven, that man might live in joy and peace in relation with the Father, and not abuse his fellow man's relation nor destroy himself by each other's hand in doing so."

Tertullian continued, "…and that the Tree of Life, which is so precious to You, will bear sprouts of all those who believe in the Son as their salvation, and that those sprouts would unite into one mighty Trunk to be the head of the new Paradise when Jesus comes to rule again, so that all shall see the unification of the Tree, and not the damnation of non-blessings that result from non-unification, until He comes again."

Tertullian spoke on, revealing the Truth known in Heaven as the Obvious Law. Then then the Holy Spirit interrupted, explaining:

"And the Tree of Knowledge in the Garden of Eden, which was not to be eaten from, was left in place—along with the presence of the Evil One and his companions—to be the measure and instrument to separate the wheat from the chaff. And later it became the later Tree of Life, which We, the Trinity, will plant after the World's Resurrection, as it sees My and the Father's and the Son's coming in the clouds, just as We resurrected our Son from death, after all had seen him hanging on the cross. And so will we then fulfill the prophecy and resurrect the world into one Tree of Life—unified as one body, on one root, in one place, with ten billion branches—replanted in the middle of the Garden for all to see and understand. Amen."

And with that Tertullian fell on his face flat in the basement of Upper Paradise, in a chamber where all the non-canonized saints were joined together to sing praises to the Lord.

"This was told to me," Tertullian attested, "on Day One of this Age—the Age of Nonprofits—which will come to a conclusion after the Tree grows to full maturity at the time You see fit to close the Age and call Your Son back down from Heaven to reenter paradise and unify the Tree again into one mighty nation, the Twelve Tribes of Israel into the Twelve Tribes of Christ. Together they shall stand as one Tree and be a blessing to all nations thereafter for one thousand years of Peace."

"And why do I continue to be asked if the Lord is a perfect and good God, asked why pain must exist as part of the life-lesson equation?" the Holy Spirit asked.

"So that the human mind can try to quantify its cost of entry with a blood payment that is equal to the cost and payment by Your Son whom You so Love. When only Grace is needed it is confusing, because the law states that without a payment there could be no will, and without a will the death is meaningless, and without the death no inheritance could be paid forward. This is the same message over and over again in its many incarnations, yet still they do not understand. Many will be sent after me to state the same message, to preach the same message, and to write the same message, but still they are a stupid lot. Like sheep who will not follow a shepherd but be eaten by wolves as they stray from the Tree of Live, You have panted for them to join. They continue to turn to themselves and their intellectual disabilities to find more answers, but this action only leads to more strife. It is like chasing butterflies for men: they must run and tire trying to catch the butterfly or the wild goose, and it is not until then that they will be still and let God be God, that the butterfly will land on them and touch them when they cannot touch it, and that the wild goose will give them wisdom of the ages, that they might learn that flying long distances towards Heaven's goal in a group allows them to fly farther than they ever could flying alone. Until they understand this, they will continue to damn themselves, living in a lake of fire and thinking they are perfect, living without Divine relation, and then blame it on you, oh Holy One… which you will never approve nor ever condone."

"Well said, my good and faithful servant. Go now and rest in Peace once more for the next thousand years before I summon you for your report and witness to all nations," She of The Holy Spirit said. Then the Holy Spirit changed back into the masculine form to address the paternal needs of the Age instead of the maternal.

A Christian who doesn't amount to much in this world should be glad, for he is great in the Lord's sight.

But a rich man should be glad that his riches mean nothing to the Lord, for he will soon be gone like a flower that has lost all its beauty and fades away, withered, killed by the scorching summer sun. So it is with rich men. They will die and leave behind all their busy activities.

James,

Your Brother in Christ

Chapter 1:9-11

Chapter 6

Life in the Limelight

It was 4 a.m. when Sonny's phone rang, waking him from a dead sleep. He rolled over and looked at Rosanne, putting the pillow over his head to try and block the noise. After several more rings, he reluctantly picked up, with a strong suspicion of who might be on the other end.

"Good morning, Mr. Silverman. Are we going fishing again?"

"No, Sonny," Andy said, "On Friday I want you to take Daisy, Rosie, myself, and the two girls you know to Neiman Marcus for a shopping spree. Be at the hanger at 5 p.m. with your wife."

"Okay," Andy quickly responded, then added, "Uhhhh, could you wait just a minute while I ask my wife? I need to ask her if she has plans."

"Sonny, she does NOT have plans, right? This is a group effort! You work for me, and she is your wife. She is your helper, so she *will* be available to help you with your job, and this means getting Johnnie a new wife. Believe me, this is how it is supposed to work. Don't worry…" Andy's voice softened a little. "She'll enjoy it!"

"I'll tell her what you said, but she may not like it." Sonny replied.

"Sonny, who's the leader of the house: you or her? Is she your helper, or are you her helper? Better grow a pair if you plan to keep working on this ship. It's Biblical. She is your helper. And you are my helper. And we all are helpers to Christ, who helps us in return, for the glory of the Kingdom of Heaven. So don't get caught up in 'who is in charge'… it's not like that. We all have one common goal: to help the Kingdom of Heaven for God's glory. Now, if she has another task she's working on for God, call me back and we can discuss, but until then, plan to meet me at 5 p.m. on Friday."

With that, Andy abruptly hung up.

"What did he say, Honey? Are you going fishing again?" Rosanne inquired.

"Nope, you're getting new shoes from Niemen Marcos this Friday, and they are going to be very expensive," he said.

"I love that store, and I love you too! You are the best husband in the whole wide world!" Roseanne exclaimed, slightly confused but delighted nonetheless.

"I know, you lucky girl, you! I'll pick you up at 4 p.m. on Friday and we'll go to the hanger together for a chopper ride."

Sonny flashed her a smile and gave her a kiss, then hopped up to make her a cup of her favorite pecan-vanilla-roast coffee before heading into the office to learn about the week's flying duties.

When Sonny arrived at the office, he met with Betty Lou Bradford, Andy's secretary.

"Betty, do you have my weekly flight plan ready? Can I have it please?" he asked.

She handed it to him, along with the phone number of Andy's favorite Houston Limousine service.

"Mr. Silverman wants you to arrange to have a limo ready to pick up your friends on Friday afternoon and take them to the hanger, and also have another limo waiting at the Galleria drop-off and pick-up area at 7 p.m. And he told me in no uncertain terms, 'Don't mess this up, or there will be hell to pay!' Got it?"

"Got it!" Sonny replied, taking his orders and walking out the door to drive over to the hangar. He was going to take Leroy over on the company's sister-chopper to a meeting at another location to have a stern discussion on a payment which needed to be collected. A local shipbuilder was behind on some pipe Andy had ordered and Leroy needed to go over and talk to the CEO about it.

As Sonny was leaving the main office and saying goodbye to Betty, he noticed a door open on the left that led to a room he had never seen before.

"What is that?" Sonny asked.

"That's Mr. Silverman's hyperbaric chamber," she said.

"Hyperbaric chamber…?" Sonny mirrored her words, confused.

"Yes, he got it to use after diving trips when he goes to the Caymans, but he also likes to take naps in there sometimes during the day to get more oxygen uploaded and recharge his electrons. He says that 'pure air' with more oxygen access to the body is the key to long life, just like in the Garden of Eden, according to his guardian angels."

"Interesting… I will have to remember that next time I am at Niemen Marcos and my wife wants something special for her birthday, hahaha!" Sonny laughed, almost in tears.

"I guess that also means pure oil is better to run my helicopter than non-pure oil…?"

"I bet Mr. Silverman would agree with you. You probably should ask him sometime, but it may take him several days to answer. And if you ask him about pure food… well, you can just count on missing Mass on Sunday!"

"Are you Catholic, Betty?" Sonny asked.

"Well, not really. I am spiritual. According to Mr. Silverman, we are all just one shoot in the big 'tree of life.' I go to a Catholic church because they talk the language of my Jesus family."

"Now you have me mixed up…. can you explain a little more? I think I am missing something here," Sonny said.

"Haven't you ever seen or read any of the plaques on the walls in Mr. Silverman's office?" Betty asked.

"Nope, can't say I have," Sonny replied.

Betty led Sonny into Andy's office, and there on the wall by the door Sonny saw several plaques. They were all famous quotes by Tertullian, the father of Western theology, written before the year 220 AD. The one over the door read: *Christians are not born, they are made*. To the left of Mr. Silverman's door, one said: *The more you mow us down, the more we grow; the blood of Christians is seed*. And to the right of his door: *Prevention of birth is a precipitation of murder*. And there were many more.

"I thought Mr. Silverman was Hebrew, not Christian," Sonny said. "He said Messianic Jew, but I didn't really know what that meant, I guess."

Laughing, Betty said, "When Mr. Silverman is asked that question, he always replies, 'Well, Jesus was Hebrew, wasn't he? Mary was a Jew, too, wasn't she? She came from Abraham, so

Christians and Jews are all some form of the same Tree of Life: one root with many sprouts, all forming one large trunk.' "

"Hmmm, too deep for me in the morning before I've had at least three cups of coffee," Sonny chuckled. "I'll have to think on that one a while and get back to you."

Then he left and headed to the hangar to pick up Leroy and take him to his meeting.

It was Wednesday night and practice was almost over for the Hurricanes and Coach Barricks. One of Coach's methods of finishing up a practice was not to let any player leave until each and every player had hit twenty free-throws in a row. If they missed one, they had to start over. Coach Barricks always said that games were won or lost at the free-throw line, so if you couldn't make a simple shot when everyone was standing around, you should find another team to play for. Johnnie was always the first to finish. He hit his first twenty without a miss. The rest of the team would shoot three or four rounds before they hit their twenty in a row.

On this particular Wednesdays night, just for fun, Coach had thought up a little game, because one player, Marcus—who was good at dunking the ball—was the worst free-throw shooter on the team, and Marcus could be there all night if the coach did not cut him some slack. Usually everyone else was in the showers and headed home while Marcus was closing down the place.

"Hey Johnnie, come over here a second," as Coach motioned to Johnnie, who was talking to Tucker, who was still shooting, having made fourteen in a row on his third set.

"I want you to help Marcus get out of here before midnight, so can you alternate shots with him?" Coach said.

"Sure thing, Coach," Johnnie said.

"But there's one catch," Coach said.

"What is that, Coach?" Sonny asked.

"As soon as he makes one, you will shoot… but blindfolded," Coach explained. By this time the other players had gathered around, and snickers could be heard coming from the back of the group. This was just another way to humble Johnnie, but also a way to seal the team into a fighting unit. Coach pulled out a red bandana he carried in his pocket and handed it to Tucker.

"Ben, here… put this on Hot Shot so he is blind and can't see," Coach ordered

"Ouch! This sucks…" Johnnie complained to Tucker. "Hey, Buddy, cut me some slack! I'm the victim here, not Marcus!"

Again, the whole team laughed. Tucker lined Johnnie up at the free-throw line just to the right of Marcus.

"Okay, begin," Coach said to Marcus.

Marcus missed his first three shots before he made one.

"Okay, Hot Shot, your chance," Coach said.

Johnnie had done this ten million times, so he was not even thinking. His brain was on automatic… but still it was a little strange not being able to see what he was shooting at. He paused and let his shot go. It hit the rim on the front, and didn't go in, but actually was closer than Marcus's first shot.

"Ha! Johnnie, I think you have met you match. Marcus is one up on you! Marcus, shoot again please."

It took Marcus four shots this time.

Tucker leaned over and whispered into Johnnie's ear, "Just shoot a little long and bounce it in… I think that will be easier."

"I am the coach, Tucker, so no outside help, please," Coach blurted out.

Johnnie thought for a moment. *I can do this, and Tucker is right. It will be a better angle if I shoot it long.*

Sure enough, Johnnie let his shot go and it hit the backboard, going in. The team jumped up with cheers of 'Yes!' together. It was a victory for the whole team. Coach liked the response, so he declared practice over and let everyone go home. The first pre-season game would be at home on Friday, and they had only one more practice tomorrow night before the beginning of the season.

Sonny still had to call his old friend, Charlotte. He had already talked to Mia, and she had responded *yes*, that she wanted to go on Friday. Both Charlotte and Mia had been popular cheerleaders in high school, so it seemed to Sonny that at least one of them would be a good fit for Johnnie as a girlfriend or even possible wife.

When Sonny could not get hold of Charlotte, he decided he had better drive over to Methodist Hospital, his old stomping grounds, and try to find her. He thought she might just be the best match for Johnnie. It was a gut feeling he had.

"Hey, Char'!" he yelled out when he spotted her getting into an elevator. "Hold that door for me! How's my favorite ER helper?"

he asked breathlessly, running into the elevator with her at the last second.

"Oh, fine… just trying to keep people out of the morgue, I guess," she said jokingly.

"Well, you've managed to keep me out!" Sonny said.

"Yeah, I should charge you overtime for that!" she said.

"Come one—it hasn't been all that bad, has it? You know, if I weren't a married man, you would have been the one for me," he said.

"Of course… story of my life: one guy away from eternal bliss," she replied.

"Well, Char', I think I can make it up to you. How would you like to meet Johnnie Spot?" Sonny asked her.

"He *is* pretty hot! Can you actually do that for me?" she asked, incredulously.

"Hey, Char', my sweet angel-girl," Sonny said, "I'll always do everything for you that I can! You're like the sweet little sister that I never had."

"So how are you going to pull off this little miracle for me?" she asked.

"My new job these days is working for Mr. Silverman, the new owner of the Hurricanes. He wants me to take his wife, Daisy, along with Rosanne, with two other girls for an evening out shopping and also to meet Johnnie."

"Two girls?" she exclaimed.

"Yes, Mia is going too. He wanted two girls for Johnnie to choose from, but I will put in a good word for you. Just leave it up to me. I am planning to set Mia up with Bobby Heatherton. He's a Mormon, and she is too, so I think that should work out fine, too," he said.

"So what is Johnnie's faith and background?" Charlotte asked.

"Well, his Mamaw is a Bible-carrying, gun-toting Baptist, and she says he is still figuring it out."

"Well, okay… as long as he is not an atheist or demon-possessed or anything like that... I don't want the rest of my life to be like dragging a dead horse across an endless God-forsaken desert!" she laughed.

"Thanks, Sis… you're the best!" Sonny said, leaning over and kissing her on the forehead.

"Someone will pick you up here in front of the hospital at 4 p.m. on Friday and bring you to us. I want you and Mia both in your scrubs! Okay?" he said.

"Whatever you say, dear! You're the boss on this one. So, if this a blind date, is he really blind?" she asked.

"Of course he is—totally! But you won't need a seeing-eye dog," he said.

At that, they both laughed and Sonny headed out the hospital for the chopper pad, so he could get back to work. He had one more call to make now and that was to the woman in charge of everything: Mamaw.

At the start of Sonny's new job, he had received a mobile phone. It was one of the first of its sort and considered cutting-edge. It was in a bag, and hence called a 'bag phone.' He could call Leroy on it at any time—whenever and wherever—and the two were to use it to coordinate Mr. Silverman's busy schedule and the business of Silverman Investments.

After using the 'bag phone' to let Leroy know he would be there at the hangar to take him to the next meeting, he dropped a call to Mamaw about Friday's game.

"Hello, Ms. Gleason, this is Leroy McGinnis," he began the conversation.

"Why, hello back at ya, Mr. McGinnis. How is my Johnnie doing with Coach Barricks and all the others?" she asked.

"He is becoming a natural Hurricane, I think! And Mr. Silverman would like you to come to Johnnie's first game on Friday," Leroy replies.

"That would be great! Unfortunately, I don't have anything to wear. I would be too embarrassed to show up in my old tattered-threads, so I think I'm gonna pass this time on the invitation. We play bridge that night, anyway, and I can watch him on television if he gets to play," she informed Sonny.

"That would really disappoint Mr. Silverman. He has reserved some seats for him and his wife, and me and my wife with you, so he would really like you to come. And he has arranged to take you and our wives shopping right before the game to Niemen's, so he is sending a Limo to pick you up on Friday afternoon. Can you be ready at 3 p.m.?"

"Why, that would be wonderful, Mr. McGinnis! I promise to wear bright blue in full support of the 'Canes, if that's okay?" Mamaw replies.

"Please wear whatever you like, Ms. Gleason. Just be ready at 3 o'clock at your house. Tony, our limousine driver, will be by to pick you up."

The Holy Spirit called for those He and She loved for their pure hearts—Luke, John, and Lazarus—to come forward.

First He—in His masculine form—spoke to Luke.

"Good and faithful servant, did you write what was requested of you, that all might hear and believe?"

"You know I did, oh Holy Spirit," Luke replied. "I acted out of full loyalty for my Father in Heaven, my love for my Savior Jesus Christ, and fear of the unknown and the unmet causations in my soul."

"You did well, my Luke. And did you record, as you were instructed, My Son's teaching to his disciples in the correct order: the Parable of the Lost Sheep, the Parable of the Lost Coin, the Parable of the Lost Son, the Parable of the Shrewd Manager, and the story of the Rich Man and Lazarus?"

"I did as I was instructed, oh Holy One," Luke replied.

"And why did you not write that final one as a Parable as well?" the Holy Spirit asked.

"Because Lazarus was there in name, was amongst us born from the line of Abraham. He was one of the men whom Jesus loved enough to bring back from death, along with the disciple John, who was allowed to skirt death by being exiled to the island of Patmos, unlike the rest, whom were martyred."

Then the Holy Spirit called Lazarus, saying, "Why is this so important to me this day in Paradise?"

"Because of the fifteen rules which You taught here as lessons for all mankind to learn," Lazarus replied.

"Tell me again those fifteen lessons, good and faithful servant," the Holy Spirit demanded.

Lazarus began reciting:

"1. Your Son loves me, Lazarus, so much that he raised me from the dead, just as You love Your Son and You raised Him from the dead."

"2. Those who believe will see the glory of God through the Resurrection."

"3. Jesus weeps for those He loves and resurrects, those just like me."

"4. Jesus comforts those who mourn and who put their faith in Him."

"5. Jesus orders those men He loves to come out of the grave."

"6. Those who see what Jesus does through others believe in Him."

"7. Jesus goes to those He loves to resurrect them.

"8. Jesus declares that He is the Resurrection and the Life and that anyone who believes in Him will never die."

"9. Jesus answers the call to come and raise another from the dead, by family members who believed in him."

"10. Jesus went back into a land that previously had tried to do him harm, with the intent to resurrect the one whom He loves.

"11. Jesus delayed His journey to allow there to be no doubt that the one He would resurrect was truly dead."

"12. The disciples of Jesus, whom He taught and loved, even the one who doubted Him the most, Thomas, wanted to go with Him on this dangerous journey, that he might die with Jesus, if needed.

"13. The Lord will forgive as many times as a person repents and asks for forgiveness."

Lazarus paused, taking a breath.

"This is good that you remembered these lessons, Lazarus of Bethany" the Holy Spirit said. "Now step forward, John, son of

Zebedee and of Salome, you whom my Son loves also. What can you add to these lessons for all to know, my good and faithful servant?" the Holy Spirit asked.

"To what Luke attests, I do also attest firmly," John said.

"Explain, my good and faithful servant," the Holy Spirit went on.

"14. That a man—anyone—who loves money more than God and doing good to help others," John spoke, "will live an eternity of want and thirst with a great chasm between himself and those who belong to God, and will not be given the relief of Living Waters."

"And finally… what else, John?" the Holy Spirit asked, "Speak loud and clear so that he Heavens might echo your voice!"

"15. That the mystery of you, and the Father, will always be a mystery in this life and world, and no one will know you except through your Son, Jesus, who came to give Living Water and lead others to their own resurrections by walking in the light; and woe to those who cause another man to stumble by leading him away from the light to walk in the darkness."

"This is all for you this day, my three servants who serve to glorify only the Father in Heaven!" the Holy Spirit announced in a fading voice.

With that, the Holy Spirit changed from an infinite mass of circling clouds speaking from on high to a smaller condensed hurricane, whose energy was concentrated in an all-knowing eye. And in the eye was the Tree that could see future events to come. For the Holy Spirit would set in motion great events that would change the world for all the saints and angels to see, so once again the world know that there was nothing left to chance on earth and no such thing as natural selection for which the Holy Spirit had not first established and ordained as the rule of order as agreed upon by the Holy Father in Heaven. Amen.

It was Friday, October 29th, Johnnie's first real game, his debut on the national basketball scene. Something special was about to happen that had been in the making for a long time, predestined according to the will of the Holy Spirit, just like the day Jesus went to the Temple to begin his ministry, on that pre-selected day, with all those around him pre-selected and chosen for their places in history, though none knew at the time that they would be woven into the Tree of Life, orchestrated into one single root with a common trunk through suffering and enlightenment.

And today it was Johnnie's turn.

A limousine went to pick up Mamaw at 3 p.m., and another went to pick up Charlotte and Mia at 4 p.m. They all met up at the hangar at 5 p.m., where Sonny and his lovely wife Rosanne were sitting waiting for them. For this occasion, Mr. Silverman had rented a corporate chopper that seated twelve. It was a granddaddy of a helicopter—even Rosanne had not seen one this big!

As if on cue, Mr. Silverman drove up with Daisy right at that moment and began the introductions.

Daisy stepped out of the car and immediately hit the ground running.

"Well, howdy! Howdy, y'all! Looks we're going to have a big party tonight, Houston-style," she said, approaching the little crowd.

Mamaw was not too sure of what to think yet. She felt out of place with all these rich people around her, all looking so prim and proper.

"I'm Daisy, the one who gets to spend all of my husband's money before he dies and goes to Heaven," Daisy said with a grin.

"You and honest Uncle Sam," Andy piped in. "Actually, I think you are making more than he is, so we need to get us a business write-off tonight. So let's go and have some fun! We can finish the introductions up in the air."

"Where are we going, the island of Puerto Rico?" Mamaw asked humorously. She did not like not knowing what to expect. She had brought an umbrella and queen-size bedsheet in her big purse, thinking these items might just come in handy if they had an engine failure and went down over the ocean.

"We are going to Niemen Marcus over at The Galleria Mall first to buy you all some comfy shoes to wear, and then we're going to see the Hurricanes beat the hell out of the fighting Ontario Bears. I have us all front-row seats, and I want Johnnie to see his Mamaw is watching him from the stands. This is going to be fun!" Mr. Silverman explained.

This was a late game, starting at 9:15, so they had plenty of time to grab some food and do a little shopping before game started, especially since they were allowed to enter the coliseum through the private backdoor, Mr. Silverman's private entrance.

They all scrambled into the chopper and set off to the Galleria Mall in West Houston on Westheimer Road at Loop 610. Sonny was flying, but he helped Rosanne into her seat first and put her seatbelt harness on, making sure she was fastened securely in. Mamaw needed help, too, and Daisy took charge getting her fastened in. Mamaw did not want to sit in the back, but next to the exit door. She clutched her purse tightly, even though the rest of the ladies had all put theirs in a large secure storage bin inside of the chopper. Mamaw was not taking any chances!

"Hey, Rosie," Mr. Silverman called out, "How did you and Sonny meet?"

"At a church dance," she replied. "I was dancing and he was the entertainment!" Then Rosanne laughed, as she always did at her own jokes. It was a family tradition where she came from.

"What kind of church?" he asked.

"A very good one, with only a few sinners," she replied, laughing some more. "We only took the remorseful sinners. All the perfect sinners went across the street to the Baptists." She then began to move her head around to see the skyline below, trying to pick out any recognizable landmarks.

Daisy chuckled at her comment and Charlotte did too.

"I am a Fundamental Baptist," Mamaw declared.

Mia showed no response to this comment.

Charlotte chimed in, saying, "Most of my friends are Baptists. They're a great bunch. What I can't figure out is how much fighting we see on television in Northern Ireland between the Catholics and the Protestants. I am Catholic. What's all the bickering about? Aren't they all Christians and just supposed to love their neighbors?"

Mamaw liked the fact that Charlotte was sticking up for the Baptists. Charlotte knew Rosie had meant no harm with her comment, but still it rubbed her the wrong way. But making jokes about things was just Rosanne's way of dealing with the stress and inequities of life, because her macular degeneration prevented her from seeing what everyone around her could see… like all the sights out the chopper windows right now.

Andy turned to Mia, who was sitting across from him, and changed the conversation.

"Tell us about working at the hospital, Mia. Do you like being a nurse? How did you meet Sonny?"

The helicopter's front four seats were facing backwards towards the back four seats, and then there were four more seats behind them, but only the two rows of seats were taken. Mamaw and Charlotte were on the outside two, Andy and Rosanne on the inside two, and Mia was in the middle. Sonny was up front and had another pilot with him today, so he could not hear what they were saying in back.

"I love being a nurse," Mia said. "It is what I believe God wants me to do. I like the neonatal part of the hospital best… helping to deliver babies. I met Sonny one day in the cafeteria. He looked like he was having a bad day, and I asked if I could sit next to him. He started talking about this friend he'd lost in Vietnam, and I could relate to it because I lost my brother there too. We both agreed it was a senseless war, where only the media and the politicians benefited."

"That's a pretty strong opinion," Andy said.

"A person either has to be strong, or die," Mia said. "That's a fact of life. I see it every day in the newborn nursery. Life is a struggle, and it begins with the first breath of air. There are no easy paths in life, only lessons to be learned."

Mamaw liked what she heard Mia saying. Mia was a fighter, and that may just be what Johnnie needed in his life to keep him on the straight and narrow. On the other hand, Charlotte was a defender with a good heart, and that was a good person to have at your side at life's loneliest times. All Mamaw knew was God was in control, so she prayed for enlightenment, all the while keeping her hands on her purse just in case the engines failed and she needed to bail out of the side door with just an umbrella and a sheet as a parachute. Mamaw was a walking paradox, always believing God would take care of her, but also always carrying a pistol and Bible, just in case she had to use either on someone who tried to hurt her or her precious Cojo, who just wanted to play ball, like Johnnie.

The ride was a short one, and in no time they landed at the Galleria, ready to go shopping.

Seven days earlier, Mamaw had received a message from the angel Verostices, who had come to her in a dream and said:

"Fear not, for the Lord is with you, and this is His message:

'Oh that you might understand! Listen to the one who will carry you like angels from on high, for His wisdom exceeds His years. Blessings will not come as you think, through the front door, but through the back, where the servant must enter: humbly, unannounced, and with the pure heart. And everything that was made from the ground is also a part of the sky, and the sea, and the stars, and just as the Holy Spirit is fluid and dwells in all things in the heart, you will be shown the plagues to come from self-damnation and lack of breath with the life it carries, withholding the blood of Christ that was spilled for you and your line.' "

This dream so scared Mamaw that she was not able to sleep the rest of that night. When she woke, her heart was racing, and all her senses told her that the dream was supernatural. The angel had told her not to be afraid, but still the message was one she could not understand. It was as if the angel were speaking some sort of prophetic code, and that was something Mamaw did not like. But she remembered that when she had been told that Johnnie would stay in Houston and play basketball there, she had not worried or feared at that message, so she would be patient and see what mysteries, if any, would show up to validate this message.

And that was the exact moment when Leroy had called her and said to be ready for a limousine to pick her up.

Mamaw had never been in anything like that before, and certainly never in a helicopter. Her roots were very simple. She had been raised poor in money and spirit, and she had maintained a life of praise and prayer to her Father in Heaven, knowing that one day she would be with Jesus and God in Heaven, because Jesus was not here on earth. This was not Heaven, and this was not Hell. This was just the testing ground to let people see their own hearts through their own actions and choices, so that they would understand their own rewards or lack thereof in the next life, absent of anger. Anger was only an emotion of the world of earth, the Holy Spirit, and the extension of Paradise in which the dimensions of the world existed. Anger was the poison that led people down the path of no return, and when Jesus came, he did so to heal that anger that destroyed, which is why he became known as and called—among other things—the 'Prince of Peace'."

When the helicopter landed one block south of the mall, one of the limousines was there to take them across the street. Daisy led the group as they all climbed into the long black vehicles, not knowing what to expect, and then the driver took them to the front doors of Niemen's. He got out of the driver's side door and opened the back side door to let them out

"I will wait here until you all return from shopping," he informed them.

Andy patted him on the shoulder as he went by him and said, "Thank you, Fred. We will be back here in less than two hours." Then Andy turned to the girls and Sonny and said, "Now let's go have some fun!"

Oh, everyone was so excited! This felt like a dozen childhood Christmases all wrapped up into one. Even Mamaw had a little jump and hop in her step when she exited the limousine. The Galleria was big and air conditioned, and Neiman's had a piano player right at the front door when they came in, playing Beethoven and other classics. It was so luxurious that only the people who lived in and around the Oaks area of west Houston could afford to shop there, or sometimes rich people from other countries who came to Houston on vacation to spend their new wealth—perhaps from their oil fortunes—on others.

The big jewelry stores there had diamonds almost as big as ice cubes and watches that were hard to look at because of the crystal surrounding the gold and platinum bands. Mamaw thought to herself that if she ever had anything like that, she would be afraid Cojo might eat it and she would never see it again, because she was having a hard time just remembering where she placed her car keys and glasses, or she would be afraid that it would be lost or stolen. She looked on in amazement and walked slowly behind the others, while the young girls dreamed and the married couples cooed like wedding doves.

"Follow me!" Andy shouted out to the entire group, and then walked right over to the ladies' shoes section of the store.

"Okay, friends," he said, "this is my gift to you. I want each of you to pick out a new pair of shoes tonight. Cost is no issue. You have one hour to shop and find something, and then we have dinner reservations in the café, before we head over to the game to see my Hurricanes play."

Everyone just stood there in disbelief. Could this be really happening, they all asked themselves.

"Sonny, this means you too. I think you need a pair of alligator cowboy boots, so I am going to have you measured for some to be custom-made, unless you find something here in the store you like better," Mr. Silverman said to him.

Sonny was shocked, and Rosanne just started jumping up and down holding onto his arm; she could hardly contain herself. Mia and Charlotte were both smiling huge from ear-to-ear, and Daisy knew exactly the shoes she wanted because she had seen them last week when she had been here.

"Well, what are we waiting for?" Andy exclaimed. And with that, the group dispersed like an army of mole rats on a mission to find the best morsels of food to eat.

Right close to where Mamaw was standing was a pair of turquoise short-topped boots that looked like something out of the

1970's disco-parade movies. *Wow, these would look great going to church*, she thought to herself, but she really wanted something in red or pink to match her 'I can do it' attitude. Just then a young man came up to her and asked if he could help her or get her something to try on, which caused her to almost faint.

After they all found what they wanted, they headed to the café to get a bite to eat. Andy had had the backroom reserved, and bottles of wine were already on the table, wrapped in towels and placed in silver buckets, ready to be poured. It was a cozy setting, and as they all entered the room they saw their names on place cards, one at the head of each dinner setting. Mozart was playing from the speaker system, and all of the waiters were dressed in black pants and white vests.

"Wow," was all any of them could say. Mamaw thought she had died and gone to Heaven, but she knew the real Heaven would be even better.

Before sitting down, Mr. Silverman asked everyone to get their wine glasses filled quickly so he could make a toast.

"Everyone has gathered here tonight for a reason. We all worship and serve our Lord Jesus Christ in many different ways, but we are all of the same root, of the same Tree of Life. God our Father has called us now to become one trunk, and not many shoots; no longer Catholic and Protestant, Hebrew and Gentile, but one common blood of and for the blood that was shed by Jesus. Though more shoots are sprouting from the trunk even as we speak, the time has come to unite us and all others. May the Hurricanes' and our hope—the new rising star, Johnnie Spot Perfect, the beacon of success that we hold so precious—help us see the light that shines for us each day in Jesus, and may we no longer live in the shadows but step into the light of God's wisdom. Amen."

Mia turned to Charlotte and said, "Do you feel like an outsider here? I think we are the bait and the fishing is about to start."

"I like this kind of fishing," Charlotte replied, smiling. "I just hope I have the right kind of bait!"

They both laughed and clinked their wine glasses and then say down to an eloquent white tablecloth in their new shoes that they had received today, for just being at the right place and the right time.

Mamaw really liked the speech, and her gray-haired head told her something big was about to happen. She liked excitement and could hurl her purse at anyone she wanted to, regardless of who they were, if they got out of line with God's will, even Mr. Silverman if he crossed any boundaries she thought were too far.

Dinner finished and the group headed back to the limousines, where Fred was waiting to chauffeur them on the five-minute ride over to helicopter to take them to the arena. Inside the 'copter was a new type of wireless telephone called a 'Bag Phone'.

Just as they were strapped in and everyone was admiring Daisy's new Christian Louboutin shoes, Andy's 'bag phone' rang. He answered it before realizing it was his sister Trixie, the one person he did not want to hear from. (To his friends he would refer to her as a 'money changer.' "Jesus was born and lived perfect, am I right?" he would say. "But he did get mad once and threw the money changers out of the temple… right? So, what do thing made him so mad that went over and turned their tables over and threw them out of his sight?") Trixie was always traveling somewhere around the world and never sat still. Though she went to church, her whole life revolved around nickels, pennies, and quarters.

"Hi, Trix," Andy said, trying to sound cheerful. "Yeah, we will be right there. All of our tickets are in the same section as light time, directly behind Coach Barricks. Just ask John at the 'will call' window and he will give you the tickets for you and Bill. Daisy needed some new shoes so we decided to stop by before the game."

Going to the game in the helicopter was exciting for everyone. New friendships were being made, and everyone was having a great time. Even Mamaw was getting comfortable with flying around above the crowds and looking at the cars below. She felt like an angel being carried on God's wings, and it was a memory she would never forget.

When they landed, guess who was there to greet them… Johnnie! Andy had asked him to be at the landing site to meet Mamaw before the first game, completely catching her off guard and surprising her! When the side door opened and she saw Johnnie standing there outside the helicopter, she almost fainted and fell out of the 'copter. Leroy got out first, and then helped Charlotte and Mia out. Johnnie did not know where they had been, but was impressed and almost speechless by their attire and curvaceous figures. The Sonny and Rosanne came off, and then Andy and Daisy, with Mamaw last.

They all proceeded to move toward Johnnie, who was standing away from the wind of the rotary blades. Mamaw hobbled over to him as fast as she could with one her bad leg somewhat numb from sitting on her left hip as she rode, and then she threw her big arms around Johnnie and gave him a kiss on the side of his cheek that left bright red lipstick as a marker on him.

"Johnnie, my boy, it is going to be a big night, and we have all come to see you play!" Mamaw yelled in his ear over the sound of the helicopter.

"Thank you, Mamaw.... this means a lot to me!" he yelled back.

"Mr. Silverman has bought us all front-row seat tickets to watch you play," she replied.

"I hope I don't disappoint you," Johnnie said. "It is going to be new for me in the big leagues, and I'm a little scared..."

"Don't worry, son, you are there to be a servant of the King, so I know you will do well!" Mamaw replied.

With that, they all climbed into the limousine that was waiting to take them over to the arena. It was a full load. On the ride over, Johnnie got introduced to both Charlotte and Mia.

"Johnnie," Sonny began the introductions, "I want you to meet a couple of my friends from the hospital. They are both nurses. This is Charlotte, and this is Mia."

"Very nice to meet you," Johnnie replied. All he wanted to focus on was the game that night, and what Charlotte was wearing was a little distracting to him. Coach Barricks always thought it was helpful to get a little testosterone going for a young single man before a game, but not too much, to the point of distraction. And right now his job and legacy were on the line.

"Where are you all going to be sitting?" Johnnie asked.

"Directly behind the team bench," Andy replied. "We could have chosen to sit in the skybox, but I like it behind the players, up close... so we can see and hear what is going on."

"Me too," Charlotte said.

Mamaw was watching the interaction closely, thinking that Charlotte was perhaps getting a little too friendly and glassy-eyed in the cozy limousine. But then she remembered doing the same thing when she had met Charlie and had picked him out as hers, wanting him to be her one and only husband and lover. Mamaw used to say:

Men just don't have the slightest clue of what is going on when a she-woman wants to catch them and make them her own. Men think they are in control, but really they are like puppets on a string, and the woman is holding all the strings.

When they got to the arena, Johnnie rushed off to the locker room. Coach Barricks was well aware of where he had been, so there was no problem with him missing the pre-game strategy planning session. The other players, however, did not know and thought he was already getting special privileges, and this wasn't even the first game yet, which made things tense even before the jump ball. Johnnie sat down next to Tucker, and some players began to taunt Johnnie as he tried to get involved in the meeting.

Coach Barricks called out the starting lineup, which the players had been waiting for since the end of last season.

"Ok, guys," Coach said, "this is how we are going to field the floor tonight. But just remember: no one is a rock star starter just yet. Everything depends on what game you show up with tonight and if you can dominate on the floor from your position. So, if you can't pull your weight, there will be someone waiting for the chance to take it away from you. Let this be your fair warning! Carlson, you will begin at point, Fredericks and Stallone forwards, Jake you are our center, and Johnnie you are out at wing."

Tucker usually played point, and he thought Johnnie would get that position, but he guessed that maybe Coach was just letting the newer Carlson get a shot early in the year. Also Harper, Orlando, and Weatherford did not make the first timeout, so Tucker was okay with a new starting line-up to go with Jake, the all-NBA center.

Back in the arena, Andy and Daisy took their seats before the game, sitting next to Sonny and Rosanne. Mamaw sat down next, then Charlotte, and then Mia, leaving two seats vacant. But Andy's sister, Trixie, came right before the tip-off with her husband. They both sat at the end of the row, as a big family would do.

Trixie was curious who the two new faces were and could not wait to begin interrogating them to glean information. Andy knew that it would not have been good to have Mamaw at the end next to Trixie, because it might have led to an all-out brawl on television, because Trixie was a Sunday churchgoer only, only interested in being seen and keeping her image good in the family.

"Hi. I'm Trixie," Andy's older sister she said to Mia. "Who do I get to thank for this meeting and sitting together for the big game?"

"Sonny and his wife invited me," Mia said. "I'm Mia. So very nice to meet you."

"Where is your husband tonight, Mia?" Trixie asked coyly. "Or… did you come alone?"

At that moment the team entered from under the mezzanine level in a big billow of smoke, with a loud canon blast, and the announcer began to welcome the crowd to the arena. Mia had heard the question but chose to ignore it. Trixie got the message, and they both sat there in total silence.

As the game got underway, the silence between the two women continued, except whenever Johnnie scored and Mia stood up to cheer, hoping he would look over and see her standing out in the crowd, and even perhaps wave and acknowledge that she was there.

By the end of the game Johnnie shined above all, with 29 points. He outscored the rest of the field on his team as a new rookie. He had a triple double for his game, with twelve rebounds and ten assists, and he was seven for eight from the free-throw line. Not bad for his first NBA game. He was a natural with a gift for the game.

Andy knew it, and so did Mamaw, because both of them could talk to angels and listened in their hearts to the voice of the Holy Spirit that led them in their daily successful walk.

At this moment, the Holy Spirit felt it was the right time to judge the works of many of the great contributors who were integrally involved to the process of delivering the 'Great Divine Plan.' So the Holy Spirit called up the sleeping souls of many referred to as the Great Rope-Makers. To these The Holy Spirit had given greater than average minds and great curiosities to solve many of the mysteries of the "Age of Pre-Digital Science" by pondering the wonders of the skies and the elements of the ground and atmosphere. He and She had given them the mental rope (i.e. the mental high IQ tool sets) to use and gain these great achievements to the glory of God in the world of Paradise for the Holy Spirit of accolades. Or they could choose to take personal credit for these and damn their own people with their own pride and weakness to Satan. Johnnie Spot Perfect was not one of those blessed with the mental mind of the Great Rope-Makers, but his physical gift was just as superior and was a spiritual calling made of the same character and rope. These were the conversations carried on in Upper Paradise by the Holy Spirit and the souls of the Great Rope-Makers in that day:

"Copernicus, Einstein, and Newton," the Holy Spirit called the three of them up from the place where they were sleeping so the angels could get a better vantage position of the stage on which this meeting was taking place. It looked as if it were trial, for many beings had been sent by the Father in Heaven as witnesses to this meeting. Christ was not present, for this was just a hearing where the Holy Spirit wanted to review the Great Plan. The beings present at the hearing were not like Cherubim, for their eyes had been removed before their creation and were gone. These beings had only ears with which to listen to the words of those being questioned, and telepathic powers to understand the mental thoughts and wavelengths given off by either their pure or impure hearts, for the words they spoke were judged more important than the deeds they did on earth and the actions they participated in, for the actions were already commanded by the Holy Spirit. These were judged along with the pastors, preachers, and disciples, for they had been given certain roles to abide in, unlike others, who were just blind sheep, and these overseen by the angels of the earthly realm to happen as established before their births, as the Holy Spirit had commanded.

"Nicolas Copernicus, did you write 'De Revolutionbus Orbium Coelestium' to honor me, or to honor yourself, oh great thinker and polymath of mathematics and science?" the Holy Spirit inquired.

"I studied the canon laws of the papal heart, to seek Your will only, oh Great One, and in doing so I found many of Your hidden truths I could not have otherwise found," Copernicus replied. The great beings all listened and measured his answers of the inquisition, and they found no fault in him yet.

"You studied medicine and the art of healing as well, Nicolas Copernicus. Did you seek to answer and forward the impetus of suffering prevention and disease, or the side of self-aggrandizement for monetary sake?" the inquisition continued.

"I studied only to seek Your knowledge, oh Holy One, as I chose to do neither with limited knowledge," he answered, and the beings once again took measure of his heart. The beings began to sense irreverence in this answer, but did not speak yet with critical words of consternation.

"And one last question: did you put your face to the ground to repent as you never married, yet you kept a mistress to satisfy your needs there under my Divine Plan, from which you benefitted?" the Holy Spirit questioned.

"I did, oh Holy One, but this was only to secure more days on earth to carry out Your will, for without the moist life-springs I found in her, I would have surely died and then left my work undone," Copernicus answered.

And when Copernicus answered 'my work' to the Holy Spirit instead of 'Your work,' as was needed in the response, the Holy Spirit commanded sternly, "Be gone with you, for your work was nothing that I did not ordain first! A lesson you still have not learned, so you will have more time this day to think about this in Paradise before your next inquisition to be judged to review of your life," the Holy Spirit belted out, and Paradise trembled at his voice.

"Albert E., come forward!" the Holy Spirit called out. With that, the soul of Einstein was made known to the Holy Spirit. "You who—among very few—know the secrets of time, light, mass, energy, and relativity… who do you say that I am?" The Holy Spirit asked him.

"You are Yahweh, He who created the heavens and the Earth, Adam and Eve, Abram and Moses, Saul and Nero, World War I, and World War II, and put the world on its pedestal in the Heavens as a blue pearl in the vast time and space of the Heavens, giving it light and keeping it from darkness, so that all will come to glorify your name…. oh, Holy One," Einstein replied.

"What you say is true," the Holy Spirit replied. "So why did I choose you—as a Hebrew—to know these things, though you were not a Christian?"

"To show that the blood of the Gentile and the Jew is one, and we are both of the same tree, and of the same root, both open to receive the water of life, and that Your love will never forsake us as you people," Einstein replied.

"This is why you were not chosen as a Prophet, Albert E." the Holy Spirit replied. "You are only correct in the world of material things, that of the world of Paradise, and not the world of Heaven and Hell. You see only the Hebrew view, but my offer and love extends to all creation, even the enemies I sent against you to conquer. I allowed you to reveal these things to My glory, to open the eyes of those who cannot see, and yet they still live in the world of Paradise Blind, as if their eyes have been removed along with their hearts."

"This I know to be true also," Einstein said. "I was never born to be a prophet, and I never asked nor sounded as one. Please forgive me of my sins, that I might serve You also. And may Your name be above all and Christ be at the side of our Father in Heaven. I see this in the stars and know this to be true!"

"By your admonition for the Trinity and the love you shared for your wife when you bought her a home with the money you made for your awards, you fulfilled the requirement of the scriptures, and you too have been saved from the fire. Go in Peace."

Then Einstein was lifted into Heaven, where he would be judged at the gate of single souls and possibly united with the Father and Jesus, and at that time allowed to praise the Trinity forever and ever, or kept in waiting until the time came again for him to be questioned for his love and obedience to the scriptures and the blood shed for him.

Then the Holy Spirit calls Isaac Newton to his presence.

"Isaac N., awake, ye, and step forward from your rest, that I might set my eyes upon you this day and also counsel you more in the ways of the Lord," the Holy Spirit roused him to his side. "You were born on Christmas day in 1642 AD, with the first name of Isaac, that of your father, just as was my chosen son of Abraham, whose wife gave birth to his son Isaac when Abraham was 100 years old. That Isaac, the forefather of David, was the first son born unto Abraham, by his first wife, Sarah, and chosen to be the father of Jacob, and known as Israel after he struggled with God. And to that Isaac would be given the title of one of the three Patriarchs to the Israelites, and the only Patriarch who did not change his name," the Holy Spirit recognized him with his pre-born title.

"I am him, oh Holy One," Isaac Newton replied. "Yea, I am him… also one who struggled with God the Father to be all that I could."

"Isaac, you were created as my perfectionist of the 'Age of Reason,' to ask many questions of the scriptures and set forth the solutions by new math, yet to be unfolded. You who were known as the Father of calculus, you who studied and wrote extensively on the Book of Kings I of the Hebrew Bible, which you translated yourself from Hebrew, though you were not Hebrew. You did well to use the skills I gave to you," the Holy Spirit declared.

"Your will and desire were always in my thoughts, my prayers, and on my hands, oh Holy Emperor and Master of the Ages," Newton replied. "I wrote everything to glorify You, making sure there were no untruths in them from my heart, investigating all by science and alchemy over which You rule forever! Let the liars lie, the sheep be sheep, and the goats be goats, as Your will be done."

"And what did you find in the end after all your searching,?" The Holy Spirit asked.

"That you created ALL that is and was, and can be: ALL the great powers of the Universe, from gravity which holds it together to the molecules of the body and soul you created with the spark of life. You created with the Trinity, ALL the Heavens, ALL the angels (good and bad), ALL the souls, all the agendas, ALL the time, space, and matter, all the forces, ALL the races, ALL the religions (true and untrue), and all the divine plans to be tested by Satan and man. And those who speak with your messengers, the angels, like Verostices, to foretell these events were shun as Rosicrucians. And then you showed me that the temple of Solomon can be measured to relate to the Heavens' hemisphere and man as its part of the love of God himself, by the equation V= (2/3) (pie) r^3.

"You speak correctly, Isaac N.," the Holy Spirit said, "but also, what conclusion did you reach?"

"I wrote," replied Newton, "for those minds of science who guard their souls too closely by uneducated minds and who value the precept of science over religion, that John's Revelation was true: A new heaven and new earth. New Jerusalem comes down from heaven prepared as a bride adorned for her husband. The marriage supper. God dwells with men, wipes away all tears from their eyes, gives them of the fountain of living water, and creates all things new, saying, it is done. The glory and felicity of the New Jerusalem is represented by a building of gold and gems, enlightened by the glory of God & the Lamb, and watered by the river of Paradise, on the banks of which grows the tree of life. Into this city the kings of the earth do bring their glory and that of the nations, and the saints reign forever and ever.[183]"

"And what date, by your mathematical analysis of the scriptures, did you make this conclusion to be?" the Holy Spirit asked.

"Only You, great one, know the true answer," Newton replied, "but I wrote as my heart led me then that the time times half a time are 42 months, or 1260 days, or three-and-a-half years, reckoning twelve months to a year and 30 days to a month, as was done in the Calendar of the primitive year. And the days of short-lived beasts being put for the years of lived ["long-lived"] kingdoms, the period of 1260 days, if dated from the complete conquest of the three kings A.C. 800, will end A.C. 2060. It may end later, but I see no reason for its ending sooner. This I mention not to assert when the time of the end shall be, but to put a stop to the rash conjectures of fanciful men who are frequently predicting the time of the end, and in so doing bring the sacred prophesies into discredit as often as their predictions fail. Christ comes as a thief in the night, and it is not for us to know the times or seasons which God hath put into his own breast."

Then the Holy Spirit said, "Thank you, good and faithful servant. You never married and kept the scriptures regarding I Corinthians 7: 8-9."

And then the Holy Spirit sent for the angels to take Isaac N. along with Albert E. to wait in line for a time until they both were called forward to the 'Gate of Souls' to answer for their obedience and loyalty, then released from the earth to pass through the gate and be forever with their Creator ("The Creator") of the Universe.

183 Revelation 3:12, Revelation 21:2

Blessed is the one who perseveres under trial because, having stood the test, that person will receive the crown of life that the Lord has promised to those who love him.

As testified by James,

Your Brother in Christ

Chapter 1:12

Chapter 7

Fall from Grace, Car Wreck, and Near-Death Experience

It has always been from the greatest heights that the lowest lows can be found, and Johnnie had just climbed his first mountain. He had proven over his first three seasons that he would be the greatest NBA player to be inducted into the Hall of Fame when he retired. Even if he chose to retire after his next season, he would still have made history on such a short career. His scoring percentages, assists, and rebounds were nothing less than incredible. He was the man of the century, making the cover of every sports magazine possible around the globe! No one had created such an affinity to watch any sport like he had. He was called "The Spot" now very lovingly because he was "spot-on" perfect in his performances, just as his name denoted him. Others could not boast such a nickname, not even the greats like Ramsey, Biden, Jones, or Calloway! He could shoot the ball like no one ever believed possible, which elicited jealousy in his competitors. Many said that Johnnie was born under a lucky star. Some said he must be blessed by God. But neither of these was true… just yet.

Johnnie was still considered a rogue son of Ishmael by the Lord Jesus, Son of the Holy Father in Heaven, because he had not fully accepted Christ nor had he become completely obedient and submissive to Christ's will. He was sort of half on board and somewhere out in Neverland, though he went to church and sat in the front pews. He was a Sunday-and-holidays Christian, and his actions showed his heart was only lukewarm for the Lord. His biologic father had never sought out God the Father before conceiving this firstborn son of his, and just as scriptures stated, he was destined to live out the sins of his father unto the third generation.[184] And now—just like so many others who lived in the world of human trials as inmates in their mortal prisons or slaves to their own self-pride, pity, and worldly ambitions—he was a sinful son, like all those born to be like wild animals without the blessing of God, yet suckling at their mother's breasts until they learned to walk.

Now Johnnie had totally fallen into love (and lust) with Charlotte for what she had to offer him in the areas of his own character flaws: safety, intimacy, and courage, which allowed him to be himself without either shame or fear of persecution. They married exactly one year after that first game meeting arranged by Mr. Silverman, and now they were expecting their first child in six months. She loved him and he loved her, just as God had designed for one man and one woman to live in holy matrimony. It was a good marriage. There was no bickering, no un-trust, no secrecy of agendas, and no polarizing selfishness between them, for The Lord hated these things in a marriage and would seek to add the full measure of Satan to them if either broke the three-way promise with God in the bonds of marriage.

Johnnie and Charlotte could stand naked before each other, each knowing the other's thoughts and flaws. And to Johnnie—the

[184] Deuteronomy 5:8

man whom God created in his own image—it would be better to never have been born than to break the holy marriage vows consecrated by the Lord, vows holy though not necessarily always happy, and all the angels in Heaven agreed. For Charlotte it was different though—very different—and her values were different, giving leeway and merit to that which Satan contrived; for she was made as of a different cloth.

"Johnnie," Charlotte said one evening while lying next to him in bed with the lights off, "don't you think we should start thinking about some names for the baby?"

"I am going to leave that to you, Sweetheart," he responded.

Johnnie always called her Sweetheart because she reminded him of the only Valentine card he had ever gotten in sixth grade from a girl named Veronica. It was pink with white doilies glued to the front and candies taped to it, and inside a note that read 'I love you always… your sweetheart, Nica.' Although it was pretty mushy back then for the taste of an adolescent boy with acne, but no one had ever told Johnnie they loved him. This was a first and only time Johnnie had known someone to have feelings for him, other than his mother Jenny. And even though Mamaw had told him she loved him many times, that did not count in his mind. He needed to hear it from a stranger, someone whose love he felt like he had earned, because this was the only thing that made sense to him. Love could not just be given, sort of like money had to be earned by sweat or else it was not really earned.

When Charlotte had first wrapped her arms around him and told him that she loved him, that was all it took for him to be down for the long count. He was knocked out by compassion and gentleness over any brawn or brute force. From that moment on,

Charlotte was his queen, and he gave her everything he could possibly afford.

"If it is a boy, how about Charlie? You know, for your grandfather… 'Charlie Spot Perfect'! Or what about 'Johnnie Spot Perfect II,' and we could call him 'Junior'? Or how about just 'Little Johnnie?' " Charlotte asked.

"I am not really okay with any of those, sweetie. Can't we just give him his own name, so he doesn't have to live in anyone else's shadow… especially not mine!" Johnnie exclaimed.

"I think it would be an honor to you and your family line, if you thought that was okay," Charlotte said. "Okay then, so what about John Charles Perfect, then we could call him JC?"

"Naw… too close to Jesus Christ, and that would make me uneasy every time I called his name. Can we talk about girl names? How about Little Charlotte, Jr.?" he now teased his wife. "I bet she will make the WNBA when she grows up and then you can have the 'Perfect' daughter you always wanted!"

"No, Johnnie, she will be the perfect daughter that YOU always wanted. I am sure she will be getting a miniature basketball every Christmas day from here on out, and you will probably install a mini basketball hoop on her crib headboard, won't you?"

"Now you're talking, Sweetheart! Now can we get some sleep? Tomorrow is going to be a long drive out to the training camp in the Hill Country," Johnnie said. He needed some rest. He was planning to drive his Ferrari to the team event they always had for teambuilding.

The Hurricanes were the undisputed reigning NBA champs. They were carried almost single-handedly by Johnnie in the playoffs and finals. Shortly after winning the finals, Johnnie renegotiated his player's 'Perfect' deal to an unprecedented 12-year unbreakable contract, with a minimum $25 million payout even if he got injured but was still able to suit up for the games. It was a no-brainer for him to take the deal, even with his weak knees.

Mamaw saw to it that Johnnie had a good CPA and actually learned to save 10% of every paycheck in a savings account—he called it his 'rainy day fund'—just in case there was ever a problem. Johnnie he was on Easy Street! But the fame started to bother him. The paparazzi were always around, leaving Johnnie and Charlotte no peace—day or night—unless they snuck around in their black BMW with the dark tinted windows, which they did whenever they wanted to go out and have some regular fun. Though Charlotte liked the BMW, Johnnie said he would buy her whatever she wanted—even her own Ferrari!—but she just liked to keep things simple, because it reminded her of her simple roots growing up in Waco, Texas, under the shadow of the Baylor Bear Stadium.

At 4 a.m. the next morning, July 1st, Johnnie got up early to drive out toward Johnson City to the BBB Ranch, just south of town. It was owned by Mr. Silverman's holding company. There the team would meet for the July 4th weekend, play a little poker, bond as a team, ride some skittish horses, play a little baseball, and strategize for the upcoming year. The coaches would watch clips of perspective draft picks and start making plans.

Most of team was meeting at the arena to ride out to the ranch on the team bus, but Johnnie had talked his way into taking his own car. He often got bored sitting in one place for too long, which sometimes led to altercations over simple annoyances, like a teammate jiggling the back of his seat or playing headphones too loud. So Andy had approved him to go on ahead and met the team at the ranch, as long as he agreed to take Leroy along to keep him out of trouble.

"Come on and get in," Johnnie said to Leroy, as he pulled up to the front of the Houston condominium where Leroy lived. It was still dark outside, and Johnnie could see Leroy standing and waiting for him on the street corner.

"And next time you better carry a gun this time of night in Houston," Johnnie added as he opened the door. "You could get yourself mugged out here this time of night."

Leroy reached into his front pocket under his blazer and pulled out a small 25 caliber pistol, showing it to Johnnie.

"I'm glad you and I are both in agreement that we need to stay safe, because you don't always have time to call the cops, right?"

"Right," Johnnie said. "I would never forgive myself if I let something bad happen just because I wasn't prepared… I couldn't do that to Charlotte! So I always try to be prepared at all times, especially since we have the baby coming… I am super-cautious and try to take *zero* chances. It would be the worst day of my life!"

"Right on, Johnnie!" Leroy said. "Spoken like a true grownup with responsibilities! I think all this marriage stuff is just now getting to you. You're finally beginning to act like the rest of the world. Join our reality as the new professional sports royalty king, and you just might have some fun in life."

They then took off down Interstate 10 through Katy, Texas, heading for San Antonio and the Texas Hill Country, leaving nothing in their wake but tread marks in the morning sunshine.

"Johnnie, how fast have you driven this thing?" Leroy asked.

"Oh, a little over 95… but that was before I got married. Besides, I figured if I got a ticket, Coach would get pretty mad, especially if I had to call him to bail me out of jail."

"No cop in Texas would ever put you in jail, Johnnie. You are 'THE HOT SHOT SPOT' ...the shot-maker, the man with the golden touch, the guy who can put the ball in the goal with \ your eyes closed!" Leroy replied.

"Thank you for the kind words, but even that won't help us if we drive through Selma and get caught speeding and carrying your concealed gun!" Johnnie replied

They both laughed hysterically, remembering the time Leroy landed in jail in Selma for going fifteen miles over the speed limit with an expired license. Leroy now had his permit to carry, as Mr. Silverman's bodyguard and security agent, as well as in the arena on game nights. So there was no real danger of them being arrested if they were stopped. But just in case, Johnnie always carried the phone numbers of Mamaw's attorney and doctor.

"Hey, Johnnie let's stop and get a beer, okay? It's the 4th of July weekend..." Leroy said.

Leroy had struggled all his life with alcoholism, and it wasn't easy trying to hide the fact that he drank now because of his loneliness and childhood wounds. They had been driving two hours now and were approaching San Marcos.

"I am getting us a twelve-pack, Johnnie Boy, and it's on me," Leroy said when Johnnie pulled up to a gas station. "Gonna be a long drive the rest of the way, and I don't want to remember too much when I get there," Leroy confided.

"So, what's going on in your life that you need so much beer these days?" Johnnie yelled after him. "Sometimes I think you swim in it... I can live on one beer per week, and you can't seem to live on one per hour." But Leroy was already gone. Johnnie leaned back in his seat and unfastened his seatbelt, waiting for his friend to return.

Ten minutes later, they were cruising down the road again, with Leroy drinking a beer in a brown paper bag.

"Can I ask you a question?" Leroy asked. "There's evidence that a Clovis culture lived in San Marcos about six thousand years before Moses, and some eight thousand years before Abraham. And I've heard it said that the San Marcos springs we'll be going past have never gone dry, not since the days of Saint Mark… sort of like with Jesus's living waters never going dry, either. What do you think about those time-seasoned questions, 'Mr. Spot Perfect,' great wizard of the basketball court?"

"I think Moses needed a better last name, ha! And Abraham needed a fifth wife to make him a little happier," Johnnie smirked back, seeing if Leroy was actually listening.

"I thought Abraham only had one wife," Leroy replied.

"Nope, my friend, he had two wives, Sarah and Keturah. Hagar was a slave, and not a wife," Johnnie replied. "And he had six children after the age of 100."

"Wow, what a stud he was!" Leroy said.

Johnnie had really been hoping he would ask about Moses, Johnnie's hero.

"I think Moses was a bigger stud," Johnnie said. "He parted the ocean so his people could get out of slavery."

Johnnie hated the fact Moses never made it into the Promised Land, just because he hit the rock too quickly when God told him only to speak to it.[185] Johnnie identified with Moses, because they both seemed to have been asked to do the something by the Lord for which they were very ill-prepared, and both did not like authority

[185] Numbers 20: 6-13

over them. But that was just how the Lord used people to do His will.

"I'll drink to that," Leroy stated groggily, by this time on his third beer and ready for a nap while Johnnie drove the rest of the way.

Servius and Verostices were meeting in a grand hallway located in Upper Paradise to prepare the event that would soon bring Johnnie back to the Lord in servant's bondage. It had been decreed by the Holy Spirit that Johnnie would become the next ambassador for the Tribe of the 'Mary & James' gene, though he was totally unaware of his calling at this time before his 'Big Event.'

The prominent archangels Michael and Gabriel were leading an entire army of 15 regiments of fighting angels in the eastern war against the angels of evil, in what was known in Paradise as the 'War of Inherent Security.' The war had been raging now for one-and-a-half epochs. After Jesus left lower Paradise (fallen Earth) to then travel to Hades for three days to oversee the management of the unbelievers, he went into upper Paradise to meet with the Holy Spirit for matters of the management of earth while he was away. After that He rose back into the Heavens to be with the Father, and to aid God Almighty in the four wars that were in the four corners. These were not left to the oversight and auspices of the Holy Spirit, who was commanding the fighting and overseeing the angels of Paradise to keep the souls of the saved and protected from the roaming bands of angels collecting up the lost and self-damned to be carried away from the bosom of God.

What a pity, the angels of the light thought as they watched over their people like sheep, while the angels of the darkness grabbed and devoured them to increase their own numbers because of the loneliness they felt from being self-forlorn. These living angels of fallen earth collecting the souls of the self-damned were known as the 'Representatives of Living Dead' in and about Paradise. But much more evil was coming after the 'Age of Non-Prophets' in the form of artificial intelligence of non-human origin known to future generations as AI drones and androids, machines thinking and acting without souls, which would be run by a company also known as 'The Unifier Corporation,' whose symbol notation would be 666. These machines would take men back to the evils of worshipping idols, such as golden calves, and then the Laws of Moses would again be carried out without the mercy of the apostles and the admonition of second chances.

This all occurred at the point in time of men of having sex with un-souled machines, which was an abomination even lower that having sex with un-souled animals or demonic angels or un-souled spirits. For the Lord had been clear in the creation of the world that the difference between Adam and the rest of creation was that Adam had a soul, and that Man was created in God's image to have a soul, which would differentiate him from other creatures, and would allow him to gain or lose perfection, based on the obedience of the heart.

These Laws were all written in scripture and would be reinstated for all at the height of the Second Age of Non-Profits when Christ would come again, if the Holy Spirit, Lord Jesus, and God the Father agreed to its renewal of the punishments ordained by the Laws of Heaven. For it was written that the world would not again be cleansed by floods as in the first days of Noah[186], but would be cleansed by the Seven Bowls of God's wrath in the final days of Armageddon. For it was witnessed in a vision—and then written down in the scriptures in God's final Revelation—by John, who lived and walked with Jesus, that these things will come to pass:

The Seven Bowls of God's Wrath[187]

Then I, John, heard a loud voice from the temple saying to the seven angels, "Go, pour out the seven bowls of God's wrath on the earth."

The first angel went and poured out his bowl on the land, and ugly, festering sores broke out on the people who had the mark of the beast and worshiped its image.

The second angel poured out his bowl on the sea, and it turned into blood like that of a dead person, and every living thing in the sea died.

The third angel poured out his bowl on the rivers and springs of water, and they became blood.

Then I heard the angel in charge of the waters say.

"You are just in these judgments, O Holy One, you who are and who were; for they have shed the blood of your holy people and your prophets, and you have given them blood to drink as they deserve."

And I heard the altar respond:

Yes, Lord God Almighty, true and just are your judgments."

The fourth angel poured out his bowl on the sun, and the sun was allowed to scorch people with fire. [9] They were seared by the

[186] Genesis 8:21-22

[187] Revelation 16

intense heat and they cursed the name of God, who had control over these plagues, but they refused to repent and glorify him.

The fifth angel poured out his bowl on the throne of the beast, and its kingdom was plunged into darkness. People gnawed their tongues in agony and cursed the God of heaven because of their pains and their sores, but they refused to repent of what they had done.

The sixth angel poured out his bowl on the great river Euphrates, and its water was dried up to prepare the way for the kings from the East.[13] Then I saw three impure spirits that looked like frogs; they came out of the mouth of the dragon, out of the mouth of the beast and out of the mouth of the false prophet. [14] They are demonic spirits that perform signs, and they go out to the kings of the whole world, to gather them for the battle on the great day of God Almighty.

Look, I come like a thief! Blessed is the one who stays awake and remains clothed, so as not to go naked and be shamefully exposed."

Then they gathered the kings together to the place that in Hebrew is called Armageddon.

The seventh angel poured out his bowl into the air, and out of the temple came a loud voice from the throne, saying, "It is done!" Then there came flashes of lightning, rumblings, peals of thunder and a severe earthquake. No earthquake like it has ever occurred since mankind has been on earth, so tremendous was the quake. The great city split into three parts, and the cities of the nations collapsed. God remembered Babylon the Great and gave her the cup filled with the wine of the fury of his wrath. Every island fled away and the mountains could not be found. From the sky huge hailstones, each weighing about a hundred pounds, fell on people.

And they cursed God on account of the plague of hail, because the plague was so terrible.

Then before these things could happen or be approved in the Great Plan, Verostices leaned forward from his commanding position over the other angels in his Legions and said to Servius, after their short but fruitful meeting:

"All has been prepared for Johnnie's 'self-ego drain' and his 'self-induced spot' to be removed, as he is washed as pure as God's purified snow falling on the highest mountaintops, overseeing the valleys and desserts below. He now has status given by the Love and Mercy of God the Father in Heaven, and all his sins are removed. And from now on and forever, he will be part of the unified everlasting living Tree of Life, springing up in Lasting Jerusalem and growing forth from the same root of Christ's suffering, which will continue to give free medicine to the world, whom the Father loves so much.

"This is motorcycle-country in Texas, Heaven for sure, because when the bluebonnets come out in full bloom after the spring rains along the rivers and roadsides, it is a sight to behold. God truly has blessed the Texas landscape with His love and color," Leroy said one day out of the blue, mysteriously, while watching the pastures and massive oak trees go by.

"Yeah, I know," Johnnie said. "I think much of the rest of the United States except Alaska has been ruined by the demonic moneychangers of the east and west coasts, just like in the Jewish synagogues of Jesus' day when Jesus threw them out! Hey, how come they don't have an NBA team in Juno yet? I think that would truly make them the next paradise here on earth!"

"If I had you, Johnnie, as my free agent, we could start one… Do you want to go and start a team? How about calling us the Killer Polar Bears?"

"Not bad, Leroy, but if we take Orlando too, we will need to be called something like the Spineless Toothless Walruses," Johnnie laughed. "Then Mr. Silverman would not be happy with us for leaving. So, I guess we'll just have stay in Houston or bring the whole team and be the Juno 'Canes."

"Okay, and they have some big earthquakes there, anyway," Leroy said, as he slammed down another beer. "So maybe we should call our new team the Juno Earthquakes?" Then he let out a big laugh.

"Probably not a good idea, buddy boy… we shouldn't use any terms that terrorize the faithful fans," Johnnie was quick to respond.

They were now on a back-winding road between Driftwood and Wimberley. Leroy had dozed off and Johnnie put in Credence Clearwater Revival's 'Bad Moon Rising' on his eight-track tape. He was rocking out, thinking about Charlotte, how good his life was, and how well everything was turning out, now that he had so much money in the bank with his new contract in place. The curves in the road were just perfect for his Ferrari to hug and drive fast. In some places in the road there was no shoulder, and even a couple of bridges that were one-car only.

He was doing about eighty on a road that was meant for half that, and making the turns like he was in a Monte Carlo race. It was exciting and fun, and Johnnie was comfortable pushing the limits of his car, because he knew just how much the car could take with him at the wheel.

As he made a hard turn to the right around a blind curve, there were two cars coming at him, one in the oncoming lane, and one trying to pass before they made it to the curve. Johnnie had no time to react before the head-on collision, with an impact that could be heard a mile away.

The accident was fatal, and Johnnie Spot Perfect and his good friend Leroy were both killed immediately, as were both of the young drivers in the other cars, who were teenagers and racing to see how fast their cars could go, playing 'chicken' to see who would back off first. All four men and boys were killed in the gruesome bloody scene of twisted metal.

Verostices and Servius were there to meet all four in their world transitions, because they were no longer of the material world of money and two paths. They had now just one path before them, and the time had come for sifting the wheat from the chaff.[188] Their souls needed to be separated from their bodies, which had been unified before their births, and be appropriately escorted to their final path. That path still was not a final destination, but a journey on which they would be judged, after which the destination would be decided and written into stone, just as the Ten Commandments had been done, And when this was done, the Tree of Life would have one more shoot and leaf to be united into its base of the common root. Phylamonas and Chalymina also came to support the scene. At least four angels were needed to carry these souls as directed by the Holy Spirit, so more angels had been summoned as escorts.

[188] Matthew 3:12

Each of the four angels hovered over each of the dead bodies, and each soul rose up toward the sky. Johnnie was immediately drawn toward Servius, and Leroy to Chalymina.

They then separated away from each other, and Johnnie looked down over the wreck and the death scene below. He could see himself lying motionless in his Ferrari with Leroy beside him. A part of Leroy's body was missing and it was too gruesome for Johnnie to look at. All he could feel was the pain that it was his fault that all these people had lost their lives… because of his momentary desire for excitement in an unexciting world. He remembered the words Mamaw had spoken to him once: *You will always make mistakes in life when you are going too fast, either driving too fast, drinking too fast, living too fast, or loving too fast.*

Then Servius lifted him up and placed him horizontally in a position and where he could look up only and not down anymore, with blinders on each side. His eyes landed on God the Father in Heaven through a portal which God had opened. It was like a giant telescope that only Johnnie could see through, and in the moment Johnnie was shocked and stunned at the events which were happening. The others were not experiencing such events, or if they were it was not apparent to Johnnie, nor did he care, for he was in the center of life now, and all he could think of was how he let Charlotte down, and his child that he knew was a son. This was just something he felt in his bosom, and knew to be true, because he had been enlightened at the time of his death. He was full of sadness and remorse.

Then God said to Johnnie, in his moment immediate transition from skin to transformed pure energy, "Who do you say that I am, Johnnie?"

"You are God," Johnnie answered.

"But you did not declare this so in your heart on earth," God reminded him. "You believed in me, but not fully, did you? You needed living proof, just like Thomas the disciple, and here I am!"

Johnnie could not really believe what is happening! It seemed like a dream. There was guilt in his heart, and he began to pray silently for grace and mercy through the blood of Christ, his Savior.

"Johnnie," God said to him, "you made your life much too complicated on earth, for it is really simple. You must never have or place any gods before Me, and you must give all thanks and praise, which is reserved for only Me, to Me alone, and no other. You must never blaspheme, for it is not your right. You must remove all hate from your heart to be pure, love your enemies to be perfect, keep my Commandments to remain submissive, and follow My spirit with honor to my Son, and glory to My cause, in order to be called Mine. In all things, you must put others' well-being before your own, living your life in service and humility. For we will meet again, and on these things you will be truly judged, and next time the Law will be more clear to you, more precise. Promise to keep these things true, and do these things patiently, and you will return to see your son born. For I have chosen him, your blood son, for you, that you might find in him someone in whom you will be well-pleased, just as I was in My Son, and he will be with you one day in Heaven as Mine is with Me. I will protect and provide for you all that you will need and not want, just as will do for your son. And in all things, avoid false gods, false idols, false prophets, false paths, false news, and false words."

"I promise you, I will do these things," Johnnie whispered. He bowed his head and kneeled, not understanding what he was kneeling on, because he was still overhead in the skies somewhere. Servius was by his side but invisible to Johnnie so that he would not disturb the moment in the history of this one soul which still needed to do more work before being delivered to his final cause. For no one had ever looked upon God and lived in the earthly world, but this was the spirit world, the world of souls still in part of Paradise, and only a few had ever felt the glory of His presence and lived to tell it, and even fewer had ever been witness it,[189] so this was an epic event of the ages.

"Then go now and be My New Leader of My Twelve Tribes as I have anointed you to carry out these things for twenty-seven years and one-half score, and then I will send another after you.

Johnnie then immediately found himself back in his body, being carried and lifted into a helicopter and then life-flighted to San Antonio to an emergency trauma hospital. He felt different, not only from the time he had with God, but different… clean. He felt very warm and much loved, like never before. He knew what had just happened: his soul had been washed clean. His life and mind were no longer stained with the insecurities of not being good enough or having to prove himself to others. He felt no remorse, no poor history, no indignity, no shame, and no obstacles that could not be broken or overcome with prayer and the help of his God. He just knew that he was simply loved by God, and that could never be removed, and he would never be the same ever again, no matter what his future now held. Johnnie was a man now to be feared and admired because he walked with God's words on his heart, with Jesus now as his brother, mentor, Savior, and the only family on his mind, with the courage and wisdom of the Holy Spirit written immortally on and stitched eternally into his soul.

---

189 Exodus 33:20

"Mr. Perfect... Mr. Perfect.... can you hear me?" Someone he did not recognize was calling his name. Johnnie could hear his name being called and could feel someone holding his hand and patting chest trying, to wake him and get a response. The hand holding his was very warm, but he could not see the face it belonged to. He felt as if he had sand in his eyes and could not open them.

All he could think about now was Leroy. This was weighing heavy on his heart, so much that he just passed out in agony thinking maybe Leroy was dead, and it was his fault. As he drifted off, he could hear in the background the whirring of a helicopter in flight. This reminded him of Mr. Silverman's chopper in Houston, going back and forth to his functions, and this would be all he remembered for the next few days, as everything just went black and Johnnie slipped out of consciousness.

In Heaven, God the Creator and Father, along with Jesus, His Son, the Christ, looked down over both Upper and Lower Paradise and over the three underworlds of Hades below, listening to the joy coming from all the other realms of their kingdoms reaching to the far ends of the universe, all praising the names of the Trinity, who ruled and controlled all, shouting that there were many rooms in the Kingdom of Heaven, just as Jesus had confirmed when on earth.[190]

Jesus then wept in front of His father for the second time, just as He had done many millennia before, at what he saw for the ones

---

[190] John 14:2

He loved as He looked down upon the fallen earth. Then He spoke to the Father.

"They have destroyed, soiled, and prostituted the land for themselves, and ruined it with subdivisions for homes, pouring concrete altars to themselves in high-rises, so there would be no more butterflies, only few deer to roam free, no wild herds of elephants, and no mighty animals that once sailed the oceans at will. The lakes and streams that the wild fowl once used for food are gone, and the beavers run from their lands where there are no trees to build with, for man has cut them all down."

"I gave Satan many ways to lead them astray," God the Father replied, "so they would know the ways of their folly. In the end, they must lose and learn they cannot build back—even these small things—yet they grow lonely and weary without Me, and yet they still do not relent, these stiff-necked people."

"It is hard for me to bear," Christ replied, "for I love them so, and yet they know not their sin and what they do, even after I taught them the better way."

"It is always for the money with them," God said, "and in the end, they will find that there is no coin or its substitute in the rooms of My mansion. For no one who idolizes money and chases it will keep Me in their heart. For remember my words to them: 'Where your treasure is, there is your heart also.' "[191]

"And for the same reason I threw the money changers out of your temple," said Jesus.

"You did well, my Son," God the Father replied. "The money-changers love their money more than they love me, and they

[191] Matthew 6:21

will never know My love as long as they love money more than they love Me."

Jesus then said to the Lord God Almighty, "When can I return? Can I return now? They are waiting for me, as I have promised to return soon. I must go and save more like Zacchaeus so they do not fall into the eternal lake of fire and self-damnation."[192]

"No, not yet," God the Father replied "You ask me constantly… when will you cease asking?"

"Never, my Father. For you know my heart is with my brothers, whom I love, each and every one," the Lord Jesus replied. "I would die for them all over again if I could save just one more who might be lost in the shuffle that is now occurring."

"You cannot save all of them," the Lord God Almighty replied. "Even as I went down and spoke to them, they denied me, despite the blessings and miracles I gave them. They are a stiff-necked people who turn their heads on prideful shoulders. And the miracles you gave and showed them also, spilling your blood to save them, landed on deaf ears and blind eyes. This is not right!"

"I beg of you, Father, to give me another chance," Jesus interceded for his people, as he would ask for a baby not yet conceived to be given a soul with the chance at eternal life.

"Your time will come soon, My Son, once the Holy Spirit counts the coming dead in the great battle of Armageddon to a number that is less than zero, and She calls forth the angels to begin the great battle to end all great battles with Satan, the Great Pretender. We three will then know and we will agree on the time of your returned arrival, just as We have designed and desired for you at the time for the final redemption of Our loved ones; for not until

[192] Luke 19

the Holy Cup of Salvation has been filled with the blood of the martyrs can this new and final war begin," God Almighty declared.

Now listen, you rich people, weep and wail because of the misery that is coming on you. Your wealth has rotted, and moths have eaten your clothes. Your gold and silver are corroded. Their corrosion will testify against you and eat your flesh like fire. You have hoarded wealth in the last days. Look! The wages you failed to pay the workers who mowed your fields are crying out against you. The cries of the harvesters have reached the ears of the Lord Almighty. You have lived on earth in luxury and self-indulgence. You have fattened yourselves in the day of slaughter. You have condemned and murdered the innocent one, who was not opposing you.

As Testified by James,
Brother of Jesus
Chapter 5:1-6

Chapter 8

Dealing With Complete Loss of Sight, Dependence on God

Johnnie was in a coma, so he did not understand the world of suffering blessed by joy which he has been reborn into yet, but the words of the Holy Spirit were repeated in his subconscious mind for three days, and thirty-three hundred times, to plant seeds that could not be removed. Servius was there to support Johnnie through the blessing and count each one, and to wake him when the last one was read. The convicting voice of the Holy Spirit spoke thus to him:

You who think you are so great, tell me a lot…

Or tell me a little, and cast your net by the ocean's shore,

By the arena that you know, or the keystone, or by the morning's door,

What breath you have, or light you know, your will cannot search nor ever find

A guardian to keep your store.

From whom, you dare not say, do not look

With any sight, no, or wisdom, yes; that hath made you what you are;

these things you can now possess and you will hold the keys to wisdom's door.

Knock as in days of old, and even if you are bold, or not…

When the years are going fast, the seasons will be blurred, and you shall feel your time going slow

In old days of past, now born anew,

You know not the things that were you, or became you, when your thin red blood ran cold,

But now your heart has been helped, restored, rejuvenated, and refilled.

Where once there was only emptiness; and your son is nearing his own ways and breath,

You will live to see the moon, not on earth, but in Paradise;

As My celestial living clock again, the angels count its beats.

And then your love can be what it was meant to be, and melt the lives of all the rest.

Oh, dear, say: where is your strength without me when you call it?

Stop, think, and surmise…

The mercy that you seek: is it just from my end?

Where is the one true love that I gave you first when you left me here abandoned,

So now at the dawn…

And in the end your heart beats again; I started it over with a second life.

And so, to whom shall it belong?

To Johnnie, Spotless, who is the longer of memories past, and is of the one,

Who has wrestled with death like Jacob to become Ishmael, and fight for your new name,

And then all spots are gone and not inherited or transferred away,

For I am He who stands alone, and stands before the servant King, who finds the sun temperate with fun and no worries about a thing.

I am He who can find healing in a smooth voice over any silence,

I am He who can yearn for life and be not moved,

When all else has been undone….

For yea, you have been in the valley of the shadow of death…

When your hand has been against me and seeds have been un-sown,

I found you to praise Me,

I AM THE One who is the one who gives all life, and keeps the rivers full.

He said to me in open verse:

All children will know my name before they know their own.

I am God, the Mighty One.

And you will not be a drake who sits for all to admire and see before it comes to die,

Be only as humble as a servant of the King

Whose desires have been lashed and dashed to a bollard by the sea.

So, will you come again to know the mighty One, the one left in your cave?

This is where you will struggle and suffer like Christ did in his own darkness for three days,

To rise and come forth in newer glory, in His own light!

To emerge on eagles' wings and dance with the angels'

And show the world His strength through good men, like you…

As angels bid well all things of the Master, He says,

"I will endure through your bloodlines

And endure all though your shame

With the might of all that lives and breathes,

You alone will know My name.

And you will lead others by your example

Where perfection can run and hide

In a game of seek and rescue;

It is there by your side.

For only a few can find pure wisdom, and no one can find whole untruth,

But when I return back to my kingdom, overhead in the clouds riding high,

I will be the greater victor, and destroy Satan alas, and take him from his roost." Amen.

And then, exactly to the minute and final second, after hearing these words exactly thirty-three hundred times, Servius whispered into Johnnie's ear.

"Johnnie, wake up… open your eyes, and do not be afraid, for the Lord God is with you." And Johnnie began to weep. His eyes opened. He looked straight up at the ceiling without expression or words. He had only tears running down his face, trying to clear whatever scales or foreign bodies he had on his eyes, for he could not see. He felt something there, but had no understanding of where he was or where he had been. He just lay there in total darkness. Then he heard Charlotte's voice.

"Johnnie, I am here, right here… for God's sake, can't you hear me?" Charlotte pleaded through tears.

"Char…?" Johnnie said.

Johnnie!" Charlotte screamed. "You are alive! It's a miracle!"

"Char, where are you? I can hear you, but I don't see you. Char? Char?" Johnnie said agitatedly, wrestling with the bed sheets.

Everyone present began to hold him down to keep him from hurting himself, both doctors and nurses. Daisy and Mr. Silverman also reached over to help, amazed that Johnnie was finally awake.

But Johnnie's eyes had both been removed in surgery due to severe lacerations to his face. The fluid had drained from both eyes and they had dried out before reaching the hospital, causing irreparable damage to his retinas. He also had severe internal damage, which they first feared would be fatal: a direct puncture wound to the liver and the pancreas, along with multiple broken bones and a possible spinal injury. If he struggled and tried to walk he would have to be restrained with arm and leg straps, because his back and legs couldn't take the strain for at least a month.

"Johnnie, I am right here. Don't struggle. You've been hurt in an accident," Char said. She was an ER nurse at Methodist, and now all her nightmares were coming true. She had never had to watch a loved one come through the doors while she was at work, and the hospital did not allow relatives to be present in the ER life support, but this was different. Charlotte missed the Emergency Room triage to keep him alive, and by the time she and the Silvermans could get there from Houston and Johnson City, Johnnie was already in a medically induced coma to try and save his life.

"I can't see you, Char. Am I in Heaven? Where are you?" Johnnie asked in a panic, flailing his arms to try to touch anything that would help him understand where he was.

Charlotte pressed her cheek against his and then kissed him on the cheek. She held his head and looked him right into his face.

"Johnnie, I am right here. I am not leaving your side. You were in a wreck, and you can't see, so please be calm. I love you, Johnnie… I love you… Please settle down, so you don't hurt yourself anymore."

He felt her warm cheek against his and immediately calmed down. He felt the breath of her words hit him in the face, and he knew she would not lie to him. His momentary confusion and panic slowly subsided.

"I have been saved, Char," Johnnie said to her.

"I know, Johnnie, the doctors here are amazing," Char replied.

"No, Sweetheart… I have been saved. God saved me, and he spoke to me," Johnnie whispered urgently.

"Johnnie, just rest now," she said. "Mr. Silverman is here, and others… we all love you. Just rest… just rest. We can talk more later, when you're thinking more clearly."

"Char, He spoke to me. He said He loves me. I can never be like I was… I am not me anymore. God loves me and I can't do anything I did before," Johnnie replied excitedly.

"Sweetheart, please just get some rest! Your body needs to heal," Charlotte said, on the verge of tears. Reality was beginning to hit her. Sure, she had her husband back, but she was about to give birth to their child, and her husband would be disabled and blind his whole life, unable to work, and she would have to take care of two people, both needing her full attention. It was just too overwhelming.

"Don't cry, my Love," Johnnie said to her soothingly. "There is no need for crying ever again. God spoke to me and told me all the answers, all the things I need to share, all the things he wants us to know."

Charlotte could no longer hear him.

Mr. Silverman was nearby, looking down at his star MVP player, wondering what was going to happen now to his future and the future of his team, his investment, and all the money he had spent on the new arena to fill the seats to pay for the debt he had accumulated.

Servius was there, too, listening to all the reactions of Johnnie's loved ones. At that moment, Servius reached over and wrapped his hands around Andy's face and whispered into his ears.

"Do you not know what the scripture teaches? 'The borrower is slave to the lender.'[193] "

God had intertwined their lives so much and Johnnie's decisions had impacted so many, that it was now becoming felt around him. Then Servius went over to Charlotte and wrapped his mighty wings all around her, with the grace given to him by the Holy Spirit to share as a comfort giver. Immediately she settled down and fell asleep on the bed at Johnnie's side in a state of exhaustion and fear. Johnnie reached over and began to stoke her hair. He could feel her body lying next to his and her breathing slowing, and he was comforted by her proximity. He then reciprocated the love she had always shown him by whispering in her ear as she slept.

---

[193] Psalms 22:7

"I will love you always, till death do us part, and even beyond, until God heals all things and we can be together in Heaven as we once were, as man and wife."

Charlotte smiled in her sleep, but Johnnie could not see it. The doctors and nurses all watched these things transpire and took mental notes, for one day the world would know their fateful story.

Then Johnnie spoke again.

"Just rest, my Sweetheart. I am not going anywhere, and when you awaken, I will share with you all the things God has told me to share with the world. He wants no more personal suffering, nor minor plagues to happen on his earth; it is his desire for them not to happen anymore. But we have not been listening, and we keep hindering ourselves. Oh cry for the world, my Love! We are all born blind as vulnerable sheep, living in a truly unenlightened, but inspired and merciful world."

As Leroy's soul was separated from his body, Chalymina wrapped his massive insulated thick wings around him, and they glowed pure translucent white. Then with a flutter of the angel's thin outer wings—delicate as a butterfly's—they rose into the Heavens, away from lower Paradise toward upper Paradise, where the Holy Spirit was waiting.

"I can fly!" Leroy shouted out as he felt the super-sonic elevation increasing and saw below him earth sinking away quickly, and with it, what was left of his lifeless body.

Upper Paradise was the most holy of all the angelic spaces for conversation and witnessing, where the Holy Spirit spent most of His and Her time, when not leaving center base to survey the earth and be with His and Her flock.

The Holy Spirit spoke to Leroy after Chalimyna dropped him off on the landing platform and then left to go back to earth and finish a new work order.

"Mr. L. McGinnis," the Holy Spirit called Leroy's name. The platform on which Leroy had been placed then began to move toward the Holy Spirit on its own. He was being drawn forward, and if a magnet was taking him from one place to another. It could not be gravity because he was not being pulled down. In a feeble moment of thinking he was still on earth, he wondered if this was referred to as anti-gravity, but those thoughts were mere ideas lodged somewhere in his mental capacity which somehow were released at this moment and then faded… maybe from a lingering prostaglandin hormone response from the body's physical death.

"Mr. L. McGinnis," the Holy Spirit repeated, "do you know where you are?"

"I do not, oh Holy One," Leroy replied, for he did not understand the separation between Heaven and Paradise yet, but now it was to be revealed.

"You are of the root of Jesus, whose blood was spilled for you, that you might be called the Tribe of the Persecuted for Righteousness Sake," explained the Holy Spirit.

"I do not understand," Leroy replied.

"Your grandfather, Gantt McGinnis, was murdered for preaching the faith in his hometown six months before your father was born. That is why your father leaned on you so much in the faith, and your spirit was bent to seek me first, before Satan turned you down the wayward path. You fought against the winds of Satan with the help of Chalimyna and your other guardian angels, who often prayed that you might not be taken by the storms which surrounded you. These were the same thoughts of you grandfather as well, which were instilled in your genetic DNA before you were born. A man in his town, named Oswald, whom he shed light on, was a coward, and he shot your grandfather through a window late one night while he was reading his Bible."

The Holy Spirit spoke on in scripture and code, but all telepathically at this point, to be knitted into the fabric of his soul now as it was being prepared for final processing. No words of praise were yet allowed to be sung from Leroy's lips, as his upper enlightenment phase had not been completed.

"I still do not understand," Leroy confessed, in a spiritual quandary which left him unsure of his future.

"Your Tribe of Jesus serves the inner core of the Tree of Life, Mr. McGinnis. It produces daily medicine for the world and keeps it alive, as dictated through the will of the Holy Trinity and the blessing of the slaughtered lamb, the Lord Savior Jesus, and the Father in Heaven. This medicine is invisible to the naked eye, but is seen through the healing of the mind and spirit of the human social path," the Holy Spirit continued speaking telepathically.

"I am only getting more confused," Leroy confessed.

"As you are supposed to be. So now look down on this movie of your life, and you will see all the people you helped whom you did not know but who were your spiritual family, to the third generation, just as your grandfather helped you…."

Leroy looked down at the images of his life playing before him. He could do nothing now until he was called back again or taken to Heaven by another angel at the appointed time.

Leroy's movie was a glorious one, and he could not believe all the good seeds sown in Jesus' name which had flourished because of his ambassadorship over them unto three generations. Many people in his movie he never knew existed, and this was an enlightenment to him and a blessing to watch for an eternity or until his calling. Others who had to watch movies of their lives, however, watched in total horror at the destruction they had contributed to souls unto the third generation, as their names were cursed and they screamed in the agony of suffering caused by their selfishness and contribution to Satan during their weak and stressful lives.

Oswald was one of these souls stuck in Lower Paradise now, waiting for a final judgment without a promising positive ending. Leroy, being enlightened to his pain in the fourth dimension, was commanded to share and carry his burden for a while by the Holy Spirit so that both could understand new roles. So Leroy began praying for Oswald in the afterlife constantly. Both knew their eventual directions as both sat still in Paradise in a constant waiting state. Both were given the task of watching movies of their own personal lives while on earth which were to never cease in a process which began over and over again and went on without end.

Three days had passed since Johnnie had woken from his coma. Servius, Chalimyna, and Phylamonas had all been with him during that time, helping to explain many of the things of the fourth dimension. When Johnnie became coherent again of his surroundings, he slowly began to touch around his bed in hopes of finding Charlotte somewhere nearby. Sonny and Rosanne were there in the room with him, but Charlotte had gone back to the hotel to take a shower. She said she would be coming back in a couple of hours. Daisy and Andy had gone back to Houston to take care of business back home, and now Mamaw was there to take their place. She had come with true and solid moral support and had been praying over Johnnie's bedside for the past three days, constantly with her Bible open, most of the time also touching him on his forehead or shoulder to be in contact with him while his body and spirit healed.

Mamaw believed in miracles; it was one of her internal strengths which allowed her to overcome anything, a gift that only those from the Tribe of Those Who Mourn were able to understand. This was something that went all the way back to Mary, the Mother of Jesus who saw her son raise Himself from grave after three days.[194]

"Char… Char...? Char!" Johnnie began to call out. Without her the bed felt like a casket instead of a hospital bed, for he was still confused about where he was. He thought maybe he was in the afterlife… but alive and blind, without eyesight? He still could not grasp that.

Sonny reached over and grabbed his right hand and squeezed it gently, speaking soothingly to him.

"Johnnie, hey, Spot Man… Johnnie, this is your buddy, Sonny. Old buddy, can you hear me? Can you understand me?"

Then Johnnie began to turn his head to the right and to the left. The words were coming into his ears but something felt wrong.

[194] Mark 16

"Johnnie, this is Sonny. Rosanne is here too. Charlotte is at the hotel and will be back soon. Mamaw is here too," he said.

"Mamaw?"

"Yes, Johnnie," Sonny said.

"Mamaw? Mamaw? Are you there? Where am I?" Johnnie pleaded.

"I am here, Mr. Servant of the King, by your side… where I have always been. Just rest, please. God has shown me some things, some great things you are going to do."

This was not what Johnnie wanted to hear in his new prison of blindness, which he was beginning to grasp. Mamaw was already pushing him in a direction he did not want to go. He needed Charlotte, her love and unconditional support.

"Charlotte, where are you?" he screamed out the name his wife, who shared his soul without judgment. And then he let out a long roar, like a dying lion. "CHARLOTTE… ARGHHHHHHHHHHHHH… HELP ME!"

But she was not there to help him. And never again would she be there for him, for she believed Johnnie was beyond her human help, and she wanted to survive in this world. She forgot her position as the good helper God had created her to be for his emotional and spiritual support, to help keep him balanced in the wake of Satan's lies. A three-way promise of marriage had been made before God at their wedding, each saying 'till death do us part,' but she had forgotten that three-way promise was to be honored on both sides to God first and to each other second, both on earth and in the world of Lost Paradise. No, she remembered it only as a two-way promise between herself and her husband, a promise which she now could not keep, for she had lost the will and understanding to lean on her Lord and let Him control her destiny.

And it became an emotional discussion on the issue of doing 'good' versus doing 'right.' This argument went all the way back to the Garden of Eden, where the serpent had circumvented God's edict for man's life in Paradise, where Eve had been misled and told that if she would like to eat of the Tree of Knowledge, she would not die, and so she gave the fruit also to Adam. It was also the argument used by lawyers, agnostics, and atheists who only believed in Lost Paradise, thus placing themselves at the center of all things, forgetting they were the center of nothing and could not even make their own hearts beat without the will of God.

Charlotte had been born into an old world of men, childbirth, babies, food, housing, money, and famine, and she would now have to learn how to cope and survive alone, which gave her an extra 'bent and flexible' advantage in life on earth but a morsel of lost advantage to lead or conquer. Charlotte was going to have a baby, who would be solely dependent on her to survive, and this became her new first priority, not her husband, whom she would now leave.

Unfortunately for Johnnie this would become his new challenging reality, forsaken as Christ was by Judas, as he moved from living in the world of Lower Paradise to the Upper Echelon of Paradise and the world of Spirits, the Holy Spirit, and the minor angelic forces. The guardian angels were considered most of the minor angelic forces because they were derived from the souls of humans and used to guide other humans on the path of righteousness, like Enoch.[195] But the major angelic forces had been created before the humans, with souls unlike those of the guardian angels—much more powerful and indestructible—as they carried out the Lord's commands, seeking out power from Heaven and infinite

[195] Genesis 5: 23-34

omnipotence given them by the Trinity in the beginning. Enoch had been given 365 years before his time was done, representing each day in an earth's orbit around the sun, giving sunlight to the bones to create the blood that would carry life to the whole body of man, and show how the Trinity was at work in the fallen Garden of Eden, as he was taken away and made into an angel that could serve like Michael and Gabriel.

The Holy Spirit called forth many of the sons and daughters of the Guardian Angels and commanded them to bring forth the three atheists and Job. There were 1100 in this count to witness the words and lesson to be spoken.

Then the sons and daughters opened a great pit, and when a hand emerged, trying to climb out, they grabbed it and fished out the one to whom it was attached… and then another… and then a third, and then the closed the great hole until ordered to open it again. The three who had emerged were then dragged on a great palate of ice by chariots pulled by mighty cherubs until they landed in front of the Holy Spirit, who spoke to them in Her angry voice.

"Did you not hear the scripture and alas turn away?" asked the Holy Spirit. "These words I spoke forcefully to each of you many times, and yet you rebuked me in the direct faces of your friends, who are my enemies."

Out in the open, wisdom calls aloud,
she raises her voice in the public square;
on top of the wall she cries out,
at the city gate she makes her speech:
How long will you who are simple love your simple ways?
How long will mockers delight in mockery
and fools hate knowledge
Repent at my rebuke!
Then I will pour out my thoughts to you,
I will make known to you my teachings.
But since you refuse to listen when I call
and no one pays attention when I stretch out my hand,
since you disregard all my advice
and do not accept my rebuke,
I in turn will laugh when disaster strikes you;
I will mock when calamity overtakes you—
when calamity overtakes you like a storm,
when disaster sweeps over you like a whirlwind,
when distress and trouble overwhelm you.
Then they will call to me but I will not answer;
they will look for me but will not find me,
since they hated knowledge
and did not choose to fear the LORD.
Since they would not accept my advice
and spurned my rebuke,
they will eat the fruit of their ways
and be filled with the fruit of their schemes.
For the waywardness of the simple will kill them,
and the complacency of fools will destroy them;

> but whoever listens to me will live in safety
> and be at ease, without fear of harm."[196]

"Now you three of many who line and crowd the everlasting nonbeliever's pit, GO BACK! For I will never see you again! This is your last chance to gaze your eyes upon me, Wisdom and Truth, and now you mock the Trinity no more!" the Holy Spirit spoke

And then the sons and daughters of the guardian angels dragged them back to where the pit lay, and Azoz, the mighty one who had left the Tribe of Ishmael for the Tribe of Isaac many generations before, opened the lid quickly—before any others could get out—and pushed the three back in, never to be heard of or seen again.

Then the Holy Spirit said to Job, "Step forward, my good and faithful servant! How many days have you rested in my care?"

"Since my birth, oh Holy One," Job answered.

"And you never forsook me, not even when I let Satan ruin your life and take your family and steal your possessions. You always trusted me, and never left my side," says the Holy Spirit.

"I have loved You from the day I knew you, oh Lord, and still love You now, and I will love You forever more, oh Holy One. Even Satan cannot pluck me from Your hand!" Job replied.

Then the Holy Spirit took the 1100 angels and turned them into a living statue, and then commissioned them to guard the Pit of the Nonbelievers. Then they began a never-ending praise song, constantly repeating these words: "Mighty is the Lord God, Our Redeemer and Savior; He rules over the highest and He rules over the lowest; He serves up his mercy and His justice over all who

[196] Proverbs 1:20-33

listen to him and obey; He measures and enforces the Trinity's Laws accordingly. Amen."

Two weeks had passed since Johnnie had been hospitalized. He slipped in and out of comas, and constantly asked about Leroy. Many of the players had come by, and Coach had warned them not to speak a word about Leroy's death. He told them simply to tell Johnnie, if he asked, that the doctors had not given a final report on Leroy and that he was still in intensive care. When Johnnie asked to be rolled over to see him, all doctors and nurses refused, saying they could not unhook him from his life support systems yet.

Charlotte did not come back to the hospital after she left that first day. She could not bear to see him one last time, and she felt it would be best is she just left and did not drag out the reality that she could not stay in the marriage anymore. Johnnie constantly asked for her too, but in his heart knew she was gone. He was utterly broken both in heart and body. He knew he had just lost everything in a single moment, including a son, whom he would now never see. He was drowning in true desperation, locked in a hospital, strapped to a bed, blind and facing a life of total darkness.

In his most recent moment of rest, Servius came to Johnnie in a dream. He was in full glory, his wings outstretched, as he spoke to Johnnie.

"Fear not, for I bring you greetings from the Lord! When you awake you will say to those who are with you these words: 'The

Trinity lives with you in your blood, so do not mix it, nor defame it. And when God breathed life into Adam, He commanded it to be with him, as He was in Christ when He was baptized. And to abuse the Trinity is to reject the blood of Christ, which was spilled for you, and which will bring plagues, famine, and disease which will leave you and your families dead, dying, and suffering by their own hands.'"

When Johnnie awoke, he did as he was told, but first he wanted to find out who was with him in the room, since he could not see anything but total darkness in front of him.

"Who is there?" Johnnie called out into his hospital room. "Please tell me… I have to know."

"Hey, Johnnie, it's me, Tucker, your best bud," Tucker said to him, reaching over to grab his shoulder and give him a kiss. "I love you like a brother, Johnnie… you know that, don't you?"

"Yes," Johnnie said. "Is anyone else in the room right now?"

"Yes," Tucker replied, "and I have a surprise… Zig is here to see you! And Mamaw is downstairs at the cafeteria."

"The Zig Man?" Johnnie recoiled into his pillow and then moved around the bed in an unconscious twitch. "Ziggie, are you there, really?"

"Hey, Spot… Brother… good to see you alive again. Man, we were worried about you!"

Tucker said, "Coach traded Orlando for Ziggie… he is now playing for us instead of Chicago!"

"That is some cool beans!" Johnnie exclaimed with an uncharacteristic joy in his voice that had been missing over the past weeks.

Right then Mamaw came into the room and saw Johnnie talking excitedly with the guys. She immediately raced over and gave him a hug, whispering in his ear, “Johnnie, I love you… how is my servant of the King? Did you have a good rest?”

Johnnie immediately recalled the dream he had just had with Servius, and proclaimed to Mamaw, Tucker and Ziggie, “I have to tell you something that just happened to me.”

The three knew that whenever Mamaw entered the room, Johnnie usually took on a more serious demeanor, which is what had once again just happened. They all three looked at Johnnie, in silence and expectation.

“I had a dream,” Johnnie began, “and in it an angel came to me and told me to say something to you. I know I will say it and then feel better, so please just bear with me and don’t think this is too weird, okay?” Johnnie confessed.

“Go ahead, Spot-Man… we are just happy you are alive and ready to go play basketball again, ain’t that right, Zig-Man?” Tucker replied.

“Tucker, what the hell are you talking about? You know I’ll never play again. I can’t see! It is impossible.”

“Never say ‘IMPOSSIBLE,’ Johnnie… I won’t allow that sort of negativity at all,” Mamaw interjected. “When you walk with the Lord, nothing is impossible. In a few days I am going to get you out of that bed and put your heels back on that court. Now,” Mamaw continued matter-of-factly, “what are you supposed to tell us?”

“Okay, Mamaw… all three of you, listen to me. This is what I am supposed to tell you all: ‘God lives with us in our blood, so we are told not to mix it (I am sure that means with unbelievers), and we are not to defame it. I was told that when God breathed life into Adam, He commanded the Trinity to be in him… and that He was in Christ at the moment when Christ was baptized… and that to abuse the Trinity is to reject the blood of Christ, which was spilled for us.

And if we do not honor His blood, the Lord God will bring plagues, famine, and disease to us and our families, which will leave them and all of us dead, dying, and suffering by our own hands.' There… that is what I am supposed to tell you," Johnnie finished emphatically.

"Spot-Man, you are starting to sound like a prophet, and that is kind of scary, you know what I mean?" Ziggie was the first to speak after hearing that news from the Holy Spirit.

"Hey, Zig, I know what you mean, but I am no prophet! It is scary to me as well. I can't see, I can't play what I love, and I can't get my wife—my soulmate!—to come tell me she still loves me! I hate my life, and now I can't even get rest from the angels, who are beginning to haunt me when I sleep. I really just want to get a gun and kill myself."

"Nonsense!" Mamaw exclaimed. "You better shut your mouth, Johnnie! God never promised you an easy life. You are already a winner from the day you were born, so don't be giving us your pity party or I will climb onto that bed so fast it will make your head spin and give you a dose of my own heavy-handed medicine! The doctors' will have to pull me off of you and you'll have go back into surgery to get a second round of bruises repaired!"

Tucker chuckled and gently grabbed Mamaw by the left arm, holding her back a little, because he half-believed she was serious… and perhaps just a little bit bipolar and could use some medicine of her own. (He wished one of the doctors had been in there to hear her rant, so he could have her examined another time!) But really he was just happy she was not his mother, because he might never want to go home for Christmas dinner again.

"Mamaw, did you hear what Johnnie said to us about his dream? What do you make of that?" Tucker asked her, trying to calm her down a little.

Ziggie leaned back in his chair as he covered his face. He was trying to hide a big grin and snicker or two about Mamaw and her uncontrollable ways.

"Johnnie is a servant of the Lord. I know and he knows it, and what's more: the Lord knows it! So as soon as we all understand this little secret, it won't be a secret anymore," Mamaw clarified.

"Okay, ma'am," Tucker said politely, "so when do you think we can get 'The-Spot' back to Houston for some good ol'-fashioned food and some nutritious healing chicken soup?"

Johnnie spoke to all of them at once in a sort of blanket statement, saying, "You can't call me Spot anymore. I don't like the name, and I won't allow it. I was washed clean by God when He talked to me."

"See there, Tucker! See what I mean?" Mamaw shook her fist at Tucker.

"I guess I see what you mean, Ms. Gleason… but, Johnnie, the whole world knows you by that name… you can't just say 'I don't want to be called Spot anymore.' "

"I just did… so please don't call me that anymore. I will fix it with Coach. Besides, I am pretty sure he will just want to get rid of me, anyway, because I am dead weight to him now, as soon as he sees me again."

"Well, maybe… let's just wait and see, Mr. Perfect," Tucker said to Johnnie. "I think he might just have a surprise for you yet."

"I don't care about that anymore. Can you try to call Char again for me? Please tell her I love her. I really miss her." Johnnie then started crying uncontrollably again, putting the pillow over his face and sobbing for over an hour. He just could not seem to come to grips with losing her in this way. He could understand the injuries he had sustained in the car wreck, but not the injuries in his heart from being abandoned. Even though his eyes couldn't see, they still shed tears of utter grief.

Then Servius came to him and whispered in his ear.

"Everything will be all right, for just as it was for Job and Paul, it will be the same for you too."

One thing Johnnie knew for sure was that he would never get married again if Charlotte did not come back to him. His life on Fallen Eden would never be the same from this day forward.

Brothers and sisters, as an example of patience in the face of suffering, take the prophets who spoke in the name of the Lord. [11] As you know, we count as blessed those who have persevered. You have heard of Job's perseverance and have seen what the Lord finally brought about. The Lord is full of compassion and mercy.

As testified by James,
Brother of Jesus
5:10-11

Chapter 9

Refusing to Give Up or Give In

For five months, Johnnie was in the trauma rehab section of the hospital learning to walk again. He was required to do physical therapy, walking up and down stairs and using multi-speed treadmills. Despite having been an athlete in perfect condition before his car wreck, much of his body was starting to atrophy from disuse, and his muscle mass had shrunk by more than thirty percent. Now his doctors were telling him it was time to go back home to Houston, but he did not want to go. He really had no friends or family there. He felt like a wine cork, bobbing on top of the ocean's waves after having been thrown overboard from a long-ago, long-gone futile celebration.

Then the Spirit of the Apostle Paul went to the Holy Spirit and asked to be heard. This was unusual for the Holy Spirit, but since it was Paul, it was granted.

"Lord, Master, and Leader of the Angels over Fallen Eden, may I beg one thing from you?" St. Paul asked.

"Ask it and it shall be done, if it is in the will and plan of the Lord God in Heaven," the Holy Spirit responded

"Thank you," St. Paul said. "Please have Phylamonas deliver these words to Johnnie, so that he might be comforted in his time of need: 'For God so loved the world that He gave His begotten Son, that whoever shall believe in Him will have everlasting life!'[197] For I was once like Johnnie, and I will pray for him, that he does not fall prey to the despondency that I, too, felt when the Lord put my feet on that new path, though I knew not if it was God's will."

"Yes, my good and faithful servant," the Holy Spirit replied. "Your heart still feels the wounds of a broken childhood through the bones of a full-grown man. You must sit at the table and constantly eat the Bread of Life, so I will carry out this request for you. that you also might be comforted as you travel back to Heaven to take your place at the table of the Apostles."

Johnnie returned to Houston and to the gym where the rest of the 'Canes team had been working out during the off-season. The remainder of the regular season had been played while Johnnie was in rehabilitation, and the Hurricanes had not made it to the playoffs that year. Coach Barracks had little time to spend visiting with Johnnie when he returned, because the team needed him to focus on the game schedule. Only Rosanne and Mia had made trips to San Antonio on a regular basis to take him homemade baked cookies and lemonade, which he could not get at the hospital. They even snuck in a couple of burgers and french fries, which were definitely not on his

[197] John 3:16

approved diet. But Johnnie always beamed at the sound of fast-food paper bags being carried into his hospital room.

To Johnnie, the hospital was more of a prison. The angels kept him busy at night in his thoughts so he would not go astray—just as they had done with Paul and Job—because it took more than human strength to maintain the will of perseverance when one felt completely abandoned and alone, a feeling Paul knew all too well.

Mamaw became his new chauffeur when he got back to Houston. He could have called a limousine to take him places, because he still had money coming in from his lucrative contract, but he chose to keep the money in the bank and put up with Mamaw and her tough army-talk.

On the first day Mamaw dropped Johnnie off at the front door of the arena, she would not get out of the car to help him. She wanted him to feel his way into the locker room using his cane, because it reminded her of Moses leading his people in the desert when he himself was trying to find his way. No mercy had God given Moses when he was waiting for that stiff-necked generation to die there in the desert, and no mercy would she give Johnnie, for she knew he had to find his own way in the darkness.

After some trepidation and bumps, Johnnie made it to the locker room and found his locker. But when he reached into the locker, he found that it has been cleaned out. Stunned and shocked, Johnnie just stood there for a moment, feeling completely abandoned.

Coach Barricks' office had a view into the locker room through a big glass window, and when he saw Johnnie standing there in confusion, he rushed out to him to try to explain and give him some insight into the business of basketball.

"Spot-Man, glad you're home!" Coach Barricks greeted him.

"No you're not, Coach," Johnnie said, turning toward the direction of his voice. "Where is my uniform? My things are gone, and this place no longer feels like home. And don't call me Spot-Man—that's not who I am anymore."

"You never did seem to mince words, Johnnie," Coach replied. "Sorry you didn't make more friends here."

"I made enough friends, Coach, to be satisfied. We all just live in different worlds. I live in the world of my heavenly Father; you live in the world of the moneychangers."

"Money makes the world go 'round, and that is why we play basketball, Johnnie."

"No, Coach… that is why *you* play basketball! I played it because I loved it, but now even that has been taken from me!" Johnnie said, almost shouting. Then he paused, becoming solemn. "Why don't you just take me somewhere and get rid of me… put me out of my misery?" Johnnie said in a quiet voice.

Coach Barricks and Mr. Silverman had met out on the fishing platform the week before and discussed the financials of the company. Attendance had dropped by half once Johnnie was not playing in the games. They had lost their momentum as a team, and their leader was gone. It was the triple-whammy of business failure, and both Coach and Andy knew it, so in a desperate move to regain the momentum they had decided to make Johnnie a manager in the front office and keep him on the payroll.

"I'd like you to come into my office, Johnnie," Coach said. "I have something to tell you." Gently, he took Johnnie by the arm and led him into his office, helping him into a seat. Just then, Zig-Man interrupted, sticking his head in to ask a question.

"Oh hi, Johnnie! Good to see you back! Hey, Coach, when is the fish-fry at your house again… this weekend or next?" Zig asked.

Since this was supposed to be a surprise party for Johnnie's return, and Zig had just blown the cover, Coach tried salvage what he could.

"Oh... uh... I need to check again with the schedule and I will let everyone know today at practice." Then he gestured for Ziggie to please leave them alone by waving him toward the door. Zig-Man got the message and promptly disappeared. Then Coach returned to his conversation with Johnnie.

"Johnnie, you may not consider us as your family, but we consider you as part of our family. This is your home, now, for both you and Mamaw. Mr. Silverman has moved your jersey and things upstairs into to front office. He is making you assistant general manager under himself. Now doesn't that sound like you have a family, and you can call this place home?" Coach asked.

Johnnie began to weep, moved by the word 'family.' He still had so many childhood wounds from his past that it was difficult for him to grasp the term 'extended family,' much less understand the meaning of what Coach had just said to him.

"Thank you, Coach, I am appreciative like you do not even know," Johnnie said.

Then coach picked up his phone and called upstairs to tell them Johnnie would be coming up in a few minutes and to please send down one of the pages to come get him so they could give him a tour of his new office. Shortly thereafter, a young attendant came down and took Johnnie by the arm and led him upstairs to where he would find his jersey hanging in a box-frame on the wall and a new place in the business of basketball.

That night while Johnnie was sleeping, Servius delivered a message to him that he would forever remember and keep in a special his place in his heart. This was the dream: He was standing at the edge of a great valley, and across from him, on the other side, he could see Mary, the mother of Jesus, along with the four brothers of Jesus: James, Joseph, Jude, and Simon…

Behind them stood twelve great tribes, and Abraham stood in front of all.

The Lord God then came down and rested in the valley, and spoke to Abraham.

"The tribes I gave to you from the seeds of Isaac were washed and transformed into the twelve tribes of my son, the Christ, who died for all. On that day of your rebirth, I spoke these words to you: 'I will make you into a great nation, and I will bless you. I will make your name great, and you will be a blessing. I will bless those who you bless, and whoever curses you I will curse; all the people will be blessed by you.'[198]

Then the Lord God continued speaking to Abraham.

"Look behind you and see the seed of Mary, which is of your seed and the seed of Isaac, but fertilized with the Spirit of the Holy Ghost. Then look behind her and see the seed of her four sons, who are of your seed and the seed of Isaac. Then look behind them and see the twelve tribes of their seeds and the seeds of the Holy Spirit who spoke to me as the Lord. And the word became flesh, and He,

[198] Genesis 12: 2-3

My Son, delivered the message at the Sermon on the Mount, distributing blessings, just as I foretold to you on the day of your rebirth."

And then the Lord God told Abraham, "Look across the valley and see the one who will unite my tribes into one root with the blessing of the Holy Spirit. He is to come, but not yet. He is to be broken before he can be used. He must be like a vase that is shattered and then put back together again, so that he knows the power of the one who sent him. And he must first be blind before he can see, so he must live by faith in the darkness, which will become his light."

Then the Lord God spoke to all those in all twelve Tribes, saying to them:

"The day will come soon when you will no longer be called many names: Jew and Gentile, Catholic and non-Catholic, Protestant and non-Protestant, Eastern and Western Orthodox, Lutheran, Methodist, Anglican, or Mormon. You will all be called the Children of Christ, the fruit of the vine, the blessing of the single root, the life given of the living water, and the medicine provided without cost to the world."

And then The Lord said to them all:

"What you see is what you do not understand, and what you understand you do not see. I tell you the truth: my Son is the only way to me, and only through Him will you find the Way, the Truth, and the Life you now seek. Follow Him and have Eternal Life in a relationship with Me.... I Am who I Am, and no one comes to me but through Him."

Then Servius took the vision from Johnnie, and he sat down beside his bed and continued the message the Holy Spirit had given to Servius to reveal to Johnnie.

"Do not tell these things to anyone yet," Servius said, "for you are to lead a great nation for twenty years, and then be replaced by another; and there are many things you will not understand. You will suffer for Christ, in His name, but he will never forsake you, for it is Him who they hate and not you. They have only darkness ahead of them for an eternity once they are judged and found guilty of sin which would not come clean."

And with that, Johnnie woke up, drenched in a sweat that covered his entire body. It was as if someone had thrown water on him, and he was not aware that his hair had turned slightly gray overnight. His heart was not racing, though, as it would be after having a nightmare, and he knew these things were all true, because when he woke it was still complete darkness before his eyes yet he had a new sense of direction and understanding that blanketed him with total peace. He knew his twenty years of suffering had now begun, and only hoped that it would pass quickly so that he could go home to be with His Father who loved him beyond any shadow of a doubt.

Johnnie began to pray. He rose from his bed sheets, got on his knees, and gave thanks while kneeing on the concrete floor. He did not try to add any padding under his knees as he leaned on his bed, head in his hands. Then looked at the sky with dismay, feeling completely beaten up. He was blind but knew the Lord was looking down on him, and he saw himself reaching up with both hands. If someone could look down on him and see him, they would see the reflection of the Lord on the cross in both eyes, but this was impossible because only the angels were with him now. Johnnie was alone except for his Lord in his heart, the Holy Spirit in his soul, and his guardian angel keeping him safe and intervening for him with the messages from above, which were defined for him in his own way to understand. Johnnie was on the road to Salvation, knowing that it was truly a journey in this life, and not a destination until he was in the next life waiting for him to receive for all the things he said, did, and thought to honor and spread the message of the King, of whom he was now a full servant.

It was morning now, and even though Johnnie could not see the morning sun in his window nor feel the warmth of the room rising in temperature, his body knew day was dawning outside. He still had a body which responded to the electrons of the sun coming over the horizon and waking his central nervous system through a series of hormones and enzymes—which all humans have and which tell them to reduce the human growth hormone amounts and increase the stomach enzyme action—so he could work and do the Lord's work, even though he knew not how. All humans responded the same way in the human diurnal biological clock, though most believed it was just the alarm clock and coffee that made them wake up, not being taught well in the education of common sense. But of course, humans still lived in the world of selfish thoughts, and selfish ways, and selfish desires, so that they never knew the impact that creation had on their lives, but still lived in the myth of evolution, in which they were the center of the universe. This was very sad in the higher multiple dimensions, where the angels and God knew the eternal truth of the moments and watched in total despair as the egos of humans caused their utter self-destruction.

The door flew open and Mamaw let Tucker and Ziggie into the room.

"Today is the first team meeting of the season to discuss the new draft selections, Johnnie, and Coach wants you to be there," Tucker announced.

Johnnie was still on his knees.

"Why?" Johnnie asked. "He wants to show me off with my walking cane as some kind of novelty… like a freak at the Barnum and Bailey Circus?"

"Get up," Ziggie ordered Johnnie, who was still kneeling at his bedside, "and quit feeling sorry for yourself! God at least made you white, so you have no complaints in my company! No sir, not even if you were blind a hundred years, you get no sympathy from me."

Tucker knew he needed to bring Ziggie along to get Johnnie out of bed and into some clothes. He had not shown up at the office to report in for two weeks. Just sitting around having a pity party all morning was not going to get the job of making the team meeting at 2:30 p.m. a reality. Zig-Man would push all the right buttons. Mamaw had called in to talk with Coach and tell him Johnnie was not doing well. Johnnie and the Zig-man had befriended each other in a playoff game Johnnie's fist year when they had met accidentally in a bar after a game where Johnnie and the 'Canes had lost by just three points. Each of them really had no family life at that time, and Johnnie was just getting to know Charlotte better. Johnnie did not ever like losing at anything, not even poker, but on that night he had lost. But though he had lost a game, he made a friend, and he forever held respect for this great player who had beat him fair and square. (Well, actually Johnnie had fallen off a ladder and hurt his hip earlier that season chasing a bug from his closet, so he had developed a limp that had slowed him down in the fourth quarter. Johnnie never let the Zig-Man know of the injury, which was okay with both them and his guardian angels, but Johnnie always knew in his heart that he would have the last laugh if it ever came up again in a fight or verbal confrontation.)

So, they got Johnnie up, put him in a business suit, and carted him off to the arena where they held their meetings, which Johnnie remembered very well. Before they entered the room where everyone was sitting, Johnnie wrenched his right arm away from Tucker's hands, who had been leading him though the hallways and doors.

"I can at least walk into the room by myself," Johnnie said to Tucker and Ziggie, "so now just leave me alone and let me walk in with some honor, guys, okay?"

This was becoming a real self-pride issue for him and sooner or later he would come out of his shell, but still Johnnie was holding onto his past and was not yet able to break free.

When Johnnie entered, the players began a loud round of applause for him and then began cheering and chanting his name.

"Spot-Man, Spot-Man…!"

Johnnie held up both hands and asked them to please be quiet, in frustration mixed with anger over his new handicap. This took a while. Finally he sat down in a seat that Tucker provided for him, the same place he had always sat in this same room. He sat in the front on the left side, next to the exit door, facing Coach, ready to hear what the owners would want to say.

Coach Barricks picked up an old tattered basketball that looked like it had seen better days and held it up in the air.

"Do you know what this is?" he said to his team.

Of course, no one would be stupid enough to act a fool and answer 'basketball.' Johnnie, who could not see what he was holding and therefore he had no idea, sat patiently waiting to hear the answer.

"This is God's air with a covering around it. Just simple old air! It is the same stuff that you and I all breathe. What makes this air different is how it was captured and made to work for us. Somehow, somewhere along the way, this square foot of air was chosen to be different from all the rest of the air. I did not choose the air, and you did not choose this air, but someone somewhere beyond our ability to know these things chose this air to glorify… what? The game you and I play. It is a game based on air, something we did not create. We think we are the ones who people come to see, but really we would be nothing without the air."

Johnnie was only half listening to Coach, somewhat distracted by the sound of the loud air conditioners whirring in the background and thinking what Servius had told him about how God created man from the beginning of time, with Adam as the first man to have a soul, before basketball and before manufacturing that could even do such a process. Why didn't he give Adam a basketball on the first day to play with? Then maybe he would not have eaten the apple because he would have had something else to occupy his time! Johnnie had zoned out. He wondered why Tucker had dragged him here against his will in the first place.

"This air is under pressure," Coach then said to the team, "and that is how it is made to work. If I did not put the air under pressure, it would not bounce, and you would not be able to dribble. Much like you guys: only under pressure do you work properly. The more pressure, the higher you should bounce. If a basketball has no pressure, it just sits on the floor and has no value."

Then Coach Barricks wished to introduce Johnnie to the team.

"Johnnie, will you please stand up?" Coach requested.

"Everyone here knows 'Sir Johnnie,' our hero. He has become my hero because of who he is, not what he has done," Coach Barricks explained. "We want to acknowledge him today as part of our new management. When he came to us, our team was flat, like a basketball that had no air in it. And then Johnnie came and put air into our team. All by himself, he put the pressure on himself, and the pressure became work, and the work became bounce, and the bounce became scores, and the scores became wins. But we would not have had that without the air first, which gave us everything else! This man still provides our air, even though he is not on the court. I expect each of you to go to him when you need help. I do not expect you to understand what he might tell you, but I do expect you to take what he says seriously, and then to have the patience to do in practice what he tells you."

Johnnie was humbled by what Coach had just said about him. He liked the name Sir Johnnie and now asked his friends to just call him 'SJ.' This would become his new identity, a way to whisk away his past. But unfortunately God would not let his past leave so easily for him… there was still plenty of pain for him to understand there. (Jesus had carried the pain of Judas with him to the cross, and Johnnie 'SJ' would also need to carry the pain of a betrayer with him, so he could come closer to the forgiveness needed to understand unconditional love given for him. He still needed to forgive Charlotte. The pain was still heavy on him like, a hot knife burning in his heart.) Johnnie sat there motionless, thinking of Charlotte and his lost life, but what else could a blind man do? Johnnie felt he had nothing else to contribute or really live for.

The commands given to him at his rebirth gave him some promise and hope, though everything still felt kind of like some sort of cruel joke from a bad dream. This was the only rational and logical explanation, as he began to question his current status as a victim and handicapped person in life.

Johnnie certainly would walk away from his team and his lucrative disability clause in his contract if he could, but last week he had been served with divorce papers from Charlotte, and now separation from the only one he loved and his future child weighed heavily on his mind. All that money he had coming would go straight to attorneys or court fees, but he did not care anymore. He just hated that he was now dependent on Mamaw again for his sustenance, and this would be ever harder for both if they had no money now to live on. Johnnie was alone again, and with so many mental problems would soon be an imposition on the others unless he could make a change that would help him cope. Of course, no one else thought anything of the sort, and the thought that he was a burden had only been put in his mind by the Evil one, planting seeds of weeds in his brain. He would have to learn to fight these thoughts and keep the blinders on, so as not to be distracted from his God-given purpose.

The usual routine for Johnnie each morning became a struggle. Mamaw would make him eggs and bacon around 7 a.m. While he ate, Johnnie would sit at the table with the news playing in the background so Mamaw could hear the state of the union from a liberal viewpoint, while Johnnie would hear what "the democrats were doing to mess up the country." Mamaw had taken up dipping snuff every day while she carried a soda can with her around so she could pit her excess saliva in there as she enjoyed the pleasures of the nicotine addiction with the added mint flavor of the tobacco leaves while she was washing dishes. Sometimes it was so strong 'Sir Johnnie,' as he was coming to be called, could smell it from afar.

"You know God is going to punish Charlotte for leaving you, SJ," Mamaw said to Johnnie as she was cooking his eggs one morning. "Women are supposed stay with their husbands till death do they part."

"Maybe," he replied.

"Do you know why I know that?" Mamaw came back at him hard with a rebuke of Charlotte's action. The divorce was not final yet, and all Johnnie had been doing was moping around thinking about it instead of working on putting his life back together and working on something constructive.

"She just wanted to be loved and for someone to give her security," Johnnie replied, "and I know I could not do that anymore. I understand her pain, Mamaw. I do not hate her like you do."

"Johnnie, please don't say that… I don't hate her! I don't hate anyone. I just believe in the deepest, most sincere part of my heart, being, and soul that we all are accountable for our actions. It was a THREE-WAY-PROMISE which was made in marriage between you, her, and God. And more importantly, not to be taken so lightly, and where most of her suffering will lie: it was a two-world promise: ONE for this world and ONE for the world of heaven. It is not as bad to break the promise with you because this world is sort of that way, but she broke her promise with God, and that is where the seeds of her anguish will be sown, until reconciled by His love and saved once again—a second time, and a third, and a fourth, and so on—until she understands and is obedient in true love, grace, submission, and mercy."

Johnnie reached around his head with his left hand and scratched an itch on the back of his neck as he smelled the plate of food that Mamaw had cooked and set down before him. It smelled enticing, and the taste of bacon was something Johnnie loved and had become the highlight of his day. Cojo also loved bacon, and Mamaw would put this dry food in his food bowel and then pour any of the bacon drippings over it that sent the dog into ecstasy over his breakfast bowl. Again, this morning, Cojo's eyes followed Mamaw back and forth as she went from the stove to the table and set out breakfast for Johnnie.

"Mamaw, I am still not sure I believe you, but I will try."

"SJ, you would not be here if I were like Charlotte. You would be on the street begging for food, with your hand outstretched, hoping to collect a quarter for a meal. You would have become a ward of the state. See the democrats like to talk about 'doing good' all the time, but they leave when the real work needs to be done, being responsible and upholding the promises of God. They want to do good with someone else's money, not their own, and they like to take a holier-than-thou attitude all the time, like they are somehow more righteous than everyone else, when in fact they are the ones who really cause the social problems to begin with. It is a double-standard hypocrisy that never ceases to amaze me!" Mamaw lashed out with her opinions.

"But didn't Jesus teach us to 'Give freely just as we received freely, so we must do that without remorse'?" Johnnie replied.

"Yes sir, SJ..., Mr. Perfect, he did! And here is where our world has gone crazy. The liberals hide behind this concept, but here is what they do to soil the beauty of Jesus's words: When they are questioned on the truth, they deny, deny, and deny more. When they are questioned on the facts, they assassinate the character of anyone who disagrees with them. It is always because of some childhood wound they had and not the victims they represent. And when it comes to money used to help a person or a tragedy or a handout, it is always someone else's, and not theirs. And for these lies they represent, they will be judged, and it will not be good, because they misrepresented the heart of Jesus with their own prideful crusades!" Mamaw ranted on. "Yes, it is our job to give freely of our own hearts, possessions, and accords, but not to have the government steal our money in the form of disingenuous taxes to give freely to others, because they have no accountability to God in doing so, just as Charlotte has no accountability taking your money from you without personally coming over here and making you breakfast or washing your sheets, and changing your underwear if you need it. She is lost and tries loving you from afar with letters pleading her cause that she is not strong enough to weather the future, is not good enough for anyone, especially God. She should pick up her cross and carry it like the rest of us and not take the easy way out because it hurts when she cries. What a pity party Satan likes to join in on! Life must be a hands-on activity… you have to show you care with your hands, and not just with good intentions. Otherwise it becomes a crusade of man's desires, and God does not like man's desires unless Christ is leading them!" Mamaw finished.

Just as Mamaw was gearing up to give Johnnie another huge earful of hard-nosed true-life living experience, there was a loud knock at the front door. Cojo jumped up for a second, looked at the door, and then finished the last bite of his delicious greased food before he racing into the front TV room to see who had come to visit.

It was Coach Thornton, a blast from the past. wanting to see and talk with his childhood student marvel.

"Well gosh, God Almighty, who do we have here today?" Mamaw said as she opened the door to greet Coach Thornton. "What brings you over this way? She asked, and then quickly added with a grin, "Wait, I bet I know… Hey, SJ… someone is here to see you!"

Cojo remembered Coach and immediately began sniffing around his shoes and pant legs. This meant 'You are okay to come in, so why are you standing here so long?! I need someone to throw my ball and give me some attention and scratch my back!'

Coach came in and they all went in together and sat down in the TV room where he had such fond memories of the night Johnnie was drafted into the spotlight of the NBA.

After Coach sat down, Johnnie made his way around the corner from the kitchen, feeling his way with his cane and making sure not to fall over any laundry baskets or other items Mamaw might have left in the floor.

"Hi, Johnnie," Coach said as he stood up out of respect as Johnnie came closer to him by the couch. "Hope all is well," he continued, trying to break the ice in the tenderness of the moment.

"I think God should have just finished me off when he had the chance," Johnnie said in a slurring mutter as he took up his place in the recliner that had become his home twelve hours out of every day except when he went up at the arena to hang out for a while.

"I brought you a gift," said says, reaching into his pocket and pulling out a card with Johnnie's name scrawled on the front on it.

"So, what did you bring me? Sunglasses so I don't go blind looking at the sun?" Johnnie snickered to himself, but Mamaw and Coach would not in his game of pity.

"No, I brought you an invitation," Coach Thornton replied.

"No shit, Coach, you brought me something I can't read as a gift. Well that is a real kick in the pants, isn't it," Johnnie sarcastically replied.

Coach Thornton reached over and gave it to Mamaw.

"Can you read this to him, Mamaw? I think he likes you better than me," he replied whimsically.

Mamaw opened the invitation, which was handwritten by Coach Thornton. Then she began to read aloud.

"Sir John, your attendance is respectfully requested at the Saving Grace Community Bible Church this Tuesday night, August 12th, 2000, at 6:30 p.m. to hear Lawrence Merriweather preach the Gospel on: Your Soul Does Not Belong to You & Thy Kingdom Come. There will be baptisms to follow at 8 p.m. sharp. Please bring your bathing suits."

There was a long silence after Mamaw stopped talking. Now it was time to see who would break the silence first. Coach Thornton had been told by his coach and mentor, Coach Bobby Gault, when he was very young that when in a contentious position, the first person who talks first loses, and Coach Thornton had nothing at stake here to lose except to try and help get Johnnie out of his self-induced depression and feeling sorry for himself. Probably three minutes went by, which seemed like an eternity to Mamaw, but Johnnie did not feel like responding and Coach did not feel like pursuing him anymore, so Coach rose and began moving toward the door. Cojo also got up to follow him, and Johnnie could hear the clippity-clop of

Cojo's toe nails hitting the wooden floor as they both headed for the door. The all of a sudden Johnnie responded.

"I think I would like to go," Johnnie said loudly as he heard the front door opening. Coach turned around and closed the door gently. He looked up to the sky and quietly said a prayer of thanks to God.

Coach came back in the room and sat down on the couch.

"Would it be ok if I come by about 5:30 to pick you up, and we can go have a burger before we show up?"

"No thanks, Coach, I just want to go to this meeting, hear what he has to say, and come home. This is hell living like this and I need to get out of the house or I will go crazy!"

Mamaw chimed in, "Okay, well that makes two of us!"

"Thanks, Mamaw, I love you too," Johnnie retorted sarcastically. "At least you can see and drive and move around without help. I live in a godforsaken world of darkness. I don't understand what I ever did to deserve this," Johnnie muttered and then got up and walked out of the room, heading upstairs to his room to go to bed.

"That's all he ever does these days, Coach," Mamaw explained with a sigh. "I hate to say it, but Spot-Man has turned into a hateful, negative, pessimistic ball of dog doo, and nothing seems to help. But I know God is still working on him, so I hope your magic works on him. This is really wearing me out!"

"I heard that Mamaw…I love you too!" Johnnie yelled down the stairs through the open door to his room. "And don't call me SPOT-MAN!"

Coach got up, saying he would be back on Tuesday. Then he leaned over to Mamaw's ear.

"Mamaw, I had a dream," he whispered. "It is going to be all right. He is almost ready for God to be able to use him… but not just yet."

"I hope so, Coach. It is either that (a miracle for him and me) or I am going to have move to Panama or somewhere far away, and he can just go back to being a ward of the state again with his bad attitude and ungrateful ways because, I have just about had all I can take!"

Later that night, Johnnie and Coach Thornton showed up at that small church to hear what Mr. Lawrence Merriweather had to say. It was much the same when Coach had heard him speak when he was just a young boy. But now, Mr. Merriweather's hair was solid gray, and he had to hold on to the pulpit when he spoke, and he had a sort of drawn-out stutter to his voice. Nonetheless, his message remained powerful and direct.

Tonight was special, at least for Johnnie, because he was about to hear something that was going to change his life. It had all been arranged by Servius and Chalymina and the Holy Spirit that Coach Thornton was finally going to have Johnnie come to grips with his destiny, much like Saul became Paul when he was knocked off his horse on the road to Damascus.

"Good evening, and may the Lord bless you and give good cheer to those of you who have answered the call of the Holy Spirit to come here tonight," Mr. Merriweather began, as he started his brief but inspiring call to come to the Lord. "I want to begin tonight with a quick review of the Book of Job, and then zoom forward to the Book of Matthew, as we apply some of the principles today from things that happened way back yonder in yester-year."

Johnnie sat quietly listening next to Coach.

"You see," the old pastor continued, "the Book of Job bears the oldest words of history and oldest story in the Bible. You would think that it would be placed first in the Bible, of course, given its status in ancient history, above much of the other facts placed before you when you open the Holy Book and gaze upon the holy words which so many people died to deliver to you tonight. Yes, people have died to give you this information, and yet we do not know all of their names, I can assure you," Mr. Merriweather said, "they are looking down on you tonight."

This, of course, made the guardian angels applaud and begin to jump and shout in the balcony, for they knew the history of which the pastor was speaking. But the humans down below could not see or hear them, which was just another example of the world spinning on in time, with the two worlds coexisting, but only one being seen or felt by those living below in the box of World I and materialism and the three dimensions of length, height, and width.

Then Mr. Merriweather began the same introduction he always gave when he held this annual meeting, calling on all the saints in the Houston area.

"I am not a pastor like the person you would hear on a Sunday, when you sit down and listen to a sermon and a choir," he said. "No sir! I am not one of those, nor do I want to be. They live a hard life. Many of them know how hard it is, and why the Book of Job is so important in the Bible. And when you leave tonight, I hope you do too!"

Mr. Merriweather looked out over the people before him in the little church room, took a breath, and then continued.

"The Holy Spirit came to me one night and changed my life. He and told me, 'Lawrence, get up! Go down to the church on the corner. There will be a man standing there on the street. Go talk to him!' And so, I did. And there WAS a man standing there on the corner. And I believe that man was an angel. And I approached him, and this is what he said to me: 'Lawrence, feed my sheep! Tell them the Truth! And let them come to me so I can use them according to my will!' And that is all he said. And then he walked away from me. I was stunned, for I had no idea what this meant. I wondered if I should quit my job with the post office and go to seminary or get a college education and a fancy degree so I could be certified by the people around me, and not seem like some kook who had lost his marbles. But no… that very next Sunday I came back to this church and prayed for God to reveal to me what this strange message could mean. And then I knew! He was preparing me as a messenger to help those He was going to use for His holy design! And they, too, would be sent to me, just as Ananias was sent to talk to Saul when he was blinded, before the Lord removed the scales from his eyes."

Now that got Johnnie's attention. He had been sitting there like a dead man without hope, but once those words landed on his ears, they touched his heart.

"You see," Mr. Merriweather continued, "Job lived about seven thousand years before Saul (who later became Saint Paul), and about nine thousand years before today. And he lived several thousand years before the great men Moses and Abraham. That is all to say: this is an old, old story! But it applies to you and me today. Someone decided to put it in your Bible, to stick it in there after all of the beginning stuff, in between a book about a lady named Esther and the songs without musical notes, called the Psalms. And I want to explain it to you in the simplest terms possible, so that you do not misunderstand why the Lord led you here tonight. So this is going to be very short and very sweet!"

His audience chuckled. Mr. Merriweather continued.

"You see, God created Adam and Eve (actual humans, I mean, not Neanderthals: a certain man and certain wo-man) and gave them souls to be good stewards of. They sinned after their creating… they wanted to know more from the Tree of Knowledge, but this was not their privilege! It had not been given to them, and now all their children and their offspring had to suffer for their lust for knowledge without enlightenment… a suffering sort of like what we in the Merriweather family like to call the 'school of hard knocks'… just like you are suffering today. And you most likely have been hit on the head just like Saul did when he was knocked off his horse, and you probably did not like it any more than Saul liked it two thousand years ago… but that is not the issue here, whether he liked it or not… the issue is: what did he DO with his life after he gained his sight again."

And once again, this got Johnnie's attention… but nothing had quite spoken to his heart directly yet... nothing that might give him deliverance from the cage of suffering he was trapped in.

"One of the sons of the sons of the sons of Adam," Mr. Merriweather continued, "was a man name whose name was Job. He was a very successful business man. He had it all! He was just minding his own business, doing what all men do every day: going to work and taking care of his family. He was blameless and upright, and he feared God and shunned evil. So he was, by our standards today, a very good man.[199] His possessions were many. He had ten children, seven thousand sheep, three thousand camels, five hundred yoke of oxen, five hundred female donkeys, and a very large household. The Bible tells us he was the greatest of all the people in the east in his day. Now that is a pretty big claim right there.... HE WAS THE GREATEST MAN IN THE EAST!"[200]

Mr. Merriweather looked around, waiting for his words to since in, before continuing.

"But then Satan went to God and asked a great question, after roaming the earth, surveying its inhabitants. He wanted to know if there was a man who could not be turned from God even if he *lost everything*. And God said, 'There is, and that is my man Job. You may take what you want from him, but do not touch him, for only I can do that.' So, God allowed Satan to ruin Job's life to see if he would turn against God and if he would curse him for what Satan had taken from him. It is said that in one day, Job lost everything. All of his household was taken and killed by Sabean raiders; all his sheep and his attendants were struck by fire from Heaven and burned alive and destroyed; his camels were was stolen by Chaldean raiders and the attendants killed by the sword; and all his children were eating and drinking wine when a storm came and killed them all. And only one single servant messenger survived to bring Job the message that he was now alone and without any possessions or family. But Job did not curse God. He fell to the ground and worshipped him, and said the Lord, 'Naked I came from my mother's womb, and naked I shall return there. The Lord gave, and

[199] Job 1:1
[200] Job 1:2-3

the Lord has taken away; blessed be the name of the Lord.' And in all this, Job did not sin nor charge God with wrongdoing."[201]

This—finally—touched the core of Johnnie's heart and he was moved, overcome. He could not sit still, and he could not keep quiet, so he stood up and interrupted the service—right then and there—once again being the disrupter he had always been, much to the chagrin of those who knew him and called him their friend.

"And what about those God touches and tears down himself??" he called out to Mr. Merriweather. "Like Job, I feel and know his pain, but my pain came from God himself, and not Satan. In know this is true in my heart, so what have I done so bad that I have to lose my eyesight and everything else good in my life? I was once the greatest man in the east, too, and had it all! But not I have nothing! I need to know what happened! They never tell this story in the church I go to. They never talk about suffering and injustice. I want to know how God can be so cruel to me and make me less than human, bumping into things, not even able to take care of myself anymore. I almost want to curse God for what he has done!"

Mr. Merriweather had done this many times before and seen many who stood like this to ask questions of him, like Johnnie had just done. He knew one person would always come and be set apart from the others (the rank-and-file sheep) to ask the hard questions, like Job had done, searching for the answers of justice, life, and soul; for they were being tested far greater than many of the others, and for them God was preparing great things. For each of the eleven years he had been doing this work for God, at the end he would always plant one red crepe myrtle on the corner of the church, representing one person who was moved and saved by God at his

[201] Job 1:14-22

sermons. This time it would be Johnnie. For even if even those who came and were moved by the Holy Spirit to repent did not see the changes themselves, the changes would be seen by the eyes of others, and these people would, at their own designated times, be the representatives and agents of God, ambassadors of change in the world, just as Saul had become an ambassador of God for change in the world when he changed into a new creation: Paul.

Saint Paul never knew that his writings would be keep for eternity and be read perpetually for thousands of years. In his time, he was only interested in fulfilling God's mission designed for him, so he set about his daily routine to do just as he was lead, and not get distracted by the pettiness or worldly traps of the day.

"My dear young man," Mr. Merriweather said to Johnnie gently, "God never promised any of us any justice on this earth. If you are looking for justice from God, you will have to wait till the next world to find out what it is in your case. None of us knows that, but what I will tell you, if you will sit down, is the rest of the story."

So Johnnie sat down and began to listen again.

"I am not the regular pastor of this church," Mr. Merriweather said, "and actually, I am not even an ordained pastor by any organization of this world. I am just a voice calling in the wind, and I have been called to stand in the wind and to preach the gospel as John the Baptist did many years ago, calling for a new age, beginning with the birth of the Lord on earth. The original Bibles that were here earlier, a few years back, have been taken up by the church members and replaced by Bibles provided by the Gideon Organization, for it was the angel Gideon who came to me that night and met me on the street corner and told me to do this. So, in tribute to those who have placed these Bibles around the world to shepherd those in lonely places of solitude, we also will pull out our Gideon

Bible and read from it tonight. Now, if you will pull out the Bible from the back of the pew in front of you and turn to page 542, please read with me the Eleventh Chapter of Job. Here you will find your place on this earth relative to your suffering. We will begin in verse 4, with Zophar the Nammathite chiding Job in his suffering. Now my question to you as we look at these words is: Are you a Zophar, or are you a Job? Zophar answers Job using Job's own words: 'You said these words: My doctrine is pure, and I am clean in your eyes. But oh, that God would speak and open His lips against you. That he would show you the secrets of wisdom! For, they would double your prudence. Know therefore that God extracts double from you that your iniquity deserves. Can you search out the deep things of God? Can you find out the limits of the Almighty? They are higher than Heaven-what can you do? Deeper than Sheol-what can you know? Their measure is longer than the earth and broader than the sea. If He passes by, imprisons, and gathers to judgment, then who can hinder him? For He knows deceitful men; he sees wickedness also. Will he not considerate it? For, an empty-headed man will be wise, when a wild donkey's colt is born a man. If you would prepare your heart, and stretch out your hands towards Him; If iniquity were in your hand, and you put it far away, and would not let wickedness dwell in your tents; then surely you could lift up your face without SPOT; yes, you could be steadfast and not fear. Because you would forget your misery, and remember it as waters passed away. And your life would be brighter than the noonday."[202]

Something stirred in Johnnie again as he sat listening intently to the sermon. And when he heard the word 'Spot,' he jumped to his feet with a surging impulse and cried out, "Forgive me, my Lord, for

[202] Job 11:4-14

I have sinned!" Then he began to weep while just standing there, limp as a wet washrag that had washed away his past, as Coach Thornton stood up and wrapped his big arm around him.

Seeing this, Mr. Merriweather did not stop preaching, for he knew there might be others there who would do the same. So he continued reading to the end of the chapter, so that all could hear the words regarding Job's life to completion.

" 'Though you were in the dark,' " he continued, " 'you would be like morning... And you would be secure, because there is hope; yes, you would dig around you, and take your rest in safety. You would lie down and no one would make you afraid; yes, many would court your favor. But the eyes of the wicked will fail, and they shall not escape, and their hope... is loss of life!'[203] "

As Johnnie continued to cry unrelentingly, Mr. Merriweather stepped away from the pulpit that he occupied for just one hour, once a year, on the anniversary of his calling. He stepped down to where Johnnie was standing with Coach Thornton at his side, and put his arm around Johnnie.

"Would you like to be baptized tonight and give your life to the Lord, so He knows for sure you are His and He is yours, forever and ever?" he asked Johnnie.

"Yes, I would," Johnnie replied.

And then the three left the congregation, walking to the back of the church, where Coach led him to sit down and rest, preparing him for the 8-o'clock baptism ceremony.

As Johnnie and Coach Thornton were in the back area sitting quietly in a corner, they took refuge in the peace and quiet of the lonely bench which has been placed there for sinners to occupy...

---

[203] Job 11:14-20

but not for long. Many had been on the bench but then had risen like the proverbial phoenix from ashes, to rise to the Heavens and make the Lord God their home. Soon a curtain would open, showing all who were waiting for the immersion process, but only one person would be there tonight. It was a special night for Johnnie, the sole person God spoke to this evening, to publicly make his profession of faith, then gather up Christ's cross and carry it daily as a symbol of being forever bound to Jesus with his soul and his life.

When Mr. Merriweather had gone back out front to finish his sermon, he went on to describe a life of carrying the cross, and referred to Matthew and the parable of the seeds cast along the path, and what it meant to come forward, repent, and be baptized like Johnnie saying, 'Blessed are your eyes because they see, and your ears because they hear. For truly I tell you, many prophets and righteous people longed to see what you see but did not see it, and to hear what you hear but did not hear it.'[204]

Johnnie was baptized that night, and he was never the same.

For a moment, as Johnnie opened the back door to leave the church, it was as if he could see again, but without his physical eyes. Not the land and the stars, or the cars parked on the street, or the people walking by. No, not the things of this world. He saw an angel, glowing white, shimmering above the twelve crepe myrtles Mr. Merriweather had planted, the last one having been planted this very day in the morning sun.

Johnnie immediately fell to the ground and held his hands over his eyes, crying, "Oh my God, I can see again!"

Then the angel spoke to him.

[204] Matthew 13:16-17

"Josiah III, Tribute, do not be afraid. I bring you greetings from the Lord. You will unite the twelve tribes of Israel. No longer will there be different churches in different lands, for you will call them all together and name them 'The Children of God,' and they will worship as one root of one tree. These twelve trees will unite to form one tree, made of one trunk, and formed of many churches, all unified again under one roof."

And then the angel vanished, and Johnnie could see no more. He was just as blind as he had been before his baptism. But that moment of vision of all the glory of the world of God and the Heavens, and also Paradise, just as John had seen in Revelation, was enough to lift his spirit so that he could walk in a world of darkness without fear or hate. He was now spotless, cleansed by the gift of mercy from the Holy Spirit and the blood of Christ, spilled for him… and spotless and true he promised he would remain, just as Job and Paul had done to the bitter end.

Is anyone among you in trouble? Let them pray. Is anyone happy? Let them sing songs of praise. Is anyone among you sick? Let them call the elders of the church to pray over them and anoint them with oil in the name of the Lord. And the prayer offered in faith will make the sick person well; the Lord will raise them up. If they have sinned, they will be forgiven. 16 Therefore confess your sins to each other and pray for each other so that you may be healed. The prayer of a righteous person is powerful and effective.

As testified by James,
Brother of Jesus

Chapter 10

Problems with the Public, Management, & the Team

It was once again time for the next epic's conclusion and the End-Of-The-Age, where the Triune God would return unto itself for revitalization and affirmation of the Great Plan from its individual Triad Godheads, which it had occupied for its limited Age-Event Time. This reunion was to reunite back into the sixty-plus dimensions the Father, the Son, and the Holy Ghost for another limited Age-Event Time, so that the Trinity could enjoy itself for another limited time, for it had been separated on its Great Plan of Holy Design for way too long.

The energy of the unification would be seismic on a universal scale, and even though the Three Godheads were separated by the different spectrum of dimensions, there was still fluidness between them as a whole. And when the Holy Spirit combined with the humans who accepted the Trinity as the creation of the universe, it became the Holy Ghost, who lived in man and reconnected his soul with Upper Paradise, from which it had been separated at the time of its human birth when sent into Fallen Eden, which was once known as Lower Paradise, with Satan as its measure.

Nothing in the universe could compare, as the three worlds coexisted, created at the same time, but would remain separated by the veils of the dimensions until the Father said it would no longer be in the Great Plan. The angels who praised and sang all day and night became silenced by the overwhelming reuniting chord-ship of the three Godheads melding into one again. It was like an infinite major chord harmonic from beginning to end, as if made up of three unique vibrating harmonics—like C, G, & E, all being played together in every possible octave—to ears who could hear all sounds throughout the universe in one multi-dimensional spectrum of space, energy, and time. It pieced every atom, every molecule, every force field, every heart, every thought, and every photon of light. It was what made the Godhead Supreme as the Creator of all time, wisdom, and creation, from the beginning and the end; the alpha and the omega; the life, truth, and manager of death; and the wisdom of the ages. None could or would ever be able to stand against the Godhead when it united into one single Triune Trinity Entity, where all things exist in thought, life, pre-life, death, and immortality, which rises above and conquers all.

Just as expected, the specter from the glow of the universe changed hues, as many stars exploded under the pressure of the harmonics colliding into one, the Holy Spirit piercing the veil between Upper Paradise and Lower Heaven, to meet with the Son and the Father, as the three united into one being. Christ had been given fourteen dimensions originally when He came down from Heaven to fulfill his sojourn on earth while living with the humans, but in Heaven he reigned over those below him with thirty-five dimensions. The Holy Spirit in Upper Paradise reigned over thirty-two dimensions in Upper and Lower Paradise, while God the Holy Father did not have a limited or measurable number of dimensions.

Like mercury, His dimensions were fluid and could be separated and reunited at any time without increasing or decreasing His power, strength, wisdom, or might. This was hard to fathom even for the angels and caretakers of the shrines to the Godheads in Heaven, as well as the greatest of all minds of all time, for it was not logical. But just as time is a fourth order geodesic and can be sent both forward and backward, according to the Trinity's will, the Great Plan was only moving forward, which gave them all a sense of direction until the Lord Father God changed His Great Plan at the time of His own preferred choice. Many times, people on earth would experience what they called a 'déjà vu experience' when the angels changed their time clocks for an instant to align with another encounter that would be in their future, or, called to witness in the past, would feel time moving backward or just slowing down.

When Christ was on earth, He ruled with His higher level fourteen dimensions. Much of it was representationally depicted and best sought out and explained by Leonardo De Vinci's drawing of the 'Vitruvian Man' living in the square box of Fallen Eden and also in the circle of Upper Paradise. The hidden secret of the dual meaning was the two-world difference, whether Man lived dimensionally outside of the 'Box of the Three Dimensions and Materialistic World,' honoring his creation and showing his center of existence as his umbilical cord, obtaining his life and soul from God, or whether Man lived dimensionally inside the 'Box of the Three Dimensions and Materialistic World,' showing his center of existence as his sex and genitals, which produced for him an extension of life without God, denying his soul separated from the One who created him from birth. The umbilical cord was the designed worldly input of human life, design, and immortality; while the genitals and urethra were an output, symbolizing the union of waste, biologic filtering, and the urges and pangs of procreation, like God Himself, draining him of his inner self and leaving him vulnerable to the faux expectation of the world itself.

God could have chosen to reverse the body lengths and proportions and given woman the upper body strength and height by the dominion in the ranked position of physicality and honorable dual-world status, but He did not. And the reason was to hold the keys to the bloodline link to the genes themselves who would carry the Holy Spirit later and be united with Christ Himself in a new human form. This new form was to be united with the Holy Spirit in a way that was different from the marriage between husband and wife, which allows sanctimonious union without involving the genitals of the world to be corrupted by the materialism that Satan often used to lead both Man and Woman astray.

The creation of physical genders and roles could have been made equal, but they were not. God does not make mistakes! This was done intentionally and with reason, just as the sun and moon were placed in perfect harmony to oversee the heating, cooling, washing, and protection of the earth and Lower Paradise throughout the Age of Fallen Earth until it would be restored back and merged in time with the Age of New Jerusalem. This was done deliberately by the Triune God in His Great Plan, making the female body—the wo-man—shorter and weaker from her waist up, not allowing her the growth she needed to gain access to the spiritual world of Heaven while on earth without her male husband leader as her soulmate to help her out of the box she was born in. This shortness to live in the box was inherently created and symbolized in the removal of one set of ribs, when she was created from Man's rib as Eve (in World I), to be Adam's helper (created in World I & World II originally), for the two of them were to enter into Paradise together as one un-cleaved soul, but then sin was allowed to enter into the Garden of Eden, and regardless of which half of the same flesh and soul Satan spoke to first, unity was deceived and the soul was torn apart.[205]

Da Vinci's effort to use World-I mathematics of World-I proportions in the World-I of three basic dimensions of height, length, and width represented 'Man', and not 'Wo-man,' represented Adam at the time of creation, which is the time he received his soul. In Evolution, man does not have a soul. He somehow evolves a body, but without a soul he is nothing more than a cow, eel, or butterfly, to live and die in the one world, never reaching the extra world created by the TTT (Triune, Triad, Trinity).

Wednesday morning came, less than ten hours since Johnnie's baptism. He felt the earth warm with the life-giving electrons sent by the sun as it turned and rolled around once more, as the night gave way to daytime. And he could also smell the bacon cooking downstairs, where Mamaw was making something delicious for her and Cojo to eat. He thought maybe on this day when he opened his eyes from sleep he would be able to see the world again, as he once had, with full color and living eyesight... but alas, this was not the case. The scales had not been removed from his eyes yet, and he was only allowed to see short small glimpses of Heaven and open Paradise when it was the will of the Lord. And that was not

[205] Genesis 3

today. But this did not dampen his spirit. He rose, got dressed, went out to where Mamaw was making breakfast, and sat down.

"It is a beautiful day out there today, isn't it, Mamaw," Johnnie said to Mamaw while her back was turned to him, cooking over the hot frying pan, which popped and sizzled from the six pieces bacon she had going (three for her and three for Cojo). For a moment she could not believe what she was hearing, almost fainting that those words were coming from Johnnie!

"Did I just hear you say, 'it is a beautiful day'?" she replied, trying to mask her surprise.

"Yep, Mamaw, you sure did!" Johnnie said.

Johnnie whistled at Cojo, who was eating near the washing machine, and Cojo immediately responded by coming to Johnnie and standing by his chair. Johnnie reached down and petted Cojo on his shoulder and gave him a scratch—which he had never done before—and it was quite enjoyable to both of them, that moment of sharing and bonding for the first time.

"I want to go in today and talk to Coach Barricks at the arena… can you take me?" Johnnie asked humbly.

Mamaw was still not sure what she was hearing. Could this actually be the change which she had been praying and waiting so patiently for?

"Today is my bridge day, SJ. I was going to Thelma's house in an hour and did not plan to be back until five or six tonight. How urgent is this?"

Instead of getting mad, as he usually did, Johnnie said, "That's okay. I can ask Coach Thornton, or even call Sonny to take me. It's not urgent, but I know I have to get up there and talk soon, before it's too late to mend some fences."

Wow, Mamaw thought to herself. This was really not like the Johnnie she knew yesterday. He really was different. It was a miracle, and now maybe her life could get back to normal, she thought to herself.

"Well, I think Mr. Abrams had a doctor's appointment today and was going to be there late," Mamaw said, "so I can drop you off, and then you can call me when you're done to pick you up. Would that suit you for today?"

"Sure, Mamaw, thank you… that would be great, and I would truly appreciate you doing that for me," Johnnie said.

"Holy Mother of Jesus," Mamaw muttered under her breath. "It is a miracle! I can't wait to see what happens now…." Johnnie was back in the ball game of life as a servant of the Lord, and this was really going to get interesting, what the Lord had in store for them both.

They both got dressed, and Johnnie went out and waited in the car until Mamaw found him sitting there all alone in the garage, waiting to leave.

"You are really in a hurry, I see," Mamaw said as she climbed in and opened the garage door with the remote control.

"I am not in a hurry, but God is, so we better not tarry unless you want to make him wait," Johnnie replied.

And with those words, Mamaw took Johnnie to the arena. When they arrived, she opened his car door and led him to the front door of the arena, so he could make his way inside. Unlike before, when she would just drop him off, this time she held him by his arm and showed him the way to the door, so he would not have any unnecessary struggles in his quest to do or say what he wanted to this day. Johnnie had put on his best suit, which he had not worn since his wedding day; and oddly enough, he had not even thought anymore about Charlotte since his baptism. That was in his past now, and he had been washed clean of the memories of pain that he associated with his betrayal. His mind was clean, and his heart pure, so no more bad thoughts would be pulling his down today, not even any rejection that he would get from the team if they saw him enter the locker room as has-been star.

Once inside the arena, Johnnie immediately went to Coach Barricks' office and sat down until he was called in to talk to him.

"Hi, Johnnie, how are you doing today?" Coach Barricks asked. "You are looking pretty sharp there… what's up, my friend?"

"I want to play again," Johnnie said bluntly.

"You… what?" Coach replied, with a highly astonished tone in his voice.

"I want to play again… well, actually God wants me to play again," Johnnie said in a slow but firm voice.

"Can you see again? Has your eyesight come back? Has there been some miracle I need to know about, because if you can see, you will play the next game!" Coach said to him, sort of jokingly.

"I don't need to see to play basketball… I only need to be able to shoot," Johnnie replied, "and I still have use of my hands and feet, so that makes me qualified to play again, according to my contract."

"You have to be kidding me, Johnnie. Mr. Silverman would not go for you suiting up again. This would be turned into a media joke if he ever put you on the court again!"

"Job did not think it was a joke when he had everything taken from him and he would not give up. I am going to pray for you and all my friends beginning now, for it is written that that when Job prayed for his friends, the Lord gave him twice as much as he had before," Johnnie said to him.

"You have me on that one, Johnnie, but I don't think Job was a basketball player making a living in front of the whole world."

"This is exactly what I am saying, Coach, and that is why I have to play again," Johnnie replied emphatically. "There are those who wonder what I will do as a blind man. Will I shout at nd curse God for what He has done to me? Never! We need more examples like Job, those who will not turn on God, not even when they have lost it all. I am being called to be that example, for my spot has been washed away and I am clean again, ready to start a new life relying on faith alone."

"That is a heap of faith, SJ, but I am not sure Mr. Silverman will agree," Coach replied.

"I want us to go talk to him right now," Johnnie said.

"Right now??"

"Yes, right now."

"How about a little coffee break, and let's talk a little more first before we go up."

"I don't need any coffee, and I am not in any sort of mood to wait," Johnnie told him.

"Ok, but before we do that, you have to do one thing for me," Coach said.

"What is that?" Johnnie asked.

"You will see here really quickly," Coach answered, leaning across his desk and pushing a button on his phone. His secretary answered on the speaker phone.

"How can I help you Mr. Barricks?" she asked.

"Would you please go get Tucker for me on the court right now and bring him to my office ASAP?" he said.

"Yes, sir," she replied.

Then there was silence again, as Johnnie sat and waited for Coach Barricks to say something. But Johnnie was content to just sit and wait… wait for the energy and courage to do what he about to do. After a few minutes, Tucker showed up, sweaty from a scrimmage going on between him and some of his second-string teammates.

"Well, hello, Spot-Man, great to see you!" Tucker said as he entered Coach Barricks' office.

"Hey there, Tuck… remember, I am no longer Spot. That was my past. You can call me SJ now. Thank you," Johnnie said.

"Okay, cool beans" Tucker said. "So, what do you need, Coach?"

"Johnnie is going with you out on the court to shoot a few baskets before he goes up to see Mr. Silverman." Coach said.

"He's what?" Tucker asked, confused.

"Please take Johnnie with you and give him a basketball… I want to see him shoot a few baskets today before he meets with Mr. Silverman."

"Ok, Coach," Tucker answered. "So, Johnnie, when was the last time you shot a ball?" Tucker asked him.

"Before my wreck," Johnnie replied quietly.

"Okay… interesting. Well, let's go and shoot some hoops," Tucker said. "I'll help you to the court."

He took Johnnie by the arm and led him back toward the door. They proceeded down the long hallway toward the court, past the team locker rooms, trainer offices, x-ray equipment, and mouth guard facilities on either side of the hall.

When they arrived to the court, Ziggie and a couple of his friends were there playing with assistant coach Malcolm Fehrueger. Coach Fehrueger was unrelenting in his conditioning. He often said that his team had never lost a game in the history of the franchise, but they sometimes just ran out of clock time every once in a while. He would have them run and run until they could run no more, and then he would have them keep running until their shoes began to come apart. If they could not run, then he would have them crawl like babies begging for mercy, or he would sit them on the bench at the beginning of the next game and give another player the chance at a starting position in the lineup. There were no egos on the Hurricane team because they never started the same five players in any given game. Johnnie was the only person with that privilege… before his wreck. And now he was going out onto the court where Coach Fehrueger was standing.

"Well, who do we have here?" Coach Fehr (as he was often called) asked, turning and stopping still in his tracks.

He blew his whistle and told those on the court to take a break. The others were in the game room watching a video of the Tarpons, who they 'Canes would be playing next season, with two newly drafted forwards and a traded center from the Argonauts.

"Coach Barricks sent us out here," Tucker replied. "He would like Johnnie to put a b-ball in his hands again and see how it feels."

"They all feel the same, Tucker, just like a fine woman made by God," Fehr said. He and Tucker both snickered at the reference.

"I don't need your pity, Coach Fehr, and I don't need your jokes," Johnnie responded. "I just want you to take me to the free-throw area and put my toes on the line."

Coach Barricks—having followed them to the court out of curiosity and respect for what Johnnie once was—was watching from the hallway.

Tucker leaned over and whispered in Johnnie's ear, "Would you prefer to leave your dress shoes on or take them off, because they have heels and that might throw you off."

"I'll leave them on, but could you help me remove my coat?" Johnnie asked humbly.

He could not see, but he could still hear the roar of the crowd that seemed to echo in his head every time he was in a gymnasium, no matter the size. It all went back to the days of Coach Thornton and middle school, where he would taunt the other players and they would taunt him back, and the game of tit-for-tat took shape in his soul of restlessness… but that was all gone. Johnnie was calm now. He dropped his coat onto the floor and stepped forward as Tucker took him to the free-throw line. A quick tug on his arm was enough to stop him, as if he were a horse with a bit in his mouth and the reins pulled tight by his rider.

"You have done this ten million times before, Johnnie. You know where the basket is. Ten feet high and fifteen feet long… that is the sweet spot."

"Don't use the word 'spot' around me, Tucker, please," Johnnie said.

"Sorry… forgot!" Tucker replied, as he handed him a ball.

Johnnie untucked his shirt and loosened his long silk blue-and-burgundy tie. He had a tie clip which held in still close to his shirt, but at the moment he was not focusing on his clothes.

"Tucker," Johnnie said, "can you move me back of forward, so my left foot is just about two inches behind the line? And I need to be just left of center, a couple of inches too, please."

Tucker wondered to himself about Johnnie's strange request, because he always lined up square, like his middle school coach had taught him to do. Coach Thornton had tweaked Johnnie's stance just enough to get his shot perfect, and this is where Johnnie wanted to stand.

At this point, Coach Barricks was getting bored and needed to take a phone call, but still he waited another minute. Johnnie then began to bounce the ball several times—one, two, three, four (just the number Mamaw had told him to do, since no one would ever be the first three. And then he let the ball go with a gentle finger roll and back spin that looked as natural as if he had done it yesterday.

The ball hit the front of the rim and bounced off.

Coach Barricks looked at Coach Fehrueger and gave him a thumbs-down sign, indicating to get Johnnie off of the court ASAP.

"Ok, Johnnie, you've had your chance," Coach Fehr said.

"I am not finished yet," Johnnie said, "and I don't take orders from you anymore… only from God. And I am staying until I hit ten in a row."

Coach Fehr was a little taken aback by his response.

"We are going to need this space for a scrimmage in a minute," he told Johnnie. "Do you want us to play around you?"

"I still have a contract with the 'Canes, and I plan to keep it, so don't try to move me off this court unless you think you can, and really I wouldn't try that if I were you," Johnnie said.

Tucker was also taken aback, but he knew Johnnie's will, and if Johnnie really wanted to stay and shoot baskets, there was no one except a full-blown British Commando team that was going to remove him from the court this day.

Tucker handed Johnnie another ball.

"Your shot landed at just about seven o'clock," he said to Johnnie, continuing, "so you might try to push it right and just a little longer this time."

That meant a little more finger-roll to Johnnie, just a tad, and that is what he did. This time Johnnie again bounced the ball four times—one, two, three, and four—and took a deep breath, and then, right before exhaling, he let the ball go. There was silence for two seconds as Johnnie counted in his head—thousand one, thousand two—and then he heard the net swish.

"Ha!" Johnnie uttered.

"How did it feel?" Tucker asked.

"Like I was just lifted out of my grave," Johnnie said. "Give me another ball…"

Coach Fehr handed his ball to Tucker, who handed it to Johnnie. Johnnie once again bounced the ball four times, took another shot, and once again hit nothing but net again.

Coach Barricks was still watching from afar, and he could see the life coming back into his friend Johnnie, who would always be 'Spot" to him. A lump collected in his throat and tears came over his eyes. Everything seemed to be almost like it used to be… except this was not reality; it was all a mirage. Johnnie was blind, and it could never be as it had been.

"Give me another ball, Tuck," Johnnie said, reaching out his big hand and holding it in front of where Tucker had just been standing.

"We are all out of balls," Coach Fehr replied. He put his hand across Tucker's chest to keep him from moving to get another.

"I am not finished… I have eight more to make before I leave, and this won't take long. I have to prove something to myself!" Johnnie began speaking louder, almost shouting.

Coach Barricks had made his way across the court and came up to Johnnie. He handed him a ball.

"Do you think you can dunk this one?" he asked Johnnie.

There was long pause as all four of them stood there momentarily in silence.

"Yes, I can, Coach," he said.

"Then let me see you do it!" Coach Barricks said.

On those words of inspiration and challenge, Johnnie bounced the ball four times and took three mighty 'mother may I' steps—just like he used to do with a blindfold on in high school—and leapt into the air. Feeling for the rim with his left hand, he shoved the ball though the hoop with his right hand and hung on the rim for just a second, feeling the exuberance he used to feel when he played the game he so loved. He had life back in his soul, and now he could not be stopped by Heaven or Hell or even the two combined, if he had any say in his future.

"Good job, Johnnie!" Coach Barricks said to him. "Be back here tomorrow morning at 8 a.m."

Then Coach turned, leaving the three of them standing there dumbfounded. He went back to his office and immediately called Andy, his employer and also his best friend, to share an idea he had.

"Mr. Silverman, do you have time to meet me for a fishing trip tonight?" he said to Andy with a lump in his throat. "This is important. We need talk."

He then hung up the phone, stuck by the realization that their next basketball season was going to be like no other the NBA had ever seen... for Johnnie, for the players in the league, and for the fans. It was going to be a show with a great finale.

After that, Coach called Sonny to get the company choppers ready for the meeting that night, even though storms were brewing on the horizon.

It was 2 p.m. on September 10, 2001, when Sonny got a phone call from Coach Barracks.

"I want to go fishing tonight. Please meet me at the hanger at midnight, Sonny, to pick me up… it's going to be a long night." Then, abruptly, Coach hung up.

Sonny sat there for a moment with the phone in his hand, confused by Coach's very short, impersonal, and non-informative message.

"Okay, so you now have that dazed and stunned look on your face again, Sonny-Honey," Rosanne said to him as he finally set down the phone in the kitchen. "What is your premonition this time? Was that Coach calling again wanting you to do something strange?" she asked while making his favorite organic lentil-and-potato soup for dinner, with her favorite cottage cheese with strawberry Jell-O pudding for dessert.

"Yes, dear," Sonny answered. "I'm guessing the guys want to go out to the oil platform tonight to discuss business again," Sonny replied.

"Did he say what about?" his wife asked. "I am curious. Did you he give you any clues?"

"No, they never do, and I won't know anything when I get there either. My job is to stay in the chopper and sleep if I need to, until they are ready to come back. I can tell you that much. They said everything else is secret."

"Yeah, I bet! You're not taking a bunch of hookers out there for an oil-rig orgy, are you?" she teased him.

"I will definitely be taking you along, if that is ever the case Rosie, but doesn't look like it's in the cards. Daisy always carries her .357 S&W with her and she knows how to use it, so there would be no survivors if something like that ever happened… you know that, right?"

"Yeah, and we would both push you all over and feed you to the sharks afterwards, sell the team, and live high and mighty till kingdom comes… you know that, don't you, Sweetheart?"

"You know I do, Babe, you know I do!" Sonny said, enjoying their teasing in that moment of marital bliss and total transparency, as they always did with each other.

"I need to catch a few Z's before I have to get up and meet him. I'm going to watch a little TV and then sleep for three hours. I'll set my alarm for 7:30 and then we can eat some dinner together before I have to head out, okay?"

"Well, I am coming with you," Rosanne said. She was no fool and she knew the world could be cold and cruel sometimes, and you never knew when a loved one might leave and never come back because of an accident or something strange happening. She had already lost a sister in a car accident and an aunt she loved to cancer. Roseanne was well familiar with suffering, and she wanted to take the opportunity to show her husband some loving before he went out the door on an unknown trip over the ocean in the middle of the night.

"Someone needs to protect you from the monsters under the bed, and I know just the outfit to wear to scare them off…"she said to her husband, and the both laughed and headed to the bedroom.

About an hour had gone by, when Sonny turned on the television to rest. He started flipping through all the channels, looking for something to fall asleep to. He stopped on a documentary made way back in the 1960's. It was black-and-white video footage showing four young girls looking at the sky and supposedly talking to Mary the Mother of Jesus in a trance. This sparked Sonny's interest, since he was not very religious after his tour in Vietnam and what he was called to do there.

Roseanne had just gone back into the other room to check on her cooking, when she heard Sonny call out to her.

"Hey, Rosie... *Sweetheart, come see this*!" he called to her. "This is really interesting."

The story was quite revealing, with the actual video footage, and made clear the undeniable connection between World I and World II, as the archangel St. Michael, Mary, and the four girls carried on direct conversations, as if they were all in the same dimension. This all happened in northern Spain in the Pena Sangra mountain range in a small village called San Sebastian de Garabandal between 1961 and 1965.

Sonny had read the Bible and knew about this sort of stuff, and this was similar to—but also somewhat different from—when the angel Gabriel came to Mary and told her a child would be born to her—the Son of the Most High—to whom the Lord would give him the throne of David, and who would rule over the descendants of Jacob (i.e. Israel) forever.[206] How could this be? Things like this did not happen in modern times. Something was a bit strange about the whole documentary, and it sent an uneasy feeling through Sonny as he watched. When the show was almost over, he saw a most

[206] Luke 1: 30-33

disturbing quote on the screen, a second message Mary had given to just one of the girls, the principal visionary.

'As my Message of the 18th of October has not been complied with,' Mary's message said, 'and as it has not been made known to the world, I am telling you that this is the last one. Previously, the cup was filling; now, it is brimming over. Many priests are following the road to perdition, and with them they are taking many more souls. Ever less importance is being given to the Holy Eucharist. We should turn the wrath of God away from us by our own efforts. If you ask His forgiveness with a sincere heart, He will pardon you. I, your Mother, through the intercession of St. Michael the Archangel, wish to tell you that you should make amends. You are now being given the last warnings. I love you very much, and I do not want your condemnation. Ask us sincerely and we shall grant your plea. You must make more sacrifices. Reflect on the Passion of Jesus.'[207]

A previous message had caused particular controversy when it was revealed that Conchita had actually written 'many cardinals, many bishops, and many priests are following the road to perdition.' She was asked many times to verify this information. The young woman stated many times that Mary stressed the importance of the priesthood, and focused attention on priests above others.[208]

Besides the two 'messages,' the visionaries forecast a 'warning', a 'miracle,' and a 'punishment' (if people would not correct their ways). The warning was described as a momentary stopping of time around the world, with all people then seeing the spiritual condition of their souls and how they should amend their

[207] 221 Garabandal, Spain - June 18, 1965

[208] 221 Garabandal, Spain - June 19, 1962

ways. Within a year of the warning, a miracle would take place, which would leave a permanent sign in Garabandal, which would be able to be seen and photographed, but not touched. The 'miracle' would occur between March and May. The 'punishment,' or 'chastisement,' would be conditional upon how humankind reacted to the preceding 'warning' and 'miracle.'

In addition to the predicted events, devotees believed a 'small' miracle took place in the early morning hours of July 19, 1961. A photo, reproduced in all books and websites on Garabandal, was said to be taken from a film in which a Holy Communion wafer materialized in Conchita's open mouth, supposedly put there by an angel. The girls often claimed that an angel gave them Communion, and they were frequently seen going through the motions of receiving the Eucharist.[209]

In January 1966, Conchita was called to the Vatican for an interview with Cardinal Ottaviani, Pro-Prefect of the Congregation for the Sacred Doctrine of the Faith. In February 1968, Conchita again went to Rome, to meet with Cardinal Francis Seper.

Sonny was a faithful man in his heart and tried to do as instructed, but sometimes he got sidetracked. He was there at the hanger as instructed at midnight sharp, while Coach Barricks was outside waiting for him to arrive.

---

[209] https://www.youtube.com/watch?v=ws76ver8J8k

"Sorry, Coach, I should have been here earlier to get the bird warmed up," Sonny said.

"What caused the delay… a big bag flat tire right when you left the house?" Coach never liked excuses from his players and always led with a far-reaching question to put the question in perspective.

"No, Coach, I lay down to rest a little before coming over and then could not wake up. I had a crazy dream. It was really ridiculous. Let's get in the air and maybe I can fill you in."

"Okay, can't wait." Coach just shook his head in sort of disgust. He did not want to explain to Mr. Silverman why he was late when he had such a big plan to tell him.

While they were flying out, Sonny had mental tapes of the Garabandal story running through his mind, repeating over and over again. Coach did not ask again why he was late, because he was thinking about how he was going to ask Mr. Silverman to put Johnnie back into his uniform and have him sit on the bench this coming season to help inspire the team to win another championship. This was 'strike one' for Sonny—though he did not know it yet—because Coach was a timely person and hated being late more than losing a competitive game. 'Everything is about having a positive attitude in life," he would tell his players, "and being late is disrespectful, inexcusable, and a sign of a loser.' Coach Barricks lived by this code and expected every else to as well.

When they arrived at the oil rig, Mr. Silverman was in his usual 'spot,' thinking about the one who used to be called 'Spot,' and wondering how he was going to pay off the massive short-term loans he had made to increase the size of the arena, which had always been totally filled when Johnnie was playing, but since the car wreck was usually over half empty.

"Hi, Andy… caught anything tonight yet?" Coach asked as he walked over from the chopper after it had landed on the bullseye tarmac.

"Yes, doing quite well tonight, actually," Andy replied. "I've caught several king mackerel, couple of nice ling, probably twenty red snapper, and one lonely barracuda!"

"Cool beans," Coach said. "Great night, huh? You can even see the Milky Way Galaxy. It is just gorgeous out here. I always feel closer to God under the stars, away from civilization."

"Me too," Andy said. "Now, what is so urgent that we needed to come out on short notice?"

"It's Johnnie…" Coach answered, somewhat hesitantly. "He wants to be a part of the team again. Actually, he is demanding it, not asking it. He wants to suit up."

Andy was silent for a moment, and just then he felt something tugging on the end of his line.

"I have something again, let's see what it is," Andy said, avoiding Coach's last comment.

He began to reel up the two hundred feet of 80-lb line on his short, stubby ocean pole. Sure enough, he had caught another mackerel.

"Daisy is going to love me tomorrow!" Andy exclaimed. "She loves to eat these things but hates cleaning them. She'll probably take them to the fish house by the ship channel and get them to fillet and freeze them, but I don't care—I just love catching them!"

He grabbed his gaff and Hook-Out pliers and then put the fish into a big oversized ice chest. Then he finally acknowledged what Coach Barricks had just revealed about Johnnie.

"So, Coach, you say Johnnie wants to be on the team again. Now, how do we do that with a one-hundred-percent-blind man? Maybe we should we make him our mascot? We could change our name from the Hurricanes to the 'Blues Brothers'."

"I am serious Andy, we have a problem," Coach said. "But… I think we can turn this sour lemon into sweet lemonade."

"Well… he is still acting like a horse's butt, isn't he?" Andy asked.

"No, Andy. He is changed. He is different. He isn't the jerk he used to be," Coach said gently. "And you're not going to believe this, but he came in today and shot free throws… and *made them*! And he dunked the ball, too! And all in a three-piece suit," Coach finished incredulously.

"So how is that going to win us more games?" Andy asked.

"Well, I am going to use him in practice as the standard of measure," Coach replied.

"And how are you going to do that?" Andy continued his questioning.

"I am going to push them all to perfection, using Johnnie as the tool."

"Okay, so maybe you can do that. But I assure you: he is not going to like being used, in any way, shape, or form," Andy said.

"I need you to leave that up to me," Coach said. "If things go right, you will have a full arena by the second home game, and you will have that extra money you need to refinance and not go broke!" Coach finished.

"You know me well, Coach. 'The Lord giveth and the Lord taketh away,' so I am just along for the ride," Andy clarified. "But on the other hand… I am curious what miracle you can pull out of your hat this time, so let's do it! But on one condition…" Mr. Silverman warned.

"What is that, Mr. Silverman?" Coach asked.

"I am not sure yet, but I will tell you later. Something tells me there is a hook here that I am unaware of, so I reserve the right to pull out if I smell something bad in the cooking of all this."

"Okay, agreed," Coach replied. "I will get on it first thing when we get back. I have a plan I think you will like."

By this time the sun was coming up, and it was time to get back.

When Sonny got home and went inside, he looked for Rosanne, who always saw his car drive up and met him at the door. It was silent this time. Rosanne was nowhere to be found.

"Rosie, Sweetie, where are you?" Sonny playfully called his wife. When he opened the door to the bathroom, he found her holding onto the vanity with both hands, sobbing uncontrollably over the sink. The sight almost put Sonny into shock. He had never seen her like this.

"Has someone died??" he asked with alarm.

"No… I don't know… yes," she answered.

Her makeup was smeared all over her face from weeping, and she was clearly very shaken up, frightened. She grabbed his hand and dragged him over to the television.

"Look at this!" she said. "Someone has run their plane into the World Trade Tower and it's on fire! All these people are trying to get out and they are trapped! They need someone to help them. I don't know what to do," she wailed, beginning once again to weep uncontrollably.

Roseanne sank down onto the couch and Sonny sat down beside her, focusing incredulously on all the panic and pandemonium he saw on the television. It was mad chaos, and no one seemed to understand what was happening. And then—right before his eyes—he watched as another plane hit the second tower.

"Oh my God," Sonny said. "Another plane just hit the other tower. What, for the love of Jesus, is going on here?"

Rosanne looked up, by now a complete basket case, crying incessantly and struggling to just stay in the room. She wanted to run out the door and leave, but did not really know where she would even go.

"We have to go now!" she yelled.

But Sonny grabbed her by the arms and held her tight, anchoring her and whispering into her ear that everything was going to be all right. She thought America was under assault by a foreign country and this was the beginning of World War III. She began to struggle against Sonny's grip, as if in a panic attack, thinking maybe the house was on fire.

"Everything is going to be all right, Honey," Sonny said to her in soothing tones. "We are far away, almost two thousand miles from New York. Let's just take a breath and think about this for a moment."

Roseanne began to take deep breaths, trying to calm herself down. After a moment, they both sat back down on the couch, where she immediately slumped in exhaustion and fell asleep. Sonny's eyes stayed glued on the television, watching incredulously as the events continued to unfold.

Then his phone rang. It is Coach Barricks.

"Sonny, Mr. Silverman wants to have a meeting at the arena this morning. Can you make it?" Coach asked.

"Right now?! Have you looked on the television and seen what is going on?" Sonny asked. "I think we are under invasion! I am having flashbacks of Saigon during our last days there."

"Yes, *right now…* Mr. Silverman wants to talk," Coach responded.

"Okay, but I have to bring my wife. She can't stay here alone. She is too upset for me to leave her. I couldn't do that to her," Sonny insisted.

"Then go ahead and bring her. I will see you in an hour at Mr. Silverman's office."

Then Coach Barricks hung up.

Sonny helped Rosanne out to the car. She sat shivering with fear. Everything felt surreal to Sonny as he drove to downtown Houston. He kept glancing overhead to see if any jetliners might be headed into any buildings on the skyline. There seemed to be a lot of commotion on the roadways, like people were bustling to get somewhere. Those whose faces he could see seemed to be focused on contacting loved ones and figuring out what to do next. The prevailing mood seemed to be panic combined with shock.

When Sonny and Rosanne arrived at the arena, the backdoor—which was usually locked—was open, so they walked right in. The place was vacant, and they took the elevator to the third floor, where Mr. Silverman's office was located. When they walked in, Coach Barricks was there, along with Mr. Silverman and Daisy, all huddled around the television, watching the events in New York City unfold. Mamaw was there as well, as was Johnnie.

A meeting had been set up to visit with Johnnie about his new position in the company (i.e. as a member of the traveling squad), but so much had happened since they had gotten back from the evening trip that things were chaotic now, to say the least. Johnnie could not see the television, so Daisy was describing the rescue operations to him. While Sonny and Rosanne were driving over, both towers had collapsed, and many were feared dead in this unbelievable catastrophe.

A speaker for the President of the United States was on every channel. She was stating that the President had been airlifted onto a plane and was in contact with his military generals on the ground, surveying the manifold events going on in the country, one of which was the US Pentagon being hit. This attack was now was being considered an act of military war.

Rosanne, who could barely see due to her macular degeneration, had been crying hard all morning. And Sonny felt like he needed to go enlist in the military again, because his country was going into WW III.

Andy had a more cool and collected head than the others, and he kept suggesting the need to let some time go by and find out what was really going on before jumping to conclusions.

Mamaw thought that maybe someone was mad at the stock market because they lost a lot of money and just wanted to destroy the system of individuals who worked for institutions that were parasites on society.

“Those people have no souls or hearts,” she said, referring to the stock market CEOs, “so maybe this is a wakeup call for them to be more human, and less like robotic money-grabbing machines.

They should feel some of the pain they have caused at the lowest levels. To them it's all about the money at the end of the day, but there ain't no hearses with big or small luggage racks, so everything they have accumulated is just borrowed anyway! Nothing belongs to them, not even the underwear they have on! Even those will rot away, just like the caskets their bones are put in!"

Johnnie just sat and groaned. He wanted to talk about his new-found desire to be a part of the team, but this was not the right time.

"Sonny, glad you're here. I need to you to take everyone here down to the hanger and get them out of town," Mr. Silverman said to him.

"Take them where?" Sonny asked, confused.

"North to Tyler… to Mamaw's old house."

"Tyler?" he stood motionless, shaking his head.

"Yes, Tyler… that is the maximum range for the choppers we have. No one will be able to take a plane anywhere. The airports are shut down. You can still fly out of Houston, and I want Daisy to be safe. Tyler is about as safe as it gets. I will call you when you get there, so get going! I'll be in touch."

"I am staying," Johnnie responded resolutely.

"No, you are leaving too," Mamaw said, and Mr. Silverman nodded in agreement.

"I refuse to live in fear anymore," Johnnie declared. "I am not leaving, and you cannot make me go. I am staying here with my boss. It will be okay. He needs someone to talk to anyway, and sometime I actually like his bad jokes."

Johnnie was adding some humor at a very tense moment, but he was also just living his faith: the Bible said not to worry, so that is what he was doing… fearlessly living the life he had been called to live.

Sonny still had the visions of Garabandal running though his head and was wondering if perhaps this was the warning the girls had spoken of: the beginning of the end. Was everyone going to die or be taken up in a single rapture, while he would be left behind? What if that happened while he was flying to Tyler? Would he look around and suddenly see no one left in the chopper with him? This thought scared him to death and causing him to do some real soul searching. Maybe he was not really the center of the universe he thought he was…?

The group departed very quickly, leaving Johnnie and Andy there alone together.

"What are you so afraid of, Mr. Silverman?" Johnnie asked, sensing his fear.

"I am not afraid," Andy replied, "but I do believe I am called to take care of my loved ones, and that is why I am sending Daisy out of town the best way I know how, in the hands of good people like Coach Barricks and Sonny. They will take care of her if something should happen to me… or rather us, now."

"And what might that be, Mr. Silverman?"

"Not sure… and that is the scary part… the unknown," he answered hesitantly.

"You are talking to a blind man who met God on his death bed," Johnnie reminded Andy. "I was pronounced dead and brought back to life just like Lazarus. So, I have to die twice, which is once more than you have to, Mr. Silverman… and I am not afraid. Once you have been where I have been, you will not have fear anymore either. Or I don't think you will, anyway. I can only speak for myself, and I am not afraid. I met the angel Gideon, and he assured me this is not the end of the world. I am to play basketball again, so that means we at least have one more season," Johnnie said, beginning to laugh hysterically. "At least one more season," he said, "unless I misinterpreted… maybe I am supposed to play basketball in Heaven. That is a wild thought. I wonder which team I would be on…will it be an all-white team or an all-black team?"

Johnnie continued to laugh, as if the events in New York were a minor event in the history of the world, but Andy was not amused as he saw on the television the faces of those being led out of the rubble. They looked ghostly and in shock, and all he could do was empathize with the children who were now orphans due to this tragic event, this evil plan to take vengeance on God's green earth.

"Well, Johnnie, guess what? You are going to play again for the Hurricanes again and wear number four again… Coach and I have decided. Coach Barricks believes your eyesight will return, but I am not so sure. He wants you to be ready, willing, and able when the time comes. So you will begin practicing with the team again next week… assuming the earth does not come to an end before then, and the skies don't come crashing down on us," Mr. Silverman said matter-of-factly.

"That will not happen, I can assure you. This old earth is going to keep spinning. God is in control, not us. And we can rest in that peace until Jesus comes again to take us home."

"How do you know that for sure?" Andy asked.

"The Good Book says so," Johnnie replied.

The two of them sat for a while longer in silence before getting up and going to Andy's house, where they would spend the next few days discussing religion, politics, race, and theology. None of these were Johnnie's strongest subjects, buy Mr. Silverman listened intently to him as if he had a PhD in all of them. It was sort of like talking to someone who could not move if he wanted to and could not be moved if he needed to be. Johnnie kept repeating the phrase 'this will all pass like water under a bridge,' and he was right… but without a lot of soul searching by everyone he knew and had relationships with, even his loyal followers, for many years to come.

Johnnie spent at least an hour in prayer each day of his life from that day on, and Andy also followed him in the calling. Andy's prayer time was not as consistent or deep, but it was all the same, for they both shared in the blessing of peace—which they both immensely enjoyed and benefited from the rest of their days on earth.

Elijah was a human being, even as we are. He prayed earnestly that it would not rain, and it did not rain on the land for three-and-a-half years. Again he prayed, and the heavens gave its rain, and the earth produced its crops.

As Testified by James,
Brother of Jesus
Chapter 5:17-18

Chapter 11

Johnnie Leads by Example with Hard Work

The horror of the September 11, 2001, attack was still hanging in the air when the Hurricanes resumed their basketball practice the following week.

(The word 'September' comes from the Latin (i.e. Roman) root word of 'septem' meaning '7th.' The septem month, which was part of the Roman calendar, was initially named as the seventh month because the Roman New Year began in March, and September was the Roman seventh month, and not the ninth as it is today in the Gregorian Judeo-Christian calendar [named by Pope Gregory, who put in leap year to correct the actual days for the earth to orbit the sun annually]. Johnnie knew it was no coincidence that the United States was attacked in September (the septem month). An angel had told Johnnie not to fear this battle, because this chapter in the world was going to be nearly a repeat of a similar battle of forces, like the Battle of Actium between Octavian, the first dictator of the Republic of Rome, and the combined forces of Mark Antony and Cleopatra on Septem 2, 31 BC. The Senate had lost control of the will of the people and had handed its power over to the rulers of the government, which became a long bloody struggle to gain its voting powers back, which it never should had relinquished; but so are the poor decisions of mankind that haunt his existence and make him dependent on God to show him the light and direct his path along a perilous journey involving Satan and the angels in his midst, which he can never foresee, foretell, or forewarn.)

Coach Barricks had a surprise for Johnnie, one he would never have guessed in a million years. He assembled his team again before bringing Johnnie out from a backroom, where he and Tucker were waiting. Tucker had brought him into the arena through a side door. Johnnie was already in his practice outfit. Tucker had had him a new jersey made with the number ‘4’ on it, and above the number was not the name ‘Spot’ anymore but rather the initials ‘SJ.’ This was a new life for Johnnie in a new world of basketball without sight, a new beginning, a new chapter in is life. And it was best to leave his past behind him and arrive on the court without any expectations, just as he had done as a new draftee fresh out of high school.

“The events of last week have made us all think about a lot of things recently… at least I have, and I bet you all have too,” Coach Barricks began addressing his team. “I know now I need to put value on things like relationships, increase my faith, and encourage others to do the same, because life is too short to chase after things which are fleeting. This year is going to be different for the Hurricanes. In fact, it is going to be different for the NBA! We are going to show the world that we do not exclude based on life events, and our door is always open if someone wants to try out for the team. Today we have a new walk-on player who wants to try out for the team. Mr. Silverman and I have both agreed this would be a good thing to do, so I want you all to meet the person I am talking about…”

At this, he motioned to Tucker, who had been waiting by a back door to the court floor to enter. Tucker pushed open the door and emerged with Johnnie from the shadows of the backroom. There was a brief moment of silence, for none of the players knew if this was a joke or not. But then Tucker began to clap and chant "SJ, SJ, SJ…"

No one knew what this meant, but they all started to do the same thing, and Johnnie held up both hands in the victory sign, with his fists pointed to the air. Then the team erupted in applause as Johnnie walked forward onto the court. Without hesitation, the team he so loved and admired surrounded him and started pushing him around in typical victory fashion. This went on for a couple of minutes, until finally Coach Barricks blew his whistle to get them back to work on the court.

"I need my first team 'alpha' and second team 'beta' to go with Coach Fehrueger," Barricks said. "Johnnie and Tucker, you two will come with me."

So Tucker grabbed Johnnie by the left arm and led him over to the side baskets, off the main court.

"Johnnie," Coach began, "Tucker and I have a surprise for you. He handed a basketball to Tucker and told him to shoot the ball in the basket they were standing under. Tucker did what Coach asked. He took the ball and reached up and did a small push shot into the ring off of the back board. When the ball went through the net, a door chime attached to the backboard sounded.

"What was that?" Johnnie asked.

"It is your new best friend, Johnnie... Tucker and I call her 'Samantha.' The device talks to you every time you shoot and make your basket, letting you know with a door chime. Tucker has a nerdy cousin who is an IT geek. We gave him the idea and he figured out how to do it for us over the past week. Tucker is getting a patent on it now so maybe he won't have to play basketball the rest of his life to support his wife. Now you will know every time you make your basket from anywhere on the court, even in the dark." Coach said.

"Please dispense with the jokes, Coach… I got the idea," Johnnie came back at him.

"It has a laser attached to the rim that, when activated, lets you know you made the shot. Tucker, move Johnnie over there to the free-throw line, and let's see this invention in action," Coach said.

"Hmmm, I already know how to make free-throws, Coach," Johnnie said.

"We all know that, but we want you to be able to make a shot from anywhere on the court. If you are going to be a part of the team again, you need to figure this out, and Samantha is going to be your new eyes."

"Can we at least call her 'Sam'?" Johnnie chuckled. "You know, I don't need any more women in my life anymore… I am over that for a while… most likely forever!"

"Johnnie, you can call the darn gismo anything you want to… but just don't call it 'Daisy' or the name of any wife or girlfriend related to the team. And not hole, whore, or anything vulgar like that, either," Coach replied.

"*Sam* is fine, Coach... I am not like that anymore. You know I am reborn and follow my Lord. He demands even higher standards than I used to have, so I hear your message loud and clear! Now let's see if Samantha… I mean Sam… is going to sing to me," Johnnie replied.

The Holy Spirit was looking down on Lower Paradise and reflecting on the great battles of the Levant. Many had come and gone. And many were more to come and go, and in each time the sons of Ishmael would aggress and take action against the sons of Isaac, though they would never hold a long victory or even gain a foot in the struggle to unseat the ancestors of half-brothers from their inheritance. The sons of Isaac would always improve in strength after each struggle, being mightier is wisdom each time, and the result being the spread of the Gospel of Christianity to even more Jewish bloodlines from the Twelve Tribes of Israel, which had morphed with time into the sanguine bloodlines of the True Believers of the Twelve Tribes of Jesus. These worldly battles between the two groups grew and existed as Jesus instructed, to show the world how to suffer well in the name of Christ, for it was written in the scriptures: *We know that in all things God works for the good of those who love him, who have been called according to his purpose.*[210]

Tucker took Johnnie by the arm and led him out onto the court toward one side, because Coach had told him what to do before

[210] Romans 8:28

the day started. He walked Johnnie over to the top of the key (the center of the three-point line), which was even farther out than the free-throw line. Once again: for a blind man, this seemed impossible, but not for someone who had once boasted in high school that he could do it in his sleep.

"Coach wants you to be able to make your next shot from here," Tucker said to Johnnie, continuing, "It's a straight-up shot, ya' know… and you can use the backboard if you want to. I don't need to tell you it is another eight feet and nine inches farther. After you get to where you can make it ten times in a row, he said you and I will be playing horse, and only one of us will be staying on the team. I am not sure if he was joking or not, but that is what he said."

"The Coach kids a lot! Why would Coach even think about keeping a blind person on the roster when he has an All-American guard like you who can make points? That is crazy and makes no sense to me, but it is God's will, I know, so hand me a ball and tell me where it goes, okay? I gotta know if I can still hit the rim, because I have not done this is soooo long." Johnnie said to him, giving him a quirky grin.

He bounced the ball four times on the wooden floor below his feet, and coiled, leaning back like a trebuchet releasing the ball with a high arc that fell just short of hitting the rim.

Now Tucker—acting like an artillery scout in an army battlefield giving reports to the gunners who were firing the canons—said, "You were straight on that shot but about a foot short, Johnnie."

Just then Tucker looked over at the rest of the team, because the court had gone silent. Everyone was just standing there as if frozen in time. Then Johnnie reared his arms and shoulders back and bounced the ball four times in his rhythmic pattern, and let his payload go once again in trebuchet fashion, and this time it hit its mark! The doorbell climbed and a red light and buzzer went off at the same time, which they had installed since the last session. The rest of the team witnessed the new miracle forming in the 'Canes' arena, and the all cheered. And once again Johnnie got the biggest kick out of hitting a shot he was not supposed to make, giving him that edge he needed to survive.

Slightly proud and cocky for a moment, Johnnie said, "I bet I can make it as a bank shot next!"

Tucker watched the old Spot determination to never give up come back into Johnnie, and he laughed to himself. He loved the old Johnnie who loved to take chances and taunt the crowds and other teams relentlessly, but Coach had told him what to say when that ol' fake god Pandora started to come out of the box again…

"Okay now, you pecker-head, let's not get too cocky, or Coach will come over here and fire both of us, ya' know... Just stay on point and let's get this next key shot down so we can both graduate the next one. I think it is going to take you at least a week to get this one down!"

Johnnie flipped the ball over to Tucker, slightly amused but not offended.

"Okay," Johnnie taunted back, "let's see you if can make it too, then, whenever I make it in, Tucker, you pecker-head." Johnnie laughed at his own joke.

"Jack it up, Tuck'!" Johnnie said, so Tucker looked at the basket, took a few bounces, and then made a back-shot that went in, so everyone could hear the chime and see the red light go off.

"You cheated, brother!" Johnnie called out. "I heard it hit the backboard. This is no fair. I wanted you to swish it like I did. You got to do it the right way," Johnnie insisted.

"There are always two ways to do things, Johnnie, and they are both equal. And one thing I have found out through much of my own suffering and walk is that life is not always fair, my friend. We win some, and we lose some… so we had better leave this one alone, and let's shoot about fifty more before I take you home, and you have to deal with Mamaw!" Tucker laughed. "If you can make it twenty times today, that will be great, and we can work on perfection tomorrow."

"Maybe for you, Tuck, that works, but 'Sir John' never loses… it is not my nature," Johnnie replied. "Well, what? I mean, God never loses! And together, all this world, all this court, all this life *He* has given us… even this basketball! I know were all made by Him. Basketball used to be MY GAME, but in reality, basketball is HIS GAME, and so are whatever other games people are playing. I think maybe they have one more lesson to learn like I did."

That evening back at home, Mamaw wanted to know how Johnnie was coming along with his process of returning back to the world and coping with his disability. She began gently fishing for information… anything other than a grunt or snort at the dinner table as he downed his second helping of stew and black-eyed peas.

"What did you do at the arena today?" she asked.

Johnnie inhaled and then exhaled slowly, and said, "I shot some baskets."

"That's some cool beans, son," she replied. Mamaw did not want to go any further with the questioning in case it might stir an angry response, but Johnnie was over those days. So, Johnnie became forthcoming with his ideas and position on the matter.

"Coach Barricks says he wants to keep me on the team as a blind man, at my request of course… pretty funny, isn't it?"

"Well, did you make any baskets?" Mamaw asked.

"I made eight out of ten with Tucker telling me what I needed to change, and fifteen out of forty without any help. That was worse than in middle school. I hated shooting and not knowing what I did wrong. And Tucker would not tell me, other than try again."

"Sounds like a pretty normal basketball practice, if you ask me," Mamaw said.

"Not to me… he just wants me to suffer, I think. He would not help when I asked him."

"I think that happens a lot in life to all of us: we ask someone to help us but we don't get the response we wanted… so what are you going to do? Sit and mope around tomorrow or try harder."

"I am blind Mamaw, don't you understand?!" Johnnie spouted out.

"Johnnie, everyone has something… You can either sit and feel sorry for yourself and be just another a victim in life, or you can give it to God, move on, and be what He wants you to be, which is someone who is useful to Him, not yourself. You can get to Heaven and when asked what you did for Him say, *Well I sat around all day feeling sorry for myself.* Now, that is not an answer that goes very far, so give it to God and then move on! You can't do anything about the past—it is over and done, so put a stake in it and get over your victim mentality. You have to play the cards you are dealt, and no one else's."

Johnnie hit his fists on the table, and his heavy silver fork went flying. He did not like to hear what Mamaw was saying, but she always spoke truth with love, and Johnnie knew in his heart she was right.

The next Morning Tucker came by to pick him up, and Johnnie was waiting on the front porch, ready when he arrived. Tucker beeped the horn once and Johnnie struggled down the three steps in front of the front door and then exactly eleven steps to the curb where Tucker's car door was open.

"Are you ready to do this today, Sir John?" Tucker asked.

"I am. Let's go." Johnnie replied.

When they arrived at the arena, the rest of the team was already scrimmaging. Tucker had been up all night with a ladder, duct tape, and a ball of twine, measuring distances on the court which were the corners of the three-point circle. He had them laid out on the ground and taped to the floor when they arrived.

"Sir John, I had an idea after I took you home last night, so I went to a hardware store and got a surprise for you… I hope you like it." Tucker said.

"What is it… another pair of sunglasses?" Johnnie asked, with a smirk on his face.

"No, buddy: a way for you to study and perfect your shot… I mean *improve* your shot," Tucker explained. "I put some tape on the floor for a chair. That will be your chair for every game. It will be your home base. Everything you do will be from this reference point. When the team sits down, you will always sit in this chair. It is exactly five feet from the corner of the court. It is your job to figure out the steps to the rest of the spots…I mean the places on the court you want to practice from. I also bought some rope twine and measured it for you from the basket to the end of the three-point line, and then also back to the chair. It is taped to the floor. I know you can't see it, but I know you can feel it with your feet. This morning I don't want to shoot the ball, I just want you to sit here and follow the twine back and forth from the three-point line to the chair. You have the distances calibrated in your head already. That is the easy part. I just need you to find your place on the court so you can make the shot with better accuracy."

"I got this Tuck," Johnnie said. "I like the way you think."

"Good, because I have to go scrimmage with the team, SJ. I am getting a little rusty and out of shape. You can begin working on this, and I will be back to discuss your thoughts on this in about an hour, ok?"

"You got it, bro'," Johnnie replied.

Then Tucker turned to run over to the group doing the full-court scrimmage, and Johnnie called after him, "Thank you... I needed this."

"No problem, man, you can do it. I have faith in you!" then Tucker headed off to play with the rest of the team.

Johnnie began his study creating a map in his mind where everything was from the chair. It became his reference point for everything on the court, the arena, and his life. It all centered on where the chair was. For a moment he just sat there and contemplated what to do next. After a few minutes he began to remove his shoes and then his socks. He stood and walked along the lines of tape and twine Tucker had strapped to the floor, because he wanted to feel them with his feet and soul. He began the pray as he walked the floor, giving everything in his life to God, the past and the present. He had done this before, but he wanted the angels to be able to hear his words because if he did not say the words out loud, God would not hear them and place them in the Book of Life. Thoughts are one thing, but words are forever. You can't take them back, and you can't use them recklessly, so you had better be faithful when you say them.

As Johnnie walked, he prayed the prayer that the angels told him Jabaaz had prayed many years ago. He did this over and over again, walking the tape on the floor until his feet were raw and he could not walk on them anymore.

"Lord please enlarge my territory," he prayed. "Help me to do *Your* will. Guide me and be with me. Protect me from evil, that I not cause any pain. Amen." This prayer he repeated over and over… over and over… over and over… until he fully understood the meaning of 'not cause pain.'

Mia and her new husband had been watching Johnnie's recovery from afar, trying to distance themselves from being too involved in the relations split between a husband and his wife. Char had been staying in contact with Mia to see how Johnnie was doing. She talked a lot about how she still cared about Johnnie as a person, just not as a person she wanted to be connected to in the future stages of her life. Char had never been really a spiritual person; religious yes, but spiritual no… She believed in the symbolic tradition and ceremony of being Catholic more than being Catholic by commitment though having a repentant heart, as each of the Popes did during her life.

Johnnie and Char were expecting their first child. So much in their lives revolved around raising a religious family which they believed would be part of their life in the afterworld, and preparing for this world of imminent dangers. Unfortunately, when it was all said and done, Paul's dissertation in the Bible that a religious life was really not that important, whereas a Godly spiritual life in relation with Jesus was. Mamaw saw everything that way, and she thought the LDS were a little kooky because of the way they claimed their religion had begun, but that being said, the LDS Mormons also believed that Christ was their Savior, just like the Catholics, Protestants, and all Gentiles, so from the Eternal message of having a relationship with Christ, it sounded to her like there would be some good LDS Mormons in Heaven too, so she did not ever stir the pot to confuse the issue or resist any of their doctrinal beliefs out in public.

This was not true for Coach Thornton. He voiced many times he was upset with the LDS secret lifestyles he had seen through the years, and he believed that in order to be a true Christian, one could not have two agendas that were separate than what was preached in the Bible, i.e. works vs. faith. Coach Thornton did not believe in 'add-ons' to the Bible's theology because then 'Where would the add-ons end?' and 'Who was to say who could add on and who could not?' The open-ended question to this led to the question of cultism or not, which most were just not eager to engage, because most of society were in some form of cult anyway, whether it was the television cult, the idolatry cult, the pornographic cult, or the get-rich cult. This was all the same to the Holy Spirit, who saw man as uneducated and without leadership, and was not amused at the many who believed that just being good was good enough to enter Heaven, which was a big error in man's meager mind of simpleton thoughts and ways.

Before Tucker went to college at Purdue, he had been assigned a Mormon roommate in a private high school dormitory. He had many late-night conversations with him about the LDS faith and what it meant to be a Mormon. From the outside, Tucker felt like the Mormons were always trying too hard to 'be good' instead of 'being right,' but also being right too, on a secondary level; but only a non-denominational cemetery could ever reveal a true answer, when all souls had left for their eternal resting places and nothing but bones were left. This was one of those things which was dealt with in the many rooms of Heaven, but Heaven could not be judged, nor measured, so was is not to be the concern of the mortals, who only tried to judge in vain.

It seemed that Mia and her husband had both converted to the LDS faith because of the stability it brought to their marriage. Both had been married before, which was becoming quite common and problematic in the current American society of rapidly changing disposals and insincere covenants. Mia had spoken many times about the 'Judas' in her life, her past husband who had abandoned her. Roger was the same. He had been married before and his wife had left him as well. He attributed it to society and living in a world of disposables. Now a person could get a non-contested divorce, and just leave a marriage without anything other than just feelings. There was no reason to follow the idea that marriage was a three-way covenant between a man, a woman, and the Holy Spirit. As many of the Lord's prophets indicated, especially Paul,[211] marriage was not designed to make people happy but designed to make them holy. The man would always be better off to control his sexual desires and not marry, but he most times was unable to do that, so he married and was consequently tied to the World I, in which he must contributed his time and focus to fulfill his obligations, in which Satan colluded with the angels of the dark to remove him from his status above the angels, while the Holy Spirit and the angels under the Holy Spirit's command defended him while he was under assault and tried to help him make better decisions, leaning on the Lord for guidance, and hopefully praying to Heaven and all the saints, and the Lord,

[211] I Corinthians: 6 & 7

Himself, to relieve his suffering and keep him safe in the world of measure, of the quick and the dead.

The Lord God then called up Lucifer to come before Him again and bow down. This would be the twelfth time He had done this since the Lord God Creator had rid the earth of the pesky un-souled dinosaurs who were put there to till the earth, breathe the air to convert the oxygen to carbon dioxide so the pants could grow, and prepare it for the coming of man. In that day, the Lord had to prepare the soil to be fertile just as a farmer would prepare his fields to plant the seed and make it grow. The Lord had to grow the plants that would be the fuel that would become the oil in the ground to allow humans to warm themselves besides cutting trees and burning bog. The Lord had to move the lands away from each other to raise the mountains so than rain would fall on one side and the currents would traverse the oceans, cooling and heating, creating warm waters to heat and cool the land so that the people would not burn under a constantly hot sun. And the Lord had to create diversity so that the people would look around and know that He was Lord, and that intelligence was not made of a digital medium, because man created digital media, and God created man. And God had shielded the earth from meteors and asteroids, and the universe was a big ocean of vast space in which cold outweighs heat, so the Lord was the Light of the Universe and the Light of Creation that could only shine in the darkness of both the dark universe and the darkness of the human heart when it was devoid of the Light.

The Lord called his Four Horsemen to go to the North, South, East, and West, to find where Satan was hiding this time. For he would be hiding in total darkness, devoid of any light, while his dark angels carried out his scourge on World I, and battled the Holy Spirit in World II for dominance of the Spirit world. Satan did not possess enough dimensions to overcome the Holy Spirit, so there would be no match in the final battle, so the Lord kept Satan in place and in subservient power to measure His mortal beings and find out which loved Him back as much as he loved them when He had created them. This was the great unknown, never yet revealed on earth: that Satan was like a disease kept like a thorn in the side of mankind, that he must suffer to show his allegiance and faith in something he could not see, but had to learn by faith and obedience, as enlightenment and wisdom were revealed though suffering and penitence.

The four Horsemen went and began the search again. They would ultimately find Satan again, for he could not hide nor move around enough in his game of hide-and-seek that the master who created him also could not find him. Even the scriptures said: *A student can never be greater than his teacher*, and so it was with Satan, who could never be greater than his Creator and Teacher, the Lord God Almighty! The Word was now out and Satan could feel the echoes of the pounding hoof beats of the Horsemen in ether-less air and the sound of angelic tidal waves searching for him throughout the Universe. He was hiding, but God would find him, and when the Horsemen found him they would send word back to the hounds of the Kingdom, and the dog angels would come and chase him down until they corralled him into a hole or cave and dug him out like a rat hiding in a field beneath the snow and grass when a wolf is hungry for his morning meal. Even the great dragon could not defend him in this day. But the dog angels were not allowed to kill the dark Angel, Satan, for it was not their privilege. They were only to report his location, so that he might be dragged before God once more and put in his place while awaiting the mighty battle Satan surely would lose. For when God created Satan and the other angels, He had not given them dimensions enough to procreate and populate themselves, nor did he give them power over man unless the Lord allowed it, as was done with Job, when God gave him His test of faith to show his obedience.

And next time the dog angels located Satan and he was brought before the mighty 'King of All Creation,' God Almighty would smite him once again, over and over until he released him again and punished him for what he had done to the women of earth (except Mary, whom he could not touch) because human women were given a higher status above the angels with mortal dimensions possessing superior beauty in man's eye. Satan loathed that God had not given the angel the dimensions needed to procreate and bear offspring, as He had done for mankind and the beast of the field, for even the animals had been given this privilege, yet the angels had not! So, when Satan was rebuked and turned and ran astray from God and cohabitated with the women of earth until God said, *no more!*, and God cleansed the earth of all wickedness through Satan, and had Noah and his family put all pure animals on the earth onto an Ark and washed all remnants of Satan's remnants in World I away. No longer would Satan be allowed to have blood on earth and have in comingled with the humans and with the animals. Only God the Father would come to do this, and later bring Himself as His own son, Jesus, to comingle His blood with Mary and the other humans, so that Satan would know he was not allowed to touch their bodies anymore or be a part of Earth in World I until he would be banished from World II and stricken from the Heavens of World III and put in the fiery pit of Hades forever for his disobedience and disloyalty to God the Father and the Trinity Triune Godhead.

This is the bane and angst which the great evil one, Satan, bore along with the stripes on his back from the whips of God's lictors who controlled Satan as he carried out the testing of man's loyalty and obedience, while trying to live in two worlds at once, like the Vitruvian man, but Man could not because he was held in World I by his loyalty and devotion to the woman, who lived only in World I and kept her husband contained with the physical companionship and company he needed to survive and thrive in all things that were created good, so that he would not be alone.[212]

Each time Satan was found by the dog angels of Heaven, he was dragged out and carried back to God for his punishment for that Age, where he was stricken multiple times upon his body to bear the marks of his dastardly deeds. Each blow would cause his body to harden so that a scale was produced on the skin, and beating on the head and spine created horns of different sizes, so that his body had become a disfiguration of all the animals on earth he has abused. He had the body of an angel, but the horns on the side of his head like a burdened oxen, horns that ran down the middle of his face like a rhino, and horns that came from each cheek like a warthog, sometimes equally walking on all fours, thus eye-to-eye with the serpent he so loved to become. The spine down his back had a row of horn spikes much like the great lizards that roamed the jungles of the southwest oceans, and the scales on his sides were reminiscent of great snakes. He had a tail as long as a shark that also carried a spine

[212] Genesis 2:18

like that of a stingray that, when hurled, could produce venom to puncture a man's heart and turn it to stone whenever he could get close enough to strike at him. His fangs could also produce venom to paralyze and allow him to devour his prey if he could reach them, and he had a tongue that could be hurled forward with a sticky end, like those of the mighty lizards of the trees, to catch children who were unprotected. All would know his weapons were many and his nets were strong to overcome the weakness and innocence of man, who only lived in five dimensions: height, length, width, time, and space.

Then the day came—as had been prophesied and proclaimed by the Father Almighty—that Satan was to be bound for one thousand years,[213] and that the time to overcome and date which only the Trinity knew would not be revealed, except by revelation to the assigned seers amongst the saints. Then the final battle would occur, in which Satan would be destroyed and put into the lake of fire along with all the cowardly, unbelieving, abominable, murderers, sexually immoral, sorcerers, idolaters, and liars, in the place called the Second Death,[214] and 'New Jerusalem' would come down from the sky, and the Son of Man would sit again on a new throne on earth as a new Tabernacle covering the entire earth and reigning in all His glory.[215] This was all laid out in the Great Plan, in which all those who loved Christ would overcome, and all those who did not would perish by their own deeds, good or bad, regardless of their bent, for they would have chosen other gods—whatever they might be—over the one true God who created them, and they would

[213] Revelation 20:1-3

[214] Revelation 21:8

[215] Revelation 21:2-3

return to the falsehoods of Evolution and other false teachings that they would return to the roots of their own beliefs. Amen.

Then the Holy Spirit called up the legitimate sons of Abraham who made up the Twelve Tribes of Judaism. He said their names one by one, as He called them to come forward: "Rueben, Simeon, Levi, Judah, Dan, Napthali, Issachar, Zebulun, Gad, Asher, Joseph, and Benjamin… come forth and stand before me!"

Then He called up the twelve Tribes of Ishmael in the same way and manner, naming them one by one as he called them for forward: "Nabaioth, Kedar, Adbeel, Mibsam, Mishma, Dumah, Massa, Hadad, Tema, Jetur, Naphish, and Kedemah come forward!"

And then finally He called up the Twelve Tribes of Jesus, naming them one by one, just as he had done twice before, saying: "James, Jude, Joses, Simon, and the first of each of the other Eight Tribes, being 12,000 of each of the Tribes of The Meek, The Poor in Spirit, The Merciful, The Pure in Heart, The Peacemakers, Those Who Mourned, Those Who Thirsted For Righteousness, and Those Who were persecuted for Righteousness Sake. In this group there were 96,000. And then He added the names of others not yet to be born to make 144,000 that would be there as His representatives in that day where He could look around and know He was Jehovah, Creator of All, Incarnate with His Son, and One with the Holy Spirit whose Ghost ruled over Man in the greatest Triune sense.

The Holy Spirit called one name from each bloodline group to represent their lineage and bent in the Great Plan, so He called Judah, Kedar, and James to stand before Him.

"Judah, like a lion who will fight any beast and is unafraid in the midst of war," the Holy Spirit said, "you held my people together for the sake of righteousness of the Lord, but you failed to accept the new blood chosen for you which also created a bloodline to go on through the Hebrew side of the Holy Mother Mary, Mother of God. Kedar, you were a prince and served your bloodlines well, but you failed to serve others unconditionally, so the lesson repeats itself, continually until your royal family learns the blessing of giving unconditional love service to your enemies, then no eternal peace can abide in or with you, for hate can never win over love. And James, you whose blood ran through your veins just as that which was spilled at the cross for the Salvation of the World, you have represented your 'Family of Believers' well. Each of you was chosen even before you were born to carry out your preordained deeds. The time will come soon when all men will see the Truth, which will strike their souls with all fulfillments and all divine purpose. In that day, New Jerusalem will become the crown jewel in the crown of Christ, and the pain and all the suffering will be gone. At that time, God, Himself, will dwell with man upon the earth, and He, Himself—and only He—will be their God.[216] All shoots rising from the root feed off the blood of Christ, and the martyrs who died for Him will unite to become one tree, whose vine will be the medicine of the world, called the Kingdom of God, which shall rule forever.

[216] Revelation 21:3

It was sad that Sonny and Rosanne's lives had changed so little immediately following Johnnie and Leroy's accident, for they lived in a world of bank cards, of weights and measures. Since Sonny had lost so many friends in Vietnam, he had become numb to the loss of close ones, and he really never could quite understand the meaning of life and death. He had a *comme-ci-comme-ça* attitude to life… except for when it came to Rosanne.

Then one day, it happened. God's conviction began calling Sonny, and all of a sudden, out of nowhere, life, religion, spirituality, and Heaven became real to him, and he needed resolution in his own heart for peace. One week after the passing of Leroy, Sonny went to Mr. Silverman and asked for permission to pay some sort of tribute to Leroy on the chopper as he flew around Houston. Andy said yes, of course, and he also offered to pay for any decals that Sonny might want to use. Andy could empathize with Sonny, because he, too, had experienced the same feelings when he lost one of his best friends in battle during the Korean war.

Together, Sonny and Andy came up with the term 'Phantom 369,' which was what Leroy had called his beloved blue corvette, which had had the license plate '369.' The number 369 was significant to Leroy because 369 Main Street was the address of the hospital in the small town of McAllen, Texas, where he had been born. His own grandfather had established the hospital as a place to care for injured border patrol agents, all in the name of patriotism and loyalty to his nation which afforded him such freedoms and liberties. *Nothing in life is free, especially not freedom,* Leroy had once said. *You have to fight twice for it: once to earn it... and then again, to keep it.*

So Sonny had a big decal made of a blue corvette with the words 'Phantom 369' running across the body of the car. One day before they took off for a meeting, he and Andy had their own moment of silence for Leroy. They knew he was up there smiling down on them for these actions, and when the chopper lifted off to head north across town for a meeting, they both felt an extra sense of pride, knowing those who looked up at them would see the blue corvette on the side of the chopper and wonder what it symbolized.

A year later, Mr. Silverman decided to spin his two private choppers off to make a separate new small business for Sonny, to give him a management desk job overseeing the operations instead of a pilot position. This would give him and Rosanne a better income to live off of, now that he had proven his loyalty to Andy and the business ventures he was involved in. Together they called the new business Phantom 369, Inc. Andy proceeded to buy six more choppers, co-signing for the debt with Sonny, and giving fifty-one percent to Sonny and Rosanne. It soon became a major small exclusive charter helicopter service in the southwest for many of the other oil tycoons of high net worth who wanted to travel short trips back and forth to their own drilling platforms for day trips but did not want to spend their own time and resources owning personal helicopters and finding trained pilots and mechanics to service them.

Bob Heatherton was now beginning to make the rotation into the first string of the game openers. Ziggy, the Zig-Man, rotated in and out with Tucker for point guard, the position Johnnie used to play, even though Johnnie was officially called the strong side forward. Bob and Mia's life was also settling down now because they had bought a home and were getting situated in the ward where they had been assigned to attend their church family life. Bob was the only member of the LDS faith on the Clear Lake Hurricane's team, so he tried to not stand out or cause any stress among the group, staying pretty mute in his faith… it was just the Mormon way. Mia supported him in what they felt God had called them to do, and they hoped one day there would be a time when they could share their faith with someone who felt called to ask about it and maybe they could live a more planned and peaceful life than they had in their current state of chaos.

Ziggy had roots in Nairobi, and his father had been a Christian leader in a church there when he was born. Given the birth name 'Zachariah,' he got the nickname 'Ziggy' when he learned to play basketball on a dirt field outside the white one-story building with a hoop nailed to its side. By the time he was just fourteen, he could dunk the ball. Whenever Ziggy went in to town, he would take a portable basketball set up he pulled on a trailer behind his bike. Then he would set it up and do basketball tricks to passersby for change, which they would put in a guitar case with a small piece of cardboard that said 'Nairobi Christian Church, please give to the Kingdom' on it. The sign had been handwritten by his father about a month before soldiers of the Islamic faith had broken into their home in the night and taken Ziggy's father away, and then executed him for spreading his Christian beliefs.

But the beliefs were too strongly instilled in the Zig-Man for him to give up what his father had been so passionate about: salvation and leading a Christ-centered life. And this was how he was discovered by oilmen who were in Nairobi looking for new opportunities in oil fields: a kid shooting baskets on his homemade hoop with profound and unbelievable accuracy. And thus the legend of Ziggy was born. The rest was history: he came to play for the University of Houston as a walk-on international transfer student with a sub-level education… and would never leave the court if there were still time on the play clock or if his relentless cheering fans were chanting his name.

Though you already know all this, I want to remind you that the Lord at one time delivered his people out of Egypt, but later destroyed those who did not believe. And the angels who did not keep their positions of authority but abandoned their proper dwelling—these he has kept in darkness, bound with everlasting chains for judgment on the great Day. In a similar way, Sodom and Gomorrah and the surrounding towns gave themselves up to sexual immorality and perversion. They serve as an example of those who suffer the punishment of eternal fire.

As Testified by Jude,
Brother of Jesus and James
Chapter 1:5-7

Chapter 12

Staying the Course as a Blind NBA Player

"Hey, Tucker," Johnnie said, "watch this…"

Johnnie reached back with the ball over his head and let a shot fly from the corner of the court. It took exactly two and nine-tenths of a second, and then… an audible swoosh, buzzer, and red light that went off as the ball went through the hoop, hitting nothing but net.

"You are almost as good at that shot, SJ, as when you had both eyes," Tucker said to him teasingly, as he saw the big grin on Johnnie's face showing the gap between his front teeth you could stick a pencil through.

"What is your true and exact distance from your humble 'Basketball Throne'?" he asked Johnnie. Tucker was referring to the folding metal chair which he had duct-taped to the floor for his blind man's bearings… Johnnie's home spot.

"I am two regular steps to the sideline and then two small steps up to the base line," Johnnie said.

"So how many can you make out of twenty shots?" Tucker asked

"That's private information," Johnnie said with a laugh. Then he follows it with, "Twelve or thirteen, looks like."

"That's not good enough, Sir John," Tucker replied. "An NBA player has to shoot at least 80 to 85 percent from there, so don't give me any crap about being blind, okay?"

"Hey, cool it! Okay, buddy?" Johnnie fired back. "You are not my coach; Coach Barricks is…"

"Yeah, but I care more for you than he does, so I am going to keep harping on you to get this through your tough skull: 'Get Tough, Get Rough, and Get Over It!... until you can make it like you used to at 90% or better. We are not playing candy grab-ass around here to lose in the finals, so we need to win, and that means 90% completion... *Comprende, amigo*?"

"I got it, *amigo*," Johnnie replied, turning to sit down in his chair as he takes a short break. Tucker came over sat sits beside him, resting his hand on Johnnie's arm.

"Hey, *amigo*, you know I am always in your corner fighting for you, right?" Tucker asked.

"I know," Johnnie replied softly.

"Do you want to hear a secret that is about you?" Tucker asked him.

"Not really… *amigo*. I don't like secrets."

"Barricks has been watching you and he has made a bet with Silverman that you can beat one of the other players in a game of Horse next week, so you had better get better or you are going to let Coach Barricks down," Tucker said.

"That is impossible; I can't play a game I can't see!" Johnnie said.

"I am just warning you so you aren't surprised, so I need you to start measuring the places, spots, on the court you want to shoot or dunk from, and I will help you get the job done," Tucker said.

Johnnie did not know that this idea was hatched by Mr. Silverman, Sonny, and Coach Barricks during a fishing trip. Andy asked Sonny if he had any ideas on how to get Johnnie motivated to keep honing his skills so the other players could watch him come back and not only shoot blind but also gain confidence to play completion on the floor. Sonny suggested he play him in a game of horse but that would be a slaughter even if Sonny was playing a man with regular eyesight. Sonny had zero basketball skills and they all three laughed when Sonny said it, but it made Andy think it really was a great idea if he could get Johnnie to think he was going to let someone down if he did not play along.

"Does this mean I will be the laughing stock of the team if I lose?" Johnnie asked.

"Well, if you lose, but the Sir Johnnie I know never loses, now does he?" Tucker asked.

"You know that I, the ol' Johnnie, never lost, Tuck… but not quite sure yet about the new Johnnie with no eyes. It is really dark in here…" he said, sort of laughing, but with a sorrowful and fearful laugh, not a laugh that Johnnie was accustomed to laughing, because old Johnnie was never afraid, and it wasn't really the fear of defeat anymore, but rather the fear of being judged as inferior because he was not in control as a man anymore, having to rely solely on God. He was not on the same playing field as the rest of his completion, anymore, and that frightened him.

"So now you know how the rest of the team used to feel when they played you, and wouldn't it be great if you could put that same fear back in them by beating one of them blind!?" Tucker said, planting a seed in his brain to grow for a while.

"Yeah, that would be great… just like old times. I would like to see them squirm a bit when I hit that half-court shot they think I can't make even with two good eyes on a good day with the air conditioning blowing in my favor!" Sir Johnnie said with a laugh, as they now seemed to connect at a real brotherhood level.

"So, what do you say, *amigo*?" Tucker asked.

"I need you to help me count steps to half-court, and then I will take it from there." Johnnie said.

They both stood in unison, and Tucker took him by the arm. They then went to the half-court line and Tucker went and got two ball caddies, each of which carried a dozen balls.

"It's time to get rough, get tough, and get over it, *amigo*," Tucker said.

"I know," Johnnie said, "but before I do, I need to do one thing."

"And what is that, *amigo*, take a bathroom break?" Tucker retorted.

"No, something more personal…"

And with that Johnnie dropped to his knees and put both hands on the floor. He laid his body all the way down and stretched out his arms and legs in a full spread-eagle position, and he began to pray. Tucker watched him as he went to the floor. He could see tears welling up in his eyes, and Johnnie whispering some sort of prayer. Johnnie just lay there for a few minutes when Tucker slowly melted away back to the team for the rest of his daily workout.

The arena had two full-sized courts, so the fact that Johnnie was lying in the middle of one of them was not a problem for the Hurricanes practicing. Andy had just come down from his office and began looking on from the mezzanine when he saw Johnnie lying on the floor. He thought maybe he had fallen or pulled a groin or muscle, so he scurried down to the floor to see what the problem might be.

By the time Mr. Silverman had made it down to the arena floor and was at the edge of the court, Johnnie had already gotten up and was shaking his arms to loosen them up as Andy approached.

"I thought you were hurt, Johnnie," Mr. Silverman said.

"Not my body, or anything you can see," Johnnie answered.

"So, what were you doing?" Mr. Silverman asked.

"Praying, Mr. Silverman… just praying," Johnnie said to him.

"Good idea, Johnnie," Mr. Silverman said. "Now, why don't we just get back to business and keep shooting the ball?"

With that, Mr. Silverman walked away and headed back to his office, where he needed to work on the beer sales contract which the entire league was bidding on to make the most profit in the upcoming season. Andy had to guarantee a certain amount of beer sales to maximize his profit… too low of an estimate left him short of available beer to sell, and too high a bid would cost him extra, reducing his net profit. These were intangible costs, and most people did not think about the cost of paving a parking lot or the air conditioning bill on a five-acre building.

Then Johnnie lifted his hand behind his head with a ball gently cradled with seventy percent of the weight held in his left hand, and he let the ball go toward the hoop… it traveled almost five seconds this time and Johnnie never heard a swish. He turned and Tucker was not there to be his eyes and tell him what went wrong. Mr. Silverman was walking away from him the other direction, and

Coach Barricks was busy coaching the rest of the team, so now Johnnie was standing at mid-court in a dark place he had never been before feeling all alone, when he heard a voice speaking to him over his left shoulder.

"Johnnie, do not be afraid, for your Lord is with you," the voice said in a warm glow of compassion. Johnnie even seemed to hear angels singing softly in the background, and there was a faint smell of lilacs and lavender coming across his nostrils that seemed to sedate his anxiety and put him at ease.

"Do not turn around. Your shot was three feet to the left and short just a little."

Johnnie was mystified by this but heard the angel's voice say to him, "Pick up another ball and try it again."

He was obedient to the voice, raising his hands like he had done so many times from the half-court line and letting the ball fly toward the net. In roughly four and a third seconds, he heard a swoosh, the ring, and the red-light buzzer go off. Coach Barricks looked over at where Johnnie was standing and could not believe he had just made a half-court throw without help. (What Coach did not know would not hurt him).

When Johnnie heard the buzzer a second time, he fell to the ground on his knees, spreading out on the floor again and beginning to pray a prayer of thanksgiving; for once again he knew he was not alone, and once again he knew he was not forsaken. 'What a wonderful feeling this is!' he thought to himself.

Tucker drove Johnnie home that evening after an amazing practice. It seemed to Tucker that Johnnie continued to beat the odds just as he always had done, but what Johnnie was doing now was different: it was super-human. Tucker had always enjoyed watching him play basketball when he was doing things no one else could do, but now he was doing things that were just plain unimaginable. Tucker knew Johnnie was 100% blind. He could not fool anyone with that part of his life. Tucker still had to open his car door to let him out and hand him things he could not find when he dropped them, and he always made sure that Johnnie made it into the house and back into Mamaw's care, because no blind person in that neighborhood would be able to defend himself if he were jumped by gang members, even though he was a global star on the basketball court. On this night, Johnnie made it home just fine. He had a new story to tell, and he was excited to get home and share with his grandmother what he had done today from half-court.

"Mamaw, I have some good news," Johnnie said as he came through the door.

"I have good news, too," Mamaw said.

Johnnie entered through the door and reached down to where be felt Cojo sniffing at his leg and gave him a rub on the head. But this time it was different, he did not feel Cojo, what he felt was another dog. It has a lot hairier, a little shorter in height, and the hair he felt was long and velvety. The dog's ears were lying down and not pointing straight up, like Cojo's did. Then it took just one second and Johnnie said, "You've got another dog? What happened to Cojo?"

"Cojo is still here. I put him in the hall bathroom so you could meet Duchess without Cojo jumping on you or bothering you," Mamaw said. "I wanted you to get to know Duchess. She is a great dog."

"Okay, so, I came in to tell you some great news, Mamaw, but you have stolen my great moment of joy."

"Why is that, son? I still want to hear what you have to say. I am very sorry… please tell me your good news. I am excited to hear what it is you have to say!"

"I am starting making my favorite shots again from half-court! I mean, I started making baskets from half-court. I can still do it! I am blind and I can still do it!" Johnnie exclaimed, slowly sitting down and starting to laugh harder and harder, until he put his head down on the kitchen table and began hitting the table with a light thump and pounding of his right hand.

"This is remarkable and also fabulous, son! You seem to be now enjoying getting back onto the court."

"Yes, Mamaw, I am… An angel helped me today. I could tell it was a woman angel by her voice."

"Oh, yeah? A woman angel? I don't remember any women angels in the Bible… but I always expected some of the angels to be women. Even though most of the women I have known in my life have all been witches, but starting with a 'B' in front. I really wish God would have made me into a man. I have always felt strongly I could do a man's job better than he could."

"Mamaw, there you go again, spoiling my moment. And what is this new dog you have…Why, I mean where did you get him, or… I mean her? Duchess is a girl name. Besides, owning and caring for one dog is enough, isn't it? Cojo already runs this house as if he were the boss man."

"I bought her for you," Mamaw said.

"I don't need a dog... I am good just the way I am," replied Johnnie.

"You may think so, but you need companionship, Sir John. No man can live alone and remain sane without a helper." Mamaw said.

"No ma'am, Mamaw, really I am good. I can barely take care of myself. How am I going to take care of a dog? I really just want to be left alone, you know that."

"Yes, I do, SJ, and I know that 'man is not supposed to be alone', so until you find another woman in your life, you need something to fill gaps and take up your time, and Duchess is your new Number One lady!"

"Yeah, I guess she will have to be blind too, if she is going to look past my faults," Johnnie laughed again at the joke he had just made, and then Johnnie reached down and pet Duchess once more. He grabbed her by the neck and gave her a good rubbing back and forth, and heard her breathing, sort of snoring, as he scratched her under her chin. She was soft and smooth, and was more rounded around her body than Cojo. Cojo was always more muscular with a hard and stiff body, stiffer hair, and boney to the touch.

"What color is she?" Johnnie asked

"Does it make a difference?"

"No, not really, but I would still like to know."

"Green...." Mamaw laughed and began to pound her fist on the couch because she thought it was a good racial joke.

"Johnnie, she is green, just the same color you and I will probably be in Heaven since no one will be the same color as here, or maybe we will all be blue, orange or purple... I think we will all get a new color of exterior just so we can all have a good laugh together or maybe you will be another color than you had here on earth as Heaven Regulation #20102: No one gets to be the same color as they had before, so you become the race you made jokes about when you sinned on earth. And probably won't have any elbows either, so we won't be able to feed ourselves or eat by ourselves; we will have to feed each other across a dining table made of tin and bamboo in order to get some ice cream or milk shakes when everyone else around down under is thirsty with dry mouth, haw-haw!"

"No, really, Mamaw, what color is she? I want to know… The rest of that is irrelevant to any sane person like me."

"She is white with brown spots. She is a Brittany Spaniel, and they are known for their good hunting, retrieving, and swimming skills."

"And what is this big collar on her I feel here for?"

"She is a service dog… a servant, just like you, Johnnie. She will help you get around places you are unfamiliar with. Like a street corner or an elevator door."

"Wow, cool beans, Mamaw. I like this! You know I never liked surprises before, especially car wrecks (ouch), but this one I like," Johnnie said, giving Duchess a big hug, grabbing her on both sides of the head, and whispering something into her ear which Mamaw could not hear. "I love you," Johnnie said softly, "and I am going to call you: Duchess Diana… not Patches or Spots or anything like that for you either, sweet girl."

"Now that you have met the new girl in your life, I want to hear more about your day at the arena," Mamaw said. "And tell me more about the angel that spoke to you."

"I did not see her. She was behind me and told me where to shoot the ball. She had me walk up and down the entire half-court, taking two steps forward each time, and then she said, 'Shoot!' So I shot. And I made about half of the shots, which caused the team to stop and watch me every time the score board went off. I felt power again, but only because the angel was there telling me what to do."

"So, this angel, did she give you her name?"

"Yes, but she said to not tell anyone."

"Please tell me, Johnnie!" Mamaw begged.

"I can't… she said not to repeat her name to people. I am just to wait for another time to be granted permission to reveal her name. She did say that I could say this: The Lord has a message for me to give to others later, but she would not tell me what the message was. All she said was, 'Remember the name *Joses*,' which she said I was allowed to say at this time."

"And what did she say the meaning was? Who is Joses?"

"I don't know! She didn't tell me. I believe I once read it is the Greek version of Joseph, sort of like Paul is for Saul…"

"And were you making baskets from the half-court area when she said that to you?"

"Yes, lots of them, and some even longer… that's what I wanted to tell you! I was really amazing…but really, I mean, *IT* WAS AMAZING!"

"What do you mean by *IT*?"

"Well, I was using my ol' unstoppable Sky Hook to shoot the ball and without much effort almost every single one was going in! The score board just kept ringing as if all the fire alarms were going off in the area at once."

"Well, maybe that shot is not so unstoppable when someone is standing in front of you, huh, now that you are blind? Doesn't this seem a little odd to you? Do you think maybe the others think your eyesight has come back a little, and maybe you aren't telling the whole truth about your condition, just to get more attention and popularity as the greatest comeback player ever in sports world history?"

"No way, Mamaw! Everyone knows I can't see. I am totally, 100% blind!!"

"Well maybe so, but some people may think your eyesight might slowly come back and this is what it is going on. So maybe you just aren't telling the truth anyone."

"No, Mamaw, slim chance of that happening! Tell you this is a true miracle of what is happening. I can't see anything. The only time I could is when I came out of the church and saw the angel Gabriel in the grouping of crepe myrtles on the corner and he spoke to me."

"But you could see then, only then, and you can't see now. This is crazy, but I guess no crazier than the story where Moses parted the Red Sea to take his people out of slavery and captivity."

"How many people have you told your angelic crepe myrtle story to?"

"Just Tucker…"

"Are you sure, *only* him? Just one other person besides me?" Mamaw double-checked.

"Yes, and I am getting worn out from your Nazi-like interrogations. I think I am going to go upstairs and get a shower."

"Hush your mouth, child boy! This was *nothing* like the Nazis, and just to make a comparison like that is an insult to the reality of all the terrible things that were done in the name of false prophecy." Mamaw paused, and then continued. "Now, better take Duchess with you. She needs to find out about everywhere you go and sleep before we take her out into the real world to walk down to the food market."

"Yes, ma'am, Mamaw… You are always the boss here… and we all know this. Let's go, Diana." Johnnie reached down as she was smelling his shoes and pant legs, and he took Diana—his new best friend—by her collar, leading her upstairs.

"Diana? Her name is Duchess! That is what she responds to," Mamaw insisted in her know-it-all voice.

"You said you gave her to me, right? So, I am giving her a name that I like, and I like Diana. I don't want to be Sir John and his Duchess. It's too corny."

"But Diana was the Roman goddess of the forest, the well-known pagan animal lover and deer whisperer. She was a false god of animal worship that the people gave gifts to for security and happiness. Paul preached against all animal worship, and Timothy died trying to turn the followers of Diana and their animal worshipers away because they were doing it in Ephesus when Mary, mother of Jesus, was there, and they were going to parade in front of Mary's home while John was taking care of her. This was a true insult for Jesus, who came to such pagans as these and shed His blood for them all, each and every single one…"

"I know the pagan story, Mamaw, of Timothy's martyrdom, so I will tell you this too. The angel said there will be a 'rude awakening' coming for the same people of today, with much suffering and a chastisement in the form of a plague, to those who worship their dogs and cats like children, just as if they were idols of them like the pagan Goddess Diana. These people never go to church and mock those who do; their hearts are never open to hear the truth of the Word, and they live in carnal sin just the same as in the days of Jesus, their ears closed to those like Paul trying to preach to them and save them from their suffering. HAVEN'T THEY SUFFERED ENOUGH?? They are lost in their prideful ways, finding pleasures in animals to adore. And the angel told me in my lifetime there is a worse day coming when people will leave the love of animals and men for the love of machines and artificial intelligence. All the trappings of Satan as he leads those sheep astray! Neither animals nor machines are born with souls. Both have been allowed into creation by the will and guidance of God (i.e. not evolution!) for their distractions, just like all things that lure away from prayer and the pursuit of purity, for these are an abomination to all those who worship them as if they were another Golden Calf to tithe to instead of tithing to the Living God."

"The woman angel told you this?" Mamaw asked incredulously.

"Yes, she told me telepathically," Johnnie replied. "No words were used for these messages. I could hear the words in my head, but the only audible words I could hear in my ears were those to direct my shooting of the basketball in World 1. Wisdom was done from my heart to her heart and back again, in World 1, because my heart was opened up and hers was poured out to fill mine. This is something you would not know because it is not your privilege."

"Now you are starting to hack me off, young man! I have just as many privileges as you," Mamaw said, jumping into a fighting stance and clenching both of her fists.

"I don't believe that to be so, Mamaw... I'm very sorry," Johnnie said to her conciliatorily.

"How about I come over, then, and whack some of those privileges out of you?" Mamaw teased her grandson.

"The angel told me that women were created to be the 'angels for man,' for him to love and cherish, just like God has His angels whom *He* loves and cherishes. They are to be God's helpmates, just as women are to be man's helpmates. When Satan refused to be God's helpmate, then God lost his love for Satan. And the same analogy goes for man's angels: if the woman is no longer the helper, as God intended in His great design, then man loses his love for her. It is true that both man and woman must help each other, but man helps woman gain access to the world of God's angels in World 2, and woman help's man gain access to the beauty and fulfillment of his own creation in World 1, of God's angels, which he can neither touch nor love, but still he lives and burns with the desire to be as God and love angels to fulfill the grand design on the path to salvation and rebuking evil.

"This is way too much for me to digest this late at night!" Mamaw interjected. "Tomorrow I am going to call Sonny to see if he will take you over for an eye exam… and maybe a brain scan as well! You still may have symptoms of a concussion, even a year after the accident. I bet Mr. Silverman would like a report on the status of you, anyway, and I would like one too. Maybe—just maybe—there is some hope that your eyesight will come back, and you don't even know it!"

"I would not bet on it, Mamaw… It's been over a year, you know, and that is a long time. Nothing good has happened so far, so I guess this is the way I will always be. I am gonna live to be an old bachelor without an angel in my life (I'm talking about Charlotte, who left me!), never to see my kid again, just wasting away on the end of a basketball bench, collecting a retirement check for existing as a freak in a freak show for television and big business, just in case they want to put me in a game to sell more airtime or season tickets. Do you catch this personal drift of mine, Mamaw? I am drifting like a cork from a bottle, floating in a huge ocean, carried by the currents, with no will or say-so of my own. And it's a lousy drift… for sure!" Johnnie concluded.

The Holy Spirit was measuring the progress of Mankind this day, counting the inventory and taking measure of the number of souls lost to pride and prejudice. During the Triune meeting, toward the end of the most recent epoch to define and calculate the length of the New Age of the Second Coming, the Most Powerful and Honorable Lord God and Father of all Hosts wanted to know how much longer this Age would go on, until the new established reunion would take place, when all his beloved children would be called home for the grand celebration and Feast of the Lamb, which would happen after the rapture, in order to bring justice over the quick and the dead.

On this particular day in Paradise, the Holy Spirit witnessed the angels of the Lord God help create and bless 360,492,671 new souls, and then cast them out upon the seven continents of land: upon the shores, alleyways, backroads, and valleys of the earth, to be distracted and measured by Satan's dark angels and worker for the underworld. These angels could not die unless the Lord Father gave them the authority to do so, and many of them had been destroyed, for they were too evil even to be allowed to be in the proximity of Paradise, and even the Lord God created and replaced them with prideful hearts to wander the earth and wave wings to fly about the skies, creating havoc and chaos in homes, churches, and sanctuaries. But the evil they did would all be washed clean with a simple prayer and request for redemption, so no evil would ever be greater than any good, so that evil could never win over good if it had been bought and wrapped in the shroud of Christ's blood of righteousness.

The Holy Spirit also took inventory of the souls which were removed from the earth each day, and today they numbered 149,367,041. These were the souls which the angels collected and brought back to the great room for processing. Only those who returned the love the Lord Jesus had given them were allowed to stay in the great room in Paradise, while others were carried away to live in non-relation with God, which was exactly how they had been living on earth. Most were placed in small rooms with locked doors and forced to watch the repeat of their lives over and over again, so they could see the ripple effect they had had on others, which had led them to perdition. It was a terrible ending for so many who had lived so happily for their short time on earth, and now were living an eternity by themselves, just watching themselves as the masters of their own destiny, which they had created for themselves and now were watching continually, over and over and over again.

During the processing this day, there were 9,321 who were allowed to stay in the big room, and they celebrated greatly for being allowed to stay. They had feasts, and singing, and the cherubim made great parades and messages in the skies that could be seen all the way in Heaven, as their names were written in the Book of Life.

These souls—all 9,321 of them—sat and watched their lives on repeat. They had entered as one big group into Heaven, as one group who now understood salvation… now understood what it meant to learn to die to self. Each had done this, and there were special ones there who had been martyred that very day, and they were the leaders of the class, holding the most esteemed places at the heads of the tables of the feasts and the parades. Some of the dark angels were made to watch as punishment for their continued pride in the zones of World 1 and World 2, for they had been captured by the dog angels after being found trying to disrupt the Great Plan as God the Father had laid out and proclaimed to the Heavens, the holy Word and verdict of His love.

After all the souls in the class were honored, they would then be allowed to pierce the veil that only saints and the Triune Triad were able to pass through. It was a holy trip, and so many dimensions needed to line up. The combination was greater than one trillion-trillion combinations needed to unlock the veil to let just one unique soul go through.

As for this class, the Holy Spirit called the three saints to meet and talk with them on this day, congratulating them on their obedience, loyalty, and love for their step-brother, Jesus of Nazareth, son of Mary, and immaculate conception of the Holy Ghost.

The Holy Spirit inhaled a huge amount of the constellation and galaxies around him, and blew out the names of St. Paul (Saul), St. Joseph (Step-Father of Jesus), and St. Joses (Full brother of Jesus).

"Paul, Joseph, and Joses…. Come Forth!" the Holy Spirit commanded, and with that the Heavens rocked with the sound and reverberations of the Holy Spirit's calling of these names, so that many angels hid and took cover until the words had passed and the saints had arrived on time. Had they not arrived within the twinkling of an eye, causing the Holy Spirit to have to call again (which only ever happened once in the history of time: when Satan had been called), then terror would hold every angel captive until the word and time had passed that the Holy Spirit would be pacified and the search vindicated in the capture of the insolent, and Paradise could proceed on without disruption or discourse amongst its inhabitants there.

"Paul, my good and faithful servant," the Holy Spirit said to him upon Paul's arrival, "please confirm your faith to our new class, and that you went so many miles without water or food on my behalf?"

"Yes, this is true: I suffered in Your name, and was assisted by the angels," Paul responded.

"And your soul was chosen from the beginning to lead other souls here to be with us, where love, service, and mercy abide."

"Yes, this is true: I suffered in your name, and I was assisted by your angels," Paul confirmed.

"And you now serve with the angels to oversee Thy Kingdom Come," the Holy Spirit said, "as both World 1 and World 2 are measured, tempered, and hammered into tempered steel, so they might see the ending of the Age and the dawn of the next."

"Yes, this is true: I suffered in your name, and now I serve you and assist alongside your angels, those whom You created to serve and never have free volition." Paul answered.

Then the Holy Spirit called forth Joseph, step-father of Jesus, to stand in His presence.

"Saint Joseph, come forward!" the Holy Spirit commanded him forward, and immediately Joseph stood before the Holy Spirit and kneeled in His shadow, for he would not come close unless he was commanded to do so. It was not his privilege, for he had not been martyred as the others had been, so he had to stand behind the line of martyrs before he was called closer.

"Joseph, come closer. Cross the line and stand before me," commanded the Holy Spirit in a mighty roar which shook the multiple dimensions of the ultra-blue light spectrum they all existed in today. They sometimes moved into other light spectrums and traveled at great speeds from one side of the universe to the other and back again, something like traveling on a train that was moving at the speed of light, but time stood still for those who moved together but aged not in World 3, the ubiquitous world, in which they currently resided and existed.

"You were obedient and were faithful when presented with the choice to cast away Mary and the Son of God when you had the chance."

"Yes, this is true: I suffered in Your name, I was obedient, and I was assisted by Your angels," Joseph replied.

"And you walked many miles to Egypt when you were told to protect my Son from King Herod's sword, for which he has been repaid many times," said the Holy Spirit.

"Yes, this is true: I suffered in Your name, I was obedient, and I was assisted by Your angels," Joseph responded.

"And you made money to provide a good home for my Son when he needed sustenance as a child, before he could work for himself," the Holy Spirit, now in the female form, said.

"Yes, this is true: I suffered in Your name, I was obedient, and I was assisted by Your angels," Joseph answered.

"You did well, for we chose you before your soul was stitched to your body in World 1, and before you could deny us as your creator, we breathed the life of honesty and purity into you so could lead the Holy Family in their cause to establish the Twelve Tribes of Jesus in the Age of Non-Prophets, who have been cleaved, reborn, and incarnated from the Twenty-Four Tribes of Hebrew prophets: Twelve Tribes from one side of Abraham's groin and Twelve Tribes from the other side of his groin."

"Yes, this is true: I suffered in Your name, I was obedient, and I was assisted by Your angels," Joseph said.

"Now the groin is one, and no longer two," said the Holy Spirit, who had been there the night when Jesus was conceived in Mary.

Then the Holy Spirit called Saint Joses to come before him/her to be reconciled once again for his new place as head of the second tribe in the Twelve Tribes of Jesus.

"Come Forth, Joses, brother by blood of Jesus,[217] full brother to James the Less,[218] third son of Mary. Now the time has come for you to be called again to serve!"

Joses stepped forward and stood before the Holy Spirit, for now he was allowed to cross over the line of the martyrs. There he stood silent, and the Holy Spirit was silent as well, for what seemed like minutes. The Heavens were silent and blanketed with a stillness that had not been observed in quite some time. It was an honor given to Joses alone, who had cared for his mother Mary after James had been martyred in 70AD as the Bishop of Jerusalem during its fall, and served as the patron of the family until John could care for Mary after his release from the island of Patmos, where he had been receiving the messages of the Revelations from God.

---

[217] Luke 3:29

[218] Mark 15:40

Legend has it that Joses was named for Mary's uncle, Jose. Joses' gift was that he loved greatly—which he, as a middle brother, had learned from Jesus—and he was often the glue of the family when Joseph and James were not around and the family needed protection and nurturing. Joses as an adult and father was called many times to spread the gospel, going sometimes with his second cousin Joseph of Arimathea to Britain. During these mission trips, he left his son under the protection and guidance of his cousin Lexus the Gladiator to be raised as his own son and be brother of Servius, as the Holy Spirit had commanded him.

"Joses, my good and faithful servant, are you ready to serve again?" the Holy Spirit finally broke the homage of silence for Mary, but in a much softer voice now, for Joses had been created with a gentle spirit, in a softer mold of design, with different gifts and talents, and not created with the persistent heart of a hunting lion, as Paul and Joseph had both been created.

"Your son, 'Spurious,' blood of your blood, and bone of you bone, second leader in the Tribe of your line who now serves in both World 1 and World 2 to close the sinful dissention between women who wear their hair too short and put on men's clothing to give them shoulders where they have none, and the frail men who have been emasculated without castration, and must sit to urinate, because Satan used rebel women to ruin them as leaders and just fathers to lead households and make wise decisions, creating democracies of schools, prisons, and courthouses, places where the Lord's commandments have lost. You are charged with the duty to undo the abominations of Satan's influence which have poisoned the waters of the free world because 'James the Just' was called to another world by the Son and the Father to begin again mirror of earth as the air has cleaned enough to breath and the temperatures have been balanced enough to bring the seasons of temperate climate changes."

"I am ready," said Joses. "I suffered in your name, and I am ready to suffer again. I was obedient and I was assisted by Your angels, and this time my son Spurious will be with me."

"And I will send Mary Madeline with you. She is there with Gabriel assisting in the Great Plan. Have you heard of my next hosen one, John, son of Jenny Gleason, who is in your downline and blood tribe?"

"I have, and I am ready again," said Joses. "I suffered in Your name, and I am ready to suffer again. I was obedient and I was assisted by Your angels, and this time my son Spurious will be with me." Joses says.

"Then go meet with Spurious and Mary. I have sent Chalymina and Verostices to be with James, and the Son, in the other world. All the Heavens will be expanded greatly with the glory of the Triune, with God the Father in the lead, as more love must be generated and given forward to offset the hate of the dark angels paid backwards, which tries to destroy the Great Plan of Salvation Generated for All," the Holy Spirit concluded.

"I am ready again," said Joses. "I suffered many times in Your name, and I am ready to suffer again. I was obedient unto death, and I was assisted by Your angels to lighten my load, and this time my son Spurious will be with me, as my strength is under duress." Joses said.

Then the Holy Spirit said to Joses, "Have you seen my honorable man Sonny? He is of your family line and in him I will also make a great leader and counselor who will speak one day for your tribe, the Mary-Joses Gene' tribe. For just as you have been called to serve for your brother James, and his tribe with Johnnie, I will call the one who looked over your son as his dear friend, Quintus, to look over the establishment of your tribe through Sonny. He is to be given his new born-again name. For just as I made Paul from Saul, and Quintus from Servius, and Metatron from Enoch, I again will make one more: Sonny will become Sunnis, charged with giving a message of obedience to all.

The Holy Spirit called all the beings from the four corners of the world said to them:

"God the Father, Jesus the Son and Savior, and I, the Holy Ghost and Great Counselor, we—the Triune Godhead—do command these things once more so no one shall be misunderstood or claim ignorance before their Mighty Council of Holy Peers. We created the angels to serve us—and no other—without question and without want in the Heavens as our ambassadors and helpers in carrying out the will of God the Father. And we created in the same likeness of the angels to be ambassadors for mankind to serve in the same likeness of the angels to helpers of Man's will on earth, just as God's will be done in Heaven. And we created Mankind to serve God and be ambassadors to God alone, not the angels, nor other men, nor idols, nor money, nor children, nor animals, nor any other graven image that should take his mind off of the Lord as he seeks constant councils and gives constant praise. And should a man decide to marry, he will have less time to serve the Lord, for he will need time to serve his wife. And she will serve her husband, where he is the head, but she is the neck that turns the head for either good or evil, when both take their eyes off the Lord."

Then the Holy Spirit concluded Her Commandments of the day, and addressed the three archangels around her, Michael, Gabriel, and Metatron.

"Go with Joses and take him to where Mary is, so that he may also watch over Johnnie to help with his comeback as a new leader in the world and in the 'Mary-James Gene Tribe.' And so it was done, in the blink of an eye. And all the angels in Heaven said: *Amen*.

It was Sunday, and Rosanne wanted to go to church today because it was communion Sunday—the fourth Sunday of the month—but Sonny was hesitant because he wanted to work in his woodshop on his only day off. He was building a picture frame out of mahogany boards he had bought at a timber shop for a picture he had painted of Rosanne from a picture he had snapped years ago of her walking along a lane of wildflowers in the morning sun. He had another of her sitting by a water fountain taken on their honeymoon, which he had painted as well, and it was his personal favorite, so it hung over the fireplace mantle. Sometimes they would cook marshmallows inside the house on an open stove flame when it was cold enough, but that was a rare occasion since Houston was on the gulf and it never got very cold. If it got into the 30s at all, it was marshmallow time, with wine and an old movie, like the "The Thorn Birds" with Richard Chamberlain.

Rosanne liked to attend the Methodist church, which was pretty close to their house, about three blocks walking distance. Sometimes she went alone because she could not get Sonny to go with her. But today was different. Rosanne felt very strongly that

Sonny should go. She had a feeling—maybe even a premonition—that something good was going to happen, though she had no idea what. Some people called it a woman's sixth sense, and some people called it being chased by demons or spirits in the world of angels, and some—those who never acted on their senses because they believed that everything had to be logical—just called it foolishness. But Rosanne was no fool. She just had a gut feeling that something good was going to happen, so she began to pester Sonny to go to church with her.

"Honey, Baby… my Sugar Pooh-bear," she said, buttering him up, "how would you like to go with me to church today? I think it's really going to be a good message today… something just tells me so. I really need you to be there to hold my hand if I get a little nervous during the sermon… okay?"

"Arrrgh," Sonny moaned. "Rosie, I work all the time. I need some down time for *me*…"

"Yes, you work all the time… so you don't have time for me when I need you. And I need you now," Rosanne insisted.

"How about let's negotiate? You can get your nails done this week so you can have some personal time, and I can finish building my picture frames so I can have some personal time, and we are even! How does that sound?" Sonny asked.

"This is not about me-time…this is about *us*-time, *comprende*?" Rosanne's replied.

"Fine," Sonny said. He knew when she started in with Spanish, it was time to just agree and move on. He remembered hearing Mamaw once, when she was coaching Johnnie on marriage before he even met Charlotte, telling him that a man may win the battle when he is in a fight with his wife, but he will never win the war, so it is better to just give up early and beg for mercy up front.

That might be good advice for newlyweds, but very bad advice for long-term relationships. He and Rosanne always worked things out without any fallout or drama. So he would go to church with her as she requested and not waste any more mental energy on the topic.

Just as Sonny reconciled that he would be going to church with Rosanne, the telephone rang. Sonny picked up and heard the Zig Man's voice on the other end.

"Hey, Ziggy, what's happening?" Sonny asked.

"If you all aren't doing anything this morning, I'd like you to go with me to my church, Mount Zion Temple over on the east side… They're gonna have a preacher my daddy knew from back home talking today and I wanted to go but did not want to go alone, so I was hoping you would go with me."

"I gotta ask the boss-lady because she just told me we were going to her church… I mean, *our* church."

"What does Ziggy want?" Rosanne asked, overhearing part of the phone conversation.

"He wants us to go with him to his church today because someone special is speaking there."

"I like it! Let's go, Sonny! Just find out what time and where to meet him," Roseanne said breathlessly.

"Okay, we can go, Zig," Sonny said into the phone. "I think I know where you mean. The same place I dropped off Johnnie once for you right?"

"Yes, service begins at 11 a.m.… see you there!" Zig replied, hanging up the phone.

Sonny glanced over at Rosanne and then got a big smile on his face.

"I always wanted to go in to Mount Zion. I hear they have some fire-and-brimstone preaching with music sung by a choir of angels there," he said.

"I've heard the same thing, so get a move on and let's head that way," she responded.

At 11 a.m. sharp, they parked the car and saw Ziggy standing outside the front door with a group of teenage girls and no other adults. Sonny and Rosanne walked up and began to say hello, when Ziggy stepped forward.

"I want to introduce you to some of my cousins from Nigeria," Ziggy said. "Well, we're family in Christ, so we call each other cousins, but we actually just met today. They are Ibo, from the Igbo Tribe, and they traveled today with Father Boniface, who is head of the Roman Catholic diocese in Orlu. These girls come from the houses of the Holy Trinity Cathedral," Ziggy explained. "They have a teacher training college there now, but it was not always like this. Today their head priest, Father Boniface, is going to talk about the slavery in Africa and specifically in their native country, and about why these girls are here in America. They really don't understand most of what I am saying, but they understand that Jesus died for them, that the Trinity rules the universe of us all, regardless of our background or race. They believe in God, the Father, as their creator and master."

Rosanne did not say anything; she just listened in awe. She was wondering to herself if this was what today was supposed to hold, or if there was there some other missing piece in all of this which she would realize later.

Sonny, on the other hand, was casual and unshaken.

"Cool beans!" he said in his typical charismatic and nonchalant manner, shaking each girl's hand, each of whom then replied 'cool beans' back to him.

Then the group as a whole all turned to the left and walked through the big double front doors of the sanctuary. They all walked forward and sat down in the third row from the raised stage at the front of the sanctuary.

The choir was just ramping up to a crescendo in their song, accompanied by an organ which had been donated from another church on the west side of town. The four risers that the choir was standing on swayed back and forth to the rhythm of the song "Shout it Out, The Lord has Risen!" The rocking of the bleachers was so pronounced that Rosanne feared they might collapse or give way in the middle of a song. She prayed for their safety and closed her eyes as the group waved their hands and stomped their feet.

After twenty minutes of sweating and singing along with the highly energetic choir, the head pastor of the church took a breath and stepped forward, clenching his microphone, which seemed to be attached to his very soul. Then he pulled out his tattered and worn Bible and began speaking the group.

"Today we are going to talk about Moses and how he led his people out of the bondage of slavery in Egypt, leading them into the Promised Land. So, let's turn in your Bibles to Exodus 7:16 and read with me."

He paused a moment and then continued.

" 'Then say to him, *The Lord God of the Hebrews has sent me to say to you: Let my people go, so that they may worship me in the wilderness. But until now you have not listened.*' "

The pastor began explaining the history of the Jews, not the Gentiles.

"Now if you are sitting here in these pews today, I am a betting you are a Gentile, and not a Jew! Am I right?"

The congregation answered, "Hallelujah, brother!" and "Amen!"

"And God the Father said He would take them to the Promised Land and be their delivery by Moses' hand… but God never promised them they would go straight there, now, did He?"

The congregation answered, "No sir, brother!" and "Uh-Uh," and "No way!"

"So," the pastor continued, "what was the point of the wilderness the Hebrews had to live in once they escaped slavery before they could get to the Promised Land? Do we here in America think we are in the Promised Land yet? Are you in God's chosen wilderness? I want you to think about what the Hebrews had to do to get out of their wilderness and where they are today… are they still in their wilderness? I am going to have my good brother, Father Boniface, talk to you about why some of us today do not believe that we have not reached the Promised Land. But I ask you this: do we *deserve* to be in the Promised Land? Is it our God-given right? Is it our privilege or is it our curse? And is it only our pride which is holding us back from being all the God Creator wants from us, to be fulfilled and at peace in our lives today? Here is an amazing man who I pray will touch your souls with wisdom, like he did when he spoke to me."

The pastor lifted his hand and motioned to where Father Boniface was seated, and then 'Father B' stood up and moved toward the center of the stage.

"I am Father Boniface," he began, "and I want you to understand the word 'catholic' means 'universal.' We do not separate ourselves into denominations like the Protestant churches do, because God is *universal*, and His laws are universal, and we do not have the God-given right to pick and choose which of His laws we wish to obey and which we choose to brush off and disobey. When God delivered his Hebrew people from their bondage under the whip and death-lash of Pharaoh's rule, He did not give them immediate freedom. In fact, He did just the opposite: he gave them a wilderness to live in to train them, to show them that they were not gods themselves, nor could they exist without His sustenance as their God, nor could they find a good direction out of the wilderness unless they had God's help. They were lost, dying, and helpless! In fact, God told them that they would not be able to leave the wilderness until two generations of them had died off first and all the prideful of those who were slaves and thought they should not have been were dead and gone! How do you like those conditions of God to his favorite people? He wanted them to know man would be a slave either to God or to themselves, and there was no in-between. This story and passage reminds me of my mother when I was a boy, and these men were just about ready to get a good old-time whooping for having bad attitudes to me because they needed to learn an important lesson, that they were not children of the earth, but children of God, and they needed to learn their place of order and position in the world before they could make it into the Promised Land, because the world and Heaven were not made to revolve around them!"

Father Boniface paused, looking around the sanctuary, then continued: "The land I come from in Africa is the country of Nigeria, or more exactly the Niger Valley, in West Africa. My family has lived there—been born, raised up, and died there—for many hundreds, and even thousands, of years. They were there even before Christopher Columbus discovered this great land of yours you call the United States of America. If fact, my people were there in Africa when Moses spoke to Pharaoh and said, 'Let my people go,' for he could very well have been speaking to my people at the same time, because we were under a ruler very much like theirs. In fact, we have many Igbo Jews now in Nigeria who believe they are descended from the lost tribes of Israel, so we are not that far apart in our spiritual life journeys. That being said… when I was a small boy, my father told me that many of our people many generations ago had a tree in the jungle which they prayed to. This was our religion, and god-worship was everywhere. We had many gods who were not the real God, though, and we also believed in reincarnation, and even that a person could come back after death as a family member, so not everyone had their own souls. I say these things so you know your country is not the only place where God is working to save people from suffering and discontent these days, for we are now a nation of Catholics who praise God and rebuke Satan."

Again Father Boniface paused, and then continued.

"While your country was being molded and formed because white people were looking for religious freedom, you needed God-led leaders like a Moses, a Columbus, an Abraham Lincoln, whom God did so choose to begin the Christianizing process. In Nigeria, we had not a Pharaoh, but an oracle with priests who settled our complaints and differences through a group they called the Aro people with their false god, Ibini Ukpabi. When a problem was brought before the oracle, and a decision was made concerning who was innocent and who was guilty, the guilty and their family were either killed in the river, caves, or along footpaths, or they were sold as slaves along with their families for money as commerce, just the same way you Americans sold your cattle and took them to market on the Chisholm Trail, or the Goodnight Trail. We have no one to blame but ourselves! Our market trail was called the *Long Ju Ju of Arochukwu*, and my people, the Igbo people, were sent to Calabar, where they were shipped out to work in sugarcane fields and do other intensive-labor jobs in the newly forming Americas when God was planting the seeds of religious freedom throughout the world in the new 'Age of Non-Prophets' and the coming 'Age of Eternal Life with Jesus Christ in relationship' with His command for His people to pick up their cross and carry it daily as a public demonstration of their faith and obedience in the Great Plan of God, the Creator and Father, to show their salvation to the world. Then God sent the same message to my country in Africa, and to many other countries in Africa and Asia, by the same British Imperialists, who were the protagonists of Christianity, to destroy the oracle and let my people go, and become Catholics, with the understanding that the only answer was the universal belief in the universal root of Jesus Christ, where all children are of the same tree and of one trunk, and not of different trees with different trunks from the same root. Because Jesus said, 'I am the vine, my Father is the vinedresser, and you are the branches.' "

Father Boniface proceeded to clear his throat and then added one final closing message with a personal clarification.

"A sinless vine must have only one root, and only one unified stalk that needs to be pruned from time to time to bear many bountiful branches of struggling pure and sinless fruit."[219]

Then the Holy Spirit called a noble army of twenty archangels, who had all once been Knights of St. John, to go with Her, to travel to the earth to see how the 'Great Plan' was developing and how the earth in all its majesty was working in the circle of life. The Knights had earned this position by being the first organization to set up a Christian Hospital on the island of Rhodes and were affectionately known as the Knights Hospitallers to their comrades. The army of archangels then transformed themselves into invisible beings of the upper second dimension, leaving Upper Paradise through the portal window they and the other angels used to defend the Christian souls from demon attacks and collect the souls of the dead and dying for due processing.

The Holy Spirit took the archangels back into the Lower Paradise dimensions of height, length, and depth, known to contemporary science as the X, Y, & Z planes of reference, where they traveled together at a height of barely where a helicopter would hover, as they took inventory of the earth and all its glory where man did not stand, sit, or lie down.

They followed each and every coastline and river, over the ins and outs of the wetlands, bayous, and river deltas. The pristine

[219] John 15:1-5

waters where the ocean salt met the fresh river bicarbonate was so refreshing that the water teemed with new life that benefitted the fish, fowl, scaled and furred animals, as well as the entire earth, for it was so beautiful now eyes had seen as great a gem in the sky as God had created here. From land with snow caps, to waters with white caps, the constant striking of lightning bolts around the globe lit it up like a magical symphony, which played its music in harmony as the trade winds cooled the deserts and made the clouds rise in the skies to cool and bring fresh rain on the crops to grow for food for both the animals and the ones who were given dominion over them.

The Holy Spirit said, “Take me to the seat of colonial America, that I might witness the birthplace of this country’s legacy.”

So they went to where the ‘Stars and Stripes’ of the flag representing freedom and allegiance to God had been born. There they saw how the British established thirteen colonies, which gave the flag thirteen stripes, made of red and white, representing the suffering and blood to win freedom and the purity and honesty to keep it. And the Holy Spirit went over all the earth and looked at how the world had been brought to this point and who was grateful for the process and who had contempt for the process, just like those who were with Moses in the wilderness, who complained, demanding that they be led into the Promised Land in their own timing instead of the timing of the Lord.

Then the Holy Spirit arrived back in Upper Paradise, along with the entourage of twenty archangels taken forthwith, each remaining totally silent during the entire trip (always silent in their obedience by not speaking out unless spoken to first). They left Lower Paradise behind, and the Holy Spirit called for the leaders of the African nations who had closed their eyes to God's plan and complained of the Great Design as if they had a say in it, and Lower Paradise was some form of democracy versus God's Republic of Devine Laws and Holy Intervention. The Holy Spirit commanded the cherubim to bring Her mighty throne, which was only a speck compared to the throne of God the Father in Heaven, and She belted out a roar that was heard across all dimensions to the far ends of the universe.

"Bring me these three at once: Huey P. Newton, Idi Amin, Walpurga Bugenhagen, and Steve Jobs!"

In the west of the land of many keys there was a great mountain; and on the side of the mountain, many doors to many dark and forbidden caves; and on each door was a series of numbers and letters, for no earthly names were allowed on these doors, nor names of any kind to mark their existence. Therein were the souls of those who existed in eternity in holding, without any valid relationship to help them endure to lengthy times of waiting in despair. It was called the Mountain of Gnashing Teeth, with its dark caves of isolation. These souls were not brought forward except to be reminded of their deeds for which they suffered at the fate of their own dealings on earth.

The main angel, who was the overseer of the Mountain of Gnashing Teeth, called to his army to bring the keys to the mountain, and so they did, but the keys were many and it took three Amazonian-sized spirits of horse stature to pull the keys in wagons and present them for opening the cave doors. The angel had to be careful because these souls were swift to escape if possible, and then they would have to be hunted down by the other angels and brought back to be punished for their deeds of misbehavior.

The first soul was Huey P. Newton.

"Unlock his door," the Holy Spirit said, "and drag him out to me, that I might gaze on this leader of this atheistic band of ingrates."

And so it was done, and the angels had to put an invisible net over the opening, so as it launched its escape from its incarceration, it immediately was tangled in the web. Immediately the soul began demanding God do all things in its time, not God's time, for it had no patience with the white man who had risked so much to make Huey a free and honorable man.

"Soul #76.cd9426-i9lm3.e3," the Holy Spirit began, for He did not refer to the unsaved souls by their earthly birth names or their multidimensional soul-designed names, "how do you plead again... for the 22nd time?"

"Not guilty, and I demand release!" the soul claimed. But this only angered the Holy Spirit more and added to the pain which would be dealt in the lake of fire later as final retribution for an ungrateful existence. To be so pompous to even hint at demanding anything from the Holy Spirit was to lose the holy gifts of mercy and grace, which were tied up with bows and reserved, saved, and bestowed for each and every living soul, even those which had been discarded for lack of empathy, and those already judged, such as these who wished for amended reconciliation with their creators, the Triune Godhead.

"How many Anglos died in the American Civil War to give black slaves their freedom, which you claim you never received?" the Holy Spirit asked.

"No white man ever died for me. They killed each other over money and traded us like cattle, only to enslave me and my ancestors. Thus it is against them and their children that I hold this unending turmoil, contempt, and hate in my heart."

Then the Holy Spirit turned, pointed at the land to the east, and called for all the soldiers of the Northern Army who had been wounded, suffered, or died—either in battle or of starvation or frozen in the winter's cold for lack of proper clothing and shelter—in those four years it took to emancipate the Africans captured and sold by their own brothers and fathers to traders bound for the British Colonies.

"Now if you choose to count them, oh damned Soul #76.cd9426-i9lm3.e3, they, as victims who suffered for you, then they number over one million (50,000 of whom were civilians), including orphans and loved ones, heartbroken because of the triple ripple effect of the pain extended to their children, which you have caused by claiming your solo victimization, which does not exist except in your hardened heart with intolerance for goodwill toward strangers!"

The more than one million souls confronting this soul from the Mountain of Gnashing Teeth then began to chatter and chant.

"Hear us, hear us, see us, see us, know us, know us, be us, be us…" they wailed, again and again, until their cry was deafening to the Holy Spirit and the angels called to this discernment of the true victims of the world.

Then Soul #76.cd9426-i9lm3.e3 began to yell in his defense, "I never knew one of them! Not one of them ever called me friend or came to my side and to give aid to my wounded soul!"

"You had to forgive first, and forget, to understand the whole truth of your consciousness. Naïve blindness of being the victim without individual responsibility is never a good excuse," the Holy Spirit roared in the face of the soul, as many of the angels hid in the corners of this space in Paradise, because much destruction had been known to occur, even sudden incineration, to those around the Holy Spirit when He went into these moods.

"And if you could count them, damned Soul #76.cd9426-i9lm3.e3, how many missionaries have also suffered, died, starved and been tortured in my name to help free the slaves like your ancestors in all countries from around the world, from the beginning of time, so that you and your family could live a life with a clean slate to then become generous, and then to give generously, because you have received also generously, because someone who did not know you and was not your race or color paid your life forward, that you might breathe free air and not fear for your life as you sleep."

"Not one, because none knew me! Not me! Those who went to other lands did not die for me, because if they looked the other way even once in their life, they missed seeing me in my misery."

"But Jesus did not miss you, and you never sought His face! And so, you have set your own measure and judgment, oh damned Soul #76.cd9426-i9lm3.e3, for those you have condemned for looking away from you one time will also carry that judgment out upon you. YOU WILL NOT be given mercy or grace, because you yourself did not give any to others first. Let it be said: you will be given over to the second death. In the lake of fire, you will be tossed one day, and the second death will never end, for it is an eternal death, and with it your name will never be uttered or remembered again."

The Holy Spirit roared once more even louder, saying, "Take it back and close its gate forever. The next time it is called will be its last!" Then the Holy Spirit called out, "Bring me the key to the gate for the one who was once named Idi Amin."

The three wagons of keys to the Mountain of Gnashing Teeth shook violently, and then the angel who was its keeper reached in and pulled from it one key which was different from the rest. It was long and curled with a length of 24 cubits, and one cubit wide. On it were holograms of faces and bodies reminiscent of the souls who had been used and destroyed in the name of self-gain. Over half a million lives of all ages and genders had been destroyed on the decimation of the country of Uganda in the 1970s AD, along with the names of his forty-three children, doing much the same and in the same style to his own people as many of his brutal dictator predecessors had done with the same self-aggrandizement ambition: Napoleon Bonaparte, Adolf Hitler, Joseph Stalin, and Mao Tse-tung. In his effort to remove God's plan for Britain to westernize the tribes of the jungles who still worshipped trees, plants, and animals, Idi Amin used race as his tool to brutalize all in his grasp into submission, even to the point of declaring himself 'His Excellency President for Life,' which stirred the Holy Spirit into an infinite rage. The Emperors of Rome, too, had made such declarations, and they were destroyed by the armies of angels who came against them as well, and the foothold of the church of Universal Laws (Catholicism) was built on the 'Site of the Rock' within its own walls and then made into a new nation within a nation!

"Bring the damned Soul #21.xr9031-i3lk8.e7 before me, that I might examine it once more," said the Holy Spirit. The angel set about the gate the great net to catch the soul as it came forth, and it was dragged after many angels pounced on it to hold it down so that it might be subdued of its pride.

"How do you plead this day, #21.xr9031-i3lk8.e7?" the Holy Spirit questioned in an intimidating and loathsome tone.

"Not guilty," said #21.xr9031-i3lk8.e7.

"But you have taken the way of Cain! The angels on both Heaven and Earth have heard your lies. You chose to live in World 1, the world of change, and you tried to change it to meet your ways. But your ways are not my ways.[220] And Eden, which I created, will one day be restored back to a world of non-change, and those who inhabit it will no longer wish for change because it is unchangeable, as was my original plan. So be gone with you, all those who live in World 1 and wanted to change it to meet their desires!"

So the angels removed #21.xr9031-i3lk8.e7 from the Holy Spirit's presence, and then an angel with a mighty bugle arrived. Winds were pulled from the four corners of Upper Paradise and then sent down into Lower Paradise, and they swept over the oceans and over all the lands until they had touched every woman on the earth, both young and old, and the angel secured the bugle to a mighty chain which was bolted to the base of the veil that led from Paradise to Heaven. Once the winds had returned, the Holy Spirit commanded the wind to thrust itself though the mighty bugle, which it did, and a mighty sound came out, which all of Heaven and earth could hear, calling out one name, which could be heard ringing in all the land.

"Walpurga Bugenhagen, come forth so that we might discuss your events on earth!"

Then a place of souls where only women were housed sprang up from the depths, a temporary place not known to many, called the Great Castle of Good Intentions. The Castle would grow each millennium according to the souls kept there, for they were the ones who believed that in doing good, all would attain salvation, but in their hearts, they knew that doing good would never overcome doing right, for which they one day would again stand and be judged.

[220] Isaiah 55:8-9

These were numbered differently, for they still had to receive their final eternal lot as their bent still needed its final straightening.

The Holy Spirit then took a great book and looked into it. It was not the Book of Life, but the Book of Pending Repentance. Then He and She looked and found the name which had nothing written next to it and called forth #CVJB-HR4U-PQ67-UN8H. The angels who attended the Great Castle then reached up into the sky amongst the stars and pulled one star down, which was a key to the castle, and opened the great gate where these women were housed. None tried to escape when the gate was opened so they had to be called by their number so that they would know who was to be judged. Then the Holy Spirit commanded #CVJB-HR4U-PQ67-UN8H come forth, and she did.

The Holy Spirit came close to her, and He and She took hold of the wind that passed through the mighty bugle and wrapped it around her so that she might feel protected in this moment of questioning.

"How do you plead, #CVJB-HR4U-PQ67-UN8H," says the Holy Spirit?

"I am not guilty in Man's eyes" said the soul, "but guilty in the eyes of God." Then the Holy Spirit took the blanket of wind from around the soul, and said once again, "How do you plead, #CVJB-HR4U-PQ67-UN8H?"

Without the feeling of protection by the blanket of the four winds to keep her warm from the cold of loneliness, she said, "Now I see that I am guilty only in the eyes of God. Just like Eve, I moved my Adam to make a mistake, which had a ripple effect and caused others to stumble."

"You are correct," said the Holy Spirit, "and because of your confession, you will be allowed to leave the Castle of Repentance and go the place the others like you now live. Together you will wait until called again for your next duty to serve in the kingdom of Upper Paradise, where free volition is not a friend but an enemy." Then the Holy Spirit continued, "Would you like to see all the souls whom you caused to stumble?"

"Please, no, Your Greatness, that would be more than I could bear," answered the soul.

But the Holy Spirit wanted to show those who had stumbled to know of the repentance that was done in Paradise and not on earth, so the Holy Spirit called for a great Mountain Range to be erected with soul #CVJB-HR4U-PQ67-UN8H on one side and the rippled souls on the other. So, it was done, and the two were separated by the mountain range, but after twelve hours of waiting, a sun shone directly overhead, above the great mountain range, and it heated them so that that the mountains melted and threw themselves into the sea which surrounded them. The rippled souls then cheered for their release from the effects of the soul which had caused them grief, and the soul which had grieved the others felt relief. They then all went together to another place where that stayed, and the one soul felt an acceptance which it had never felt before.

And the Holy Spirit was happy that another soul had found its path to repentance, albeit late, but had fulfilled the requirements of obedience to a higher calling, where all would wait and be judged together when the universal time came for them to honor their covenant, which would be read over them at the time of their creation when they were set apart as single blessed souls.

It was then the Holy Spirit took a break from His and Her formal duties as counselor and manager over the earth, which He and She needed, to see how earth was doing with its many blessings which had been poured on it recently. The Holy Spirit lived and existed in many millions of singular dimensions in a multi-plurality of space and time, in both planer and warped galactic time zones. This allowed the Holy Spirit to live in each believer as their spiritual guide and conscience and be the same in all beings at the same time. It could be visualized in earth-terms as a single current of electricity which ran through all things at the same time at the same voltage, never fluctuating, so that all things were measured at the same time, but resistance could be felt in the voltage, as certain people turned from the force and did not let it run as it was designed to from the beginning of creation. When the Holy Spirit did this and took inventory of the voltage of all the individuals on earth, it was like a great collection of electro-magnetic waves, which all converged at a single point of convergence, and the power was almost overwhelming to the Holy Spirit, especially if the total number was below the mark of seven. When it was above seven, the Holy Spirit was not concerned, and on this day, it was 7.3829018462121, so the Holy Spirit could go on with His and Her business of monitoring Upper Paradise and keeping the angels busy with their Holy Chores.

So the Holy Spirit continued with the calling up of those who had lived their lives under the mark of seven and dragged down the rest of the world with their resistance to the Holy Spirit's will and design. A new soul had arrived and had not been processed yet, so the Holy Spirit called for the one known as Steve Jobs, typically referred to by his peers as the smartest man of recent time in the Age of Non-Prophets. He was no longer in his earthly skin and bones, neither of which he was able to bring with him to Upper Paradise, nor did he bring any sacks of wealth or clout with him as he was called up for holy questioning.

"Bring me #OOTR-DSMN-``89-GFR5 from the Torrent!" the Holy Spirit roared, as angels were sent out to bring the Torrent before the Holy Spirit.

This was a difficult task and a usual thing in Upper Paradise because of the size of the Torrent. With souls all moving in a circle and bumping into each other as they went around and around, they cursed each other every moment, for they were not free to have space between them any more than the rings of debris around Saturn had around each particle. But the angels were able to put mighty magnets at each pole and pull it across the sky from the Dark Hole Abyss in which it was normally kept.

When it arrived, the Holy Spirit reached into the sky and pulled down a magnificent staff which was curved at the end to reach into the Torrent with precision and pull out the soul He and She wished for examination. The Torrent was traveling fast in a circle and it looked like just one big mass of jelly as the angels would describe it among themselves, but with precision the Holy Spirit plunged the Holy Staff into the Torrent and waited for a moment until the correct soul had be collared for the interrogation. The staff wiggled and went left and right, much like a fish on a line, but this was no fish but rather the soul of a very confident being who had run from his destiny in order to seek a more self-defeating role for fame and fortune.

The Holy Spirit pulled His and Her staff from the Torrent and with it the soul who had been collared to stand judgment this moment. This would not be the final judgment because that would be done by the Father in Heaven, but the Father would take the Council of the Holy Spirit into consideration for all those who were set aside in the Torrent for softening before their final judgment day.

"Soul #OOTR-DSMN-``89-GFR5, how do you like the way your days are being spent here in Upper Paradise while you await Final Judgment?" the Holy Spirit called out, though He and She already knew the answer the soul would give.

"I see no logic to this ending, this continuum as it is presented, or this hypothetical treatment of my life based on my actions while lived on earth," the soul replied to the Great Holy Spirit and Master of all things good and bad on Earth. "I was a good man, and I sought good in all things, taking the high road always where injustice was found."

"And who are you to decide what is just and unjust?" the Holy Spirit roared at the soul, showing no respect for that which gave no respect to the Holy Spirit on earth. "Were you not baptized with the oath given to have the Lord Jesus as your Savior, to follow and obey Him, and claim only Him as your relationship with Heaven?"

"I did," replied #OOTR-DSMN-``89-GFR5.

"And how do you plead?" asked the Holy Spirit as He and She turned many colors, beginning to pulse up and down, as lightning began to crash around and strike, and the angels sought cover.

"Innocent!" answered #OOTR-DSMN-``89-GFR5.

"After making a covenant with the Son of the Lord God, Creator and Master of the Universe, for whom I am His conscience and Council," the Holy Spirit said, "you chose to follow a human prophet of World 1, seeking council and enlightenment by meditation, when you should have sought council from me… How dare you!"

The Holy Spirit then began to exude fumes like a mighty volcano with heat radiating from its core. The heat went from a state of divine fusion to unbridled fission, and then began to get so hot in became like a giant round star, the greatest in the universe. Its heat was so great that it began to melt much of Paradise around it, but then the veil from Heaven opened and Jesus, the Son of God, was standing there.

"Oh Holy One, Lamb of the Universe, Morning Star to the Father in Heaven, I greet you on this day you have blessed us with your kindness and generosity. Your Peace is welcome here with us," the Holy Spirit said, and then began to settle down from His and Her unusual state of irritation, even to the point of being civil.

Then Jesus spoke.

"Many times countries have received plagues and judgments by the wrath of the Holy Spirit," Jesus began, "who saw evil upon the earth, and many times the Father in Heaven allowed these judgments to occur because of one man. Moses was sent to Pharaoh, David to Goliath, Eisenhower to Hitler, and many thousands more, and now we must send another man to undo the curses you have brought on man with your evil of self-indulgence on the earth. The Passive-Aggressive are always the most cunning, and like Satan, himself, they will present two gifts to their prey: one gift in a big box with shiny beautiful paper and a big bow on top, supposedly representing the value inside, and another gift in a small box without paper, but with mud and blood on it, to symbolize impurity and defeat, and not a bow on top but tears wept on it to represent suffering which will happen if the victim chooses this box. And so each time the victim chooses the beauty over non-beauty, form over function, good-intention over the righteousness of clarity of purpose and fulfillment, the unknown of chaos and disorder over the known of peace and harmony, he then creates a ripple effect, which causes the Holy Spirit grief to defend His and Her loved ones, because now they live to be first guilty, where once they lived to be first free and innocent. The Wisdom of the Ages sees no value in such gifts of beauty, just as Satan saw beauty in himself when he separated his will from the Father, and he was cast out and not a vagabond on the earth, roaming and looking for his final mark. I say to you, #OOTR-DSMN-``89-GFR5, here are your charges with which you will be charged one day after you once again are called from the Torrent to answer these claims from the other souls who are in the Torrent with you."

The Jesus called for Enoch, a.k.a. the angel Metatron, who was called to hold all the charges of all those in his hands who would be brought before the Lord to be judged and to pull from them just one soul's earthly deeds.

And this is what Jesus read:

"You put in all people's hands the future 666 tracking, for which they have all lost their freedom. Never again will they find peace without being guarded and sought after by evil inside their homes as they are watched and listened to, for you destroyed the future relationship of all God's children for putting in their hands the gateway to pornography which would steal their childhoods, take from them first their sense of purity, and ruin relationships before they could even begin to seed and sprout. You made all men constantly look down and praise artificial intelligence because that is where Eternal Hell exists, instead of looking up and praising God, in Whom Eternal Life exists. You have done these things to the detriment of the world! And now you have caused the Holy Spirit more work and more unsettlement, and you claim innocence before the Holy Spirit, but no one stands here innocent but me, who died for you, and yet you denied me in front of others. Be gone with you, back to the Torrent, where you may no longer see anything but the backs of those you stepped on in life, taking them into a more imperfect world ruled by darkness, loneliness, dependence, computer slavery, and anxiety."

And so the angels threw #OOTR-DSMN-``89-GFR5 back into the Torrent, which swept him away once again into the big circle which he chose as his eternal resting place, and they carried the Torrent back to the place of loneliness and solitude from where it once came.

Then the veil closed in front of Jesus, the Lamb, and Jesus returned back to Heaven to sit by His Father's side, where His Father constantly said, "In Him, I am well pleased."

After Jesus returned back to Heaven, the Holy Spirit rested again for a time, and then commenced as the Mighty General who carried out the divine plan on earth. The time had come for his archangel, Servius, to meet Johnnie, so He and She called up the angel which had been converted from its soul and now lived an eternal life moving between Upper Paradise and Lower Paradise, constantly doing the Father's will.

Make no mistake, a human soul may never be elevated to God's status, where choice is given on the same level of the Triune Triad Godhead, but becoming an angel was somewhat common for those souls chosen from the beginning of creation to carry out the holy duties of the divine plan, for they had been obedient on earth to the point of being martyred, and for them obedience was still a requirement in Paradise so that their loyalty and trust in their Father would never be questioned or impugned.

"Servius, come forth!" the Holy Spirit called for the angel who had as a man carried the Gospel with Luke after the loss of Paul on the earth. "How is the plan developing on earth, the planet which I cleaned from all Paleozoic Life so they could live in Eden?"

"We are controlling the temperatures, as you requested, for the balance and seasons and blessings of the rain and heat for all the world to be fruitful in its season of planting, just like a woman's womb, oh, Great One," said Servius to the Holy Spirit. "You designed and have controlled the last earthy Ice Age well; for now, it has been almost 35 million years since the heating began, and 13,000 years since the Son has been allowed to visit again and check on His people, so in that time it has warmed enough that the season of ice caps may be gone from the heat of the mantle warming. We do not let the mantle warm too much, so the process is slow enough that they may carry on their business and acts of honoring and praising the Father without distraction of impending peril."

"Have you measured the cracks in the mantle to see if it is time to move the continents again and reset the earth on a different axis?" the Holy Spirit asked. "The tides will certainly wash the earth clean again like in the days of Noah, and we must prepare Johnnie and the others for that time to come. The oceans will rise at least 1200 feet in an instant and in some places even more, so no ship or person in the zone shall survive. They will call on my name and if it is the first time it will not be heard or answered," said the Holy Spirit.

"The mantle is secure, but the faults are growing larger over the most lost, and many will be swallowed in future days just as in past days. We are ready for your command, Oh Great One," Servius replied.

"And who is the most prepared for the next coming calamity?" asked the Holy Ghost now.

"I believe it is the ones known as the Church of Christ by Latter Saints, yet we all know that the alleged angel Moroni was just a man," answered Servius. "For just as I am in the heart of the Holy Spirit a tool to fish for men in lost seas, so was Moroni a tool in his day, so all might be fishers of men around the globe and fish in whatever body of water they might be bent to serve. For fish are of many breeds and kinds, just as you created man to be many breeds and kinds, the difference being you created man in your image with a pre-destined soul to receive eternal relation with you if he withstood the measure of the predesigned evil one."

"You have gained much wisdom, Servius, as a good angelic observer, caring for the will of the Father in Heaven to be carried out in His time, and not man's time; so yea, you shall be rewarded with your next duty, just as Verostices and Chalymina were given their holy duties to watch over Paul in his last days. Now it is time for you to earn much of your past so you can understand your future and put much into perspective, that you might be fulfilled in your creation," stated the Holy Spirit.

Then the Holy Spirit roared out, "Bring me the Great Crystal of Gobal!"

And the angels were sent out and began to roll the clear round crystal, which was mined on the planet Gobal into a perfect shape of the earth. It had many of the secrets stored in it from days past which the Holy Spirit wanted Servius to see and know. Then the Great Crystal was before them, and it was beautiful in its perfection, radiant beyond measure, and noteworthy of praise simply because the Father had created it in His love for obedience, yet with a disdain for hate and loose lips.

"Here you will find your past from before you were born from your mother's womb," the Holy Spirit said. The Holy Spirit commanded the rock to speak and it did so, with clarity and affirmation, just as the burning bush had done for Abraham in his day of loyal obedience.

The Rock of Gobal began to move inside, and a vision of a story began to unfold. Here is what the Rock said:

"Servius, from before your soul was created, we go back from you father, Tilius, who changed his name from Tullius, to your great great- great- great- great- great-grandfather, Servius Tullius, almost six hundred years prior. He was the sixth king of Rome, and he did many great things in his day, for he knew not the evil in worshipping pagan gods and for these things he will not be judged, but for other things he will be judged, as all who lived in that day. Of these things which the Deity of the Triad Triune Godhead grieves the most is his erection of the Temple to the Goddess Diana in the Aventine in Rome."

The rock showed the Temple and how many citizens of Rome came there to pray, giving praise to the animals, which gave them sustenance and food, as well as the companionship of lost souls when they had nowhere else to turn except to the Lord of Hosts.

The Rock of Gobal then turned to a second theme and began with a picture of a great parade in Ephesus to honor the goddess Diana. It was planned for the street where Mary, the mother of Jesus, lived with John, as he was taking care of her as the Lord Jesus had commanded him to do. And when Timothy, who was Bishop of Ephesus, heard of this group who were going to protest that Christians were moving to their town to meet and pray with John and Mary, Timothy tried to stop the parade, but the mob beat him in a side street and killed him for standing in their way of loving animals over the Lord of Hosts.

Then the Rock said, "And to all those who worship animals as their children and put them to bed and have funerals for their lost lives: you will be judged for these things you have done; for like the angels who only worship God, Man is only approved to worship God, and in his place no other gods are allowed to be praised because he is a jealous God; and their place is not in a realm of love or worship to take the place of God. If you spend one minute with your pet, how much time do you spend with your God? And in this you find which is your God and which is your destiny as a child of creation with the loss of an eternal relationship after your pet has died. They are to be servants of man, as bees that pollinate the flower, and vultures that clean the dead from making you sick from disease, and also food for man when he is hungry, regardless if they are cured or not; and this is all for animals the of the field, sky, and sea. All were to be born without souls and without reincarnation ability, just as man was before he was given his eternal soul to be a steward of. All non-humans are to be like angels to man, to worship and to serve him, and not the other way around, for God does not worship the angels. Animals were created for the dominion of man, and when they cease to survive on the earth from man's carelessness, then man will cease to be alive on the earth as well. For man's fate is that of the animals, who were not chosen to be given the legacy of holy creation. When these animals are destroyed, then the great time clock of man—which began with next to last Ice Age, when Adam and Eve were given the first souls, created to be above the angels, no longer like animals, but separated from the rest—when this happens, the earth will stop turning, and the moon will hide its face from the sun as the tides no longer cleanse the earth, and the oceans will all dry up under the scorching heat of the sun, thus causing an explosion created from inside out. The magnetic poles of dry magma will draw the remnants even closer to its solar parent than it has ever been before. The earth will fall toward the sun in pieces, and a smaller planet will break away from the earth, and it will take its own new orbit to become a new blue jewel, holding all the water necessary for life in the sky. Those there again will long to hide, but God will find them there too, because he has placed them there to once again make a new beginning and covenant for a new age; and with them will be a great test and strain which they must pass through before they can be worthy to call themselves children of God. Amen."

Woe to them! They have taken the way of Cain; they have rushed for profit into Balaam's error; they have been destroyed in Korah's rebellion.

These people are blemishes at your love feasts, eating with you without the slightest qualm—shepherds who feed only themselves. They are clouds without rain, blown along by the wind; autumn trees, without fruit and uprooted—twice dead. They are wild waves of the sea, foaming up their shame; wandering stars, for whom blackest darkness has been reserved forever.

As Testified by Jude,
Brother of Jesus and James
Chapter 1:11-13

Chapter 13

Living Faith with 100% Blindness Forever

It was again early on a Sunday morning, about 4:30 a.m., when Johnnie's eyes opened. He could not sleep anymore. He tossed and turned in bed for a while before deciding to get up and pray. It was even too early for Cojo because even a dog needs eight hours of sleep to recharge its body for the next day of burden, whatever that might be.

Johnnie felt compelled to get up and pray this morning because of his heavy heart. He went to his Bible to hold and pray for understanding for what God would have him learn that day, and when he opened it, he of course could not see anything, so he just sat and reflected on the events in his life. On the inside, written on the first page of his Bible, was an inscription from Coach Thornton, given to him that first day he joined the coach's basketball team, which changed his life when he was just a teen. The inscription read: 'To Johnnie, may you learn what all Christians eventually learn, and that is *Pick up your cross, and carry it daily*. I will pray that when you do, the weight of your cross will be light. Many Blessings, Coach Thornton.'

Johnnie picked up his Bible, and opened it to that page. He could not read the words written, but he rubbed his hand over that page as if to feel the meaning and power still held locked within the ink on its pages. He prayed about his calling and found peace in the light of his mission, that he was not the first nor would he be the last to wear the shoes of a blind ambassador for Jesus who would preach the humble truths of salvation through a life of submission and suffering. Jesus did that, and showed the world how it was to be done. While Jesus walked as his public display to the place where he would be crucified, he was mocked, spit upon, cursed at, and ridiculed for his faith in His Father, yet he never wavered or gave up his power to those who tried to steal it from him by putting him on their level. He chose the higher path, the higher road to salvation, and the higher calling to live as God called him that day on his rebirth, to be nothing more and nothing less than who he was created to be, and who he had been designed by creation to be. This was his cross!

As he ran his hand past the pages in his book and over the words that so many people had died to bring to him, an angel appeared to him. Yes, even a blind man can see angels, for they are usually seen directly in the brain as a wavelength, sent from a different dimension, and not in this World as we know it, which is why no one else can see them when only one or two people can.

"Fear not," said the angel, for it was Servius! "I have been sent by the Lord to bring you good news."

Johnnie just sat there holding his Bible in amazement, frozen completely still as he felt he was in some form of a time-warp somewhere, anywhere, but not here. He could not fathom what was going on, for he was blind and could not see! So how could this even be happening? It was not logical. And even more, he knew it was not possible… so he just sat there in mental confoundment, but still he listened intently in his wonderment in the moment.

"Remember what Paul wrote to the Hebrews," the angel said. "Christ is the High Priest, the Son of God, who has gone to Heaven. Paul was the man born chosen to represent other men in their dealings with God. He was subject to the same weaknesses you have, and that is why he had to offer sacrifices, for both Man's sins and his own human sin. No one can become a high priest just because he wants the honor; he must be called for God for this work, just as Aaron was. That is why Christ did not exalt himself to become high priest. No, he was chosen by God, who said to him, 'You are my Son; today I have become your Father,' and also at another time, 'You are a priest forever in the line of Melchizedek.'[221] "

Then the angel vanished.

This all was quite strange to Johnnie. He reached over and grabbed his heart to see if it was racing form the fear he felt, but it was not, because the angel had told him to 'fear not.' Well, he felt at peace with the event, but it was so strange that he could only pray to see what God would have him do with this information, for he knew not what it meant. And as he prayed, he felt compelled to go to church this morning, even though it did not seem right, for he knew he was already saved, and he had already had made his prayers heard for this day before sunrise. Then the message which The Holy Spirit sent came to his heart, as his guardian angels whispered in both his left and right ears simultaneously, while he still felt the calling from the miraculous vision he had just had.

---

[221] Hebrews 5: 1-6

"Today you must go to church not for you, but for someone else who will be there and will meet you there," his angels whispered.

'Hmmm,' Johnnie thought, 'this will be interesting.' So he called Sonny this time, and not Tucker. Something told him it should be Sonny who should go with him. Then he got on the phone, with Mamaw listening (she often picked up the phone downstairs in her bedroom and eavesdropped, because the shared line in the old house only had one phone number and phone line into the house).

"Hey, Sonnius, my buddy," Johnnie said. (Sonnius was a code name which Mr. Silverman used for him when he wanted him to come quickly and not ask any questions.) "Can you give me a lift to church today? I want to go to the one down the corner that has all the crepe myrtles on the corner."

"Can I bring my sweetie Rosanne with me?" Sonny replied.

"Sure can, and I might even let her ride shotgun in front if she is nice to me," Johnnie said, smiling and showing the big gap between is front teeth.

He also had quite a bit of acne scarring on his face from a bout of bad acne when he was in school. He remembered once when the basketball hit him in the face when he wasn't looking right on his left cheek and so many blisters on his face popped that the towel which he wiped the blood off with was bright red from the hit. He never forgot that and always had a heart for those he felt were some form of outcast because of their looks or the victim of poverty when they could not afford to get medicines like the rich kids who could afford to have nice skin and clean clothes to go to school in. Mamaw always tried to gently push him in the correct direction, but most times Johnnie just wanted to play the victim, so he let the things happen to him so he could justify all the events in the world as stacked against him, but no more. But through his blindness he had come to understand that God owed him nothing and he was there only to be measured against Satan just like Job and Paul, and he was not going to let a little bad memory get him down today because it was the morning of 'Fear Not', which to him meant 'Look out, world, because Johnnie Perfect is coming to town, and he is going to kick someone's butt and take some names!'

"Do you want to go to church with me this morning, Mamaw?" Johnnie yelled downstairs to her bedroom.

"No, you go ahead, and I will see you when you get home. Who are you going with?" she asked.

"Sonny and Rosanne," he shouted out in a half-muted voice. Then he began to get ready, and waited for them by the front door until they arrived in about an hour.

The pastor of the small church, of course, recognized Johnnie from aired NBA games on TV as he entered the small sanctuary and headed for an open seat on a front pew. The music had already started. They were singing an old hymn which was a favorite of his and many others in that small church called 'It is well with my Soul.' The second stanza particularly touched Johnnie that day:

Though Satan should buffet, though trials could come, Let this blessed assurance control;

That Christ has regarded my helpless estate, and hath shed His own blood for my soul...

It is well; it is well with my soul.

Then after the song, the pastor began to tell the story of how and why that song was written. A man named Horatio G. Spafford was the composer in 1873, just eight years after the Civil War had ended. Two years before, his business had been destroyed in the Great Fire of Chicago, and before that he had lost his young son to scarlet fever. He worked hard and regained his business status, so on November of 1873 he sent his wife, Anna, and their four daughters to Europe aboard a French ocean liner, the Villa du Havre. Mr. Spafford planned to stay and work a couple of days and then take another ship and meet them in Europe. After four days at sea, the Villa du Harve collided with another ship, the Loch Earn, and the Villa du Harve sank, and with it the remaining four children of Horatio and Anna were drowned at sea. Mr. Spafford, who had not left yet, received a telegram from his wife which said, "Saved alone, what shall I do?" So Mr. Spafford booked passage on the next available ship to meet his wife, and after four days at sea, the captain called Mr. Spafford out onto the deck and told him that this was the place where his children had gone down. It was also the place where Mr. Spafford sat and prayed and wrote the words you just sang… by a man in unbelievable grief, called "It is well with my soul."

The pastor went on to preach on what a man has when he loses everything… he has only God, nothing else. And Johnnie knew exactly what the pastor was preaching about. Johnnie could not hear much of the sermon past that point of revelation, sitting in the small church with the crepe myrtles outside, where he had seen the angel who spoke to him, but he knew he was there for a purpose, though still he knew not what.

When the sermon was over, the pastor did something he had not done before: he asked all those in the congregation to meet three people before they left, which was entirely unusual for the small church. After this, Johnnie felt a small arm pulling at his right sleeve from behind. He slowly turned around, as did Sonny and Rosanne, to see a family seated behind them: a husband and wife with four small children, all of whom were girls. The mother and father said hello to Sonny and Rosanne, and then they introduced themselves to Johnnie. The girl who had pulled on Johnnie's sleeve was named Elizabeth, or Lizzy, for short. Lizzy was the firecracker in the family and never shied away from being the first in any group to say or do something to start things rolling. In this case it was her touch which caused everyone to turn to each other and begin the initial words, which would become a lifelong friendship.

"Hi, we are the Morgans. I am Paul, and this is my wife, Cindy," the father said

"And I am Lizzy," the child in the middle boasted with her hair in braided pigtails down both sides.

Johnnie sort of smiled back, and then began to leave, when the family asked Johnnie if he would like to join them at their house for a Life Group they were having after the sermon. Lunch would be provided.

"He sure would!" Sonny answered for Johnnie, who gave him a look that said, *What are you saying there, brother? I have nothing in common with this family and four small children. I just need to go home and sit and wait for the next basketball practice so I can get on with my life....*

"We live at 404 Rockcliffe Drive, and lunch is in thirty minutes. We hope to see all of you there, okay?" Mr. Morgan said.

"That is so gracious… we would love to join you," Rosanne said.

So Sonny and Rosanne made the decision for Johnnie: he was going to eat lunch at a stranger's house. But then he remembered why he was supposed to go to church in the first place: it was not about him… even though as he had been listening to the song by Mr. Spafford, he had felt it *was* all about him, a very strange feeling indeed for Johnnie.

On the way over, Sonny and Rosanne stopped to tell Mamaw where they were going and that they would see her later that afternoon. It was sort of like going to the park or a picnic to get out of the house and get some fresh air, but Johnnie was blind, so he was always afraid he would knock over someone else's furniture and break it, and he was very uncomfortable going into someone's house where he could fall over items in his way. The arena was different. It was made of just long hallways without clutter, so a person could drive a truck through and not hit anything. A home with children with toys spread out on the floor was the equivalent of a war zone with minefields to fall over, so Johnnie was not looking forward to the outing, but he went along anyway.

Once they arrived at 404 Rockcliffe Drive, the three got out of their car and knocked on the door. Lizzy was there to let them in, and she was just a miniature shadow standing in front of Johnnie, with his big basketball frame of a body.

"Come in," Lizzy said. "My mommy is making pizza in the kitchen."

When Johnnie, Sonny, and Rosanne entered the home, there were several families already there from the church, as well as the pastor. It was pretty much half of the church congregation, with lots of children running up and down the stairs, creating a great commotion of noise in a game room at the top of the stairs. One could not really consider it a thunder of noise, but more like screaming chaos, as if one of the children were laughing in terrible pain. Johnnie listened to all of the noise and wished it were the cheers of basketball fans around him seated in the stands. But he had settled down a bit and was at peace with some, but not much, family commotion surrounding him, because he knew he only had to bear it for an hour or two, that it was temporary. If it took much longer, he would look for an exit in a gracious manner and excuse himself. So, he took a seat on the couch and waited to see what would happen to him this day.

The pastor was already sitting on the couch at the other end, and Sonny and Rosanne had left to mingle for a moment around the punch bowl.

"Who is there?" Johnnie heard a voice say from his right side.

"I am Johnnie," he replied.

"And what is your last name?" the pastor questioned Johnnie, prying a little deeper.

"Perfect… I am, Johnnie Perfect.

"Wow, I would like to thank you for attending our church today, Mr. Perfect," the pastor began talking with a little more excitement. "Are you having a good week so far?"

"Not exactly… I have had better," Johnnie replied. "But so far, not too bad."

"What does that mean?"

"Well, our new season basketball season is beginning, and I think Horatio Spafford and I have a lot in common: he lost all he had on a ship and in the water, and I lost all I had in a car and on the road" Johnnie said.

"I have heard, and I am sorry about your wreck. Did you know I am blind too?" asked the pastor.

"Blind… you too? Why has no one told me?" Johnnie exclaimed.

"Well, not exactly blind like you, but I am blind to many of the truths you seem to know, and I don't," said the pastor.

"What does that mean, blind but not like me?"

"I have heard that you have seen and heard an angel who lives in our crepe myrtles," the pastor continued.

"Yes, I have, but I don't talk about it. We all have guardian angels, even you, Pastor. We are just not enlightened to listen to them. Mine talks to me all the time, and now I know what their signs are, telling me what to do and what not to do. They have twenty-six levels, but only a few levels are assigned to travel back and forth to earth at a time. But I have been told not to speak about it, so I had better be quiet now," Johnnie finished.

"That is fine by me," the pastor said. "I would not want you to do anything that was not approved by God in your heart. Guardian angels, huh? Well, at least you have been told something and given insight into what others have not, correct? This is something we all pray for everyday as pastors, and we hope to be spoken to just like you have. Next week I might research and talk on the matter."

"It is not the blessing you think, Pastor. I would prefer to be like you and not know that much about how everything works… some parts of the future… or anything of the sort. I think I would be happier in this world being ignorant of all the pain and suffering that surrounds us, and living in blind bliss like the rest of the world. Seems like a better existence, with less suffering."

"So see, you are not really blind, are you?" the pastor asked. "You have sight the rest of the world doesn't. You are the opposite of blind, with clear vision. Sometimes suffering is a good thing. It can give us clear vision where others have none! Jesus suffered. Most everyone in the Bible suffered. None of them ever denied they knew the truth… It is the story of all Christians who come to know God, and who He is, and why we are who we are. How we live and deal with suffering is our testimony for the nonbelievers to see."

"I understand, Pastor, but I still don't like suffering. Our basketball season is beginning soon, and I want to see and play again. It is my true love," Johnnie said. Then Johnnie stood, beginning to feel uneasy with the questioning. He hoped Sonny and Rosanne would see him standing and would come and rescue him from the probing pastor.

"It is quite funny how God seems to take the things we most love from us, to make us see more clearly through His eyes. Did you know that Mr. Spafford later remarried and God blessed him with another child?" asked the pastor, "Did I get to that far in the sermon? I don't remember. But he did. God blessed him again for his loyalty, faith, submission, and obedience."

Johnnie sat down and said, "No, sir, you did not. I guess that was the part I was waiting for…"

"Yes, Johnnie, it is the part we are all waiting for. I'll tell you a secret. Most people don't know when I get up to preach about the suffering I live with daily. I lost my daughter to cancer when she was only three years old about ten years ago, and then I lost my wife in a hiking accident shortly after that. Both were the light of my life.

After that I just wanted to go die and be with them in Heaven, but God told me no. He had other plans for me. And now I am a pastor and try to relieve other people's suffering through my own experiences. Without my suffering, how would I be able to connect on a level that they will understand? I think it is the part where Jesus said to go and pick up your cross and carry it daily. We all have suffering stories we can tell. I have not gotten remarried yet, maybe never will. And I would like to have another child, but I don't believe I will ever overcome the loss of my wife and daughter unless I give it to God and He makes it all right in my soul, just as you will probably never overcome the loss of your eyesight. I will pray for you, and I hope you will pray for me too. Just like Horatio, we both need it to be good with our souls," he finished.

"I hear you, and I never thought pastors needed prayers," Johnnie said. "You are the ones leading us as sheep, and giving us the messages of hope and faith. You should have it together more perfectly than us, shouldn't you?"

"You would think so, Johnnie, but we are just human too, so we don't. But we are held to a high standard, so we live in sort of a bubble and have to be conservative in our words and actions. We have learned to lean on God a little more than the rest of the world by faith, and we try to show it, and hope others see it, just like you do, I think. And if we were spoken to by angels more, then maybe our message would be more clear, and that is why I think you came to the church today, so I could learn to listen to the Holy Spirit more and see if I can get my angels to help guide me too… just like Paul did."

"I never thought of it that way. I am truly so sorry to hear about your loss of your daughter and your wife. That must be pretty tough. I lost my wife too. But it is not as bad as yours. Mine just left me and did not say good bye, but I feel like she died and left me. Or at least I was the one who felt like I died, which hurts more because I am still living and I still love and miss her."

"Those like you and Horatio are fortunate, but they do not understand it at the time. God will always put a Judas, a disease, or a mountain that they have to climb in their life, so they can learn the meaning of unconditional love, Mr. Johnnie Spot Perfect. This is one of the paradoxes we all get to learn. God loves us so much that He makes us see His love and learn from it as we must unconditionally love others. It is one of the toughest lessons I think we have to go through."

"Please don't call me Spot," Johnnie said to the pastor.

"Why not?" the pastor asked.

"Because God washed my spots away… I am clean of those things. I am now spotless." Johnnie said.

"Then I guess you had better start living life without any fears anymore, without living in the past or having any regrets like you just mentioned. Those are spots in my book, how about yours?"

"Yeah, I know, but this is tougher than facing death itself, I think. I wish I had died in that wreck." Johnnie said.

"No, you don't, Johnnie. God has given you a second chance, and He is counting on you to lead others by your example... so don't blow it. This has never been about you! It has always been about Him! You will come to see that soon. You already answered that question when you said you died already. How tough was that?"

"Next time we die, I think it should be a little quicker and easier. At least I pray for that!" Johnnie said, and they both laughed a little crazily as Rosanne walked up and put her arm on Johnnie's shoulder.

"Are you two enjoying each other's company?" she asked.

"We are telling secrets," the pastor said. "Isn't this right, Mr. Spotless and Mr. Perfect?"

"That is right," Johnnie replied. "So where did Sonny go? He should be in on this enlightening conversation."

"Sonny is outside with the other men. They are standing around the BBQ pit under the big cypress trees talking about football."

"Football and not basketball?" Johnnie asked.

"Nope… sorry hun, it is purely a football group out there, so you better keep your tongue tied and your britches on, and get out there ASAP I think, and go with the flow on this one. Let's go, and please don't rock the boat, okay?" Rosanne said.

"Will you lead me out there?" Johnnie asked. "I want to hear what the real world talks about when I am not the center of the conversations."

"Okey-doke," Rosanne said with a big grin.

As she began to help Johnnie get up and walk toward the patio door, there was a loud crash that came from the back yard, followed by loud screaming. Rosanne let go of Johnnie's arm immediately and turned to run over to the back yard to see where Sonny was.

"Oh, Jesus, please let Sonny be okay… I need him," she prayed under he breath.

A huge cypress tree under which all the men were standing had had a big top branch—at least twelve feet long—come loose and crashing to the ground. It must have weighed several hundred pounds, maybe even a thousand pounds, because it was at least fifteen inches thick where it connected to the center of the tree. It was the length of a piano, and must have been there for at least fifteen or twenty years, just waiting to fall off in a wind or rain storm, having dried out or something. Who would think that it would break right now?

Just as Rosanne got to the patio doors, she looked outside toward the backyard fence and saw two men lying face down on the ground with a huge dead tree limb stretched across their bodies. One had been pierced by a large pointed branch. They both lay there motionless. As she focused for a moment on the scene, she screamed out loud but could not even hear herself.

"Sonny… no!!"

She immediately ran outside, grabbing and pushing the patio door all the way open behind her. She needed to see for herself if it was really Sonny under the tree limb or if was it someone else. How could this be? They had just left the house for a few minutes for an afternoon visit with a church group, and now this accident had happened? Could God be this cruel? *This just can't be happening*, she thought to herself. It was all so surreal as someone called 911 to get help for the two victims, while she just stood there hysterically crying in dire disbelief.

Sonny had been the one of the two people who had been struck with the falling tree branch, He was also the one who had been mortally pieced. There was no recovery for him. His guardian angel was there and had been preparing him for the journey which he was about to take. But before he left the earth, he was allowed to take one last look around from the angel's perspective.

"Sonnius, you are released from your body now," his angel said to him.

"I can fly!" Sonny said.

It was an amazing feeling and he could see a light far away which was drawing him away from the tree and the house which he had last stood by.

"Where is my Rosanne? Can she come with me?" Sonny asked.

"No, not yet, but she will be with you later. It has all been arranged," the angel said.

"Can I see her?" Sonny asked the angel, who was beautiful in his own right. He had massive wings which spread from one side of the sky to the other. This was not a lower assigned angel, but one who had a special function. He was a special concierge angel who helped keep the earth on track while the other angels fought evil, promoting truth to the souls who could hear the Lord's voice.

"I will let you see her, but fear not, for her life will be taken care of. The Lord has already seen to it, for you. You have been a good steward of the Lord, and so your efforts will have the ripple effect of grace and mercy, as you gave to others. For those who were selfish and gave no grace and mercy, their ripple effect will be the opposite, and their families will bear the suffering of their sad ways," explained the angel.

Then the angel took Sonnius by the hand and they went down closer to the accident scene. Rosanne was incessantly crying and pushing her head into Johnnie's big shoulder. Since he could not see the accident scene, Johnnie could only try to help pacify those who were suffering there, hoping he could be of some consolation in the moment of grief until the medics and ambulance arrived.

The pastor had almost fainted at the sight of the other man, who had been a deacon in his church. He had a wife and three small children all under the age of ten, and this was a terrible blow to the whole family. The pastor immediately kept all the children inside the house, trying to calm the group in the terror of what had just happened, but already some of the children were looking from the windows of the second-floor bedroom and asking questions if their daddy was going to be all right.

These were the times which pastors could not prepare for. Sermons, marriages, and funerals were the easy stuff, but onsite dealing with immediate loss and life changes had little to do with preparation and more to do with being available as support and just keeping one's feelings contained for the moment, and not being drawn into the chaos of death and destruction; acting as a beacon of light around the others.

Sonny did not like what he saw.

"I am all right… I am okay," he yelled out to his Rosanne, but she could not hear him. It was like he was in some form of heavy viscous medium where his words just bounced back toward him and could not penetrate through the clear layer of film that stood in front of him.

"You are in a different dimension now, Sonnius. And she cannot hear you," the angel explained.

"What dimension?" Sonny asked. "And why are you calling me Sonnius instead of my real name, Sonny?"

"Sonnius is your angelic name. This is what I have been sent to tell you. Not all souls get to be angels, but you have been pre-selected to do so. And you have passed the test," the angel said.

"An angel? What kind of angel? I just hope they have air conditioning where I am supposed to go," Sonny laughed as he began to kid with the big angel, who was really intimidating him right now.

"These are things I do not know, Sonnius. I am just supposed to take you for processing before the Holy Spirit. It is time now for us to leave and go to Upper Paradise," the angel replied.

Then the angel grabbed Sonny by his hand and wrapped him inside his smaller inner wings, completely encircling Sony's body as they proceeded to be lifted toward the light in the sky, just like a hug magnet, which began to pull harder and harder the more they moved it its direction. Sonny could not tell completely, but it seemed also as though there were also an opposite kind of repelling force, which was pushing him away from the earth as the magnetic force was pulling him toward the light of Paradise. Then all of a sudden, once again, he let out a big loud yell in which said.

"I can fly!" he yelled, but no one could hear him as he and the angel headed for the other end of the universe in a distant galaxy, somewhere where only the angels ever went and where believers long to be.

When Sonny arrived in Upper Paradise, the accompanying angel assigned to him landed outside the big double gates with the message of salvation written on them. The two of them entered the same way as the other angels did who were carrying recaptured believers' souls from earth as well as from other parts of the universe where other creations were happening at the same time. Earth was not the only planet (or designed space of creation) where God the Father had set up the system of orderly love, grace, and mercy to grow over and conquer evil and the mis-system of self-righteousness. Here the massive walls of God's Kingdom could not be penetrated by anything of greater power because no such thing existed. These walls were created to be a symbol of God's greatness as much as his omnipotent power and everlasting eternal peace. Sonny did not know what to do or where to go, so his guardian angel took him inside to where he was put in a queue with others who had arrived that same day.

"Sonnius," the angel said to him telepathically by looking directly and unblinking into his eyes with his own eyes of many colors, which also had many stars in each, "you will stay here until you name is called and then you will answer for the life you led. Do you understand?"

"I do," said Sonny.

At that point another group of angels came down upon him and began tending to his needs, asking, "Do you have questions or other things which you need to know?"

Sonny, overwhelmed, stammered, "Not… not at this time."

So they began to take him through a sort of metamorphosis in dimensions where he felt strange things happening which he did not understand. He was not allowed to leave his place in line, but now he seemed to be new and clean, unlike how he had been when he was traveling from earth to Paradise. Then one of the angels brought a mirror and put it in front of him so he could see the transformation. Sonny had been given a new body, and it was not like the one he had before. It was simply stunning and quite beautiful. The colors in his body were not like anything he had ever seen before.

"Why do I have colors, and the other angels do not?" he asked, confused.

One of the angels answered, "Because you have not been sanctified yet by the Holy Spirit."

"Sanctified? What does that mean?" he asked.

"Acceptance into Paradise is one thing, but sanctification by the Holy Spirit is another," the angel explained. "There are many parts of Heaven with many rooms and pieces that even we as angels do not know, and we do not ask. All is judged and sorted by the Holy Spirit, and then we all learn together as one with the Triune Godhead. Do not be afraid, for your name is already in the Book of Life, so your sanctification will come early and soon."

This was really strange to Sonny, but at least he was at peace, and harmony was at the core of his present existence.

After some time, Sonny's name was called by one of the attending angels, and he was to get prepared to go before the Holy Spirit for his presentation.

"Sonnius, come forth!" the booming voice of the Holy Spirit called Sonny by his angelic name, sending chills though his new body, as he could sense the judgment which was about to happen.

Three days later, the funeral for Sonny's body took place. It was also the opening week of the basketball season. All of the members of the team attended. Not a single member missed. They wore white carnations on their lapels to signify their love for Sonny. Mr. Silverman, Daisy, Mamaw, and most of the congregation of the small church were there too. It was just Sonny, Rosanne, and Johnnie who had attended the weekend prior, but now the whole group was in one place to honor the life of someone who gave so much and never asked questions, for that was not his way.

Though Sonny and Rosanne were not members there, the pastor of the church insisted that he be the one to do the eulogy for Sonny Francis. He felt led to do it, and that God had called him to be 'the one' in their lives at the end, much like the ship captain who had been called to take Horatio Spafford on his journey to visit the last resting place of his four daughters, and also he felt there was a connection made that weekend with Rosanne, who needed nurturing now, and he did not want to lose contact with her after the emotions of loss and heartache set in, after the realization of loss happened and the crowds dissipated.

During the entire funeral Johnnie and Daisy did not leave Rosanne's side. The crowd was so big that not everyone could be seated. Some late attendees had to stand outside for the service, and clouds began to gather overhead, so the group outside began to leave about halfway through, expecting a possible rain shower to close the event. Not many would take the journey over to the gravesite, but a few knew where it would be since Sonny had always wanted to be buried next to his mother, whose body was in a family plot just a couple of miles away.

"I have two things I want to say today to honor this fine man whose journey is not over," the pastor began, "for he now lives in Heaven, which is the final journey, and we do not know much about it, but we are sure that he is there because we know that he was a believer, and that is all that matters. Sonny showed it by who he was. The word *believes* comes from the compound root word meaning 'by life.' This means what we believe in is directly shown by how we live our lives, by what we do and what others observe in our lives. Sonny did this by how he lived his life, so we know he was a believer, even though much of the time he kept his faith to himself."

The pastor paused before continuing.

"On every grave marker there are two numbers: One date for the year a person came to this earth, and another date the year a person is called away from it, with a dash in the middle to represent a person's entire life. It is usually a very small mark made in stone, about the size of a thumb nail, without words or pictures… just a straight solid line without a story to tell. So, we—those who are left behind—must tell the story of the dash, which becomes silent and obsolete, until our dash becomes the same. There is one person whom we all know here who did not get a grave stone with two dates and a dash representing his life on it, and that person is Jesus Christ. If fact, many scholars are unsure of the years in which He was brought to this earth and left this earth, but His dash is constantly told, and then retold, over and over again, so no one will forget the legacy He left here and why He came."

Then the pastor went on to talk about Sonny's life as a Christian and how sometimes life does not turn out the way we think is should, but God has a bigger plan, and all souls are here on earth on loan, just like everything else. We get to keep nothing, for everything is only temporary, and from the dust we came, and back to dust we will all go, except the part of us that can only be seen by the angels and the Triune God, who created us for 'their Purpose'… Amen.

The new basketball season began again, and Coach Barricks had a meeting with the team. He announced that Johnnie had been elevated to Player-Coach. In the off season, the team had begun to really admire what Johnnie was doing to improve his own skills by staying late just to shoot free throws and long balls from his pre-designated 'spots' he had selected on the floor. Many times he would bet one of his teammates he could make his shot when he was hot from a spot, and then he would put it through the hoop just to listen to the entire team whoop and holler in the background. It became his sense of total satisfaction by still beating the odds of him against the world.

His guardian angels also would get involved, and if the ball was just a little off, they would give it a love tap to make sure it would go in. Most times, Johnnie did not need the extra help, but this really strengthened his attitude just when he needed it, and it was all part of the 'Great Plan' designed for him to be a world leader for Christ, even though he did not know any of this yet.

When it came time for the first game of the season, Coach Barricks asked Johnnie to lead the team in a prayer before the game, as well as to say a few words to help motivate the guys.

"Dear Father," Johnnie began, "please let us be good stewards of the gifts and talents you have given us, and help always to remember that you are in control… not us. And help us not to fall into the trap of thinking that we can do anything apart from you, so help us to remember to thank you first before we speak, think, or do anything that might cause you grief over the things you have given us and which we love so much, namely our lives, our families, our hopes, and our dreams. In Jesus Christ we pray and give thanks! Amen."

Then he turned to the team and said, "Guys, they are just as talented as us, and just as conditioned as us, and they put their shorts on one leg at a time, just like us. The difference is who wants this win more: Them or us? I want it more, but I can't play. You guys have to be my eyes and my heart, and most of all my dreams. When you get on the court, you are not promised anything for tomorrow. You may not make it home tonight, or you may lose a loved one during the game in an accident. All you have is right now. And if you do not live this moment for something greater than yourself, you will never be fulfilled. You will always regret your lives, and you certainly won't have a happy when you die and get to the other side. I have been there, and I saw what is waiting. Do this for God, that He will be proud of you. Do this for the city, so that you might bring honor to those who cheer for you. And do this for me, so that I might have my prayers answered that one day I will be able to see again and lead you in victory, as I have always wanted to do. Let this night be like no other! And also do this for Sonny, because he is looking down, I am sure, and watching to see this season begin with a win, which will cause the angels to sing and Heaven to rock with pride as we give this win to Him!!!"

Then the team gave one last roar and jump of commotion, and ran onto the court to take their positions for the announcer's introduction. Tucker would be playing this night in the starting lineup along with Ziggy, who would make Johnnie proud with his long shots, which no one could cover.

But you, dear friends, by building yourselves up in your most holy faith and praying in the Holy Spirit, keep yourselves in God's love as you wait for the mercy of our Lord Jesus Christ to bring you to eternal life.

As Testified by Jude,
Brother of Jesus and James
Chapter 1:20-21

Chapter 14

A Prayer and the Impossible Challenge

The day of deliverance and rebirth had finally come. For Johnnie, this day was to be bittersweet. He slowly awoke, almost having to force his eyes open, because he had never really slept. The night before the seventh game in the championships was always the worst… how could he sleep? Tonight he would be the only man ever to suit up for a national NBA final title game who could not even see the game.

He would have to depend on the sound of the crowd and the commentary from Elwood Murphy, the commentator, to find out each point and foul, every turnover or injury that might come. Everyone in the stands would be able to watch it happening, millions on television would watch it in real time, even the people who didn't care to watch it still could if they wanted to tape it for later. And by now the whole world knew Johnnie would not get to play unless the 'Canes were up by an ungodly amount, or maybe he got to take a free throw for a technical foul as just a fun shot for big laughs if he missed and airtime advertising sales, but if that was the case, then Johnnie would refuse to do it.

This wouldn't happen, though. The War Horses were playing with the Hurricanes and their crushing empire as the best team ever, like a cat playing with a mouse before it had it for lunch! Coming back from being down three games to one would be a NBA miracle in itself. Nobody today believed they would come even close to beating the Austin War Horses tonight. Yesterday Johnnie heard the Las Vegas Odds-Line was 2 to 1 in favor of the War Horses, and if anybody knew outcomes and predictions, it was the bet makers who made a living doing it.

Johnnie now sat up in bed to collect his thoughts. In a couple of hours, at 8:45 a.m., the team was meeting downstairs in the grand hall to go over some last-minute items before taking a bus over to the coliseum. It was a memorable trip that he had made so many times before, and he knew every inch of the way from when he could once see the traffic and the arches over the Mississippi River. St. Louis was a great town for barbecue as well as basketball championships, but the lonely drive today was not like the one he remembered in Seattle, where the sky was blue and the trees were straight and green like long stalks of grass stuck on a hill.

In Seattle they had won their first title in five games over the Lewisville Miners and then again in San Louis on game six over the Washington Castles. All he could think of all morning long was 'Nobody was going to make a circus out of me because of my misfortune.' He could hear Mamaw's voice clearly when she spoke to him at age 14: 'Johnnie, never start anything you can't finish, and always do it with respect! And better not forget to clean up after yourself whatever mess you make because no one likes a sloppy person… or I may have to come back from the grave and whoop your ass!'

At that moment, Johnnie gave out a big chuckle while sitting in bed, shaking his head and thinking how much he missed his grandmother. He wished she could be here tonight, but her health was not good so she had stayed close to home. It would be his very last game NBA for sure.

The team would finish the season with one less veteran salary to pay, which was the plan from the main office. The college draft had a lot of new talent to choose from, and George Barker, the GM, had kept to his promise to bring in some fresh muscle and bones. Johnnie could stay until the end of this season, then have his contract bought out with all perks and scoring options, and then move on with clearing the way for one more man to be on the 'Cane roster. There would be no pay for scoring options, since the wreck happened three months before the previous season had begun.

Winning the Western Division would pay well, with TV rights for the season, and if they just happened to win the game tonight, the NBA Title Bonus would be all he needed to live out a long easy life for many decades to come. But of course, Zing Chou was not going to let that happen. Every time the War Horses got twelve or more points ahead, Zing erupted like a machine and carried the ball to the hoop, like an apostle on a death mission into the enemy frontlines. Every time he charged, and three hundred and ten pounds and size twenty-four sneakers was unstoppable, unless his opponent wanted to leave the court in a body bag. And then there was the other half of the deadly duo, Sir Francis Ott. Not quite the seven-feet-two-inches tall as Zing Chou, but almost, he could clean more rebounds off the backboard than a twelve-armed octopus. Ott was incredible for sure, and if any ball went in the air toward him, he claimed it and made the job of collecting rebounds as the NBA's Champion look easy.

By now it was time for a pre-game shower. Because the team had stayed in this same hotel three years ago, Johnnie knew the whole layout. He had not wanted a roommate, and he didn't want any help, ever. About 8:30 a.m., good ol' Tucker would usually come by to get him, and then they would go to the team meeting together. The rest of the guys would all be sitting around just vegging out, jamming with their headphones on, psyching themselves out with hip-hop music or breathing to upbeat music that made them invincible, but not Johnnie. No headphones he ever wore. He needed his ears like a sixth sense to overcome his loss of sight. He could tell if a man was sweating or not, by just the way his breath came off his chest. His perception of sound was getting so good he could make a coyote searching for a field mouse under a six-inch blanket of fresh snow blush!

Ever since he was a kid, Johnnie kept the first ball he had ever scored with by his bedside. He would pick it up when he awoke and then carry it with him and set it on the kitchen table when he would eat breakfast. This was sort of a ritual he did every day, and never had it been broken since he was only 48 inches tall, and today was no different.

But like every big game day, breakfast would be done as a team. They would all go downstairs for the morning head count and attitude check. The whole team would be there and Johnnie, as always, was expected to give a pep talk just like he did before every big game. Now he contemplated what he would say. Sitting in his chair he could only think back to what his Mamaw would say. More than likely she would get out her Bible and read him the story of David and how he slew Goliath with one small precise throw. He hit his mark, and history still talks about his courage today and the small boy who killed the giant. But Johnnie did not have anything to use like a slingshot as his weapon; he only had his two arms to use. Plus, David had had his eyes, and Johnnie did not. How depressing, Johnnie thought to himself, but then the strength of Mamaw would come upon him and she would speak of his guardian angel that watched over him, and he remembered Azoz and Shemenea and his wreck, and he was not afraid anymore. He would take on this challenge just as Daniel had done with the lion, without fear of dying, either physically, mentally, spiritually, or emotionally. No one could hurt him anymore… he was over it! 'God, help me please!' he whispered to himself in a silent prayer.

Then came the knock on the door he was waiting for. There were three hard quick knocks, followed by two soft ones. It was Tucker. Johnnie smiled and his chin flexed at the sound. His eyebrows rose a bit, pushing his head toward the door, and a deep lump filled his throat.

"Come in, Buddy" he said to Tucker from his chair.

"How's Houston's Hero doing this morning?" Tucker quietly asked as he poked his head into the room before entering.

Tucker never knew if he would catch Johnnie in a moment of prayer on his knees or standing on the balcony's edge ready to jump. Tucker's palms would always be wet with sweat as he entered his best friend's room. His heart always broke, too, when he looked upon the great champion, realizing he would never play again. It was like looking at a great horse like Secretariat who had been fenced into some backyard pasture, or even worse, a broken-down stable, forced to watch the Kentucky Derby when he had once outrun the greatest horses in the world, but no one would put him in the race because he was too old or too lame.

"If you brought a gun with you, please shoot me!" Johnnie said.

He was kidding, of course. Johnnie always used humor to overcome the reality of the situation. Houston and the world would be watching him to see how he would react to their loss tonight, with cameras on him most of the game.

"Not happening, Buddy," Tucker replied. "I got your jersey clean for you here. They washed it with the rest of the team, so it would get some sweat on it, more work you get paid for but never do…" Tucker laughed out loud, teasing Johnnie.

"Yeah, but my work is mental… yours is easier, you heap of fly-infested dung-do."

Both of them laughed hysterically, which took the edge off the moment. Tucker beat on the wall and got a tear in his eye as he watched the man who was his hero struggle with what he saw as God's greatest injustice to one man to whom He had given so much talent!

"I checked the Las Vegas odds for tonight," Tucker said. "You want to know what the line is for the game?"

"No, I don't want to know," Johnnie replied.

"No problem… I am good with that. Everyone knows it's going to be close, anyway," Tucker said. "Oh, and they added an extra column… the Johnnie column."

"You mean they are betting on me and I am not even playing?" Johnnie asked.

"Of course! Las Vegas has a bet for everything!"

"Oh, great, now I am a sideshow. I might as well go sign up for the Barnum and Bailey Circus. What are my odds?" he asked.

"Ten to one coach will put you in (just to get the crowd going if we are behind); thirty-five to one if you get fouled and make a free throw. And guess what the odds are for you making a shot from the floor?"

“How about a million to one at long-shot odds?” Johnnie laughed.

“Hey, that was pretty close! That was what it was this morning,” Tucker said, laughing as he rolled on the bed being silly, “and then I saw where a couple of your fans bet on you heavily at those crazy odds, so they were lowered to 500,000 to one.”

Tucker began pointing at himself in wild signs of almost ecstasy, but of course Johnnie could not see him as he just sat in dumb confoundment.

Tucker threw him his jersey and hit him in the face. That was Tucker’s way of playing with him and getting him a little mad, just to knock him out of his pity party which Johnnie seemed to have more and more these days. Johnnie always wore #4. It was the number which he had made famous. It was also the number which he first used at the Catholic academy in seventh grade. He had kept it as his signature number his entire life, even after his accident, and he believed it was Jesus that gave him that number to keep him perfect.

On that day when he first got it from Coach Thornton, his coach had said to him, ‘Only Jesus, God, and the Holy Spirit are allowed at this school to wear the jerseys #1, #2, and #3… so #4 was always open for anyone with the guts to put it on!’ He remembered these words every day, and as he sat there in his dark prison and listened to Tucker’s chiding him on, Johnnie stopped for a moment and remembered that he was to be totally humble. But he lived in a cruel world where the outside of a man—his money, clothes, and status—was the measure of a man instead of the inside. He sank into his dark world for just a moment as Tucker waited for him to move or do something because the team was waiting for them to show before the morning prayer. In his mind, Johnnie went back in time and saw his Mamaw saying to him over a morning bowl of breakfast cereal, 'It wasn't the color of a man's skin which God cared about, but only the color of his heart.'

Johnnie paused a moment and asked for forgiveness from his Lord for being arrogant this morning and forgiveness for even thinking that they might even lose the game, for it was God's will not his that would happen this day. The sun would come up and the sun would go down without even an inkling of what Johnnie would say or do unless it was in God's will that it be done. Johnnie could not even control the beating of his own heart, so he certainly could not control the destiny of his own life, so he might as well just carry on, and whatever lot the day brought him, he would wear it as a badge of honor so all would see his actions and what he believed, proof that he was forever a servant of his King. Resolved, Johnnie stood up and put on his flip-flops, picked up his famous tattered basketball with #4 marked on it from seventh grade, and went with Tucker to the team breakfast downstairs.

When they arrived, the guys started to cheer. They were hungry. And even though Johnnie was the heart and soul of the team, they knew it was they who would put the points on the board if they were going to win tonight. Johnnie knew he could only stand by and be there for support. He thought they would have done better to have gotten rid of him and acquired a pit bull for a mascot and named it Hurricane than to have him lingering on the bench, taking up space. To him, at least a spunky dog could attack the other team if a fight broke out on the floor and get in a bite or two and cripple a shooter. So, Johnnie was reconciled to do nothing but wear his #4 jersey for a show of support, sit down at the of the end of the bench, and pray that his team did not get humiliated on national television.

Coach Barricks praised Johnnie once more as he entered the dining hall.

"Here comes our leader," he said, "the one who has taken us here to these finals before and has destroyed our competition. With Johnnie here, no team can beat us… never, no how, not ever! The other team doesn't have even an ice cube's chance in hell of surviving another game to try and take this championship from us!"

And the team went wild. Some began to stand on their chairs and chant, "Johnnie, Johnnie, Johnnie," but Johnnie soon got them to stop as he humbly came into the pre-game meeting.

"Say something to the team," Coach Barricks said to Johnnie as he struggled to find a chair to sit in that would not move out from under him as he sat down to listen.

"Guys, this day belongs to you. Don't let anyone steal your joy," Johnnie encouraged his teammates. "Whatever the outcome, you have a lot to be thankful for, so it all begins with your hearts, not your hands, or your eyes. Take it from me. It is not *if* you win that is important, it is *how* you win, because God is watching and He knows two things: your character and your heart. So don't cheat either one, and tonight will end up to us in the final minutes."

Once again, the team began chanting, "Johnnie, Johnnie, Johnnie…," but again he put his hands up and motioned for silence. Since he had been made a player-coach, he felt he could give some advice on how the game should go.

"Tucker, you know you can outperform any of these guys if you just believe with courage, so I am giving you the authority to believe in yourself. So don't go out there and think about anything else except cutting your way to the basket. You will find a way! And Zig-Man, you won't need any help from the corners because I have heard you once lived on a street corner, so you know what to do when you are backed against a wall. B.H. (Bobby Heatherton), you owe me one for making sure you got down the aisle and married that sweet wife of yours, so you make sure you don't let her and me down tonight if you get the last shot. Just focus on the rim and not the crowds. You have an eye for the basket that supersedes what I think even the angels can see. And Rocket Man, make sure you don't throw the ball away on those long passes when you rebound the ball… the game will be won and lost on our mistakes only. If we have twelve and they have ten, we will lose, so do not count anything but your mistakes, because we will all live and die by you having a perfect game without mistakes. We are counting on you to keep your head cool and not lose it in the final moments, okay?"

Then Johnnie moved his head slowly from left to right making believe he could see his team in a show of realism, but all he really could do was listen for the slightest sounds of any shuffling of feet or arms moving on the tables and judge the temperament of his small crowd by their silence.

"So tonight, when you suit up in your red and blue jerseys, please say a prayer that you will enlarge your own territory through strength and by God's authority. Be not afraid of anything, and make this place your everlasting home, because if you don't, the world will never remember you, even on the following day. You will be as dead men who never existed, with bones left to rot wherever they lie down to rest. Second place is always for the losers! So, give this one game your very best each second of the clock until it is over, and you won't be sorry that one day when you have your last curtain call before you go to the next world to see your maker, your life will not have been lived in vain!"

And with those words Johnnie's voice faded to silence, and then he said no more words, not even an utterance, till game time, when it was time to take the floor.

Johnnie went back to is room for the rest of the day to steadily wait for game time to begin. All players were confined to their hotel and not permitted to leave their assigned floor after their lunch was over. At exactly 6:30 p.m., Johnnie took his last relaxing shower of the day and began to dress himself for the game.

For the last three hours he had been listening to the cable news sports shows discussing the game and who the strongest players on each team were, and who was projected to win that night. Johnnie's name came up quite often as the leader of the team, their blind player-coach; and as he listened, he thought about how television worked: creating, fabricating, and embellishing stories that were inflated, just to sell airtime to advertisers who fed off gullible viewers.

Whether they were fake or not was a matter of looking through the smoke and mirrors of deception used to lure in the gullible just to make money. It was just a form of twisted hypocrisy, and only the older generation knew what truth really was. And this was all part of a sad commentary on human existence where the world revolved around money, entertainment, sex, music, and lies, where the people paid to live some momentary fantasy to avoid living a peaceful life which God had graciously given them initially to enjoy. This was the typical thought pattern which Satan used in their minds to steal their thoughts: 'I need a fix to breach my boredom, so I will go with the flow, like sheep jumping over a cliff, because there is no danger in being an innocent blind participant, is there?'

So Johnnie also thought, 'Am I going to be just another blind participant tonight, like one of the sheep, or is God going to show me something I can share with the world in a way no-one else can?' He knew that each person was given certain gifts and talents that no one else had, but what gifts and talents could a blind man possess if all he could do was sit on a bench and watch a game played from afar, if he never gets to get in and play in the game? He kept asking himself these things and it kept him restless. If he had any courage, he thought to himself, he would just go over to the balcony and jump off, but what would that solve? Maybe it might help with his internal stress and pain, but it certainly would not honor God nor give anyone in his life any happiness, which is what he felt his mission was. To take the easy way out was actually a form of self-pity, and a cowardly act of misguided self-righteousness, which God definitely would not approve. So, what should he do?

So, Johnnie went to his knees and began to pray that he might know his destiny. He rested his chest against the mattress of his hotel bed and he leaned forward, pressing against the bed that took care of him in his sleep and looking up toward the sky in an effort to plead his case to the One who created him.

"Gracious Father in Heaven, hear my prayer!" Johnnie began. "You know my heart like no other. You can see all, and I am just one more speck on the ball of spinning mud you have created in the vast universe and cosmic space we call the universe. If I could change words and take away the meaning of them, I would rename this place and call it Eden again, and you would be the master we could all see. But you chose to leave us vulnerable and without clear vision, so we suffer as a world needing your light now more than ever. Give me understanding, dear Lord, that I might know my purpose, and give me faith, oh Lord, that I might be at peace with your will. It is too difficult to just know that you are out there somewhere watching, and I am supposed to be a role model for you, but I need a clue as to what I am supposed to be doing in this unsure place of money, sex, and trappings of fools. I just want to come home to you and stop this insanity of listlessness and idleness without any impact for good over evil."

A tear then welled up in each of Johnnie's eyes, as he became silent and did not know what else to say to plead his case for the world. He was not pleading for himself, but for a distraught people he felt knew nothing for their own salvation and were just being led down a road of slow death, much like cattle going to the slaughter yard to end up under cellophane and be nothing more than a dinner on someone's table! It was a sad world which Johnnie lived in because he never confided in anyone. As a child he felt that he had the gift of prophecy, and now his gift seemed to be all but lost in his incapacity to do anything in the world in which everyone else lived, while he lived in a world of darkness, alone.

Then Servius-Quintus, his guardian angel, whom the Holy Spirit had assigned to bring Johnnie back to the world of reality and the Kingdom of God, appeared to him.

"Formadus, be not afraid!" said Servius-Quintus to Johnnie.

Johnnie looked up and saw a shining body raised up, floating above the front of the curtains which hung before the big windows in his hotel room.

"Formadus…? I am not Formadus…" Johnnie said boldly, now seeing in his mind images as if his eyes were working again.

The scales had been lifted from his sight for just a moment. 'What in the heck is going on here,' he thought to himself. Johnnie reached up with both hands and rubbed his eye sockets, thinking this must be a dream. Or was it the miracle of healing he had been waiting for? Perhaps he had fallen asleep and he did not know it, so he was just having one of those dreams where it seemed real, when really it was all just some crazy warped form of mental weed planted in his subconscious brain which had no meaning at all.

"Formadus (i.e. Josiah), you were created in the beginning to serve the Lord, and your day has come to do what many dream of but only a few humans ever experience," the angel said to him.

"But I am not Formadus. I am Johnnie Perfect," Johnnie said to the angel. "I don't know anything about Formadus or what you are speaking about."

"Silence!" commanded the angel. "And stop your obstinacy! Who are you to ask questions of the Lord and what His will is for you? Repent! Follow these orders. You will go to the game tonight and you will play… and you will see for only a moment."

At that moment a second angel appeared. This had not happened since Saul had scales placed on is eyes on his journey to Damascus. Saul and Johnnie were similar. They both were headstrong, persistent, noble in thought and character, common-sense smart, and articulate. Saul had his scales for only three days because he was a quick learner. Johnnie had his on for much longer because he was more obstinate and still needed more instruction and suffering.

The Holy Spirit had been watching the conversation between Quintus Servius and Johnnie, when He and She decided to send Azoz, the angel who had been sent to speak with Joseph when Mary was engaged to him and became with child by the Holy Spirit.

Azoz then spoke to Johnnie. "Why are you so reluctant to do the Lord's will? Have not your scales been lifted so you can see the angels and receive their holy message?"

"But this is just a dream," Johnnie replied, "for I am lying asleep, and at some point I will awaken, I believe, and I will be blind once more… nothing will have changed!"

"Oh, how you are wrong, Mr. Perfect! You will see one day when you gain your full education, but you are not ready," replied Azoz.

Then Azoz called to the wind, and a mighty storm stirred in the room. The curtains began to swirl violently and both large lampstands blew from the desktops near the windows. The clock, which was situated directly between the two beds, went crashing against the opposite wall, and all three layers of bedsheets were ripped from under him. Johnnie stood in utter amazement at what was happening.

"Joseph, Son of David," Azoz then called into the wind that was still there, which had been created by the Holy Spirit, "the winds of the Holy Spirit say to you: come forth!"

The message was delivered directly to Heaven, for Joseph did not reside in Upper Paradise with the lower guardian angels and the Holy Spirit. And Joseph came down from Heaven, where he spent his days worshipping alongside the upper angels and the saints who resided there with the Lord Jesus-Emmanuel, meaning 'God is With Us,' and with God the Father, who was known to all there as the Great 'I Am.'

Joseph was not shining in radiant white, like the two angels who stood on either side of him. But he was like nothing Johnnie had ever seen. Joseph had a perfect body. He had perfect everything. Johnnie could not explain it, but it looked as though Joseph had stepped out of a sauna. He had on only a sheet, his body was wet, his hair was curled with bows tied in it, and his hands and feet were formed perfectly as if they had never done work. The bows represented that nothing would cover his head in Heaven, only the shadow of the Holy Spirit, which all those in Heaven carried with them when they were there, as the Holy Spirit was also there always as part of the Triune Godhead, but also presided over Upper Paradise at the same time. It was one of the many unexplainable dimensions which the Triune shared, but the rules were known by all, and all the angels and saints knew their place, where they could go, and whom they were allowed to visit.

"Johnnie," Joseph said to him, "do you know the scriptures. Do you know my story?"

Johnnie humbled himself before Joseph, but not the angels, whom he did not understand. But he understood Joseph, which is why the Holy Spirit had sent him. And sometimes the Holy Spirit would send Mary as well in an apparition to young girls who knew they were being spoken to, like Fatima, and then Conchita at Garabandal.

"Yes, I do," Johnnie replied.

Then Joseph began to tell his story again to remind Johnnie of the history of Christ, the bringing forth of the Living Truth and the Living Word. This story also ran in the room in which Joseph stayed while he was in Heaven, playing over and over the story of his life living faithfully as a servant of the Child King who had been placed under his care as a blended family. He was to be the step-father and protector of the Lord God, born as a defenseless babe, and he wanted Johnnie to know what he went through to be faithful to what he had been asked and assigned to do as his earthly job.

"Do you remember my legacy, that I was a man of stern principle, and when I found out that Mary, to whom I was betrothed, was a virgin when she conceived through the Holy Spirit, my doubts ran rampant. How was this true? To me it was impossible that she might be pregnant in an unearthly way," said Joseph.

"I remember the scriptures,"[222] answered Johnnie.

"Do you remember the scripture that an angel of the Lord came to me and said, 'Do not hesitate to take Mary as your wife! For her child has been conceived of the Holy Spirit, and this will fulfill the message of the prophets. He was to be called Emmanuel, and I was to give him his Earth name Jesus; for even He the Lord has his earth name Jesus and His Kingdom name Emmanuel, for the Lord God is Jesus Emmanuel, the Christ Lord 'God' and the Savior to the world.' "

"I do," responded Johnnie.

"Josiah, you were given this name before your earthly birth, just as Emmanuel was given his name before his earthly birth. I was given the Heavenly name Jesse, for I was in the line of David, and my great-grandfather was Amos. We have all been assigned Heavenly names before we were born and have been given earthly deeds to carry out the will of the Lord. So, Johnnie-Josiah, just like the others, you have been called to do as I have done, and do as you are commanded. I brought Mary home to be my wife. She remained a virgin until her Son was born and I named him 'Jesus.' You are commanded to follow in the line of David, for you carry the Mary-James gene, as we all carried the Abraham-Sarah gene. When the twelve tribes of Israel ceased and Jesus was born of the Holy Spirit, then the Twelve Tribes of Jesus began, and you are in one of the lines. Blessed are you to know this and to be commanded also to carry on your tribe along with the eleven others," Joseph said.

---

[222] Matthew 1:18-19

"In my day," Joseph continued, "the Lord sent an angel to me to warn me of Herod, and that I must protect the baby Lord God, so I must flee to another country that He might be safe until the time for Him to return and assume His rightful throne in his ministry. Then he sent another angel to inform me that Herod had died and I must return to our home, but then he sent yet another angel to tell me that Herod's son, Archelaus, was waiting there to harm us, so we must then go to Galilee instead and live in Nazareth. This I was told to fulfill the prediction of the Prophets concerning the Messiah, 'that He shall be called a Nazarene'."

"Grace and mercy be upon you Joseph-Jesse," said Johnnie. "I am humbled and honored that the Holy Spirit has revealed this to me."

"But this is not all," said Joseph. "The Son of Man had a voice before He had His voice, given by the Holy Spirit and proclaiming His coming, and that was the voice of John. The Son of Man had a sign before he was born given by the Holy Spirit proclaiming his time had come, and this was the Star, which shined first in the east and then in the west, and this was the sign given in his day."

"I do not understand," said Johnnie.

"The Lord God must give His sign, proclaiming His Son will come again, before He arrives, and until then, you must do as the angels tell you. If they say go to Egypt, then you do as they say. If they say go to Nazareth, then you must go as they say. If they say you are to walk with one foot in front of the other behind them, then you must do as they say. Did not Abraham take his son upon the mountain to sacrifice him as God commanded? But He was stopped by the Lord just to test his faithfulness. Oh yes, Johnnie-Josiah, you will be tested as well—and many time—to measure your obedience against the distractions of Satan himself. Just as Servius-Quintus, Azuz-Azor, Saul-Paulus, and I, Joseph-Jesse, have done. But you will not fall along your path. The angels will strengthen you, and the Holy Spirit will give you the words to say at the right time to say them. Until then, silence, confidence, and humility will be your armor. You will run and not stumble. You will work and not fail at your endeavors. Go now and think on these things, and know the Lord God will never forsake you, just as He will never forsake any of us whom He loves."

And with that said, the two angels and Joseph raised themselves up into the skies, and went straight up out of sight. The room was put back into place, and Johnnie kept his eyesight for a few minutes, until there was a knock at the door.

Johnnie sat there in amazement. He could see his surroundings. The room was put back together as if nothing had ever happened. The sheets were tightly arranged back on the bed. The clock and lamps were back in place. He went to the windows and opened the sash. He opened the glass door and stood on the balcony, looking over the earth as if he had a new perspective for his purpose. For just a moment, he was in ecstasy. He understood now why all of his pain and suffering had come to this point of understanding. His mind had been infused with all forms of knowledge and wisdom he had never known before, and for once in his life he was now comfortable in the skin he lived in. Johnnie was at peace, and this peace would never leave him till the day he died many years later, at the age of 86. The Holy Spirit had already assigned a place for Johnnie-Josiah to be buried. It would be on a hill outside the city of Jerusalem, and around him would be a circle of twelve crepe myrtles, symbolizing the twelve tribes of Jesus, completing the prophecy and scriptures: 'For the first shall be last, and the last shall be first.'

Then Johnnie heard a knock at his hotel door. He turned back toward the door in response to the noise, and when he did, the scales once again covered his eyes and he could not see. This was once again a shock to him, for he was suddenly thrust back into to the world of darkness, but he was truly blind no more! What Johnnie-Josiah Spotless Perfect could see was more than any other living person on the earth. He had the knowledge of his creator with him, and he stirred not in his soul anymore for want nor concern.

He said loudly toward the door between himself and the new world that he would join, "Come in… my door is now unlocked forever."

Tucker stuck his head in to see Johnnie halfway out onto the balcony with twenty-five floors below to the hard concrete, and he thought to himself that Johnnie had lost it and was going to jump.

"Johnnie, stop!" Tucker yelled. "Don't do it... don't jump!"

A big grin came over Johnnie's face, that big famous huge grin from ear to ear with the gap between his teeth a person could stick a pencil through.

"Don't worry, my friend," Johnnie said to Tucker, "that ending is not going to happen, ever. Can you please get Mamaw on the phone for me? I would like to talk to her before the game begins."

"Andy flew her in for the game last night. He wanted to surprise you. She is going to be at the game and will give you a hug before you get on the bus. She will be in the stands with Rosanne and Daisy," Tucker said.

"Wow! Okay, but still I want to talk to her this minute before she leaves her hotel room."

As always, friends and family stayed on the fifteenth floor for good luck. Seemed the teal always won when the fifteenth floor was used, and this game it was just ten floors below the main team floor. And they always had a small gathering and rally before each playoff and championship game for the team as they loaded onto their team bus to be driven over to the coliseum arena, exactly two hours before game time. Each wanted them to arrive as a unit, play as a unit, and leave as a unit… that was the team attitude and team motto.

Although time was getting close and he would see her in fifteen minutes, Johnnie had something he wanted to share with Mamaw before he went down the elevator. This was important and could not wait.

Tucker said, "But you will see her in front of the bus in a few minutes."

"This can't wait, Tuck, I need you to please call her room and get her on the phone for me. I want to tell her something ASAP. No, I *need* to tell her something ASAP."

Tucker went over and picked up the phone there, close to where the clock had just been sent flying, he touched the four keys, 1531, for Johnnie, and then handed the phone to him. He had been visiting with her during the day to give her insight on how Johnnie was handling the pressure of this important game.

"Hello…" Johnnie heard Mamaw say on the other end of the line.

"Hi, Mamaw…" said Johnnie, "I have something I want to… *need to* tell you."

"And what is that, young man? You need to be thinking about the game tonight. Just focus in case you have to play. I will see you in a few minutes, okay? So, get ready and get downstairs," she barked her orders into the phone, commanding Johnnie as she had always done.

"Mamaw, I just wanted to tell you *Thank You* from my heart. And how much I truly appreciate today what you have done for me in the past," Johnnie said.

Complete and utter silence followed. It was totally quiet on the other end of the phone where Mamaw was standing. She was awestruck and had to sit down. The silence lasted for at least ten seconds, and then she said, "What did you just say, Johnnie? Did I hear you right?" Mamaw then repeated herself two more times… fading finally into a whisper.

"Mamaw, I called to tell you *THANK YOU*, and also that *I LOVE YOU*," Johnnie said, with a slight quiver in his voice. Then he spoke louder with confidence and boldness. "I know this is a strange time, Mamaw, but I could not wait. Thank you for what you have done for me; and also I love you for who you are. You have put up with quite a lot from me and my bad attitude. I have never stopped to tell you this, and also how much you mean to me. God has been good to me, I know, and I wanted to let you know that even in my darkest times, I can now see the truth, and the goodness you have brought into my life."

Once again there was more silence on the end where Mamaw was. The silence went on and on, so Johnnie thought for a moment that she might have fainted and now maybe someone may need to go down and check on her. Tucker also was silent and could not believe what he was hearing wither. This was coming from Johnnie, who always had some form of pride combined with disdain lurking somewhere in his heart. But now he had reached a new bottom in his humility, much like a knight who was not bound to take care of the lost, poor, sick, and dying with his greater cause of noble chivalry.

Both guardian angels, Servius-Quintus and Azuz-Azor, were watching over him after his apparition. They were listening overhead to the new born-again Johnnie, and they both gave a big grin of relief. Some men were like that. Some were caught by the net of the Holy Spirit and collected like cod in vast numbers caught all at once, and others like the great blue marlin which had to be stalked, baited, hooked, and gaffed to be caught and brought onto the boatman's catch. The everlasting light of Holy Enlightenment had just been achieved in Johnnie Perfect now, and he was ready to begin his mission on earth as an ambassador of Christ and the Gospel for which Christ stood. Even some men who had helped the position of the church's papacy had never had a True Enlightenment apparition of this nature, or known the true direction of the church as a whole.

As Johnnie just stood there holding the phone, Tucker did not hear him say anything for a minute or two, except one thing.

"Whatever happens from here on out, Mamaw," Johnnie said into the phone, "it won't be because of me. I know I am nothing except what God wants me to be. So, I will do my best in whatever He commands, that I make my life worthy of His calling."

Then Johnnie hung up and sat down for a minute of prayer. He was packed and ready for the bus. Finally, he turned to Tucker and spoke.

"Let's go. I am ready to get this show on the road."

They entered the hallway and met several members of the team getting on the elevators. Everyone was stoic and quiet. There were no high-fives, egos, or silly dances that were part of the preparation for the game tonight right now. It was all serious at this moment and about taking care of business.

Only one thing was on the mind of Johnnie. He knew the angels were with him always now, and they could remove the scales from his eyes whenever they wanted or needed. If he was ever asked to play at all, he was not sure if they would do that for him or if he would play blind and look like a fool, but he knew that was not God's intent. Like Joseph, he knew now that he was called, and the Holy Spirit surely would not let him down. And the angels would intervene on his behalf when needed to protect and care for new world order of the Twelve Tribes of Jesus.

The team loaded onto the bus. Each was displayed a calm countenance while they listened to music of their choice on headphones. Johnnie no longer chose his favorite Credence Clear Water Revival, but now he was an Elvis Presley fan. Since the accident he always started his bus rides to the games with 'Rock of Ages' from Elvis's church albums, and then would end with 'If I Can Dream' before the game got started.

Today was no different. The bus arrived on time. All the members of the team unloaded in an orderly fashion, with Johnnie and Tucker waiting to be the last, remaining on the bus patiently waiting for all the others to get off. Tuckered looked across the lot and saw where the War Horses' bus had already arrived. He knew that Sir Francis Ott and the others were inside, methodically discussing their agendas on how to dismantle the Hurricanes' offense. He did not say anything to Johnnie, but Johnnie had been here before and knew the routine.

"Are they here yet?" he asked Tucker.

It was like two prizefighters getting ramped up for a pugilistic battering unlike no other where there would be no true winner, but only survivors. The spoils would go to the team that could outlast the other by sheer determination, so this was a war of will power as much as physical stamina.

"They are here," Tucker answered.

"What's the report on their injury list? Will Zing Chou start on the floor tonight?" Johnnie asked.

"Yes. The say his Achilles tendon was good enough so that he will surely dominate at least those he stands in front because of his massive arm length," Tucker replied.

Johnnie reaches up and grabbed his chin and rubbed the stubble he kept as a half-beard. He never shaved on game day. It was another tradition with him. He had heard once that Romans did not shave before a battle because they wanted their weapons sharp to cut their opponents in battle, so this was a tradition he carried out in mental preparation for the games, even though no one was going to die. It was all symbolic.

"Do you think we are going to win?" Tucker asked Johnnie.

"Do you have as much faith as a small mustard seed?" Johnnie replied.

"The only faith I have is that I will be sitting next to you, brother, and hope Sir Francis comes up limping in the fourth quarter so we have a chance to gain the last momentum. I just want the last shot!" Tucker said.

"Then you are an idiot," Johnnie said. "History will only remember you for your last famous deed. If you want glory and fame, you will surly fall on your face and fail."

"I didn't mean it that way," Tucker said.

"That is okay… it is natural to want to do everything to win, but somehow, I think there is more to this game tonight that will be a ripple effect not attributed to who the winner and loser is, but who has faith or not."

"Well, I have the faith," Tucker said.

"But do you have the courage of Joseph?" Johnnie replied.

"What does that mean?"

"It means that life is a journey… not a destination, my friend. We sometimes believe life is all about the events that surround us, but really it is how we react to those events which are our legacy," Johnnie replied. "How many Samurai died on the field or after a battle because they followed a leader who lost the day in the heat of battle? It is no different for all of us. We are all warriors but without weapons, just actions. May God be with us, and may the angels protect us as we strive do the right thing for His Glory," Johnnie added before they went inside for the final pep-talk by Coach Barricks.

The Holy Spirit called many of the higher angels together in Upper Paradise to see the events unfold on this grand day on earth. John the Baptist had been the last great prophet given instruction to prophesy for the coming of the Living Word before Jesus' first coming. Since then there had been the Age of Non-Prophets and the Silencing of the Angels. The Triune Triad Godhead had ordered the silence of prophets and angels so the world would be mute, just as Zachariah had been muted before the birth of John.[223] For the earth had been muted now for two thousand years, and now it was time to begin the birth pains again.

A star had been sent to show the 'Wise Men' of the day, who were great scientists and good kings, the birth of the baby in the manger, and notice had gone out to the bad kings that their reign was

[223] Luke 1:20

coming to an end so they should shudder in fear that they had no hold on their lands anymore.

The same was going on now in Upper Paradise. The angels were becoming more restless and involved in the preparation for the second coming of the Lord Jesus, so more miracles were beginning to be seen by the people. But still many preparations were to be made, just as when Moses was sent to deliver God's people from slavery in Egypt, many sufferings still had to happen for them to believe, and these sufferings were starting now. The people of the world, in their quest for ease combined with universal self-satisfaction and indulgence, were no different than the Romans who had ruled during Christ's first coming. They were arrogant and a people of many laws who ruled by micro-managing instead of ruling by the nature of the pure heart.

Purity was what the Holy Spirit was searching for in the heart of man, and nothing but impurities in the smelting of good iron processes could be found. If iron sharpened iron, this iron was no longer usable.[224] So the Holy Spirit called the angels and spoke to them.

"Go out unto all the lands and breathe the breath of the Seven Plagues upon the people," the Holy Spirit said, "so that they will know that I am God. They are Autism, Dementia, Obesity, Diabetes, Cancer, Acid Stomach, and Sleep Apnea, for these things will cause them to die early and I will take from them the world I have given them because they have not been good stewards of all that has been given. This will hold them close to my bosom until the day comes when the Lord Christ will once again come to offer them Salvation, saving them from the things they have created for themselves by

[224] Proverbs 27:17

putting their faith in the world instead of the Kingdom to Come.[225] For in the promise given by God Himself, blessed will be those who come to him as children, not as adults, and not as prideful individuals, but those seeking mercy over justice and those who care more for others than care for themselves."

Then the Holy Spirit began to shake with a great quiver that shook upper Paradise, and the shock waves went all the way to Heaven and were felt by the Lord God and the Son Christ the Savior. They were felt on earth as well as the whole universe, and like birth pains getting ready for the delivery process, all knew the time was coming when the Lord Jesus would be sent again to reconcile justice upon the earth and to remove from it all those who would not be made to withstand the coming evil and peace to follow.

"New prophets were being born to tell the story of Christ coming again," the Holy Spirit continued, "along with new false prophets and more atheists born to confuse the people. All these were born by God with the assigned tasks of culling the sheep, and many with subversive intentions were being given new places of high esteem, like good sheep ready to be sheered for the harvest. The people will be called by the shepherds daily, one The Good Shepherd and the other The Bad Shepherd. Like two gifts which are presented together to be chosen from, one will present a gift that will be beautifully presented to the foolish person with intentions to snare like a trap, but the other gift will be presented unmarked with inherent beauty, unremarkable, but will have great value inside after the blemishes are washed from it stones. The cap-rock on the temple will finally be put into place, and all those who go to Jerusalem singing their praises of the Lord on High will be redeemed and all

---

[225] Luke 17:20

their sorrows washed away with all their inequities," said the Holy Ghost.

Now it was time for Sonnius to go before the Holy Spirit. All things prepared which recorded his life, creating his testimony, were to be presented before the Lord now and recorded and entered into His eternal record.

"Sonnius Hermetus, come forth!" the Holy Spirit commanded.

The floors and chambers of Upper Paradise shook with great strength and might when the Holy Spirit called the name of him who was born in the line of Moses. There had been no walls present in his first meeting with the Holy Spirit. The floors and walls of this chamber in Upper Paradise were all there, so that he felt confined in his meeting and different from the previous meeting.

"Sonnius Hermetus," repeated the Holy Spirit, "your record shows that you were a good and faithful servant your whole life, preparing yourself for this day. How did you know to do these things that we sowed into your heart?"

Sonny thought but he could not speak, for he had been muted this moment so that an angel would answer for him.

"The Lord God Almighty taught him to love the Father with all his heart, his might, his strength, and his soul, and to love his neighbor as himself," said his overseeing angel, "since Sonnius was born again and took the oath of obedience. His record shows this: that he gave unconditional love to all whom You put in his way, for freely he accepted what You gave, and in turn freely he gave all away."

"This is true, for many of the angels have reported these acts of Sonnius!"

"Then does Sonnius choose to extend his stewardship in Paradise, as in the line of Moses, as an angel, of does he choose to stay in the Upper or Lower chambers and fulfill his assigned acts and duties in retirement?" the Holy Spirit asked.

At this point Sonnius became unmuted, and he wished to speak for himself. His voice came to him, and he spoke to the Holy Spirit.

"I have but one request, and that is to look after my loved one, Rosanne, who has not followed me yet."

"But she already has angels to do that, so your effort would not be with her," answered the Holy Spirit. "And in Lower Paradise you will once again be presented with struggles which you will not bear here. It will be more difficult if you choose to be connected in this way. The dimensions between lower Paradise and earth are connected, so those who go in and out may endure many hardships."

"This is my desire, oh Holy Spirit," Sonnius replied, "for You created me to serve those who cannot see Your Truth, so I am bound to this oath, and this gives me the greatest pleasure permissible."

"This is not your privilege, Sonnius, to choose your position," the Holy Spirit replied.

Then the Holy Spirit sent Sonnius to a great Room of Enlightenment with others who had taken the same oath as he had, so that they would understand the Great Promise and Plan created from the beginning for earth. They all watched and learned of the seven plagues which had been sent to the earth in Moses day, and then the current seven which began in 1946, a year after the close if WWII. These were the great harvesters of the people which kept them in need of their Savior after He again sorted the world into sheep and goats. If the sheep had just chosen to be content in their current state, then they would not have received these new plagues, but they did not, so these new chastisements followed, as foretold in the days of old which God the Father knew they would choose, and like sheep they again would follow bad shepherds and make life miserable living amongst the wolves, so their children and grandchildren would be carried off and devoured as the victims they were, because they knew no other light.

There in the great Room of Enlightenment, Sonnius sat with the others who were all family in the line of Moses; and Moses was there too, leading at his position as head of the messengers.

John, the Last Prophet in the Age of Prophets, from the line of Moses, and cousin to Jesus, from the line of David, was born to Elizabeth, descendant of Aaron, who was the brother of Moses. These all were in the room except Jesus; He was in Heaven sitting at the right side of God, the Father. Johnnie would not come to this room later because he was in the line of David, who was in the line of Abraham, and not in this line of prophets. Both Paul and Servius Quintus were there. This is what Sonnuis heard as he entered the room:

Moses was preaching to his family line.

"When the first Seven Plagues were brought upon Pharaoh," Moses said, "I was sent to tell him with the voice of the Holy Spirit saying, 'Let my people go from this place! For they are on a journey to be released from slavery, and then led to the Promised Land. You will show them. For I, God in Heaven, will be your strength and be your witness.' And God finally let them go. But did make I it to the Promised land? No! I did not… for I smote the rock when the Lord said to just speak to it, so I was held back until the day of my passing, even though I begged for my people to receive mercy."

Moses repeated the story of Genesis, Leviticus, Numbers, and Deuteronomy for the 12,345,760,324,834th time.

Then after these freed bondsmen lived in the desert until the next two generations passed, so they could be cleansed and venerated, the Lord spoke to Joshua and told him the same thing, and the Lord God also told Paul, and then Servius, the same thing, just as he told Moses, followed by Joshua, and now it was Sonnuis' turn to be paired with Johnnie from the line of Abraham, for the Lord God always sent them out in at least pairs with a legion of guardian angels for protection, one to proclaim the coming of the Word and message, and the other to deliver on the proclamation. This was witnessed as Paul went to and fro with his guardian angels to deliver the proclamation.

The torch was always passed from one generation to the next. They would all receive their general instruction with divine wisdom gleaned in the great room of Enlightenment by someone from a generation before, and then receive their orders directly from the Holy Spirit as She and He guided the Great Plan out on earth. Seven thousand earth years had now elapsed since Adam and Eve had received the first two souls and been given the promise of redemption if they followed the rules of the chosen. These two sinned against the Lord, and their family was cursed with the murder of one son against the other, and so it had continued through the course of the seven covenants until Christ came again to finish the last one.

Then Servius Quintus was called forward, and he said these things to the line of prophets who sat there waiting patiently for their time to reflect on the fruit of their earthly deeds. Quintus had been sent to serve alongside Luke so that the Book of Acts would get completed, then after He too would spread the Gospel and affect and inspire Tertullian to write and affect the papal leaders to listen at the great meetings of the ecumenical councils to enact the Truth of the Holy Triune and deliver the message of the Triad state of the universe, being Heaven, Hell, and Earth, divided into the sixty-plus dimensions of the states of Upper and Lower Paradise and the Great Veils which separated them by the worlds they existed in and the angels who guarded the inhabitants there.

All was to the Glory of God the Father and to the Triune in which He existed in Three Parts. 'Holy, Holy, Holy,' the angels sang as they praised and honored the Creators of all things good and evil, true and untrue, where justice and mercy reigned over chaos, and darkness created by the bondsmen of the Dark Angel.

Now Sonnius was listening closely and watching for his direction, since he had chosen to return to earth and was expected to watch over and support Johnnie Perfect as he developed his mission to bring light on the course of the new Seven Plagues which were now emerging on the earth, covering it with a new dark blanket, and stealing the livelihood and lifeblood itself from all those who continued to live in denial and repeat the sins of the Hebrews, who had turned against Moses originally as their leader and then praised Aaron's golden calf in the Age of the Lord's many prophets, who had called for the coming of Christ the first time.

Many martyrs died in those days and many more would die in this age, the new Age of the coming of the Tribulation and Rapture. The next generation of new prophets would prophesy for Christ to come again, pleading again for His return soon as the second coming in a new body which would be given to Him after his death and Resurrection over all things, fulfilling in Him the Promise for all to see, believe, and praise until a new world would be created and this cycle repeated itself all over again as a speck of dust in the annuls of time, known as the Last Great Chance for Mankind to redeem his own children given to him by God, as the church was redeemed by Christ in the Book of Revelation. Amen.

The start time had arrived for game seven of the finals between the Hurricanes and the War Horses. Both teams stood in tunnels leading from their locker rooms to opposing sides of the floor where the game would be played. Though symbolic, Johnnie felt that this game was the epitome of what life on earth had to offer for all mankind. There were two great forces preparing to clash in an orchestrated event of titans, in which only one would prove victorious over the other. In Johnnie's mind this would be similar to Armageddon without loss of life, but that remained to be seen.

Also in his mind were his fond memories of Charlotte when he was immersed in overwhelming love, which made his life seem to be fulfilled with every dream he could possibly imagine, but as he was thinking these things, Chalymina, whispered into his ear that marriage is a 'three-way covenant' which included the Almighty himself, and not a 'two-way covenant' between and man and woman only, so it was not so easily erased from the records of Heaven, even though man may erase it on paper at a courthouse on earth, if one side decided to break it.

"Johnnie, you are still married in Heaven to Charlotte and she bore you a son, and for this reason you shall not be married again here on earth; all other forms of sex you pursue are acts of adultery, and for these things you will be judged."[226]

Johnnie then heard the team's names being called, and his was the last name to be heard over the loudspeakers. Tucker had already run out onto the floor. It was right then he recognized the voice of Marty Morrison, the legendary voice of the Hurricane franchise, announcing his own name again, and the crowd erupted and stood to their feet chanting, 'Johnnie, Johnnie…' And once again Johnnie felt extremely valuable in his creation, and he praised God for his strange and mysterious life, but this too would pass in a fleeting moment of solitude, once the game began and the athletic war was at hand.

When the spotlights turned off from Johnnie standing on the sideline, he felt a slight tug on his arm to escort him to his seat. It was Rosanne, his angel who now kept close by his side.

"Johnnie, Johnnie…" he heard her gentle voice say to him, "Mr. Silverman has asked me to be your guide helper tonight. I will take you to your seat. Will it be okay if I sit next to you? It would make Sonny happy, I think, too!"

"Well okay, let's go," Johnnie said, and they both proceeded to the two chairs at the end of the bench.

They sat for a few minutes, and then it was time for the national anthem to be sung. This game it was a young fifth-grade girl from one of the local talent agencies who was going to do the honors of the song. She sang wonderfully, and all those in attendance watched and put their hands over their hearts to honor the fallen of the military who had died giving freedom to those in the stands and on the court, those who now benefited from the blood they had shed.

---

[226] Matthew 5:32, Matthew 15:19

Johnnie could only think of the blood that Jesus had shed for him to give him freedom, not only from governmental rule but also from worldly rule by those who tried to take from him what he had already given away to his Lord. So now he was immune to the laws of the physical world, and not many knew it around him but those who had done the same.

When the tip-off happened, it looked like a scene from the Bible when David met Goliath in the valley between Sokoh and Azekah.[227] Zing was a monster of a man for the War Horses, standing almost a foot above everyone else, and he could move around the court as nimbly as Tucker could on his best day, or almost… at least on his worst day. Sir Francis Ott, seemed to think any ball in the air was his, and he made no mistake early letting everyone on the court feel his presence when the ball came off of the backboard and a rebound was ensuing.

The others there were all focused, and the game went back and forth with mostly nothing but the sound of the net swishing from three-point range and an occasional dunk by Ott or Zing on the other team, or the Zig Man on Johnnie's team. Ziggy was well adept at going between a gauntlet of defenders as he twisted and turned his body in unusual contortions to make it to the basket and make the basket. He was the leading person in free throws, since Johnnie had been taken from the game, and now Ziggy would be invaluable in his ability to make the other team foul, hoping to get them into foul trouble early.

Both Tucker and Heatherton were able to keep the lead far enough out in front by their high percentage of three-point scoring, but everyone knew that magic may not last. Tucker was known to be

---

[227] 1 Samuel 17

a hot and cold shooter, whose consistency was not his best attribute. So far in the first quarter he was three for four, and each time he would post up for a shot, Rosanne would squeeze at Johnnie arm unknowing and scream, 'Go Tucker!' so Johnnie had a real feeling for the score of the game.

Rosanne gave him a real play-by-play of the game, even though her eyesight was diminished by her severe macular degeneration from her Stargart's disease. She could see just enough by moving her head around from side to side to read the big red score on the eighty-foot overhead arena board, and taking her cues from the movement and reactions of the players' moving shadows on the court, she could relay what the momentum of the game was to Johnnie.

"This is a war like no other!" Rosanne screamed during one point about six minutes into the game.

Each team was fast to start and would not give up. The lead changed back and forth many times early in the game, and with the time running out before the first buzzer, the War Horses made the last shot of the first quarter, ending in a 27-26 advantage.

Mr. Silverman and Daisy had invited Mamaw to be with them in the executive box seats tonight. It seemed she was good luck for the team, and when she sat in with the Silvermans, the team always seemed to find a way to win. Andy was not sure if it was just the luck of the crazy lady with the wild glasses, handbag, and cinnamon flavored cigars, but whatever luck she had, Mr. Silverman wanted all of it this night when everything seemed to be on the edge of either continuing or closing on the age of the Johnnie Spot Perfect Television and Media Dynasty.

Before the second quarter began, Coach Barricks pulled his team around him and used every coaching skill he knew to try and get his team to keep their will iron-clad and focused. This was simply a matter of which team would make the least number mistakes, because both teams represented the epitome of great skills combined with the greatest athletes, the best that big money could buy in the world of growing network sports entertainment and leading world-class power players. Many of the players were becoming household names, with salaries that stifled many of the rock-and-roll bands of the sixties, seventies, and eighties.

"If anyone cannot give me 110% in the second quarter, I need you to tell me now," Coach said to them, "because if you can't I will put someone in who can. If we go into half time and we are not ahead, there will be hell to pay."

The buzzer then sounded for the second quarter to begin, and the team huddle broke up as the team went back on the floor for another round of sweat-induced demolition basketball.

As Johnnie listened to the play-by-play description that Rosanne was giving him, he could not help but feel like life would be easier with companionship, which he missed so much after Charlotte had left. Now that Rosanne was a widow, he thought maybe this was God's way of helping him make it through the rest of his life… 'But would this be fair to her?' he wondered. She had just lost the love of her life and had not healed yet. He knew it took at least three years to overcome the loss of a loved one, and he had not even healed yet from his own loss, so these were crazy thoughts at a crazy time. He just needed to focus on the game and let God be God, and hope for the best in all situations, including the rite of passage for death at the time in which God called whomever He wanted home at the time of His bidding.

The war on the basketball court was getting crazier and crazier as Rosanne was calling the game from her vantage point of half-truth and half-make-believe. Bob Heatherton just got his feet taken out from underneath him and had an elbow blow to his nose when Coach Barricks called a timeout for the trainers to look at him. They took him to the bench and sat him beside Johnnie to take a look, and Bob's nose was definitely broken. Johnnie could not see it but could hear the trainers asking Bob to try and blow the blood out and if he could breathe enough to keep going.

"I can't feel anything except like a soda bottle has been shoved up in between my eyes," Bob said. "I can breathe but not sure how long I will last."

The trainers got a piece of tape that they put across the bridge of his nose, and while he was out the War Horses went up by nine points. This was discouraging to Coach Barricks, so he came over to see how Bob was doing. He wanted to know if Bob could go back in. He needed a spark to keep the game momentum going and a few buckets by Bob, his wounded warrior, might just do the trick.

"How are you doing, Bobby? Are you good to go back in? I need someone to drive the middle of the lane and split the defense so Tucker can shoot from outside," he said.

"I can do it, Coach!" Bob said.

There was only about a minute-and-a-half left until half was completed, so Coach called his final timeout of the first half play to put Bob back in. Ziggy needed a rest, too, so he put in Johnson, who rarely played, but Ziggy needed to come out so he could watch and see where the weaknesses were from the bench.

As play resumed, Bob got the ball and immediately drove to the basket and scored with a back-side layup that seemed impossible from the opposite side he favored. The crowd roared and began to chant, 'Bobby, Bobby…' and this got Johnnie's emotions going because he was happy the crowd was cheering and supporting his team, but he wished, somehow, they would call his name instead. But it was not going to happen because his time in the limelight had already come and gone. When the buzzer sounded for the end to the second quarter, it was a 51-52 game, and the Hurricanes were behind.

In the locker room, Coach Barricks was frazzled and could not believe his team was behind. Bob getting hurt was a big blow, but it could have been anyone who got injured and the same result would have happened.

"We gotta stay healthy, guys, in the second half," Coach admonished. "We gotta play smart too. No fouls! Don't lose your cool and take a punch at anyone. A single foul and free throw could be all there is between a big fat paycheck for you after this is over, or a ride home on a Greyhound bus if you screw this thing up!"

"Ziggy, you have to take charge, man!" Coach continued, shouting. "What do you think you are doing hiding in the corner waiting for someone to give you an assist? Get those feet moving and come more to the middle. I need you to help double team on Sir Ott. Johnson is doing a good job backing up Jones behind Zing Chou, but we need to get all the rebounds on our side of the court. Keep pressing and pressing until you can't press anymore!"

Couch began to get a little hysterical, so he asked Johnnie to say something to get the team going again.

"Johnnie, what are your thoughts on what is going on?" Coach asked.

About that time Mr. Silverman came into the locker room to listen to what was going on. This was not a usual thing for him to do, but Daisy insisted that he go down and see how Bob was doing. He leaned against the wall and hung back in the background to see if the team would come out flat or fired up in the few minutes they had to reconvene before the time was up and they had to go back out for the final two quarters.

"Johnnie," Coach said, "give us some insight and wisdom. This is our last chance to be either mere lazy hound dogs or heroes."

The room went quiet for a moment and then Johnnie began to talk.

"When I was in my wreck… I died," Johnnie said. "I felt myself float up over the scene where I laid there. They were doing CPR on me, and I knew I was dead. But God would not let me die. I wanted to. I did not want to go back because I was tired and the place where I was felt like relief. And that is where you guys are today. But God showed be that there were only two paths in front of me. One was to my left and the other to my right. He made me chose. There were no other choices, just like right now. You guys are going to have to choose. You can get tired and throw in the towel, or you can get a supernatural faith that you will overcome by perseverance and strength. I believed that somehow I was not finished, and look at me now. I can't see, but I am here, aren't I? I was dead, but now I am alive, aren't I? You need to live this second half by faith, and give up all personal thoughts you have on what is right and wrong about how the game is going, because guess what? You don't have any control over it anyway. Did Sonny have control over the tree that fell on him? Did Leroy have any control over those boys who hit our car head-on and killed him? No! And you don't have any control over how this game ends. All you have control over is your desire to win and do the right thing. That is it! I need you guys to go out there and be my eyes so tomorrow I can feel the victory with you that I long to enjoy. This is not a game for you but a game of willpower for me. They are thinking the same thing, and everyone puts their pants on one leg at a time, but in the end the team that wants it more will win. I want this, guys, so for Heaven's sake if you don't want this, stay here in the locker room! I want only winners on the floor tonight, and no losers! Don't come back here in this room holding your heads down if they kick your butt because I don't want to listen to you. I hate losing, and if I were Mr. Silverman, I would fire you all if you can't win this game on sheer desire and willpower. So, I have said my piece. Give all you have and leave nothing out there on the court but blood, sweat, and tears, and tomorrow we will all celebrate together as one big victorious family!"

Upon those statements, the team began to chant again and again, 'Johnnie, Johnnie, Johnnie…' and then a frenzied craze came over them and they all jumped up and ran onto the floor. Coach Barricks, all the staff, and the trainers, followed the team down and out the tunnel toward the floor while Johnnie just sat there on the bench in his dark solitude. Andy had heard everything he said and walked his direction from the back of the locker room. Chalymina had been there all the time helping Johnnie with the words to say. Johnnie just felt alone, but somehow the connection he had with the team gave him hope in his heart that he was still valuable.

"That was a great speech you gave, Johnnie… quite inspiring!" Andy said.

"It was all true, Mr. Silverman. I did not embellish a thing there," Johnnie answered.

"They look up to you as their hero. We all need heroes, Johnnie."

"I let Leroy down. He died because if me. I am not anyone's hero, Mr. Silverman. I don't know what I am, but I am not anyone's hero."

"Johnnie, perception is reality here on this earth. To them you are their hero. It is a role you need to lean on. Whether you are a hero or not, the whole world remembers you as one, so I am thinking you need to stay in that role for your own good, or else just go dig yourself a grave and jump in. Does that make sense to you? Attitude is everything in life. You just changed their attitudes, and now I am here to help you change yours. God is watching you, Johnnie, I know He is, and He wants the best for you. And me too! You just need to allow what needs to happen to happen, and to quit fighting His will all the time with your selfish thoughts and ambitions. Just give in! I did..."

Johnnie went silent again. He just sat there, looking at nothing. His eyes were trying to focus on the floor and the game, but he could see nothing but the darkness of full blindness. All he could think of at that moment were reflections of memories of when he had been a young hopeful basketball player, sitting in Coach Thornton's office while he had the whole world in front of him, but Coach Thornton had told him to let his ego go. Coach told him then that it would only get in the way of his personal success in life and also in the 'thereafter,' which was a lesson he was still trying to learn.

It was now time for the last half of the game, and Mr. Silverman escorted Johnnie back out on the court to sit next to Rosanne at the end of the bench. This was the lineup that went from the most important players, who sat closest to the coaches and the mid-court area, to the second-team laggards, who occupied the end of the bench where Johnnie sat over on the end with Rosanne acting as his eyes and ears. This was how life seemed to Johnnie: second place was for losers; the world only remembered the winners who could make it to first place.

The game began again, and the ball was brought in bounds by the War Horses. It was just ten clicks of the clock before they had scored with a powerful dunking of the ball through the basket by Zing Chou, who was on a crusade to make sure his team would end the evening in first place and be remembered as the team who beat the legacy of Johnnie and the Hurricanes and put their dynasty to rest.

But God would not let this happen so easily, and the plans of the Master's Great Divine Agenda could not be thwarted. While the world was busy watching the on-goings of the distractions of entertainment, the Holy Spirit called Servius Quintus to His side.

"Go now and reveal to Johnnie his destiny," the Holy Spirit commanded. "Now is the time for his enlightenment!"

The clouds about the Holy Spirit began to darken, and the winds began to swirl. Lightning began flashing all around the existing universe, and a low-grade booming of thunder began rumbling. The ground where the Holy Spirit stood began to shake, and in an instant Servius was gone and arrived at the place where Johnnie was seated at the right hand of the weakest player on the team. He was like David, who was out in the fields while all his brothers were brought forward and measured for the position of kingship, though none were worthy of the choice.

"Johnnie," Servius called to him. "Fear not, for the Lord is with you."

Then Johnnie lifted his head and looked up toward the arena lights, closed his eyes, and fell into a deep state of unconsciousness, as if someone had drugged him with sodium barbital for a medical surgery in the hospital.

"Johnnie," Servius continued, "those who have come before you have paved your way and have bested many great odds against them with perils which seemed insurmountable to them in their time, but they overcame them not by their own hands but by the will of the Holy Spirit… Ezekiel, Obadiah, and David, to name a few. They have come to tell you that the Lord will not forsake you. Bear Him as your cross and nothing will overcome you on any day the world comes to judge you."

Johnnie sat once more in amazement, looking upward, as several angels gathered around him. They seemed to be following him and talking to him even in his lowest hours, but no one could hear nor see these things as they happened.

"These things I will tell you," Servius continued, "for you to remember when you are spoken to by mortal men. First, their evil is placed in the hope of false beliefs and agendas which you will recognize as false gods and idols. Second, their actions will be as guardians and protectors of false ideas and agendas who steal from the individual his freedoms and serve their own needs for money and power. And third, they will do evil things through character assassination, bearing false witness, and speaking lies to those who know no other way except to react in poor faith, so that you, Johnnie, will not talk with them except with words provided by the Holy Spirit. Remember this: 'Seek ye first the Kingdom of God and all shall be given unto you.' "

Then Servius went on to further enlighten Johnnie, who could hardly fathom the depths of the images he was seeing in his blindness.

The game seemed to be falling apart for the Hurricanes. Almost seven minutes of the second half had passed without a single score by their team. Then, much to Rosanne's amazement, she looked over at Johnnie in her despair and saw that he had fallen asleep. He was snoring during their shellacking in the third quarter!

With his head face-down and with his chin resting upon his breastbone, he was asleep, totally out like a light. Just like a boxer who had connected to a right hook of an adversary in the heat of a pugilistic match, he was out for the ten count. Rosanne could not believe it! What kind of spell was he under? This was the biggest game to this day, and he could not even stay awake to see it through?

But this was the will of the Father in order to make sure all knew just what was happening in the big scheme of things. While the cameras of the national television stations were scanning the crowds for interest and folly, they noticed Johnnie's sleeping, evidently showing a severe lack of interest in the surrounding game, and it became a televised moment on the big screen, ala' grandeur! This sight of his sleeping sent utter shockwaves throughout the loyal following of the Hurricane hearts around the world watching game seven, which would decide the world champions, and their champion was asleep!

All if this together just seemed to be too much, and the whole fan base began sinking into the inevitable quicksand of failure and defeat, just wanting the game clock to hurry up and pass away to lessen the suffering.

At that moment, Coach Barricks also looked up and saw on the screen the image of Johnnie sleeping at the end of the bench. The shocked crowds were all pointing at the big screen overhead, and no one was watching the game anymore. It was a total distraction from the purpose they were all there, and Coach thought to himself that this was the one thing he had hoped would not happen: a major distraction which would cause his team to lose faith in the heat of the battle and stop fighting. So Coach Barricks called his second timeout of the second half to get his team to refocus right before the last quarter was to begin.

It was an amazing sight: the collection of saints who came down to the game. At least three thousand angels had gathered and were hovering over Johnnie at his end of the arena. This group was distracted from the goings-on of the game. Then Johnnie raised his head and looked up, and there, in the middle of the group, was Jesus.

Jesus called out three times to his loyal and faithful servant.

"Johnnie, Johnnie, Johnnie… why hast thou forsaken me in your heart? Do you not see all that I have done for you? I have brought you here and made this world ready to accept you, but still you doubt your purpose. How can this be?" the Lord Jesus said to him.

But Johnnie could not speak. He could only observe in this unusual dream state. Then again from his seat he rose out of his body and went up with the angels to look down on the arena and see the world from the angels' viewpoint. Now he could see clearly the world as it was created from the other dimensions. Johnnie went forward and knelt before Christ the King, Son of the Living God, who reigned with the authority of the full Triune Godhead, where He stood there unmoving in His authority over everything far and near.

"Johnnie," Jesus continued, "I show this to you so you will be confident in your words and actions. No more days shall you walk the earth in blindness… no more days shall you hold your head low for your small wisdom, and no more nights will you sleep and wake to a world where darkness rules over men's hearts without discernment. Now you shall see the power of the Lord made to guide again through your voice. But beware, for even Moses was tempted to do his own will and fell from grace in his final days. Go and lead with the purpose of the Holy Spirit, and be confident that the Lord will not forsake you as you speak the will of the Lord."

Then—just as fast as Johnnie had been put into the deep sleep state to gain his knowledge of the three worlds which co-existed in a unified sate of reality—he awoke and was once again blind no more!

Johnnie opened his eyelids and saw the arena around him filled with people, and the despondency they felt in the final minutes of the game they loved so much to watch. He saw Rosanne sitting beside him biting her lower lip as if trying to divert the pain and agony she felt, somehow wanting the win for Sonny more than for herself. And as he looked down the complete lineup of the team players—some with towels over their heads trying to cover the embarrassment of the moment, and others just looking forlorn as if there was no hope left in their future—Johnnie focused on Coach Barricks, who was like General Custer commanding his brigade in the heat of a losing battle in which he neither had ammunition nor the will to fight left in the overwhelming odds of a losing battle.

As Johnnie stared at him, Coach Barricks turned back to look at Johnnie to see if he was still sleeping or had woken on the end of the bench. As he turned, his eyes met Johnnie's eyes, and they both became fixated on each other. Coach could see Johnnie's eyes were now focusing back on him, not like before. They were intense. And without a moment's hesitation, he jumped up and walked down the line of players and knelt by Johnnie's feet.

"You can see again! I can tell! You can, can't you?" Coach Barricks blurted out at him.

He was in total disbelief of what had just occurred, and he was overwhelmed for what this meant to Johnnie, whom he loved so much as a player and a person. The whole world of the basketball game became insignificant to Coach as he looked into Johnnie's eyes and saw something he had never seen before… a sense of purity that he could not fathom in his wildest dreams.

Rosanne also looked over and saw Johnnie's countenance had changed.

"Holy moly!" Rosanne said aloud, "And I thought he was just sleeping. What just happened? I was too busy watching the game to even see what went on with you."

"You've got to stop the clock!" Johnnie said to Coach urgently. "Call your last timeout."

Coach turned around while still kneeling and saw that the time clock had just three minutes left in the entire game, and the score was 102 to 85. The War Horses had expanded their lead to seventeen points and all hope was dwindling away for the faithful in Houston.

A referee calling the game on the sideline next to them whisked by, and Coach immediately rose and stepped forward in front of him, calling their final timeout. Time seemed to freeze as the television cameras started focusing on Coach and their long-lost star known as 'Spot'… the Spot Man who could hit a shot from anywhere on the court. He and the couch were having a discussion on the far end of the bench, and Mr. Silverman saw what was happening from his owner's booth at the top of the arena. Andy stood up and leaned forward, unable to believe his eyes, and turned to Daisy.

"Look! Johnnie is up and he can see again!" he yelled to her.

Mamaw, who was sitting next to Daisy, was just finishing up a flask of bourbon she had snuck into the game in her big purse, because she liked to mix it with sodas. She looked over and saw all of the commotion.

"Oh my God, they have let McCracken out!" she whispered to herself.

Coach Barricks had little time to regroup his team. He asked Johnnie if he could play.

"Sure can, Coach… put me in!" Johnnie replied. "This is going to be fun!"

By this time the crowds in the arena were chanting together, 'Johnnie, Johnnie…' and the noise was so loud that Coach Barricks could barely hear himself talking to the players.

"Johnson, you are coming out; Johnnie you are going in. Tucker, you are moving to floater, outside wing, and Ziggy you will hold tight in the paint."

The War Horses now felt as if they had been hornswoggled, but they were ahead by seventeen, so this night could not be taken away from them even with the help of the legendary MVP who had crushed so many opponents before. Plus, they had Ming Chou, who could chew up little animals and spit them out if he wanted too.

It was the Hurricanes' ball, and they immediately scored. Tucker drove the paint and performed one of his amazing lay-ups, which rattled the War Horses. They miss-threw on their inbounds toss, and Johnnie's long reach grabbed the ball away and dunked it with authority, causing the backboard to rattle under his weight. In just twelve seconds, the score was 102-89, and the crowd could feel the momentum changing.

The War Horses again threw the ball in, this time they to Sir Francis, who was across the court as far from Johnnie as possible, and he began to try and run out the clock, but Ziggy was able to steal the ball and immediately threw a long ball down to Johnnie, who again dunked the ball with authority and pushed the War Horses' lead down to eleven, at 102-91.

Now, with just over two minutes left in the third quarter, the War Horses collected their composure and began to work the clock, but Coach had Heatherton foul one of the poorer free-throw shooters on the team… Zing Chou. Oh, but he paid a price. Zing hit him with his elbow as he knew what Bobby was going to do, and it almost took his head off in the play. Bobby went to the floor, and the referee had to call a medical timeout.

Coach Barricks pulled his team into a final huddle. He put Johnson back in.

"We need some outside three-point shots to win this game, guys," he said to the team. "Don't be afraid to pull the trigger, but if Johnnie is open… well, I am not saying you *have* to pass to him, but if you shoot and miss, this will be your last game under me!"

Those were some pretty strong words, but Coach always told it like it was, and the guys knew what he meant: that they would be looking for another team next year, but more importantly that they would be looking for another leader, because Johnnie was back, and they knew they could count on him.

The arena was buzzing with frenzied excitement, and the television cameramen were having a hard time selecting what to film while the timeout was happening. Even the ushers and security guards were cheering around the mezzanine railings, and everyone could feel the electricity being generated with the rebirth of Johnnie.

The horn sounded, and both teams took the floor once more. Tucker passed the ball in from mid-court to Johnnie, who took exactly three steps and launched a long sky hook from half-court that looked like it might hit the overhead scoreboard. It took a long two-and-a-half seconds to reach the rim, where it hit nothing but net. Once again, the crowd went into frenzy.

The angels had spread out now around the arena, and to them it felt almost as if they had gone back in time to the days of Peter and Paul and were in the coliseum where the crowds were chanting in a frenzy, but for blood and death. This was a more gentle equation of might and superiority, but the end game was all the same: 'Conquer the crowds in the arena; capture their hearts, and you will lead them all the rest of their living days.'

They angels were also there to help. This would not just be an affirmation of Johnnie's new life but a ripple effect that would begin now and reach all the way around the world. The War Horses may have taken Troy in the days of old by deception and cunning ingenuity, but their time to leave the game in utter defeat had come.

Ziggy knew he could stay with Johnnie on an offense charge, so he went shoulder-to-shoulder with him and stretched for a quick three-point shot from the corner. The ball went in.

The Hurricanes had now scored twelve unanswered points, and the crowd watching was beside themselves. Tucker was inspired and took a long jump-shot after getting an assist from Johnson because they had double-teamed Johnnie, and Tucker's three points went in. After another War Horse miss, Johnson drove the paint straight up, splitting the big men of Zing and Sir Francis, and his layup bounced back from the highest part of the backboard and it went in.

For the next minute, both teams struggled to take hold on to the lead, but in the end the War Horses maintained a two-point lead as the clock ticked down. Since the Hurricanes had taken their last timeout, there needed to be a plan, but no one seemed to have one except run and gun and hope that Johnnie would get the last shot. Tucker had different plans, and he intentionally leapt over Sir Francis in an attempt, not to foul him, but to get an injury timeout for the team. And it worked.

The game stopped with just three seconds left on the clock, and the Hurricanes had possession of the ball, but Tucker went out for the last time. He and Heatherton were now out of the game. Coach Barricks had to make a quick adjustment and called for a player who had not graced the floor all season with the opportunity to throw it in.

"Bono, get over here!" he shouted toward the bench.

It was Bono who had practiced most with Johnnie before his accident with throw-ins, and they had devised a last chance play two years before, and hoped now it would work. Johnnie already knew what was happening and they had no time to get anything together. The throw-in would be from half-court again, and Johnnie would take his position behind the half-court line along with Ziggy, while Johnson went for the tip-in, just in case the long show did not make it in.

They would need three points to win and two points to tie and cause the game to go into overtime, but a tie was not in Johnnie's nature. It was either a complete win with a comeback to be talked about through the ages or just another loss to compare with all the others which came and went from generation to generation.

There was not a person sitting in the arena as the throw-in was made. Bono held the ball up and clapped his left hand to make a smack on the ball, and Ziggy ran in front of Johnnie to act as a block so he could catch the ball and shoot. Bono's heart was thumping so hard it seemed his heart was lodged in his throat, and he felt like adrenalin was almost squirting from his ears. His hands were shaking as he let the ball fly high so it could not be knocked away as Johnnie retrieved it from the pass. Sir Francis then came to double-team with Zing, and from behind the half-court some twenty feet away, Johnnie leaned backwards and let a sky hook fly with his big hands.

The ball seemed to take forever to reach the basket. All eyes were fixated on the ball. As the angels looked on, they could see all heads moving in the entire stadium move in unison as the ball careened through the air on its journey of fate: either doom and loss, or immortality and victory.

This was the legacy of Johnnie Spot Perfect. He never did anything halfway. It was either with the persistence of an eagle swooping down on its next meal and carrying it off in glory, or making a miss at the prey and finding that success would have to wait just one more day. But inevitably it would come to pass that all would see the eagle rising in victory to build a shelter in the lion's mouth for the lamb to live and reign.

The final score was 121-122, with Johnnie, God, and the Hurricanes prevailing that day on simple pure faith, a lot of determination and hope to succeed, and one small miracle with help from the angels, whom the Holy Spirit had called forth to bless the world with one more inkling of mercy… which no one ever deserved.

To him who is able to keep you from stumbling and to present you before his glorious presence without fault and with great joy— to the only God our Savior be glory, majesty, power and authority, through Jesus Christ our Lord, before all ages, now and forevermore! Amen.

As Testified by Jude,
Brother of Jesus and James
Chapter 1:24-25

Post-Log

Ben Tucker and Bob Heatherton both thought it would be fun to make a sizable bet of one-thousand dollars each on the super-long 500,000:1 Las Vegas odds that Johnnie Spot Perfect would make a shot in the final minute of play in the seventh game. It was against all NBA rules for them to gamble while playing, but their belief in God as a current-day miracle worker, combined with their witnessing the superhuman phenom—called Johnnie Perfect—and the miracles they had already seen him accomplish, caused them to believe he would be able to make at least one shot the last night of his career, if given just one more chance; and they were willing to take the chance of being expelled from the NBA, too, if word got out. Besides, no one would find out unless they actually won the bet.

Their payoff was each a huge $500 million dollars net, and when combined together it was $1 billion before taxes, which almost bankrupted the long-standing bookie system in Las Vegas. No one else had taken that long-odds bet because no one believed a blind man could ever make a shot, even if it was Johnnie Perfect. But God worked in mysterious ways. All those who had joined in his trials with him, in the life of Johnnie Spot Perfect, knew his legacy. And Johnnie's revelation—reliving the story of Matthew 19—was the thing he talked about after that night and how he was saved by the grace of God.

No way did Ben or Tucker want to hinder their chances of getting into Heaven by profiting from the legacy of Johnnie's pain, so they put all the winnings into a non-profit gifting foundation they called the Johnnie Perfect Prize Endowment Foundation, which took nominations from around the globe for lost and underprivileged persons of any age. The foundation sought out and chose one special recipient every year who best exemplified the effort to promote the Twelve Tribes of Jesus into one family, the One Holy Tree from the One Holy Root which God had planted, to unite all believers of all nations into one combined trunk of the Tree of Life.

They called the prize awarded from Johnnie's winnings 'The Perfect Prize,' to shine in comparison with the more established 'Nobel Prize,' which symbolized peace but did nothing to place emphasis on the sanctity of God's divine will or to acknowledge Jesus as the Savior to the world. The Nobel Prize was more secular, mankind's happenstance, which was only half-truth, but half un-truth.

The first prize in 1986 was awarded posthumously in memoriam to Mr. Andy Silverman. Mr. Silverman passed away suddenly in the locker room after the last game of Johnnie's career. He was at peace, though, for he knew it was his time to go, and in his last dying breath he asked those around him not to call for any paramedics, so that he could pass quietly. He had served his purpose for God, and he knew he had lived his life well.

Daisy knew this might happen because they had discussed just such an occurrence on several occasions. The money was fun while they had it, but in his will he left his entire oil estate to several non-profit organizations, primarily to the Red Cross, who took care of the poor and needy around the world using just donations from Christ-minded individuals. From the prize money, though, Daisy received a small amount every year to make sure that she was provided for, and eventually she moved in with Mamaw and Cojo, as they all benefitted from each other's wisdom and company.

Each night before going to bed, Mamaw would pray and read the last page of her Bible to herself in her room. She had always been extremely comforted by it ever since Mr. Gleason had passed, as this chapter spoke more to her than any other part of the Bible, because she had seen what God had done for her in her life, and now she understood the meaning of the River in Eden restored as the "Living Water" in Revelation 22. Without it she knew she would have died in the Dessert of Life. And now she understood what the Tree of Life was, with its single common root. For the same Tree of Life and of Knowledge of Good and Evil revealed in Genesis, when Satan was present, but not in Eden Restored, was now as she believed it to be. But still she did not believe in holding on to it as a mystery. Only those who like John would be able to testify to the truth of his Revelation. But all those who believe agree that Jesus is Lord and He will come again, and all eagerly await His arrival.

Mamaw read this over and over again to herself quietly in her room, as she raised her right hand each time to the Lord in praise, so that all the angels and saints could see right to her heart, which loved and never hated.

Reflection and Review

Revelation Chapter 22 and the Tree of Life

Then the angel showed me the river of the water of life, as clear as crystal, flowing from the throne of God and of the Lamb 2 down the middle of the great street of the city. On each side of the river stood the Tree of Life, bearing twelve crops of fruit, yielding its fruit every month. And the leaves of the tree are for the healing of the nations. 3 No longer will there be any curse. The throne of God and of the Lamb will be in the city, and his servants will serve him. 4 They will see his face, and his name will be on their foreheads. 5 There will be no more night. They will not need the light of a lamp or the light of the sun, for the Lord God will give them light. And they will reign forever and ever.

6 The angel said to me, "These words are trustworthy and true. The Lord, the God who inspires the prophets, sent his angel to show his servants the things that must soon take place."

7 "Look, I am coming soon! Blessed is the one who keeps the words of the prophecy written in this scroll."

8 I, John, am the one who heard and saw these things. And when I had heard and seen them, I fell down to worship at the feet of the angel who had been showing them to me. 9 But he said to me, "Don't do that! I am a fellow servant with you and with your fellow

prophets and with all who keep the words of this scroll. Worship God!"

10 Then he told me, "Do not seal up the words of the prophecy of this scroll, because the time is near. 11 Let the one who does wrong continue to do wrong; let the vile person continue to be vile; let the one who does right continue to do right; and let the holy person continue to be holy."

12 "Look, I am coming soon! My reward is with me, and I will give to each person according to what they have done. 13 I am the Alpha and the Omega, the First and the Last, the Beginning and the End.

14 "Blessed are those who wash their robes, that they may have the right to the Tree of Life and may go through the gates into the city. 15 Outside are the dogs, those who practice magic arts, the sexually immoral, the murderers, the idolaters and everyone who loves and practices falsehood.

16 "I, Jesus, have sent my angel to give you this testimony for the churches. I am the Root and the Offspring of David, and the bright Morning Star."

17 The Spirit and the bride say, "Come!" And let the one who hears say, "Come!" Let the one who is thirsty come; and let the one who wishes take the free gift of the water of life.

18 I warn everyone who hears the words of the prophecy of this scroll: If anyone adds anything to them, God will add to that person the plagues described in this scroll. 19 And if anyone takes words away from this scroll of prophecy, God will take away from that person any share in the tree of life and in the Holy City, which are described in this scroll.

20 He who testifies to these things says, "Yes, I am coming soon."

Amen. Come, Lord Jesus.[21]
The grace of the Lord Jesus be with God's people. Amen.

Dedication

This book is dedicated to the millions of Christians who have suffered or been imprisoned, threatened, demeaned, ridiculed, tortured, murdered, or crucified for putting their faith and hope in their Lord Jesus Christ. The most recent five-thousand-year period of history has fulfilled numerous prophecies of unimaginable and improbable statistical odds, which— when combined with the blood of countless eyewitnesses and martyrs willing to stand unwavering in their deepest beliefs for their salvation—have unequivocally stood the test of time and shown that Jesus Christ is the Son of God, born of the Virgin Mary, that He is the Messiah who was prophesied as the one who would return and rule, sent from Heaven to save the lost, that He lived a full life without sin and gave up His own life so that all people might know Him, have a relationship with Him, and procure their own eternal life.

Jesus proclaimed His place in the highest position above all others, created or born, by stating the single most powerful sentence ever uttered: "I am the Way, the Truth, and the Life, and no one comes to the Father but by Me." He proved his Lordship over everyone and everything by raising Himself from the dead, conquering the grave, and revealing Himself to those who would not believe He could do this, both then and now. He sits at the right hand of God the Father, reigning with full dominion as Lord and Savior over the earth and everything in it, from the beginning to the end, from Alpha to Omega, and everything in between.

May the Lord's will be done forever in earnest by mankind, with joyful hearts, humility, submission, and obedience in the process. And may He return soon. May all those with deaf ears hear, all those with blind eyes see, and all those with hardened hearts soften and understand the meaning of unconditional love which awaits those who answer the knock of freedom and open the door of self-worth where He stands, before He arrives to judge the lost, the wicked, and the dead.

May this book bring glory to all of God's kingdom, touching any failing hearts which may have been lost, broken, or stolen, with a reverence for Jesus Christ and for that which He has done for the whole world, living in the spirit in which this book was written.

Mamaw-isms:

1. Ignorance is bliss.

2. Time to let Cracken out.

3. The man may be the head of the home, but the woman is the neck… and the neck controls where the head goes or he has no home.

4. What goes around comes around… and God is watching you closer than Santa.

Author's Comments

The Twelve Tribes of Israel are mentioned in the Bible several times and have great historical significance, even today.

Abraham, whom God blessed, left everything that was his to his son Isaac,[228] whom God blessed after Abraham's death.[229] Jacob received Isaac's blessing,[230] then wrestled with God and was renamed Israel,[231] and then blessed his twelve sons to become the Twelve Tribes of Israel.[232]

Abraham's brother, Nahor, had twelve sons, who did not become their own tribes,[233] but Abraham's son Ishmael had twelve sons who settled along the border of Egypt to become Twelve Tribal Rulers, who lived in hostility to all their brothers.[234]

Moses wrote down everything the LORD had said. He got up early the next morning and built an altar at the foot of the mountain and set up twelve stone pillars, representing the twelve tribes of Israel.[235]

---

[228] Genesis 25:5
[229] Genesis 25:11
[230] Genesis 27:27-29
[231] Genesis 35:10
[232] Genesis 49:28
[233] Genesis 22:20-24
[234] Genesis 25:13-18
[235] Exodus 24:4

Joshua, leading his army into battle, chose twelve men from the tribes of Israel, one from each tribe.[236]

Elijah the Prophet took twelve stones, one for each of the tribes descended from Jacob, to whom the word of the Lord had come, saying, "Your name shall be Israel."[237]

Ezekiel, also a prophet, wrote, "This is what the Sovereign Lord says: 'These are the boundaries of the land that you will divide among the twelve tribes of Israel as their inheritance, with two portions for Joseph.' "[238]

To his disciples, Jesus said, "Truly I tell you, at the renewal of all things, when the Son of Man sits on his glorious throne, you who have followed me will also sit on twelve thrones, judging the twelve tribes of Israel."[239]

Jesus also reminded his disciples, "You are those who have stood by me in my trials. And I confer on you a kingdom, just as my Father conferred one on me, that you may eat and drink at my table in my kingdom and sit on thrones, judging the twelve tribes of Israel."[240]

To John, the disciple whom Jesus dearly loved, was revealed in a vision images of the New Jerusalem to come: "It had a great, high wall with twelve gates, and with twelve angels at the gates. On the gates were written the names of the twelve tribes of Israel."[241]

---

[236] Exodus 3:12

[237] I Kings 18:31

[238] Ezekiel 47:13

[239] Matthew 19:28

[240] Luke 22:29-30

[241] Revelation 21:12

James, the brother of Jesus, referred to Twelve Tribes, but did not reference Israel: "To the twelve tribes scattered among the nations: Greetings."[242]

Matthew was the disciple who wrote down the patriarchal lineage of Christ through Joseph, even though Joseph was not the biologic father. This line goes back to the son of Israel named Judah (not Rueben, the firstborn).[243]

Moses wrote the lineage of Abraham's sons. This would be the lineage to Christ, the Son of God. Judah was Israel's fourth son, who begot Perez, who was Judah's fourth son.[244]

Why this is important is because the first-born son, Rueben, of the Father of All Nations, had a mortal father: Jacob (Israel). Jesus would not have a mortal father, so he could not be the line. The line could not come through the next two sons because Simeon, Israel's second son, and, Levi, Israel's third son, took it upon themselves to destroy a whole city when a man defiled their sister, Dinah. Israel said to these two sons, "You have brought trouble to me by making a stench to the Canaanites and the Perizzites, the people living in this land. We are few in number, and if they join forces against me and attack me, I and my household will be destroyed." So, they could not be the lines because they were callous enough to let the line be destroyed.[245]

So, the next in line was Judah, Israel's fourth son. Thus, there were fourteen generations in all from Abraham to David, fourteen

---

[242] James 1:1
[243] Matthew 1:2-3
[244] Genesis 46:8-12
[245] Genesis 34:30

from David to the Exile to Babylon, and fourteen from the Exile to Christ.[246]

After the forty-two generations passed and Christ was born, a new tribe—the Christians, rooted together from the seeds of the Twelve Tribes of Israel—sprang forth and grew into twelve new tribes of one trunk and one Tree of Life, which had begun through the lineage of Mary and the Holy Spirit. This new lineage set all things new. Christ resumed the place of man as the Second Adam. Mary resumed the place as the Mother of all Nations, taking the place of Rebekah, whose children were born mortal, and not divine. Because Christ was without sin, he would have to die without children because he could not unite his body in any perfect way, and all men and women were created imperfect.

The disciple John Mark—also known as Mark, the author of the Gospel of Mark—stated that Jesus had four brothers: James, Joses (or Joseph), Jude, and Simon, who were of the same maternal mother, Mary.[247]

No longer were the sons of Ishmael and his Twelve Descendant Tribes at odds with all men forever, nor were the sons of Isaac and the Twelve Descendant Tribes of Israel the only inheritors if the Kingdom of Heaven forever, for now, in the new Age of Non-Prophets, after Christ's resurrection, the world would begin a new era of the Twelve Christian Tribes, united to face all obstacles together for the glory of the our Lord until His Kingdom Comes: those from the four brothers of Jesus (by Mary) and those who represented one of each of the eight Beatitudes.[248]

---

[246] Matthew 1:17

[247] Mark 6:3 & Matthew 13:55-56

[248] Matthew 5:3-12

They are these Twelve Tribes of Christianity and Servants of the King on Earth today:

The Tribe of James
(...carriers of the Mary-James gene)
The Angel Verostices
Johnnie Spot Perfect
Charlie & the Ghost of Charlie

The Tribe of Joses
(...carriers of the Mary-Joses gene)
The Angel Spurious
Sonny Francis
Lawrence Merriweather

The Tribe of Jude
(...carriers of the Mary-Jude gene)
The Angel Shemenea
Coach Burkhart
Mia Richardson
Coach Gault
Mia Heatherton

The Tribe of Simon
(...carriers of the Mary-Simon gene)
The Angel Sextus
Andy Silverman
Charlotte Mendez

The Tribe of the Poor in Spirit
(...for theirs is the Kingdom of Heaven)
The Apostle Matthew
The Apostle Thaddaeus
Pope Francis
The Angel Azoz (who was martyred after he left the Sons of Ishmael to join the sons of Isaac for the love of his young bride)
Jamie
Mia and Bob Heatherton

The Tribe of Those Who Morn
(...for they are ones to be comforted)
The Apostle Philip
The Angel Phylamonas
Mamaw Gleason
Rosanne Francis

The Tribe of the Meek
(...for they will inherit the earth)
The Apostle James
Jenny Gleason
Sarah Ferguson
Ziggie, the Zig Man

The Tribe of Those Who Hunger & Thirst for Righteousness
(...for they will be filled)
The Apostle Bartholomew
Coach Thornton
Knights of Columbus
Knights Templar

Freemasons

The Tribe of the Merciful
(...for they will be shown mercy)
The Apostle Thomas
The Angel Mormon
Knights Hospitaller

The Tribe of the Pure in Heart
(...for they shall see God)
The Apostle Paul
The Disciple Luke
The Disciple Barnabas
The Disciple John Mark
Pope Benedict XVI
Reverend Billy Graham

The Tribe of the Peacemakers
(...for they will be called the Sons of God)
The Apostle John
Bobby McIntyre
Ben Tucker
Betty Joe Bradford

The Tribe of those Persecuted for Righteousness' sake
(...for theirs is the Kingdom of Heaven also)
The Apostle Peter
The Disciple Timothy
The Baron of Temple.
Knights Templar, etc....

Leroy McGinnis
Leonardo di Vinci

May this insight into the history of Salvation be an enlightenment to bless and enrich you lives till Christ comes again.

Your Brother in Christ,

Q

The Good and Faithful Servant

Forget not to show love unto strangers: for thereby some have entertained angels unawares.

Hebrews 13:2

Glossary

Characters

Johnnie "Spot" Perfect

a.k.a JJ, Spot, Sir-John, Formudus, Josiah III; born Johnnie Johnson in south central Los Angeles by a midwife in an apartment; has no birth certificate; carrier of the Mary-James gene

Jenny Gleason

Johnnie's biological mother; born and raised in a middle-class family in Houston, Texas; voted 'most popular' and 'most likely to succeed' by her Katy high school senior class; carrier of the Mary-James gene

Marcus Johnson

a.k.a John Johnson, Sr., the name he used on the streets to hide his identity while doing crime; Johnnie's biological father; drug dealer and pimp; many childhood wounds; frustrated high school basketball star kicked off college team for insubordination; angry, full of hate, and racially motivated; crusader for minority injustice; raised by his grandmother; lived in a community where 90% of the children did not know who their father was, and where silence, suffering, and domination by gang violence was the neighborhood code for survival

Jaimie Johnson

Johnnie's half-brother and childhood friend; his mother, along with Johnnie's mother, was a drug addict and prostitute for Marcus Johnson

Mamaw Stuart Gleason

a.k.a. Bea; Johnnie's maternal grandmother; born and raised in Tyler, Texas; brought up Southern Baptist

Charles Frank Gleason

Mamaw's late husband; family migrated to Texas from a farm in Virginia when he was a small boy; along with his twin brother, carrier of the Mary-James gene

Cojo

Mamaw's dog, i.e. 'God' spelled backwards; adopted from the Westside Rescue Dog Shelter by Jenny for her eighth birthday when she was in elementary school; especially chosen by Phylamonas for Jenny to find and then later for Johnnie to inherit; knew his job was to protect and serve those who had rescued him, just as Jesus was sent to protect and serve the world He loved; unable to speak and communicate as he desired, much like the people he was sent to protect and serve

Bobby Thornton

Boys' basketball coach at St. Stephen's Catholic High School in Houston; graduated from community college with an engineering degree but found more satisfaction in helping to raise young boys who were struggling with missing or deficient father figures

Sonny Francis

a.k.a Sonnius Hermutus; member of a Presbyterian congregation; grew up in a 99.9% Hispanic Catholic population in Hidalgo County in south Texas, the poorest county in the nation with the highest unemployment rate, which hit 22% during the Vietnam War, where "white flight" had occurred as the Anglo population left the Rio Grande Valley after colonizing it, where food stamps were the norm, where a "me first" mentality pervaded: what could be received from instead of contributed to society

Rosanne Francis

a.k.a. Rosie; wife of Sonny, whom she met in high school, four years her senior, but she did not begin dating until after he had returned to the States from Vietnam, injured and suffering from PTSD; has familial macular degeneration and rare form of Stargeart's Disease, which is carried as a recessive gene in her family; two other sisters also suffer from this, and all three sisters have some partial vision but will continue to lose more and more eyesight as they age until likely completely blind and dependent on others for help by their 80s; never had children; attended a non-denominational church growing up but prefers to attend the Methodist Church as an adult

Bobby McIntyre

Grew up in the wide-open spaces of northern United States; did not believe in violence and was a conscientious objector; wanted to dodge the draft and go to Canada but father shamed him into the service; grew up in a 99% white community, a hard-working class that believed the only good money was that which was earned with sweat and an honest day's labor; mother (who had been part of a dying culture of women's liberation, misogynism, and the media's incessant fight for victim's equality, which left men without male identities in the late 20th century) passed away when he was in middle school

Charlotte

Born in Baton Rouge, Louisiana; mother and father divorced soon after her birth, giving her up for adoption; raised in a Catholic household in Houston; went to LSU nursing school and afterward moved back to Houston to be with adopted relatives

Andy Silverman

a.k.a. "the Baron of Corpus Christi"; born to a Jewish family; converted to a Christian-Jewish faith after meeting Daisy; owner of the Houston Hurricanes basketball team

Daisy Silverman

Born into a Greek Orthodox family and baptized as Desaria Fatima Caras, but converted to a Jewish Christian faith after meeting Andy

Trixie

Andy's sister; married to a very successful businessman, with whom she spends time riding his-and-her Harley Davidson motorcycles across the US or on cruise ships to play golf in foreign countries; spends four months a year traveling with Hollywood movie stars

Leroy McGinnis

Does not attend church much, but occasionally attends Unity Church; father was a customs officer for the US Border Patrol; likes to study all forms of information but is slow to act in many ways; known as a fence-sitter

Coach Barricks

Played college basketball at Notre Dame while a psychology major; frustrated by his own two sons' failure to accomplish anything in life except stay home and do menial jobs, thus further frustrating their mother, who is already upset by her husband's frequent absence from home due to work and travel

Ben Tucker

Member of the LDS faith; does not drink, smoke, curse, or tell obscene jokes

Mia

Member of the LDS faith; believes a woman's main purpose is to provide a good home life and raise lots of children; bore five children, all of whom became successful members of society

Betty Lou Bradford

Divorced single mother who just wants a steady income; real estate agent on the side; does not have any children

Antonio

Raised in the projects of Chicago; never knew his father; survived on the streets by staying out of trouble, doing odd jobs (like delivering packages on his bicycle), and playing basketball

Orlando

Only one in his family to attend college; attended on basketball scholarship, but could not pass his basic courses; was drafted early into the NBA, thus never finished his college degree; does not know how to manage his money and ends up broke after a successful but short four-year NBA career

Ziggie

a.k.a. Zig-Man; charismatic personality; raised primarily by his grandmother because his father traveled so much; becomes a sports commentator after retiring from a basketball career with two NBA championship rings to his credit

Malcolm Fehrueger

Assistant coach for the Houston Hurricanes; known as "The Enforcer" by all who play under him

Mr. Lawrence Merriweather

Born-again Christian called by God to preach amongst the people of Houston, though not an ordained minister

Paul and Cindy Morgan

Steadfast members of the community church who believe in helping neighbors first before sending missionaries off to foreign lands; want to make impact in local communities, since 80% of locals do not attend church

Historical Figures

Bellamino Begatti

A 20th-century Italian archaeologist and Catholic priest of the Franciscan Order who laid the foundation work for the discovery of the Mary-James gene

Horatio G. Spafford

Prominent American lawyer and Presbyterian church elder; best known for penning the Christian hymn *It Is Well With My Soul* following a family tragedy in which his four daughters died aboard the S.S. Ville du Havre

Barnabas the Apostle

Born Joseph, a Cypriot Jew; early Christian convert, becoming one of the prominent Christian disciples in Jerusalem; Apostle who disseminated the word of the Gospel as he preached alongside Paul on many occasions

<u>Three Worlds of the Triune Godhead</u>

1. Heaven

Where God the Father resides and rules, and where Jesus Christ resides to be with His Father when He is not taking care of His sheep

2. Paradise

a. Upper Paradise

Where the Holy Spirit/Ghost resides at the request of the Lord God Father in Heaven, administering over the will of both the Lord God Father and the Lord Savior Jesus Christ, and ruling over the battle sanctum of good angels vs. evil angels, until the new age of perfection is declared

b. Lower Paradise

Where the Lord Savior Jesus Christ rules at the request of the Lord God Father in Heaven, overseeing the Holy Spirit/Ghost and guardian angels

3. Hell / Hades / Lake of Fire

a.k.a. Fallen Paradise, where lost souls reside (by their own choice to rebel against Paradise) and are housed individually in anguish, apart from all others, in a constant state of suffering; void of all joy, peace, hope, love, happiness, freedom, support, communication, or meaningful relationship for all eternity

<u>Guardian Angels</u>

Azoz
Verostices
Shemenea
Phylamonas
Chalymina
Gabriel

Historical Events

Los Angeles Riots (April-May 1992)

Large-scale race riots in Los Angeles County causing over $1 billion of destruction through looting, arson, assault, and murder. 63 people were killed, 2,883 people injured, and over 1,200 arrested. Governor Pete Wilson deployed the California State Guard, and President George H.W. Bush deployed two military combat divisions (the 7th Infantry Division and the 1st Marine Division) to put down the social unrest and restore order.

Garabandal (1961-1965)

Multiple apparitions of the archangel Michael and of Mary, the blessed mother of Jesus, were seen by four young school girls in the small village of San Sebastian de Garabandal, in northern Spain

9/11 (September 11, 2001)

A series of four coordinated attacks by Islamic Terrorists using hijacked passenger airliners to strike key sites on the east coast of the United States. The New York City Twin Towers were destroyed as well as parts of the United States Military Pentagon. The attacks killed 2,996 people, injured over 6,000 others, left over 2,000 children without one or both of their parents, and caused over $10 billion dollars in infrastructure and property damage.

Definitions

Spot

A blemish, imperfection, difference in shade or color seen by the eyes; not a part of something bigger; negative term for incompatibility

Sin

Imperfect, blemished; an archer's term for an arrow which has gone astray

Perfect

Without blemish or defect, without sin; an archer's term for an arrow which hits the center mark, like Jesus—the only arrow sent by God—which hit its perfect mark

Bridge to Book Three

Thy Kingdom Come

Medical Electron Regeneration & the Seven Plagues of 2020

It is now the end of the "Age of Non-Prophets," with miracles on earth happening every day. The Twelve Tribes of Jesus are coming together to form one mighty world tree, but still many miracles need to happen before the rapture can occur. The outlanders and their drones have evolved in their lies and untruths, and they have put together a plan to hunt and destroy all Christians who tarry from their spiritual callings by orders of 666.

Creator God, the Holy Father, Papa, in Heaven's proper, senses something is wrong with the Holy Spirit's ability to absorb all the pain created by man's own self-indulgent hand.

It has taken, now, over one thousand summer-solstice years and one thousand winter-solstice passing years of repetitive motion around the young yellow star, which the humans call their sun, to get to this point. The IAU have humorously coded it as 101.a, a new millennial name, and they have built spaceships to go out and seek the world of angels to conquer. The first number unit of 101.a designates the amount of time needed to travel to the Lord's silent motioning clock-moon and then back in the S. Hawking EMF transporter cell, which was designed to move matter at the speed of light. The second unit stands for the base magnetic field gravity between the 101.a and the earth, which keeps it in its constant trajectory of harmony. And the third unit designates the speed of light to travel from 101.a to the edge of the galaxy. The 'a' represents the beginning points of all three measurements as the center of the measurements, with the Pleiades representing the "z" or the final frontier to locate new allies in life somewhere out there in the galaxies. By using this methodology, a new form of time-space and relativity has been breached and named Pedulnomics by the timekeepers, where time is now proven and measured as not linear but as a basic fourth order geodesic, which allows the mechanism of time travel. This is the time space where the angels live and exist, which is not visible to the naked human eye, much like light itself is not visible, but what it shines on is….

Mankind has doomed itself into a death spiral of intellectual moron-ism by making the 'pursuit of science' combined with 'hyperbole and philosophy of its newly found secular gods.' This habit worshipping the questions of "What if?" instead of "What is?" began in the Garden of Eden. The quest to unlock the meaning of the "Tree of Knowledge of Good and Evil" (Genesis 2:17) is making a mockery of the Lord's blessings, and the Lord's patience is wearing thin. Jesus was sent to unlock the Door of Truth, and yet the door remains shut. God, the Holy Father, looks down on His creation in Lower Paradise and watches intensely over His children (both those of men, the mortals, and those of the eternal living angels). He surveys all the Heavens around Him, which He fully created for His pleasure, and understands that more must be done to lead His sheepish creations, "the mortals," away from their evil and imperfect ways.

But they are blind and cannot see because of their obstinacies. Almost everything they do destroys them from within. Too soon they will realize that the enemy which they were born to face was none other than themselves. No other enemy is as cunning, powerful, and elusive as the mortal nature of desire, greed, and fame that lurks within. The mortals are deaf. They hear but they cannot hear. The Words of the Good News have been spoken all around them day and night, but the Word has been rebuked and thrown to the snakes for a life of self-indulgence. Hearty is the attitude that just a little sin will not kill them; but unknowingly it is just a little sin that acts like slow venom and is the most insidious. Death comes not by the greater auspices of external war, but by the lesser auspices of inner strife, because the death they see is just of the first world they live in and not the second world into which they go. Satan has been given just enough power over them with enough reason to seduce them into their weaknesses, and the dark angel has also been given the ability to woo them away from the Trinity using deceptive expectations of enhanced self-grandeur combined with immediate pleasurable gratification, which has led to justified self-indulgence.

The good angels all now grieve alongside the Holy Spirit as the He-and-She "Godhead" aches and mourns for ALL the lost souls of their creation, which the Triune made but cannot make to come home. All are called! But most mortals are distracted with urges of the moment, never hearing the call because it is like music with the sound of demonic discord, a paradox to the sin of reason. The bad angels all sit and wait for the final battle of solidarity and destruction.

Each good (not perfect) personal angel was named one-by-one, with the given purpose to be called as a witness for the ones they guarded during the Great Trial on Judgment Day. The other twenty-six levels of angels were given other purposes at their creation, known only to the Trinity who created them. The personal angels will be the ones who carry out the sentences on the mortals to whom they were assigned and who did not open the door when Christ knocked on their hearts. Thus the personal angels cry, for they tried so hard but their actions could not fully pierce the Veil of Lower Paradise. Everything was muted according to the reception setting of the mortal, as the he-and-she nature of the human was moved in the depths of their hearts.

And now also Jesus, the Lord over the world, and Highest Giver-of-Mercy in Heaven and earth, also aches and mourns, and He can also be heard crying in harmony with the Holy Spirit; for it was He who voluntarily went and paid the ultimate price of "Holy Blood and Holy Life" which was so great that it shook all of the Heavens… and still the world which they created goes awry down the material pathway of lusts. The Lord God Almighty, Ultimate Ruler and Final Judge, the Holy Father in Heaven, gives no mercy, for He leaves this to His Son and the Holy Ghost to do. He only delivers justice and stands all-omnipotent to those who blaspheme His name and follow their own dead-end ways. The world still has so many lost who know not His name, that both the Son and the Holy Spirit are hurting. The guardian angels report over and over each moment that more seek all things made by Mankind than seek things made by the Triune, and this grieves the Trinity. This happens as the dark angels of the underworld hear and listen to their victories, and they look forward to the task of caring for more inmates of Eternal Hell, whose names will be bound and lost forever.

Then after a time, at the end of the Seventh Epoch of Hebrew history, it is declared that the time has come for the end of grieving and consoling, so the Holy Spirit, along with God the Father in Heaven and the Son Jesus, tear down the barrier known as the Veil between Upper Paradise and Lower Heaven, and they begin to wander in and out of each other to gain strength from each for the judgment time to come. The Holy Spirit calls forth three of His-and-Her most loyal guardian angels who all served mankind on earth well unto each their callings: Saint Luke the Greater, Saint Servius the Lesser, and Saint Andrew III, the Promise Keeper (a.k.a. Andy Silverman). Each comes immediately into the presence of the Holy Spirit upon the pedestal of His-and-Her divine paradise inhabitance, and then the Counselor of Paradise, who is below Heaven and above Hades, questions the angels for the Holy Spirit to their bare bones of existence, to open their hearts, using the temperance of a galactic hurricane and the presence of a cosmic collision.

"Luke, the one I loved for your pure heart in caring for the sick, step forward first!" The Holy Spirit commands. "Have you consulted with Servius, Verostices, and Phylamonas on finalizing the forthcoming plagues which the world is to endure?"

"I have, oh Great One!" Luke replies.

"And you carry out my orders for what purpose?" the Holy Spirit interrogates.

"For man has not sought your love hard enough, nor have they repented of their wicked ways; and they continue to rebel in their own foolish selfishness and self-glory," Luke answers.

"Have they kept my commandments?" the Holy Spirit inquires.

"No! All ten of your Commandments they have repeatedly violated, and it is an insult to our Father in Heaven!" Luke replies.

"And their leaders do not hold them accountable, for they are not believers in their hearts and must be tested more thoroughly."

"Luke, you may step back, my good and faithful servant, and let Q pass by. Now, Servius! Step forward again… come! For you have shown your worth promoting my Eternal Kingdom with your promises kept unto death. You loved as no other those whom I sent you to call. You knew the true meaning of putting others first and understood the truth of the parable of the Good Samaritan. Your legacy is untarnished, and now you will call more souls to my Kingdom with your message of service as my infinite Good Helper."

The Holy Spirit begins to shake, and with a mighty tidal wave greater than a million tsunamis of energy, like rolling ocean storms across the universe, He-and-She begins to rain upon these three souls as they, united into one voice, stand in the presence of the Holy Spirit.

"Have you seen to the millions of abandoned and aborted children whom the unloving have discarded into their trash dumps, though I sent them as miracles of my own Creation?" the Holy Spirit laments.

"I have witnessed these, my God, and each cries out for justice to their Creator each and every day from the Grave-of-the-Unknown-Names, waiting for their chance to become part of the Tree of Life. Their hands are raised from the pits they endure, reaching out to those who bound them there through their own selfishness, with the ripple effect of ages of sin. They have been denied their chance to become fish and brought the Blessing of the Ages, as well as sheep lost in the wilderness of fallen forests, while those who denied them the Living Water slept in their lost beds, and laughed at pending death as they were created by You and destroyed by Man, which reviles my Lord Jesus of Men and Savior of All."

While Servius witnesses to the Holy Spirit, angel blood, which is similar to Christ's blood but not as perfect, begins again oozing from his forehead, spilling out in the seven colors of the skin which created the seven original nations. This bleeding represents the pain of the lost souls which he represents in the counsel of the Holy Court, just as Jesus Christ oozed holy mortal blood from his head, praying, before his time was up to leave the earth, as he was delivered into the hands of the Holy Spirit in the form of the ubiquitous internal Ghost.

"And what am I to do with your pain, oh Holy One? You must command me in your divine wisdom and omnipotence, for I cannot be the bearer of all your pain, nor can any other being you have created, for we are only instruments of your love and everlasting will! None who are created less than you can do this, not even the cherubim can; or we all would fall from grace without your mercy to protect us and your paradise in every action and moment," Servius finished in a whisper, becoming more reverent, as he witnesses and feels divine pain.

"Servius, you will now again begin to show to ALL my pain… to ALL nations the Seven Plagues," the Holy Spirit continues. "For only by this suffering and early destruction then will they be enlightened to their own self-abuses and turn from their own condemned ways. They have turned their faces away from me again and again, so they must face the plagues for their own good in order to realize their places in creation. And again, over and over, they must again sit in ash cloth and turn to repentance to accept the blood of my Son, which was spilled for them, or they will know only the pain of death without the cross, and eternal isolation combined with eternal loss. Their own futures and eternal blessings they can change only by modifying their own worldly actions and walking forward with a complete change of heart, walking in complete obedience to the Holy Scriptures, ordained by Jesus and monitored by the Holy Spirit… for so it is written! And now we will see if they repent and die or just die without repenting. The souls of their fathers and forefathers lie in state as they wait for the seeds of their actions in teaching their children to either bear the fruit of the Holy Spirit and bless others with their relations or remain dormant in the fields of the cemeteries where perdition lies waiting for its final judgment."

"Servius, now step back!" the Holy Spirit commands. "And now let me gaze on the face of my servant, Andrew, the Promise Keeper," the Holy Spirit demands. "And what did Verostices tell you, Andrew, that sets you apart from the rest?"

"That I am to prophesize in the ears of the next generation when I am told to do so, for now the TIME HAS COME that they will listen, for in my breath will be the words with which I carry your words and will," Andrew replies.

"And how sure are you of this, Andrew?" the Holy Spirit inquires.

"You were there when I was created, and you gave me my gifts to be used in this day. You were there when I received my salvation with Christ. You were there when I left the earth to be in your presences. And you have kept me close by your side as you have told me you would, until my actions are complete and I rise with the other saints on the Day of Atonement to lead in the charge of the world's final resting place," Andrew replies.

"You are correct, my servant, who can speak for me so well. For you have done well with the other tasks you were assigned and now you will carry my words forward so that medicine can be delivered to all nations who suffer with the Plagues of self-suffocation and the polluted blood of man without the cleansing of the blood of Christ to glean from anymore," the Holy Spirit replies. "Now, explain this to me in human terms, oh great seer of the saints," the Holy Spirit chides him.

"The people will continue to be moneychangers only and forget the main reason why they were created, which is to serve each other," Andrew explains. "Their children will become ever more autistic in alarming numbers, so that they must care for their own and turn their eyes downward away from you, looking at screens which reflect their own robot image. Their elderly will increase in brain death, as if held underwater, so that they will have the attention of a child, their bodies ballooning up like rubber full of air so they can no longer run if they want to and must be carried by machines because they cannot walk or sleep. Their bodies will no longer fight natural infections and disease from within, so they will self-destruct from cancer until it eats them up from inside. Their stomachs will no longer process the nutrition you have given them, so that they get sick from putting food in their mouths, and they will no longer rest at night to recharge for energy each day because their throats will close down like rope upon their necks until they roar like lions in their sleep, which will be heard as the signs of impending death. To all these you will decrease their days on earth, and it will be measured by the 'Human Death Index,' until they realize the meaning of full repentance and they grasp the 'Trinity's Life Index.' And until then they will live in the darkness separated from the mercy, grace, and love you graciously offer to them for free through the living blood of Jesus Christ, their one and only True Living Savior."

Then Andrew pauses for a moment and remains silent, until he is released back to his place in Paradise, to wait for the next time he will be called to serve and reveal the nature of the inflammation which is destroying the world by the Seven Plagues.

Then the Holy Spirit says to the three angels, "I tell you the Truth: Before my Son came to each of you, there were the days of Moses and the Plagues I sent the world due to my anger toward the stiff-necked and evil men, but because of my Son's generosity, even I have repented, and now each and every plague of mankind which causes them grief and misery is because they have done these to themselves. Before this Age, in the Age of Prophets, I spoke to them and gave them the Laws, but now in the "Age of Non-Prophets," I give them myself, the Great Counselor, to discover the Laws and follow their own path with the purity of heart in my Son Christ or the destruction of their hearts through their own plagues they set forth on themselves. Eden is no longer the place of peace and mercy as in the day I created it, but now a place of bad decisions sought out by man and the new bad apple which is constantly put before him. As long as he does not repent and does not follow the true course of my laws set out by the spilled blood of our Son, Jesus Christ, men shall ever be the prisoners of their own design. Man and woman will be slaves of their own impurities, and suffer of their own prideful choices without the medicine of knowledge or the living waters of mercy until Christ voluntarily comes again to again deliver those who do not believe but will believe in the End. All that they need—or will ever need—is that which I have already given to them, and they need no more forevermore. The answer I give to them now, which they do not understand still, is how to find eternal life combined with my precious gifts of mercy, grace, love, health, faith, hope, harmony, peace, joy, and the greatest gift of all: the Blessing of Eternal Salvation forever more. Amen.

Your Brother in Christ,
Q

36676795R00263

Made in the USA
Columbia, SC
26 November 2018